URSULA'S ARM

Penny Kline

Copyright © 2011 Penny Kline

The moral right of the author has been asserted.

Apart from any fair dealing for the purposes of research or private study, or criticism or review, as permitted under the Copyright, Designs and Patents Act 1988, this publication may only be reproduced, stored or transmitted, in any form or by any means, with the prior permission in writing of the publishers, or in the case of reprographic reproduction in accordance with the terms of licences issued by the Copyright Licensing Agency. Enquiries concerning reproduction outside those terms should be sent to the publishers.

Extracts from Dr. Marie Stopes' "Married Love" by kind permission of Dr. Harry Stopes-Roe and the Galton Institute.

Matador
5 Weir Road
Kibworth Beauchamp
Leicester LE8 0LQ, UK
Tel: (+44) 116 279 2299
Fax: (+44) 116 279 2277
Email: books@troubador.co.uk
Web: www.troubador.co.uk/matador

ISBN 978 1848767 348

British Library Cataloguing in Publication Data.
A catalogue record for this book is available from the British Library.

Typeset in 11pt Palatino by Troubador Publishing Ltd, Leicester, UK

Matador is an imprint of Troubador Publishing Ltd

Printed in Great Britain by the MPG Books Group, Bodmin and King's Lynn

For Paul

CHAPTER ONE

'It is inherent in human nature to have an inclination to consider a thing untrue if one does not like it, and after that it is easy to find arguments against it.'
(Sigmund Freud)

This is the story of me and Leo. Or is it me and Mrs Moberley. Or me and all the women like me. Me, me, me but until you understand yourself you are incapable of understanding anyone else. This is a story about love – and sex of course although when it all began "sex" was not a word that crossed my lips. So much was unmentionable: it was too frightening or too painful.

I remember hearing about a man who fell out of a train. It had reached the station but when he opened the door it was still in motion and he lost his balance and tumbled onto the platform. One of those freak accidents it must have been, because there was no serious injury apart from a finger that suffered nerve damage and ever after hung limply so that he was unable to move it at all.

The point of the story is that a few months later he asked his doctor to cut it off. It seemed he had no interest in the appearance of his hand, just loathed the floppiness of the finger and wanted it removed.

When I told Archie the story he gave me a quizzical look but made no comment about my arm. A not uncommon response, he said, but of interest to those who concern themselves with the intricacies of the human mind. He smiled and I expected him to add, "and all that palaver", but he never did. I remember that.

Before he retired Archie was a specialist. Dr Archie Ingham. Even Muriel never calls him Archibald. I started working for him straight after my nineteenth birthday, which I had celebrated by having my hair cut in a bob, and I stayed for two and a half years, my first job, my only job.

In the beginning I was the slowest typist you can imagine but Archie was endlessly patient, he always is, ideal for a doctor, strong yet gentle, like the father in one of those comforting children's stories. And his height and his thick white hair add to his reassuring image

The first time he and Muriel invited me to *The Gables* Leo was away at Cambridge, studying Ancient History. "What a pity you've missed him," Muriel kept repeating, so it was no surprise when she invited me again one Sunday in July after he had returned home for the vacation. Looking back I should have been flattered because I think it was deliberate match making. We had tea in the garden and I felt a bit of a fool because Muriel is mad on gardening whereas I can hardly tell a lupin from a delphinium.

All the time she was showing me round the beds she hung onto her hat for fear a gust of wind carried it away. For some reason I can still recall that hat, greenish-blue it was, the shade that looks green against a strong blue but blue against a vivid green, and with a white bow on its brown velvet band. Even for nineteen-twenty-five it was old-fashioned and because the colour was so strong it accentuated the paleness of her skin and the unusual colour of her eyes. Hazel with tiny flecks of yellow I think they are except I never look at them long enough to be certain.

Do you like flowers she asked, and of course I said I did, adding how the rain earlier in the day had left drops of water on the petals and made everything smell fresh and clean. She laughed, just being pleasant I expect, but the whole occasion was daunting and I felt a small flicker of fear, like being given a Maths test at school and knowing there would be problems I failed to understand.

Bear with me because Muriel is an important part of the story. I dislike jokes about mother-in-laws but she was archetypal – daunting, critical, possessive, although I can see now that everything we feel or do has a reason.

When we first met I thought Leo looked like Archie, but later I could see the likeness to his mother was stronger. His eyes are blue like his father's, but his nose and mouth are more like Muriel's and before her hair started turning grey I expect it was a lovely glossy chestnut brown, like Leo's.

I forget what I was wearing that day, something unsophisticated I expect, but kind Archie read my mind and said I looked delightful, and me being so ignorant about the plants helped to break the ice with Leo and later he wrote me a letter – nothing very romantic I'm afraid – and I wrote back, and he wrote again, inviting me to stay the weekend in Cambridge in a small hotel quite close to his college. And that was how it all began.

After he started work at Kingslade we found a little house in Highgate, well within walking distance of the preparatory school and only a mile or so from

Hampstead Heath. I used to wonder if he felt he had failed to follow in his father's footsteps. No, not failed, a schoolmaster is a perfectly respectable profession, although I sometimes think his fascination with the Great Doctor, as he liked to call him, may have had something to do with wanting to please Archie because Freud started life as a medical man and it was not until he was almost thirty that his interest turned to psychoanalysis.

I know all this now, in fact I'm quite an expert on the subject – Anna O and poor Frau Emmy – but, amazing as it may seem when Leo gave me that first article to read I completely failed to make the connection.

It was a Saturday, it must have been because Enid had the afternoon off and Leo was worried about leaving me on my own.

'Put your feet up.' He pushed the hideous octagonal footstool towards me, the one that Muriel had provided when I first became ill. 'I won't be long.' Then he scratched at a mark on the Persian rug and it reminded me what a useless wife I was and how I must tell Enid to be more careful with the furniture polish.

'I need more typing paper,' he said, 'and while I'm at the shops I'll buy you some of those blackcurrant cough pastilles.'

'Boiled sweets are better,' I told him, 'something to suck. Oh Leo, I nearly forgot to tell you, yesterday Enid made me the most disgusting concoction, layers of onions and turnips covered with sugar, and the juice expressed into a jug. I hadn't the heart to refuse a spoonful.'

He nodded vaguely and I knew he was thinking about something else. 'I wondered if this might interest you.' He placed a sheaf of papers on the little inlaid table. 'I'll leave it here where you can reach.'

To be honest I had been looking forward to starting the new Dorothy L. Sayers, immersing myself in the world of Lord Peter Wimsey and his faithful manservant, Bunter. Still at least the article was in English – I was good at French at school but we never studied German – although, as I was soon to discover, it was pretty hard going and the translation probably contributed to its indigestibility, if there is such a word.

The American Journal of Psychology. Lecture, delivered by Professor Sigmund Freud at Clark University in Worcester, Massachusetts. Pulled up close to the fire – it was chilly for April – and not much bothered if the heat penetrated my stockings and made my legs all red and shiny, I struggled through "wish-fulfilments" and "catalytic ferment", "hysterical conversion" and "suppressed libidinous excitations."

Did Leo think a shared interest would bring us closer? Before my stupid arm we had both been too busy to worry about such things – after two years of marriage you expect to run out of conversation – but now that I was more or less housebound the differences between us had become more noticeable.

Sometimes, looking back, I think about all the things we could have discussed. Freud hypnotised his patients as a way of persuading them to disclose their secrets but can you imagine Leo divulging such things? Dropping little hints maybe, although I always think what's left to the imagination tends to be more disconcerting than when someone just spits it out. Women are often accused of talking in riddles when half the time they are simply trying to be sensitive to other people's feelings. Or else they are afraid of being rebuffed. Is that something Freud wrote about? I doubt it.

Sublimation, repression, the transfer of tender emotion and enmity. Poring over the blotchy print, reading and re-reading, I failed to hear Leo return from the shops and when he joined me in the drawing room was a little shocked to see how agitated he looked.

'What is it?' I was afraid he must have witnessed an accident or learned a friend of ours was ill in hospital, or worse. But he was only thinking about the journal article.

'Did you read it Ursa?' My name is Ursula but Leo prefers a diminutive. Ursa, the feminine of ursus, the bear. Latin of course.

'Most of it,' I told him, though in fact I had read every word. 'I found the style of writing rather trying.'

'Yes, the language does take a little getting used to.' He rubbed the bridge of his nose, a gesture that usually means he has something important to say, something I may not want to hear.

Crossing to the window he began fiddling with the tassels on one of the cords that hold back the curtains. He has long arms, ape's arms his mother likes to say fondly, and his sleeves are always too short. I remember thinking he ought to have his jackets made for him, except sitting at a desk most of the day the elbows tend to wear out. His neck is long too. I like his neck, especially the back of it where his hair comes to a point.

'I've been giving it some thought.' He cleared his throat, another warning signal. 'Now the doctors are satisfied there's no neurological problem I feel we ought to try a different tack.'

'What kind of a tack?'

'A year or two back a leader in *The Times* expressed surprise that psychoanalysis seemed to be enjoying so swift and wide a popularity. These days it's an accepted form of treatment.'

'What is it exactly?'

'There's a Mrs Moberley, who as coincidence would have it lives less than a mile from here, close to Hampstead Heath. She's highly recommended.'

'Who by?'

He stared at me and I waited for the correction, *by whom*, but it never came.

'Apparently she's visited Europe and New York. She's well versed in Freudian theory but likes to keep an open mind as to the underlying basis of the patient's symptoms.'

'She's one of your psychoanalysts?' I struggled not to cough. 'I thought they were all men.'

'Oh no, there are several women practising in London.' He was still looking in my direction but over my left shoulder. 'I thought you might feel happier with a woman.'

Solomon had climbed up onto my knees and started kneading my thighs. My left one felt the pin pricks of his claws but my right one, it was always the right hand side, felt numb apart from an uncomfortable tingling sensation. I touched his ear and it flicked in annoyance. Then he started to purr and I thought, it's all right for you puss cat, with not a worry in the world as long as Leo fails to notice where you sharpened your claws on the sideboard.

'So you think it's all up here.' I tapped my temple. 'You think I'm mental.'

'Of course not, how can you say such a thing?' His voice rasped with anger, or was it fear? 'Forget I ever mentioned the woman. We'll get more opinions. I'll have another word with Father.'

'He's a skin specialist.'

'But he knows the best people in other fields.'

'What fields?' I wished Archie were there to stick up for me. 'I've been examined from top to toe, my spine, my ribs, my eyes. Prodded and poked, asked endless questions, many of them quite unrelated to my symptoms. Anyway I'm not seeing that Dr Predicate again.'

'Prendicott,' Leo corrected.

'Or the one with breath like Irish stew that kept leaning over me, and wondered why I twisted my head away from him.'

'Let me talk to Father.' He moved towards me and I thought he was going to kiss me but if he had been going to he thought better of it. A wife, one of whose arms hangs lifelessly by her side, is not an attractive proposition.

'I'll see to the tea things,' he said, leaving the room but returning almost at once. 'Where does the milk jug live? No don't get up, I'll look in the cupboard. And the sugar bowl?'

'Neither of us takes sugar in our tea Leo.'

'Nor we do.'

He looked quite sad and suddenly I wanted to cry, for myself, for both of us. To console him, tell him how guilty I felt, one minute wanting to be looked after, the next protesting that I disliked being treated like an invalid. But the words refused to come. My throat was too dry and scratchy.

'I'm sorry Ursa.' He was standing in the doorway, wondering what I was thinking, what I wanted him to do. 'It's just that I'm so worried about you.'

'I know.' I managed a cheerful smile. 'There's a cake in the tin on the sideboard. Madeira. Enid says it sunk in the middle but I'm sure it will taste delicious.'

A whole week passed and no mention was made of Mrs Moberley but the spectre of her hung in the air between us. Leo was cross with me, I could tell, but when I asked him he denied it. Being angry with a sick person is not the done thing except I was not even certain he believed I was ill. He could easily think I was a sham, coughing unnecessarily and making the silly habit worse, claiming I was incapable of moving my arm when all the time, if I had made a little more effort, I could have exercised it back to its normal strength.

It was Saturday morning and out of a sense of duty he was sitting opposite me, reading *The Times*, and because it was the school holidays he was wearing the cream v-neck sweater I had given him for his birthday. At the time I was not sure he liked it, even though being Leo he had insisted it was exactly what he wanted.

'Has the cricket season started yet?' I asked.

'Not the full season but the South Africans played a one day match at Godalming against an invited eleven.'

'What does that mean, an invited eleven?'

But he had stopped listening.

He reads *The Times* from start to finish and leaves the old copies in the scullery in case they come in useful. I read the *News in brief* part and sometimes run my eyes down the births, marriage and deaths section, although I dislike the way they have it on the front page. Surely that ought to be for news. A daughter, a son, a son, a daughter. If they gave the babies' names it would be more interesting. Of course, because of my arm I am rather clumsy and the paper often ends up in a muddle, something that irritates Leo considerably.

At the moment all I could see was an advertisement for cigarettes. *Players No.3. 20 for one shilling and fourpence. Definitely superior in flavour and cool smoking qualities.* How could a cigarette be cool? I had never smoked and never intended to although I suppose cigarettes might have calmed my nerves and made me appear more sophisticated.

Solomon had jumped down, leaving earthy paw marks on my skirt. I waited for Leo to finish whatever he was reading, and turn to the next page, then told him the identity of the murderer in my Agatha Christie and asked if he agreed that it was a bit of a cheat.

'A kindred spirit.'

'How you mean?' But he had no interest in *The Murder of Roger Ackroyd*.

'Listen to this.' He started reading: "Dr Bolton, delivering a lecture on *Mind and Brain*, claimed we were threatened by an exacerbation of world hysteria by the discovery of what he could only call the myth of the unconscious mind, based on Freud's theory of dream interpretation.'

'Why did you say "a kindred spirit"?'

'You and this Bolton chap.'

'Actually I did have an awfully peculiar dream last night. No don't worry I can't remember much of it. Other people's dreams are boring aren't they, except to one of your psychoanalysts I suppose. It was all about cleaning kid slippers. Your mother was standing over me and she said you had to mix fuller's earth with powdered something or other, I forget.'

The doorbell rang and Leo looked quite startled. 'Are you expecting someone?'

'It's probably the laundry.'

'On Saturday?'

'Oh yes.' I was listening to the sounds in the hall, stumping feet like big boys playing a noisy game.

'Odd kind of dream.' Leo broke off as Enid's head came round the door. 'What is fuller's earth?'

'Mrs Bryant,' Enid announced, wiping her hands on her apron and jumping aside as my sister pushed past her, talking loudly.

'Raining! You still don't appear to have an umbrella stand so I had to lean mine against that carved chair that used to be Mother's. The girls are at home with Sidney and I'm leaving Christopher with Enid. He's asleep so he won't disturb whatever she was in the middle of. How are you both?'

Leo folded *The Times* and stood up. 'Enid will be going home in half an hour.'

'What?' Joyce glared at him as if he had said something entirely irrelevant. 'I've come to see Ursula but I can't stay long. Sidney's rushing round like a scalded cat. Only two weeks until Easter and the chap who was taking the Good Friday service has succumbed to shingles.'

'Poor man.' Leo closed the door behind him, and Joyce settled herself in his chair, patting the cushion appreciatively. 'Still warm. Why isn't he at school? They have lessons on Saturday mornings don't they? Of course, it's the holidays, silly me. How are you, how's the arm? Have you tried Ovaltine, after such a dreary old winter they say it restores vitality. All codswallop I expect.'

She was wearing her familiar shapeless wool suit and a navy blue hat, the kind you expect to see on an elderly maiden aunt, and I found myself wondering what Muriel would make of the outfit. All right for a vicar's wife perhaps, but hardly suitable for someone like me. In the paper it said there was a sale at Harrods. Half price fur coats, Canadian mink reduced from nine hundred guineas to only four hundred and fifty. *Only* four hundred and fifty!

'Nice to see you smiling.' Joyce looked at me curiously. 'What's the joke?'

'Nothing. I was just thinking about something I read in the paper.'

'So you haven't been out. Fresh air Ursula, does a power of good, and as far as I know there's nothing wrong with your leg muscles. I spoke to Muriel and she agrees a hundred percent.'

'Yes I'm sure you're both right.' Joyce is only five years older than me but when she and my mother-in-law got together, which thankfully was not often, I felt like a child, with the two of them behaving as though they had far more in common than I could possibly have with either of them.

'Christopher's cutting a tooth.' Joyce caught at the hair that had escaped from the tight roll at the back of her neck. 'I was up half the night, propping my eyes open with matchsticks in a manner of speaking, tried to pacify him with a malted rusk but to no avail. You wait till it's your turn. They're easier when they're newborn, just feed and sleep.'

She gabbled away, talking about her other children, both girls, and how Sybil, the eight-year-old was soon going to be taller than her older sister Helen who was nine and what a rumpus that was going to create, and I listened with half an ear, relieved that so far no mention had been made of the possible cause of my "illness" although I guessed she had come with that in mind.

In the beginning everyone had asked how the paralysis had come about. Not that they ever used the unmentionable word. "The arm", was how most people referred to it. Was it gradual or did you wake up one morning and there it was, hanging limply by your side? Yes, it was quite sudden I would tell them although in truth it was difficult to remember. Looking back I could have felt the occasional twinge during the preceding weeks, but put it down to over zealous gardening, or lifting my robust nephew out of his pram.

Of course Joyce had asked endless questions. *How do you dress yourself? I suppose Leo has to help you. And you must have to be careful how you pick up your cup.* Not really, I simply turn it round so the handle is on the left.

Sisterly concern was how Leo described it but in the end it was a rebuke from him that had offended her, reducing her visits from three times a week to once or twice a month.

Drawing up her chair until she was unnervingly close she rooted about in her bag, searching for something that turned out to be a small leather-bound notebook, then looked up, meeting my eyes and giving me what she thought was a warm, sympathetic smile. 'Is Enid pulling her weight?'

I laughed, partly because it was such a peculiar thing to say and partly because, apart from her surprisingly shapely legs, Enid was rather sturdily built. 'Actually I don't know what I'd do without her. She's sweet, so kind and thoughtful, almost like a younger sister.'

'She's the maid!'

'I know but that doesn't mean she can't be a friend.'

'Yes it does. Honestly Ursula, I despair of you. She's only nineteen and in your present situation I think someone older, more experienced, would be better. How are you sleeping?'

'Dr Sawyer gave me some tablets.'

'And they do the trick? Good. What's your bed like? Not too soft I hope. No, I don't imagine so. As I recall your bedroom's Spartan, all that ultra modern furniture Archie and Muriel gave you and Leo for a wedding present.'

'I've grown to rather like it,' I said, noticing for the first time that Joyce's hands had freckles on the back. 'It's Gordon Russell, his furniture was exhibited at the British Empire Exhibition, that's what Muriel told me, and the chest of drawers she gave us is made from a holly tree. Muriel says it's absurd to believe things have to be old to be beautiful.'

Joyce thought about this for a moment, scanning the room as if she needed to check the rest of our furniture, but it was not a subject that interested her. 'Anyway I saw her yesterday.'

'Who?'

'Muriel. I called round at *The Gables*.' She had adopted the deliberately casual voice of a child confessing a minor misdemeanour, the kind of tone that deceives no one. 'She says Leo wants you to see some woman, a quack by the sound of it.'

'She's a Freudian analyst.'

'And you've dug in your heels, sensible old you. Muriel's appalled.'

'Is she?' Appalled was one of Joyce's favourite words but Muriel tended to favour something less extreme. I once heard her admitting to being "a little perturbed," and one of her favourite expressions was, "what an awful shame."

'Anyway you're not going.' Joyce drew in breath and her chest strained against her collarless beige blouse. 'Has Muriel been round to talk to you about it or am I the first?'

'We're going to lunch there tomorrow.'

'Good. Have you heard of a man called Charcot? I expect Leo's mentioned him. French so you don't pronounce the "t". I thought I'd better check him out, found a tome in the reference library and discovered nearly all his patients were women with symptoms like yours.' She turned to one of the pages in her notebook. 'Do you ever experience a choking sensation or a pain down there? Is your skin particularly sensitive?'

'Where?'

'I don't think it matters where. Pains in the ovaries and mammary glands suggested to Charcot that those regions were hysterical zones. Yes I know it's your arm, but according to Charcot your kind of complaints are all of a piece. It appears he believed himself an expert on the female body.'

I stretched out my good arm towards the notebook but she replaced it in her bag and snapped the catch shut. 'No need to read it, I can tell you the salient points, and you know what my writing's like. He used an ovary compressor, a fearful looking contraption with screws and bolts.'

'What for?'

She stared at me, expecting me to shudder. 'To

reinvigorate the organs and stimulate muscles.'

'Anyway I don't see what it's got to do with the woman Leo wants me to see.'

'I'm coming to that.' Her voice softened a fraction. 'Freud was, or still is for all I know, a disciple of this Charcot chap. They both practise hypnotism, putting you into a trance so that against your will you tell them about your childhood and…' She broke off and I wondered if she was thinking about our own childhood or was it because, as I had begun to suspect, her knowledge of Freud was almost as sketchy as my own.

'Putting you in a trance,' she repeated, 'so you talk about all kind of unmentionable things that doubtless provide an unhealthy thrill for the analyst.'

'I don't know why you're telling me all this.' I suppressed an aching yawn that I knew would be interpreted as yet another of my symptoms. 'I may have a useless arm but my mind is still functioning perfectly well and I've already decided not to see the wretched woman.'

CHAPTER TWO

'I'm glad I have no unconscious mind.'
(Dr Brian Bolton)

It was Muriel's birthday and as usual she had insisted neither Leo nor I bought her a present except I hate to think what would have happened if we had decided to take her at her word. This year she had added: *I'm far too old to celebrate such occasions. Besides you should be saving, putting aside as much as you can manage.*

The reason for economising was never mentioned but we both knew only too well what it was. Bringing up a family was expensive, especially the first born who would require a crib, a bath, a nursing chair – whatever that was supposed to be – quite apart from all the nappies and nightdresses, vests, matinée jackets and bootees.

Leo was on edge, most likely because his mother had telephoned him the previous evening to tell him what she thought of Mrs Moberley. Not Mrs Moberley herself, of course, but her work as an analyst. Like my sister Joyce, Muriel would have said in no uncertain terms what she thought of Freud's outlandish ideas and since the subject was sure to come up during lunch I was bracing myself for an argument, one that would exclude me no doubt, but might upset Archie.

The journey from Highgate to Richmond took longer than usual. Since "my arm" Leo had driven slowly, afraid an emergency might force him to brake suddenly and I would be unable to stop myself being jerked out my seat. And today he had another reason to take extra care. The car was new, a Morris Oxford Tourer, a family car.

'How are you feeling?' He kept his eyes on the road ahead but I could tell from his voice he was frowning.

'I haven't coughed at all today. I had such a good night's sleep.'

He was silent and I regretted my last remark. A good night's sleep, alone in my twin bed, was what he would be thinking.

So much of our life together had become a cause for embarrassment, and pain. We carried out our normal routine, the one we had established since the early days of my "illness", but most of our conversation was about cough mixtures and cures for headaches, or now and again the detective novel I was reading, or whether Enid had given Solomon too many scraps and he was becoming stout. Lately of course there had been Mrs Moberley and the journal article, not that we had spent much time discussing it, just the odd comment made by Leo who quickly changed the subject for fear of upsetting me.

As we crossed Hammersmith Bridge large drops of rain splashed on the windscreen and Leo cursed under his breath. 'Still, you won't want to go for a walk will you, let alone have a game of croquet? It's all that time between lunch and tea I dread. Let's hope my mother doesn't suggest we play Plant-It.'

I laughed. Plant-It was a children's board game with little coloured squares. Muriel revelled in it, shaking the dice in their Bakelite pot, shouting with glee if she threw two sixes, and fitting in her cardboard squares of lobelia or alyssum, carrots or spring onions. I thought it must bring back memories of when Leo was a little boy, or perhaps it appealed to her love of gardening.

'Why do you say *my* mother?' I asked, 'why not "Mother", that's what you call her.'

'You don't call her anything.'

'Don't I? Yes I do. Well, she's not my mother.'

He gave a good-humoured snort. 'How's your head?'

'Don't keep asking, Leo, it makes me worse. That's all you ever say to me. How are you Ursa, feeling a little better Ursa?'

'I'm worried about you.'

'Bored with me more like.'

'Don't be silly.' He turned his head to look at a house he had always admired. Set back from the road it had a monkey puzzle tree in the front garden and a path leading up to an imposing front door.'

'Is that where you'd like to live?' I asked but he ignored my question, concentrating on the road ahead although the traffic was lighter than usual.

'Not long now.' His voice was studiously jolly. 'I think this is the best route don't you?'

'To travel hopefully is a better thing than to arrive.'

He sighed and I made an apologetic face. 'You know I never feel very hungry and then your mother starts asking if there's something wrong with the food and would I prefer it if she cooked me a lightly boiled egg.'

'Since the doctor said you were to rest you're unlikely to work up much of an appetite.' He drummed his fingers on the steering wheel and it reminded me of Toad of Toad Hall, except nothing about Leo is toad-like. If anything he is more like Ratty, or Badger I suppose.

'Quite comfortable isn't it?' he said.

'Your new car, yes it is.'

'*Our* new car.'

'Leo?'

'Now what?'

'I do love you.'

'Because I bought us a new car?' His jaw clenched and I thought, now it's your turn to bite your tongue, but the moment had passed and it was better to close my eyes and think my own thoughts. Think about Archie and the house he believed was too large for them now Leo had left home even though Muriel would have died rather than abandon her garden.

The Gables had been built at the turn of the century, a long, low place with a steeply pitched roof, the sweeping gables that gave it its name, three sets of chimney pots, and windows set in stone surrounds. They had a gardener who did the heavy work, a man called Percy with a glass eye, or possibly it was a squint, who was responsible for cutting back the creeper and mowing the grass. "But I never let him near the herbaceous borders," Muriel had told me in an aghast voice, "or my fruit trees or the strawberry bed."

Would she and Archie stay at *The Gables* forever? Muriel was only fifty-six and Archie two years older. To my shame I found myself imagining a time when Archie was a widower and had come to live with us in Highgate. In my daydream he had retired from his practice and was home all day. The dining room could be his study – he might want to write a book about dermatology – and I would take care not to disturb him but we would have lunch together and if the weather was fine go for a walk on Hampstead Heath. He was such good company and because I had worked for him for two years and seven months I sometimes felt he knew me better than Leo did.

After I left school I had lived at home for a while, helping Mother recover from Father's death. That was how my presence in the house was described although, as I quickly discovered, my mother preferred to be alone. Father's illness, coming so soon after Uncle Edward being killed in The War, had made her morbid, obsessed with death, and when she did talk to me, which was not often, it was about the pointlessness of life, of being born, getting married, having children, then seeing them married off, and soon there would be more children on the way.

I realise now she was suffering from depression but since she had plenty to make her unhappy it would have been wrong to call it an illness. *After your father died I was no longer the most important person in the world to somebody.* The times I heard her say that. Of course, thinking about it now I should have protested, "you *are* to me". But it would have been a lie because if my sister Joyce is right mothers love their children far more than children love their mothers.

One afternoon a friend of Mother's had called round and talked at length about a doctor she knew, a specialist, who was in need of a secretary. Later it dawned on me that Mother and her friend must have planned the whole thing behind my back. Why bother? Why not come straight out with it? But that was never Mother's way. *It would be good for you Ursula, give you the opportunity to meet people, see the world.*

We had done a little typing at school and after a brief refresher course where we were taught shorthand as well I began working for Archie in the mornings. Later, partly because my typing speed was nothing to write home about and partly because another doctor joined the practice, my hours were increased so that I stayed on until four o'clock every day except Friday.

I still lived with Mother but we saw little of each other during the week as she retired to bed early and got up after I left for work. Mabel, her maid, cooked the evening meal, which was just as well since Mother was fussy about what she ate and complained the way I boiled the potatoes gave her indigestion. Her stomach had always been a problem but in the end it was a severe dose of influenza that saw her off. In the words of our family doctor, she turned her face to the wall and decided to join my father.

Was it possible to do that, to give up and stop trying to get well? If it was perhaps it was something I had inherited from her. No, that made no sense. My cough drove me up the wall and as for my arm, and of course it had to be my right one, I was bored silly with sitting about incapable of doing much more than read a book, play clock patience, or stroke the cat.

One of the many neurologists who had examined me had suggested my symptoms might be the result of delayed grief, and when questioned about my mother's illness and subsequent death I had nodded vaguely, agreeing it was a possibility. After all I could hardly admit that it had been a relief when she died. She had been wretched without Father so all in all it was a blessing, even Joyce had admitted as much…

As we turned the corner I opened my eyes and the house came into view and a moment later the Morris crunched up the gravel drive – the gates had been left open for us – and Leo pulled up with a yank of the hand brake.

I asked if he had remembered the present and he pointed to the neatly wrapped parcel by his feet. 'Fuller's chocolates, Mother's favourites. Only a token, she can't object to that, can she?'

'I'm sure she'll be delighted,' I said, adding, 'especially since you chose them yourself.' So in spite of all my good intentions I was unable to contain my resentment. Leo, the adored son, and me the daughter-in-law who had failed to live up to expectations.

Muriel had heard the car and come out into the porch. She raised a hand in greeting and I noticed she was wearing a new dress, a grey one with a square neck and a kind of cape attached. Since the skirt of it came almost to her ankles it would draw attention to mine, which stopped just below the knee, and the fact that practically everyone my age wore dresses that length would not prevent Muriel from inspecting me as though I were some kind of freak. *Harvey Nichols has some very smart two-piece suits, Ursula, and quite reasonably priced, only seven and a half guineas.* Still, I was wearing the spring hat she had bought for me on one of her shopping trips. *Thirty-nine and six, from Marshall and Snelgrove, straw with a felt brim and appliqué.* I disliked it but had told her how becoming I thought it was and she had given me one of her looks then smiled to herself as though she had won a battle that was well worth fighting.

Was I over-sensitive? Leo thought so. Only the trouble with his mother, while most people smile much as a dog wags its tail, Muriel's smiles were rationed, brief little twitches of her rather prettily shaped lips and since her eyes, like Leo's, were large and round they gave her a slightly surprised look which I sometimes mistook for disapproval.

'Leo!' She kissed him so close to his mouth it made me flinch. 'And Ursula dear how are you?' Her lips barely brushed my cheek and I thought about Joyce and the sensitive skin that should have been one of my symptoms. Of course, my arm meant that most people tended to treat me as though I might break.

The rain had stopped and after the birthday greetings Muriel suggested a brief tour of the garden. 'The crocuses have been rather silly this year.' She pointed at a grassy bank. 'They came out too soon then got done in by the frost and wind.'

I started to cough and in order to draw attention away from me she hurried towards the magnolia that was in full bloom. 'Look Leo, it's come out in your honour.'

'It's lovely,' I spluttered, remembering how once she had told me its proper name was *Magnolia loebneri* which should not be confused with *Magnolia salicifolia.* I am good at memorising Latin names, possibly because of all that learning by heart we had to do at school, that and all the medical terms I picked up while working for Archie.

Had the sun been shining the mass of white star-shaped flowers would have looked even more attractive. Still, although the sky was overcast the day was warm and muggy and I wished I had chosen a thinner dress, or at least left off the thick vest that everyone insisted I wear.

'I can remember when you planted it.' Leo touched a petal with his fingertip. 'Looks as if it's covered in snow.'

'Or pocket handkerchiefs,' I added, and that gave Muriel an opportunity to express surprise that I was confusing it with the actual handkerchief tree, real name *Davidia*, that was due to burst into flower in about a month's time.

'Oh yes I forgot.' I hid my face in the yellow forsythia but it had no scent so I felt an idiot and moved on to a plant with dark shiny leaves, then another covered in tight little buds, and all the time I was trying to think of an excuse to go into the house and find Archie.

Pink tulips, a red camellia, and the flowering currant that smelled of tomcats and always made me want to giggle. It looked as though we were in for a full-scale tour but with a cry of delight Muriel's eyes suddenly alighted on the gleaming brass radiator on Leo's new car.

'Leo, you never said! What a splendid vehicle and how clever of you to choose it.'

Seizing my chance, I murmured something about wanting to sit down, thinking all the while that since both my legs were in good working order if only my stupid arm decided to function properly I would be cured and there would be no need for second opinions, let alone a crackpot psychoanalyst.

As I entered the hall Archie was coming down the stairs. I saw the tips of his brogues, and felt a small contraction in my chest, then the whole of him came into view and he held out his arms.

'Ursula, how are you?'

'Hello Archie.' He made me feel he was asking about *me*, not just my arm, or my headaches, or the awful chronic cough.

'Don't worry,' he murmured, and I guessed he was referring to Mrs Moberley.

'No, I won't.'

'It will be all right, you'll see.'

'Yes I know.' I could feel the steady thump of his heart which meant he must be able to tell how fast my own was beating. More than ever I needed his warmth, his strong kind face with its straight nose, with a slight kink on the bridge, the brightness of his blue eyes, and the thickness of his prematurely white hair. He and Leo were roughly the same height but Archie was more heavily built and had the beginnings of a tummy, the effect of Vera's stodgy meals, although today being Sunday Muriel would have prepared the lunch.

We stood together, only moving apart when we heard Muriel and Leo coming through the porch.

'She's looking a little better.' Muriel spoke briskly, like a nurse bringing the doctor up to date on one of his patients. 'A bit more colour in her cheeks. Are you allowed a small sherry Ursula?' She took hold of my good arm and guided me into the drawing room. 'Is she Leo?'

'I don't see why not.'

'Actually I don't think I will thank you, I'm not very fond of sherry.'

Archie laughed. 'Something else we have in common.'

Muriel's eyebrows lifted a fraction. 'Something else?'

'Our liking for dogs,' he explained. 'Don't worry, I know all about their muddy paws and moulting jackets. In any case they need to live in the country although I see a fair number of them on my walks, some of them quite hefty looking creatures.'

Archie's walks took place in Richmond Park, less than a quarter of a mile from *The Gables*. He walked before breakfast and again, if it was still light, after he returned from work. No wonder he looked so fit and so much younger than his fifty-eight years.

I thought I could smell roast beef, or it could be lamb. Horseradish with beef, mint sauce with lamb. My sister Joyce had provided me with recipes for both and thrown up her hands in horror when she discovered a jar of ready-made horseradish that Enid had bought in the market. Stiff white table napkins and brown raffia place mats. A crystal water jug and sparkling glasses with not a sign of a smear in sight. Enid was not as fastidious as Vera, and I doubted if either of them could reach Muriel's high standards.

She and Leo were standing by the French windows that led to the terrace, talking earnestly and sipping their dry sherry while Muriel fiddled with his hair with her free hand. I paused by a puzzle laid out on the rosewood table, and picked up a piece that looked as if it would fit into Hampton Court maze but it was too large.

'Over a thousand pieces,' Archie laughed, 'strange things, human beings, can you imagine any other species cutting up a picture then spending several hours putting it together again.'

'An ape might enjoy it,' Leo grinned at us over his shoulder, 'a chimpanzee I mean. Apparently they're awfully like us in hundreds of ways.'

'Keeps me occupied,' Muriel said, joining in the general merriment since the remark had come from Leo, 'Archie's jealous because he's no good at jigsaws.'

'How true.' Archie crossed to the window and I watched the three of them, feeling a confusion of emotions that were best ignored. Husband and wife, then parents and son, going back twenty years or more, long before I had come on the scene.

When I first met her I wondered why Muriel only had one child. Now I knew it was because in her eyes Leo was perfect, there was no need for another. The two of them were so close, almost like lovers. No, that was ridiculous. Mothers are always close to their sons. If I had been a boy my mother would probably have doted on me in much the same way.

'Excuse me a moment,' I said, 'I'm just going up to the bathroom.'

For a horrible moment I thought Muriel was going to accompany me but if she had been going to Leo's frown had changed her mind. Archie would have realised I needed to get away and, to be fair, so would Leo, but such a thought would never have entered Muriel's head.

Running cold water in the basin I splashed a little on my forehead and neck, being careful not to wet my hair, then dried myself with the clean hand towel that Muriel had provided. The tiles were another of Muriel's "finds", white with blue drawings of Shakespearian characters, Titania, Ophelia, and one that could have been Rosalind in "As You Like It" or Kate in "The Taming of the Shrew". How would you tell the difference?

Did she and Archie have a bathroom each? Cautiously I opened a small wall cabinet and stood on tiptoe to see the top shelf. Green bath salts in a glass jar. A bottle of something that could have been perfume but was more likely to be medicinal. Nothing masculine, no shaving soap or cut throat razor. Nothing that smelled of Archie. Everywhere was spotlessly, almost clinically clean and suddenly I felt so overcome with weariness I wondered how I was going to get through lunch. I would have to though or the fuss would be unendurable.

When I returned to the drawing room they were discussing the proposed channel tunnel and Muriel was saying she was against it because people would desert the resorts on the south coast.

'But the French will travel to England,' Leo said.

Muriel's face brightened. 'Yes you're right Leo. 'Living on an island the English are a seafaring people, Britannia rules the waves and all that, but the French are nervous of crossing in a boat and would prefer a tunnel. In any case, it'll never happen. Absurd. Far too ambitious.'

Archie winked at me and I smiled back, but not too much in case he thought I was laughing at Muriel.

During lunch Muriel asked after Joyce. 'She dropped by on Friday,' she explained, 'she's worried about you Ursula, we all are.'

Archie gave her a look as though to say "not now Muriel" but she took no notice. 'She wanted my opinion on Leo's Mrs Moberley. She's been reading a book about hypnotism. Apparently the man who invented it held ceremonies out of doors under previously magnetized oak trees. I ask you!'

'What's that got to do with Mrs Moberley?' Leo was cutting my food into bite-size pieces as one might for a small child. 'Mesmer died over a hundred years ago and nobody goes along with that magnetic rubbish these days. Anyway I wish Joyce would mind her own business.'

'Oh I don't think that's quite fair.' Muriel gave him a fond but mildly reproving frown. 'After all she is

Ursula's sister. She only wants what's best for her.'

I gazed round the dining room with its highly polished parquet floor and the panelled walls that gave it a slightly gloomy feel. The first time I visited the house I had asked about the carved coat of arms on the stone chimneypiece and Archie had laughed and said it had nothing to do with him, an affectation of the previous owners.

'Well Ursula?' Muriel said and I was obliged to ask her to repeat the question.

'I wondered how you felt about this silly business. After all you're the one who would have to be hypnotised.'

'I've only read what Leo showed me.' The rush-bottomed chairs, Muriel's pride and joy, may have looked stylish but they were extremely uncomfortable. All I wanted was to finish the meal, have another obligatory stroll round the garden, then leave. If I could have talked properly to Archie it would have been different but I knew that was not going to be possible. Muriel had a way of herding us all together like a flock of sheep and any conversation in which she was not included put her nose out of joint, as though she imagined we must be talking about her, which in truth was hardly ever the case.

The pudding was Apple Charlotte. Soon after Leo and I were married Muriel had given me some recipes she had copied into a little loose-leaf notebook. Apple Charlotte was one of them. *Peel, core and cut a pound of apples into thick slices. Mix together breadcrumbs and suet, brown sugar and grated lemon.* Enid and I had followed the instructions religiously but been obliged to substitute the double sheet of greased paper for a single one, all we had left. Perhaps that was why it had tasted rather dry.

Needless to say, Muriel's pudding was perfection. Leo complimented her on the meal and I added my appreciation although something, almost certainly not the food, had given me a headache. Still, the coughing had stopped. It was odd how one symptom seemed to replace another. My right arm remained lifeless by my side but various bodily sensations came and went for no good reason I could tell. The pins and needles in my thigh, the blurry vision which I attributed to too much reading, and lately bouts of breathlessness, and palpitations of the heart although these rarely lasted more than a few minutes.

'Mesmer influenced Charcot a good deal,' Archie remarked, unexpectedly returning to the subject of hypnotism. 'Charcot was a brilliant neurologist, but as far as his patients were concerned a rather cold and distant man I believe. Be that as it may he seems to have made a strong impression on Freud. What do you think about all this Ursula? Leo pulling you in one direction, your sister and mother-in-law in the other.'

'As I said, I don't know much about it.' I was a little upset that Archie too had been reading up on the subject, but grateful that he was interested in my opinion. 'Joyce thinks my symptoms could be called hysterical but are much more likely to indicate an underlying disease.'

Leo came in angrily. 'Is that what she said?'

'I'm restless, hard to please, and over emotional.'

'A trifle unfair.' Muriel held the spoon above the pudding dish, offering a second helping, which I declined with a shake of my aching head. 'Still, I know she means well. You're very taken with this talking treatment Leo but there's no evidence it does any good for someone with Ursula's complaints and I imagine it could easily make her considerably worse.'

I opened my mouth to say I had no intention of visiting Mrs Moberley, but no words came out. For the past ten days I had been adamant. Giving in would have been an admission I had something wrong with my mind, and besides the thought of visiting Mrs Moberley's consulting room filled me with dread. Mrs Moberley. The name conjured up an image of a medium at a séance, dressed in flowing garments, sitting in a darkened room, swinging a pocket watch above my head as I drifted into a trance.

Leo had started telling his parents how, when Freud's lectures became available, a number of chief librarians had placed them in reference rooms for genuine students only, where no harm could come about through prurient curiosity. Archie found this amusing but Muriel pursed her lips and I suspected she agreed with the librarians.

'Thank goodness not everyone is so narrow minded,' Leo continued, 'in fact only last week I read about a school that proposes to establish methods in keeping with psychoanalysis.'

'What would that require exactly?' Archie paused with a mouthful of Apple Charlotte on his spoon.

'I couldn't tell you exactly but I do know that many cases of clumsiness or an inability to learn certain lessons can be rectified by analysis.'

Muriel looked highly sceptical. 'In the wrong hands I imagine things might easily get out of hand.'

What could get out of hand, I expected Leo to ask, but he had stopped eating his lunch and was staring at me.

'Now what's the matter?' he asked, unable to contain his exasperation. 'What ever are you doing?'

'Nothing.' The skin under the strap on one my shoes felt as though an insect had bitten it. I kicked off both shoes and scratched it with the big toe of my other foot. 'Actually I was thinking about your beloved Doctor Freud.'

'What about him?'

My throat ached. I thought how Leo always accused me of being contrary, of changing my mind for no good reason he could see and refusing to discuss things rationally. In that case I might as well live up to my reputation.

'I'll see her,' I said, watching with some satisfaction as Leo's spoon clattered onto his plate and spattered stewed apple on the spotless cloth. 'Mrs Moberley.' I spoke the name as one might announce an honoured guest arriving at a society party. 'I'll go and see her as soon as you can make the arrangements.'

CHAPTER THREE

'We know that with every voluntary movement it is the idea of the result to be achieved which initiates the relevant muscular contraction. It is not very hard to see that the idea that this contraction is impossible will impede the movement.'

(Josef Breuer)

Archie drove me there in the Daimler. I had been expecting Muriel to accompany him and the sight of Archie, alone, raised my spirits so much I almost forgot the ordeal ahead. It would be all right. I would stay for the allotted fifty minutes – the "therapeutic hour" – and at the end of it I would thank her for her time and trouble and even pretend I was prepared to come back.

One thing I was certain about. I had no intention of allowing her to hypnotise me. *One can see that the patient has sore places in his soul life but one is afraid to touch them lest his suffering be increased.* But from everything I had read pain was what Freud was all about.

Ever since Leo telephoned to make the appointment I had been building up a picture of the house in Inverness Gardens. Surrounded by dark trees with twisted branches, the kind of place where a murder might well have taken place. And in my mind's eye I always arrived there in the pouring rain. So it was a surprise to wake on the fateful morning and find the sun had reached the end of my bed and particles of dust were dancing in the shaft of light.

The first problem was what to wear. Leo was no help and I could tell he thought my questions frivolous but he was not the one preparing to enter the lion's den. Dress too casually and I would be seen as a wretched downtrodden creature. *The patient cares little for her appearance, an indication of her distressed mental condition.* Put on my best clothes and I would be vain and shallow, a spoilt little girl set on drawing attention to myself. *Her dress would not have looked out of place at a society wedding and I am inclined to believe the patient relishes the interest her symptoms have elicited.*

In the end I chose my blue frock with a v-shaped neckline and buttoned cuffs. Blue was my favourite colour, my lucky colour, and I needed all the luck I could muster. A matching loosely belted jacket would complete the outfit.

As I searched through my wardrobe Leo had hovered by the door. 'I have to go now but Father will be here quite soon. In the meantime I suggest you rest.'

'I'll read my book. Oh no I've finished it.'

'Then why not start your new Miss Silver Mystery.' He was almost as nervous as I was. 'I wish I could drive you there myself but I know you find the Daimler more comfortable.'

'Don't expect a miracle.'

'Of course not, psychoanalysis doesn't work like that. All the same, good analysts are few and far between and according to my sources Mrs Moberley is one of the best.'

'Go on Leo or you'll be late.'

'Goodbye then.' He kissed my forehead. 'Need any help with those beads?'

'No thank you.' I lifted out my matching earrings,

the ones that looked like drops of water. 'Enid will be here in an hour. She enjoys fastening my jewellery.'

'Good old Enid,' he laughed.

'Yes good old Enid.'

Archie arrived early and came through the hall singing. I heard Enid give a little squeal of pleasure and knew he had said something flattering, or something that had made her laugh.

'Sun's shining Ursula, a good portent wouldn't you say?'

I pulled a face because the weather might be nice but nothing else about the day was agreeable. 'It's so kind of you Archie. Did you have to cancel one of your appointments? If you did I feel awful about it. And I expect the patient does too.'

He gave my good arm a squeeze. 'Hadn't you better wear something warmer over that jacket?'

'Best be on safe side Mrs Ingham.' Enid helped me into my coat, wound my scarf round my neck and pulled on my gloves. 'I'm making a cottage pie for your lunch, with plenty of Yorkshire Relish just how you like it.'

'Thank you Enid but I'm afraid I may have lost my appetite.'

'Or you could be ravenous.' Archie winked at Enid and she frowned her disapproval as though to say, what is poor Mrs Ingham letting herself in for.

As we drove off, I looked back over my shoulder as if I might never see the house again. The first time we viewed it Leo had thought the front door, with its bubbly glass in the shape of a peacock's tail, a bit vulgar but he had liked the wrought iron gate and railings, and the brickwork arch that framed the big downstairs window. We were lucky living in such a pleasant part of London. Sometimes I wished we had a better view, not just the fronts or backs of other houses, but that would have cost far more and, as my mother used to say, it was ungracious to dwell on what you lacked when you ought to be thanking God for your blessings.

Archie was driving with his usual gay abandon, letting me think he was approaching a junction too fast, but always braking in plenty of time.

'There's no rush,' I told him, 'we don't want to get there early.'

'Trust me.' He chuckled to himself. 'Chauffeurs can calculate their journeys accurately down to the last minute.'

'I'm not sure I want to be put into a trance Archie.'

'You can't be hypnotised against your will.'

'Are you sure about that?'

'Quite sure. Besides no one has ever been able to force you to do something contrary to your wishes.'

'Is that what you think?' I was uncertain whether he was joking or being serious.

'Not a criticism Ursula.' He patted my knee with a large warm hand. 'A compliment as well you know.'

We passed the turning to the station, then the bookshop, the chemist, and the little shop that sold pipes and tobacco and tins of snuff. If Leo's description was correct Inverness Gardens should be the next but one on the left. Two more minutes and there would be no going back. No losing my nerve. It had been my decision and however forbidding the house turned out to be I was not so feeble that I would ask Archie to drive me straight back home again.

He was peering at the names of the roads and it occurred to me he might need glasses for driving but was too vain to buy a pair.

'How's the arm?' he asked.

'Same as usual.'

'You're bound to feel a little apprehensive.' He turned into Inverness Gardens and I reminded him that the house was number eighty.

'Down the far end,' he said, putting on a silly voice of mock horror.

'It's not funny Archie.'

'No but it will be jolly interesting finding out what she's like.'

'It's all right for you.'

'An adventure Ursula, look on it as an adventure. And if she restores you to good health that will be an extra bonus.'

When we pulled up opposite the house it was almost a disappointment. Red brick with a grey tiled roof and bay windows. No trees or shrubs only a single climbing plant with pale delicate flowers that trailed over the top of the downstairs window and continued on its way to the first floor. Muriel would have known what it was. Wisteria perhaps. No that was the one with long mauve flowers and Mrs Moberley's were white.

There, I had spoken her name, if only in my head.

I suppose I had expected somewhere grander, more like *The Gables*, and in an instant my vision of her had been transformed from an intimidating duchess-like figure to a frumpish middle-aged woman with a round, featureless face. Was she married? Did she have children? I should have asked Leo except I doubted his enquiries would have included her private life. Who were these people who had recommended her? I should have asked that too although knowing Leo he would have prevaricated, like a parent with an over-inquisitive child.

'Well then.' Archie cleared his throat and I wondered what he really thought about psychoanalysis. 'Not particularly forbidding is it.'

I managed a feeble smile but my body had started to tremble and a moment later I was overtaken by a fit of coughing that left me flushed and out of breath.

Archie consulted his watch. 'Wait a couple of minutes until you feel calmer then take the plunge?'

'I don't know anything about her.'

'I'm sure Leo will have done his homework.'

'I'm his guinea pig. Someone to test out Freud's talking cure. Do you think it's all tosh Archie?'

He gave an unconvincing laugh. 'Not being an expert I keep an open mind. Let's see how this first visit goes shall we, and take it from there.'

'Leo says my arm is the result of a childhood trauma.'

'Leo says a lot of things.'

'I thought you agreed with him,' I began, but he put a finger to his lips. 'All right I won't say another word but whatever she's like trying to cure me will be a thankless task.'

I was watching the house, half expecting to see her face at the window like the wicked fairy in Hansel and Gretel. So I had been wrong about the exterior of the place but the consulting room would be much as I imagined it, heavy brocade curtains, a thick dark carpet, and lacy antimacassars on the backs of big, ugly chairs. Not that I would be sitting on one of them. According to everything I had read the patient lay stretched out on a couch and was not allowed to see the analyst while the treatment was taking place. Did that mean a servant would let me in? Then what would happen? I would be led to the consulting room where Mrs Moberley would be sitting with her back turned, and a faceless voice would instruct me to lie down please Mrs Ingham.

Archie had opened the passenger door. 'I'll take a leisurely walk across the Heath and back then wait for you in the car.'

'Will you leave it here?'

'What do you think? Down the end there might be best.' He pointed to a row of lime trees. 'That way you won't have far to walk and Mrs Moberley won't accuse me of lurking about, trying to peer through her windows.'

'Oh I'm sure she wouldn't do that.' But he was joking, except according to Freud there are no jokes. People say what they mean with a little laugh and if it comes out rude or upsetting they pretend they were only joking.

Archie kissed my cheek and I resisted the temptation to take out my compact and dab more powder on my face.

'Off you go,' he said, sounding as unconcerned as he could, 'and I'll see you in about fifty minutes.'

'Exactly fifty minutes.'

'Of course.'

I watched him stroll away, heartily wishing I could accompany him then started up the path, trying not to touch the cracks between the diamond shaped tiles, and paused by the blue front door before reaching out to press the brass bell.

The woman who answered was tall and thin with a narrow, slightly bony face and short fair hair that grew like a feathery cloud round her head. 'Mrs Ingham?'

'Yes.' I followed her into the hall, assuming she must be the maid and expecting her to knock on an inner door and announce my arrival. But after she had hung up my coat she held out her hand.

'I'm Mrs Moberley. We're in the room at the back.'

I grasped her hand with my left one, feeling awkward and self-conscious although when she took my coat she had paid no attention to my arm and I wondered if she had forgotten about it. Perhaps she suspected I was a fake and was trying to catch me out. *You moved your arm. Yes, you did, I saw you.*

Her hair was too fine to be fashionable but for someone her age – I guessed she must be about forty – her clothes were surprisingly up-to-date. A pleated skirt that stopped just below her knees and a loose-fitting jacket with two patch pockets that caught my eye immediately because one of them had a small notebook poking out. Information she had written down on the strength of Leo's telephone call? Or was it for the notes she would make either while I was there or straight after I left?

My mouth was so dry I had to try hard not to keep licking my lips. Fifty minutes to endure but when it ended I would be free and when I told Leo how excruciating it had been he was not so hard-hearted that he would want me to go through it again.

The room I was shown into was rather like our dining room at home but less cluttered. No ornaments or pictures although one wall was almost entirely covered by a tapestry depicting flowers and trees and tropical birds. I could smell furniture polish and found myself wondering if Mrs Moberley had a maid like Enid who enjoyed rubbing in liberal amounts of the stuff. Where was the maid? Probably in the kitchen, banned on pain of death from catching sight of the patients in case she gave away their shameful secret to her friends and acquaintances. *You know that lady with the husband who's a master at the boys' preparatory school…*

'Do sit down.' She gestured towards a sagging armchair that faced her own which was on the opposite side of the fireplace.

'Thank you.' My voice came out in a squeak and I cleared my throat in the vain hope that she would think I had a frog in it and the high pitch had nothing to do with nerves. Her chair was higher than mine, something that made me feel at even more of a disadvantage, but that was probably part of the treatment.

To steady myself I fixed my gaze on the small table beside her, taking in the lamp with its glass shade, the clock whose face I was unable to see, and a black fountain pen with its lid unscrewed.

Most of the polished wood floor between our two chairs was covered in a large oriental rug and another smaller rug had been placed in front of an antique bureau, partially obscured by a folding screen, again with a pattern of leaves and exotic birds. Muriel would have liked it, I thought, although she always claimed British birds were the best, not so ostentatious. She has a little stone bath by her summerhouse and a rustic bird table in the middle of her lawn, but I never feed the ones that come into our garden because it would only encourage Solomon to pounce on them. There's a swing in Muriel's garden too that used to be Leo's and now hangs motionless, awaiting another generation of children.

'Oh Dora!' Without warning Mrs Moberley rose swiftly from her chair. 'When did you sneak in, back to the kitchen you go.'

'Not on my account,' I said, sounding stiff and formal like someone in a Jane Austen novel. 'I like cats, we have one at home, a tabby. Yours is a Devon blue isn't it?'

She said nothing, keeping her attention focussed on the cat as it settled itself on the rug, stuck one leg in the air and began washing itself in that unabashed position cats adopt, regardless of who is watching them. I could see the top of my head reflected in an oval mirror with a gilt frame and I touched my hair to feel if it was sticking up and at the same moment she spoke, startling me for a second time.

'What is your cat's name?'

'*My* cat?' It was such an unexpected question. 'He's called Solomon.'

'In all his glory.' She smiled and I tried to smile back but my face was set in an expressionless mask.

'How did you get here Mrs Ingham, did your husband bring you?'

'No, my father-in-law.'

'He lives in Highgate too?'

'No, Richmond.' I was unable to meet her eyes. 'Near the park.'

'How did you feel about coming to see me?'

'Oh.' I looked beyond her at a shabby chaise longue that must be "the couch". Quite attractive with its pattern of pale orange and yellow flowers but not very comfortable to lie on. 'I suppose I was just grateful you could fit me in so soon.'

Was the furniture polish to hide the smell of cigarettes? It had never occurred to me that she would smoke. Not in her consulting room surely but it does tend to get into your clothes. Of course I could be quite wrong. Just thinking about chocolate makes me certain I can smell it.

The first half hour had been relatively painless and consisted of me providing her with what she described as "a short case history". But now she had stopped talking and was watching me intently, like a strict governess waiting for her charge to recite the poem she had been set to learn. What did she want me to say? *Whatever comes into your head*, that was what Leo had instructed, but supposing it was something quite irrelevant, like won't leaving the top off your fountain pen mean the ink dries up.

'It was my husband's idea I came here.' Heat started to creep up my neck and she would notice the redness and think what a goose I was. 'Because of my symptoms and there not being anything wrong with me, medically speaking. I expect he explained about all the doctors and specialists who've examined me. He's a great admirer of Freud. Leo is I mean. Actually he has been for a long time, not just because…' My voice trailed away.

'And you?'

'I just want to get better.' I met her eyes at last, expecting an encouraging comment. *Yes of course you do.* But she was sitting with her hands in her lap, waiting for me to continue.

It was unfair. She ought to be making things easier for me and at first I had thought she was going to, talking about cats, smiling. Now her face reminded me of our History mistress at school. Miss Wesley – we called her "the weasel" – had the same alarmingly heavy-lidded eyes and unyielding expression.

'My sister disapproves,' I said, 'and so does Muriel, that's Leo's mother, my mother-in-law.'

'And your own parents?'

'They're both dead. Leo and Muriel and Archie are my family now.'

'Archie is your father-in-law?'

I nodded.

'So you were faced with a fair amount of opposition but you still decided to come.'

'To please Leo, to get back in his good books. No, that's not true. This may sound terribly rude but I think it was because Joyce and Muriel kept going on at me, saying what a beastly thing psychoanalysis is and what appalling things would be done to me. Joyce thinks Freud is poppycock.'

She was silent and I was afraid I had offended her but when she spoke again I could tell she was quite unperturbed. 'I expect you wanted to be allowed to make up your own mind.'

'Yes.' My left hand was squeezing my thigh and I was short of breath as though I had run up a steep hill. It was a test. To find out what I was like, why I was ill. But what was I supposed to say? Only I had to say something because the silences were unendurable.

'I have a cough,' I said, 'a chronic one, and headaches, mostly in the afternoon. And my arm of course. You know about my arm?'

'I'd like to hear about it from you.'

'I can't move it. There's no strength. I woke up one morning and it felt weak. No it was worse than that, it was completely useless. At first I thought it must be pins and needles, I must have been lying on it, but an hour later it was no better and it's stayed the same ever since. The doctors say there's nothing wrong with it. And the cough, there's nothing wrong with my lungs either. And the headaches, but plenty of people get headaches don't they. I know I ought to be able to pull myself together. Is that what you think? Only I'll need to tell Leo.'

'Shall we get to know each other a little first? You'll want to be as confident as you can be that I'll be able to help you. And the same applies to me of course.'

Another silence. I wanted to stroke the cat but she was out of reach so instead I stared down at my shoes which were new with small bows on them and pointed toes. It was no use, she would have waited all morning or at least until it was time for me to leave.

'But how will I know if you can help?' I asked, 'and how will you know if I'm suitable?'

'Would you like to come back?'

'Oh, you mean it takes more than one visit. Yes I can see it must be difficult.'

'Tell me about your family.'

I flinched and although she gave no sign of it I knew she had noticed. 'Only me and Leo.'

'And your sister.'

'Oh yes… Joyce, she's called Joyce. She's five years older than me, married to a vicar with a busy parish in Ealing and they've got three children, two little girls and a baby called Christopher. Leo wants children.'

When my words were met with another silence I found it difficult to conceal my exasperation. With a normal conversation one person speaks and the other one interrupts to say something else, and so it continues. Awkward silences only happen if someone causes offence and there's going to be a falling out.

I thought about my father and how my mother used to complain he never listened. Of course after he died she never said a bad word about him and if I mentioned him she looked away as though she thought me heartless and unfeeling. All the photographs were put away in a drawer so that sometimes it was difficult to remember what he had looked like. Not very tall, I think, with a long body and shortish legs, but quite handsome in a rakish kind of way. Once, when I was about seven or eight he had showed me how to cut a pear in half. I expect I remember because it was so unlike him. "One person cuts,' he said, "and the other chooses. That way it guarantees that the one who cuts is careful to end up with two identical halves." I used to think about that rare moment when, before my stupid arm happened, I shared some fruit or a piece of cake between me and Leo. Although the halves were never the same and I always gave him the larger of the two.

Mrs Moberley picked up the clock. 'Your thoughts are a long way away.'

'Oh I'm sorry, I was thinking about my father. I've no idea why. He died when I was at boarding school. Joyce was there too so it was her job to tell me.' I hesitated then began talking too fast. 'Joyce thought I'd be hypnotised and Leo said I would have to lie on a couch. Only we haven't begun yet have we, you haven't decided if I'm suitable. I'm sure I've said all the wrong things.'

'There are no wrong things Mrs Ingham.'

'I wish you'd call me Ursula or is that against the rules.'

She smiled and I noticed that one of her front teeth crossed over the other, but only a little.

'If I did come again,' I said, 'I'm not sure I'd want to be hypnotised or goodness knows what I might say and supposing I couldn't remember what I'd told you and lay awake afterwards night after night trying to remember. Leo says something bad must have happened during my childhood and the reason I can't recall it is because I don't want to, because it was so shocking.'

'You seem to be surrounded by experts.'

'Yes, I do, don't I.' I laughed, a real laugh, nothing to do with my nerves. 'Am I suitable? I thought it would be awful coming here. I thought you would be much older and dressed all in black.'

'Like a witch.'

'You have got a cat,' I said, proud of my boldness, then added quickly. 'But she's not the right colour.'

'No, she's not.' Mrs Moberley stood up and locked her hands behind her head. 'What do you think Ursula, shall we say three times a week, Monday, Wednesday, and Friday? Does this time of day suit you or would you prefer the afternoon?'

Archie was waiting for me in the Daimler. He leaned across to open the passenger door and I climbed in backwards, a technique I had perfected since my arm became defunct.

'Well?' he asked.

'It wasn't quite as bad as I expected. Although it's easy to say that now it's over.'

'You looked exhausted.'

'Yes I am a bit.' But I was suitable for treatment, and everyone would be pleased, except later it crossed my mind that Mrs Moberley might be glad of a new patient, any new patient, for the money I mean.

A week ago when the treatment was being discussed Archie had offered to pay and after a token protest Leo had agreed, but only if it was a loan because he had helped us out before when we bought our house. I had a little money my mother had left me but Archie had insisted that must be invested and would enable us, among other things, to hire a maid. He could afford to help, he was better off than Leo would ever be, but if only for that reason I knew it had been hard for Leo to agree to a second loan that in all probability would turn out to be a gift.

It was such a relief to be back in the car I felt like a schoolgirl who has finished her prep and been allowed out to play.

'I don't know how much it will cost, Archie.'

'Don't worry about that.'

'Or how long it will last.'

'As long as is necessary. I have complete confidence in you to continue until you're back to your old self.'

My old self. Why did his words send a slight chill down my back? Try not to think about it, not now. Try not to think about anything. I leaned back and the car moved off – it was facing in the right direction – and in no time at all we had reached the main road with its familiar sound of hooting traffic and clanking buses and I thought how good it would be to be home.

'I've agreed to see her three times a week. At two o'clock.' I opened my eyes and wriggled myself into an upright position.

'Good.' Archie glanced at me a fraction too long and had to turn the steering wheel fast to avoid the kerb.

'I'm afraid I may not be able to take you every time but you can always get a cab.'

'Or walk. Yes I think I'll walk.'

'Are you sure?'

'There's nothing wrong with my legs.'

'I thought you sometimes felt a tingling sensation.'

'No that's gone.'

The tension between us was something I had never felt before and I think it must have been the fact that I had met Mrs Moberley and Archie had not. Part of me wanted to tell him everything, about the consulting room with its two armchairs and chaise longue, about the table with its lamp, clock and a pen, about Dora the cat. But another, fiercer part wanted to keep it to myself. I felt oddly excited then guilty because I was being impetuous – a word my mother often used to describe me to her friends – and perhaps it was that flaw in my character that was responsible for my illness.

'Anyway.' Archie slowed down to allow a pretty girl, with a hat with its brim turned up, to cross the road ahead of us. 'You've broken the ice and next time will be easier.'

'Thank you for taking me Archie, I'd hate to have gone there by myself. And as you say, next time won't be nearly so bad.' I felt terribly tired and desperately needed to be on my own but perhaps I ought to offer him some of Enid's cottage pie. 'Would you like to stay for lunch or do you have to hurry back to your patients?'

'Do you want me to stay?'

'Only if you'd like to. I'll be all right, Enid's there.'

'You're fond of her aren't you?'

I screwed up my face, making out it was a strange thing for him to say, and instantly felt disloyal to Enid.

'Yes I am actually. I know she's only nineteen but she's so kind and so good-natured, just the sort of person I would have liked to have as a nanny.'

'Did you have a nanny when you were little?'

'No.'

'Nor did Leo. Muriel wanted to do everything herself.'

'Yes I can imagine. I'm sure she was awfully efficient.'

He threw back his head and laughed. 'She was Ursula, she was indeed. Leo was lucky to have such a devoted mother and now he's a lucky man having you for a wife.'

'Is he?' I refused to be humoured. 'I doubt if he sees it that way. Do you think talking will make me better? It's no disgrace seeing a psychoanalyst is it? In fact, looked at from one point of view I'm fortunate to have the opportunity.'

'That's the spirit.'

'Yes it is, isn't it?'

And now we could both laugh because the tension between us had disappeared and with any luck the sensation would return to my arm and there would be no more coughing or headaches and I would be cured.

My elation was short lived. How could talking provide a cure for a cough, let alone an insensible arm? A full analysis meant five times a week, for forty-two weeks of the year, but in my case Mrs Moberley thought three sessions a week would be sufficient. What did that mean? I should have asked her but at the time I was too unsure of myself and she might have refused to give a reason, or responded to my question with one of her own. *I wonder why you are unable to trust my judgement*

Mrs Ingham. But how could I trust her when I knew so little about her?

Leo had put a bookmark in *The Collected Papers of Freud, Volume 1* so I could study the section about hysterical symptoms. Apparently it was impossible to discover their cause by interrogation, partly because the patient found the experience disagreeable, but mainly because he was unable to remember.

Since most of Freud's patients seemed to be women it was odd that he always used "he" when he spelled out his ideas. There was the case of a girl who while sitting at the bedside of a sick person had let her arm hang over the back of the chair so that it went "to sleep". Did Leo think the memory of something like that was what had happened to me? What sick person? My father had been taken ill while I was away from home and right up to her death my mother had disliked having me in her bedroom for more than a few minutes at a time.

When I mentioned this to Leo he had thrust his hands in his trouser pockets and said giving me the book had been a mistake. 'Don't read any more, just stick to a few simple facts. Psychoanalysis is a way of investigating the unconscious mind, its conflicts and fantasies. Without the help of an expert this material is buried too deep to be recalled with any accuracy.' But what was the unconscious mind? I knew all about fantasies but how could you tell if everyone else had ones like your own? In fact I was pretty sure they did not or it would be something people talked about. Only perhaps not.

As soon as he returned from work I assumed Leo would be thirsting to hear about Mrs Moberley, in which case I would have felt duty bound to tell him at least part of what had taken place. However, like Archie, he had said little, aside from expressing faint surprise when I told him about the three times a week instead of five.

Later when we were both in bed I suggested it might be because she was so busy. 'It was kind of her to agree to see me so soon. I'm sure she must have patients with far more serious problems.'

'No I don't think that's the reason.' Yet again his tone implied he had some superior knowledge of how these things worked.

'What then?'

He rolled over and lay on his back and I watched him out of one eye with the other half of my face buried in my pillow. Light from the street lamp filtered through the chintz curtains and the short distance between our two beds meant I could see his expression, the slight frown, the drawing together of his dark eyebrows.

'Either she decided three times would be sufficient,' he said, talking so quietly that anyone listening would have thought there must be a child asleep in the next room, 'or else she thinks going there more often might put a strain on your physical health. Are you sure you can walk that far?'

'Quite sure.'

'You say that now but I think a cab would be better.'

'I'll manage, Leo, really I will.'

'If you say so.' He turned back on his side and mumbled something it was difficult to catch. I did hear though.

'Well let's hope it works and your arm – and our marriage – return to normal in every sense of the word.'

CHAPTER FOUR

'One reason the Anglo-Saxon race occupies such a leading position today is because it has refused to look on man as of necessity a lustful animal.'
(Lord Astor, writing in *The Times*)

If it had been left up to me I would have spent most of the day in the kitchen. But Enid might have found my presence a strain. Have you tried peeling potatoes with one hand? I was useless, a burden, and Enid wanted to get on with her work not waste time entertaining me. Still, now and again did no harm.

Gathering up my pad and pen I paused in front of the grandmother clock and listened. Just as I thought, the pendulum had stopped. Clocks were Leo's domain but seeing the motionless pendulum gave me a superstitious sense of foreboding. If I managed to start it again I would have to change the hands to the correct time and in my clumsy condition I might damage them. I could ask Enid to help but I knew what she would say. *Best leave it to Mr Ingham, he understands mechanical things.*

Balancing my writing materials on the revolving bookcase I opened the clock door and gave the brass pendulum a tap. It swung too fast then settled into a slow tick-tock and I told myself if it was still going when I came back my arm would regain its strength by the end of July but if it had stopped I would be condemned to live with it for the rest of my life.

Enid was making a pie, chopping up apples on the draining board and humming a tune she must have heard on the wireless.

'That's from an American musical isn't it? What's it called?'

She giggled.

'No, tell me Enid, you always know the latest songs.'

'Silly.' She started singing under her breath, choosing an octave too low so that her voice came out like a man's. '*Fish got to swim, birds got to fly. I'm going to love that man till I die. Can't help loving that man of mine.*' She broke off laughing. 'Only in America they don't say "that", they say "dat". Was there something you needed Mrs Ingham?'

'I'm bored.'

'Sit yourself down then and I'll make a pot of tea.'

Most of the rooms in the house were on the small side but the kitchen was an exception. The walls were white but the woodwork had been painted bottle green and there were plenty of shelves where storage jars and crockery could be displayed. Enid took a pride in keeping everything bright and shiny – *but warm and cosy too Mrs Ingham* – and the room was large enough to have a table in the middle where the two of us could sit together exchanging gossip, not that I had anything of much interest to tell her.

'The thing is Enid if I stay in one place for too long I start to ache.'

'Course you do.' She made a sound like a mother hen.

'And I want to write a letter,' I explained, 'and it's quite impossible on that wobbly-legged coffee table.'

'Clever of you writing with your wrong hand.'

'Not really, it's barely legible.' I sensed she wanted to hear about my new treatment, not that it would be starting until the following week, but I had told her I was suitable and she had congratulated me warmly even though I doubted she had a clue what it was all about.

Three days had passed since my visit to Inverness Gardens and Mrs Moberley had been rarely out of my mind. Every word either of us had spoken had been recollected over and over along with a string of questions I wanted to ask but never would. What did she think of me? Was I like all her other patients? Did they all suffer from hysterical symptoms? I would never be able to ask because I knew what her reply would be. *I can understand your curiosity but I'm sure you must realise…* Yes, yes, yes, but I need to know how bad I am, I need to compare.

Speculating about her other patients had triggered memories like the time my mother gave away my wooden spinning top to some children who lived down the road. *You never played with it Ursula.* And the time at school when I fell out with my best friend and she made friends with two other girls and none of them would have anything to do with me for nearly a week. Disagreeable recollections of minor injustices and rejections, and nothing to do with Mrs Moberley, so why had they come flooding back?

Before I joined Enid in the kitchen I had read a report in *The Times* of the annual lunch at the Tavistock-Square Clinic for Functional Disorders held at the Hotel Russell. What was a functional disorder? Nobody had bothered to explain but if it meant you had something that prevented you from functioning properly then presumably my arm fell into that category. A speaker at the lunch had claimed that mental havoc was being wrought by today's rush and noise. What rush and noise? In my case it seemed an improbable cause.

'I was listening to the wireless earlier on Enid and you'll never believe it, they had a talk about folding and ironing table linen!'

She smiled, not sure if I meant the programme was a good idea or an affront to women who had better things to think about.

'Solomon brought in a starling,' she said.

'Oh no, I wish he wouldn't.'

'Still alive it was but a bit groggy. I shut him in the scullery and put the bird on the shed roof to give it a chance to recover, poor thing.'

'Oh I do hope it does. You are brave Enid. I'm terrified of dead and injured birds.'

'Course you're not. How could you be afraid of something dead?'

'I know, isn't it ridiculous. I think it's because I got a fright when I was a child. I was running through long grass and I almost stepped on the body of a crow.'

'Well that accounts for it then. Is Mrs Bryant the same?'

'No I'm certain she's not.' Not my sister Joyce who prided herself on being down-to-earth and matter-of-fact. 'Was it still windy when you went in the garden? Only I wouldn't want the bird to get blown off the roof.'

'Not too bad. Wind had dropped. Quite warm for the beginning of May wouldn't you say?' She held up a tin. 'Look, apricots, Goddess brand, they were selling them in the market ever so reasonable.'

My pen had rolled onto the floor. Enid crouched to

retrieve it and when she straightened up her face was as red as a turkey's crop, not just the usual two bright spots on her cheeks, but diffused all over. Leo said it was gypsy blood that was responsible for her black hair and swarthy complexion but it was only guesswork, we knew next to nothing of her background. A colleague of Leo's had recommended the family – one of Enid's cousins worked for his wife – and since they lived not too far away, in Kentish Town, Leo had made further inquiries and Enid had come for a trial period. Of course, being Leo he had insisted on letting a whole month go by before he announced we wanted her to stay but I had told her at the end of the first week. *Our secret Enid. Yes of course Mrs Ingham. Thank you Mrs Ingham.*

She had handed me the pen. Now she stood clasping and unclasping her hands and I guessed there must be something she wanted to say but was not sure if now would be an appropriate moment.

'I'm seeing Mrs Moberley on Monday,' I said, 'I can walk there, it's not far.'

'The exercise will do you good.'

'Yes.' I half expected her to offer to accompany me but obviously the idea had never crossed her mind.

'Everything all right Enid?'

'Me?' But the screech of laughter had come out too quickly.

'What is it? Do tell me. Has Mr Ingham said something?'

I was all prepared for her to repeat Leo's name, play for time, but she was silent, staring down at the damp linoleum. Telling her there was no need to mop every morning or to use the suction cleaner on *all* the carpets every single day had been a waste of time. As far as

Enid was concerned every particle of dust that was banished, every germ destroyed, meant she was doing her bit to aid my recovery.

Her hands were still tightly clasped.

'What is it then Enid?' I started to cough but only because the stove burned anthracite and the fumes tickled the back of my throat.

She patted her thick wiry hair with both hands as though to compose herself for a difficult task. 'It's about my Jim,' she said.

'Jim who takes you to the pictures?'

'That's the one.' She gave another loud screech. 'I'll put the soup on to heat, barley cream, one of your favourites, takes ever so long to cook so I started it yesterday but I've still to sieve it and add the scalded milk.'

'You and Jim are courting?'

'In a manner of speaking.'

'In a manner of speaking,' I teased, 'what's that supposed to mean? Where did you meet him?'

'That's just it, you'd never believe. On the top of a bus it was, the Hammersmith one.' Tears of merriment ran down her cheeks and she wiped her eyes with a teacloth. 'Now look what you've made me do. Thing was I'd missed the one before, run for it but the driver pulled away. Cursed him I did and all the time if I'd reached it – '

'You'd never have met Jim.'

'Destiny, is that what you think too?'

I smiled. I had never seen her so animated. 'You're fond of him, are you Enid? How long have you known him? Have you taken him home to meet your parents?'

She wound the tea cloth round her fingers. 'He wants us to get wed.'

'Does he?' My chest tightened and I started to cough again 'That's wonderful Enid,' I spluttered. 'You must bring him round, introduce him.'

'He'd like that, Mrs Ingham, we both would.'

'Why not next…' I began but the coughing was so bad I was unable to finish. After the wedding she would leave. Then what would happen? She had been with us for two years, helping to prepare the house before we returned from our honeymoon then coming from ten in the morning to four in the afternoon to clean and do the washing, and now most of the cooking and shopping since after I became ill she had agreed to increase her hours. How would I manage without her? Find someone else I suppose but whoever it was could never replace Enid. Since my illness I had come to rely on her more and more and Archie was right when he said I was fond of her. How could she leave me in the lurch and now of all times?

I accepted the glass of water she placed on the table beside me and asked if she had fixed a date.

She swallowed uncertainly, returning to the soup then sliding the pan off the hot plate and joining me at the table. 'Don't you worry I've told my Jim it won't be for a while yet, not until Mrs Ingham's well again.'

'But you can't put off the wedding because of me.'

'No hurry is there and when I told Mum she agreed. Got nothing against Jim, says he seems a decent enough fellow, but she doesn't believe in rushing things. You should hear the way she goes on about men!'

I could smell the soup and it was making me feel queasy. 'What does she say Enid?'

She gave me a sly smile. 'Their little ways.'

'What kind of little ways?' I was eager to hear more.

'Oh I couldn't repeat it.'

'Yes you could.'

'Not like us though are they.' She stood up again and started stirring the soup vigorously. 'Made different.'

'Yes I suppose that's right.' What did she mean exactly? 'Little boys do tend to be noisier than little girls, and rougher, but not always. I used to be a bit of a tomboy.'

'Did you Mrs Ingham? I can't imagine that.'

'I was good at climbing trees and I longed for a train set, laid out with stations and points and a turntable so you could shunt the engine. I had a friend whose brother kept trains in the attic, and a farm and a zoo and soldiers, it was heaven.'

'Must have been.' But she was thinking about something else.

'Does Jim live in Kentish Town?' I asked.

'Tufnell Park. His mother works at the Eye Hospital, cleaning and that, *and* she takes in washing.'

I nodded, uncomfortably aware that however well we got on sooner or later we always came up against the fact that I was from a more well-to-do background. I hated her to think I was different and I hated the way she accepted that some people were better off than others and, in her own often repeated words, that "things were the way God intended and it all worked out for the best in the end."

'All right if you marry a good provider,' she said, returning to the subject of men, 'and make sure he's not one what's handy with his fists.'

'No I should think not.' Did her father get drunk and take it out on her mother? The only thing I knew about him was that he delivered coal, had done all his life, and I had a sudden picture of him coming home in the evening with a grimy face and washing in a tin bath by the hearth. I was curious to know if they had plumbing but there were questions I could never ask, divides we could never cross.

'Watch out for yourself on a Friday night.' She wiped her hands on her apron as though she was wiping away an unpleasant memory. 'That's what she told me and I said she needn't worry on that account, my Jim was as gentle as a lamb.'

'Is he? I'm so glad Enid. So glad you've met someone you really like, I mean love.'

Her head swivelled round and she stared at me for a moment before opening a drawer and finding a second wooden spoon so she could take a sip from the pan of soup and test the heat. 'Mum's had her work cut out with the seven of us and when Eric and little Jim were on the way she had a bad time.'

'One of the twins is called Jim too.' To my shame I realised I had lost track of the names of her brothers and sisters. Two girls and five boys as far as I could remember and Enid was in the middle and had helped look after the youngest two.

'Jim's not his real name, that's Peter, but my Dad thinks Peter's a bit fancy. Are you going to have your soup in here Mrs Ingham?'

'Yes I think I will, it's so much easier than balancing it on that table in the drawing room. You have some too.'

'Later maybe.'

'No have it now Enid, I want to tell you about Mrs Moberley, the lady who's going to make my arm work again.'

She filled the bowls and took two soup spoons from the cutlery box. 'Slice of bread and butter?'

'No thank you, but you have some.'

'Go on then, tell me about Mrs – what did you say her name is?'

'Moberley. Well, let's think, she's tall and slim, even her face is thin. And her hands and feet I expect. I forgot to look.'

Enid nodded. 'What colour hair or has it turned grey?'

'Oh no, she's younger than I expected. Fair hair, very fine, not cut in a fashionable style but rather pretty. I'm seeing her again, starting on Monday. Mondays, Wednesdays and Fridays.'

'That's nice.'

'Yes.' I was thinking about Enid's mother with her seven children, and always short of cash no doubt. And here was me with not a care in the world apart from my stupid arm and Archie was going to pay for me to talk about myself for three hours a week, well three lots of fifty minutes, and Muriel and Joyce thought it would make me even worse. 'I hate being like this Enid.'

'Course you do.'

'Mr Ingham thinks my symptoms are because something bad happened to me when I was a child.'

'What kind of a bad thing?'

'A death I suppose. Something like that.'

She thought about this for a moment. 'My uncle Len died in The War.'

'Did he Enid? So did mine. Uncle Edward he was called, my mother's brother.'

'Most people know someone who was killed and with some it's five or six.'

I sipped my boiling hot soup. 'I should count my blessings, not mope around feeling sorry for myself.'

'That's not you Mrs Ingham or you wouldn't be sitting here would you, you'd have taken to your bed.'

'Yes I suppose you're right.' I wanted to hug her, beg her not to leave, not yet. 'Does your Jim come from a large family?'

'My Jim?' She let out another squeal of laughter. 'Three of 'em, all boys. Jim's the youngest, his father died before he was born.'

'In The War.'

'No it was his chest. Turned down for the army then died anyway. Doesn't make sense does it although they say it's God's will. When you've finished your soup there's some prune mould left over from yesterday, just what the doctor ordered.'

Later I sat on the lawn and had another go at writing a letter to my friend Midge. We only have one tree in the garden, a laburnum that since it was May was in full flower and cast a dappled shade over the lawn. The seeds are poisonous so it was lucky we had no children although I used to worry when Joyce came round with the girls. Not now they were older of course, but when we first moved Helen had been nearly seven and Sybil only six and I was the one who had to keep reminding them.

Joyce thinks I fuss but I see no point in taking risks. *Children have to learn for themselves Ursula*. Learn how it feels to have your stomach pumped out I wanted to say, but of course I kept my opinion to myself. No matter what age you are your older sister is still your older sister and it's amazing how hard it is not to slip back into how things were when you were little.

I was nine when I was sent away to school. Joyce had only started there the previous year but because she was five years older I had very little to do with her. Unlike me she was good at sewing and flower painting, anything where you had to use your hands, whereas I preferred languages, French and Latin, and the kind of English Chaucer wrote. Strange how different we are and I sometimes wonder if we were born that way or if it was our upbringing although my mother treated us both the same, at least I'm fairly certain she did.

The school building was early Victorian with a high tower at one end and a low crenellated wall along the edge of the roof that made it look a bit like a castle. It would be wrong to say I was unhappy there. I was at first, I wept buckets, but that must be the same with all children who are separated from their parents when they are still so young.

I remember the first time my mother said goodbye. We were standing in the hallway with its smell of camphor and its polished floor where you slid on pain of death. *Be a good girl and I'll see you in no time at all.* She kissed me, an awkward kind of kiss that landed somewhere between my forehead and my nose, and I hoped nobody was watching. Eleven weeks I thought, an eternity, but because you have to, you adjust quite quickly. Woken at seven by matron jangling a bell outside the dormitory, wash in cold water, put on your liberty bodice, with suspenders attached, black stockings, petticoat, gym slip. Each article of clothing had to be marked with your own particular number. Mine was thirty-six.

As well as languages I enjoyed the music – I learned to play the piano but only up to grade five – and the games, netball and hockey in the winter terms, rounders and tennis in the summer. I was quite good at tennis, good enough to be in the house four, and I enjoyed netball although when I was thirteen I broke my finger when a girl called Bettine Bailey who suffered from boils jumped up high and knocked the ball out of my hand. Later she was made head girl.

The reason I had abandoned my letter to my friend Midge and started thinking about school was in case Mrs Moberley asked me, in case that was where the trauma took place. I found it hard to believe it did although I do remember how guilty I often felt and I think that must have been because we had religion rammed down our throats, morning, noon and night. Three services every Sunday, sitting in the school chapel wearing our hats, felt in winter and straw in summer, and gloves whatever the weather. It was stuffy and girls often fainted, or pretended to, especially when the candles were snuffed out and the smell got up your nose. If one girl fainted there was nearly always another and another, something Miss Dalgleish described as hysteria.

There, I knew I had heard the word before.

On weekdays special times were allotted so we could say our prayers and I prayed for my mother and father – *please God make them happy* – except even then I knew it was a lost cause. What else? No running in the corridors, no slouching or you were given a deportment mark. Walks in a crocodile, a bath twice a week. Oh, and the knickers, thick and navy blue, and underneath a pair of thin white ones called linings. Funny how you remember the little details like that and forget all about the lessons. I could have done quite well – I was usually among the top four or five in the class – but most of the teachers were unqualified. Even so, my parents would never have dreamed of sending us to the local county secondary school. Much too common.

Midge was my best friend and we had remained in touch ever since although we hardly ever saw each other – the last time was at Leo and my wedding – because she lived in Paris and she was single and had a job as an interior decorator. And she was not unattractive, in fact she was exceptionally nice looking with big greeny-grey eyes and bright auburn hair.

I was still making notes when Leo came home, looking rather pleased with himself, which could have been because I had agreed to see an analyst or might have been because of something that had happened during his day.

'Boarding school,' I told him, 'in case Mrs Moberley asks.'

'It don't think it works quite like that.' So he was going to take his usual superior attitude. 'It's all a question of associations, that's why I keep telling you to say whatever comes into your head.'

'But what if nothing does?'

'Oh come on.' He had carried a deck chair into the garden and was having difficulty fixing it at the correct height. 'You mean nothing of special significance. That's just the point, you don't know what is and isn't important. Freud laid great stress on patients not omitting any thought or idea, particularly if it was uncomfortable or painful. Are you sure you're warm enough out here?'

'Enid's getting married.'

'Married?' That had wiped the condescending expression off his face.

'To Jim who takes her to the pictures but they haven't fixed a date. She said they were waiting until I was better but I told her they couldn't possibly do that.'

'If that's what she wants.'

I sighed. Men are so literal, taking everything at face value and totally unaware of what people are really thinking. 'She was being considerate. Anyway I suggested she bring Jim to meet us and she seemed rather pleased. I wonder what he's like. What do you think?'

'I haven't an idea.'

'Guess.'

'What's the point, we'll find out soon enough. How's your cough been today?'

I folded up my notes and pushed them into the pocket in my skirt. 'Actually I've hardly coughed at all.'

If I stretched my neck I could see Solomon asleep on the roof of the shed. Did that mean he had caught the starling all over again? I could ask Leo to check, see if there were any feathers or other parts he had rejected as too indigestible, claws, or the beak.

I shuddered and Leo thought it was because the sun had disappeared behind a cloud and immediately suggested we go indoors.

'No, I like it out here. Look at the laburnum, it's the best it's ever been. There was a photograph of cherry orchards in *The Times* today. *Cherry Orchards in Kent*, quite close to where my parents used to live. You know you said something distressing must have happened when I was child, only I've been thinking and there wasn't anything, apart from nearly stepping on a dead bird.'

'You mean you can't remember anything. You could

have blocked it out of your memory or it could have happened when you were only four or five. No-one can recall things from such a young age, not without the help of an analyst.'

'I can. We had a dog that let us dress her in a bonnet and wheel her round in a pram. I wish you liked dogs Leo, it would be a friend for Solomon.'

He cast his eyes to the heavens, just as I had known he would, and started giving me a lecture on my inability to accept that pets were not people and that interpreting their behaviour in the same way that you might a human being was not only absurd but also unfair on the animal.

'In the paper it said an Airedale dog had bitten off a man's finger.'

'Its owner's I hope.'

'Oh Leo.' When I first knew him had he talked like a schoolmaster or was it something that happened to you when you spent your days in front of classes of horrid little boys? The first time I visited him in Cambridge I was so nervous I had been glad of the way he took over, making all the decisions and escorting me round buildings of historic interest without ever asking if it was how I wanted to spend my weekend. Of course later, when we got to know each other better, things changed a bit. I'm not a submissive person, never have been, in fact my mother used to accuse me of being too fond of getting my own way, but since my illness I had been forced to rely not only on Leo but also on Archie and Muriel, and sometimes I had a sneaking suspicion Leo rather liked it that way.

'Time you went inside,' he said firmly, 'I know it's warm for the time of year but in your state of health you have to be careful, watch out you don't catch a chill.'

'Ne'er cast a clout till May be out.' I let him pull me up from my deckchair and slide an arm round my waist. 'Did you know the South Africans are playing Surrey at the Oval today?'

'You're not interested in cricket.'

'No but you are. And the Queen opened a new wing at the Elizabeth Garrett Anderson hospital in Euston Road.'

He sighed. 'What is all this Ursa?'

'Since I don't go anywhere there's nothing to talk about except what's in the paper. How were the boys today?'

'Same as usual.'

'Are some of them awfully clever?'

'One or two. Most are pretty average.' He looked tired and there was a dejected expression in his eyes that I blamed entirely on myself. Poor Leo, I reached up to untidy his sleeked back hair and he gave me a lopsided smile. 'Now what?' he asked, 'why the mournful face?'

'No reason.'

'Fibber, you must have been thinking of something.'

'Just the starling Solomon caught this morning. Enid saved it and put it on top of the shed but I think he may have been watching her.'

That night I slept fitfully, waking at four in the morning with a start and afraid I would have to add palpitations to my list of symptoms. But it was only a dream. Mrs Moberley might ask about my dreams but if she did this was definitely one I would keep to myself.

I was walking by the sea with Archie, just the two of us except now and again I was aware of a shadowy figure in the background. The tide had started to come in and a big wave splashed over our bare feet and Archie took hold of my arm to steady me and his fingers accidentally brushed my breast. The wind was blowing hard and strands of hair covered my face, long hair like I used to have before it was shingled. With his two hands Archie parted it and kissed me, gently at first then harder, much harder so that I lost my balance and fell, landing on my knees on the warm, damp sand. A sea bird was hovering overhead, crying and wailing, and something heavy pressed against my chest, and with an anguished cry of my own I reached out with both arms and…

And then I realised Solomon had climbed onto my bed and curled up on my stomach. So in spite of Freud's clever *interpretations* it shows where dreams come from and how easy it is to read all kinds of silly meanings into them when in truth there's a quite simple explanation, like a cat on your bed and the dawn chorus starting up outside your window.

CHAPTER FIVE

'Recollection without affect is nearly always quite ineffective.'
(Sigmund Freud)

Today I was on the couch. There had been no compulsion. Mrs Moberley had allowed me to choose whether I sat on the chair like last time or lay flat out on my back.

'Which would be best?' I had dithered between the two. 'What do you think?'

Needless to say there had been no reply.

'All right but I think I'd better take off my shoes.'

Once I was on the couch I wished I had chosen the chair. I felt helpless, like a child. How could I speak to her on equal terms when she was sitting up and I was lying down? Out of the corner of my eye I could see her profile, the thin straight nose and high cheekbones, but not her expression although from her tone of voice when I arrived I suspected she was having second thoughts as to my suitability.

Leaving home with more than enough time to reach Inverness Gardens at two I had walked slowly, all the while devising a plan. Holding on tight to the wrought iron rail on the steps leading down to the main road I made a decision that if I spoke and she remained silent I would pretend she had responded, fill in the blanks in my head and carry on regardless. Long silences made me nervous and surely one of the reasons I was seeing a psychoanalyst was to lessen my anxiety. Of course it was perfectly possible that was all part of the treatment, like allowing an abscess to grow larger and more painful until finally it bursts and the putrefying poison oozes out.

I considered asking her if that was how the treatment worked but decided against it. I thought I could feel a small hole in the toe of one of my stockings. How embarrassing although I doubted if Mrs Moberley would notice and even if she did she would be unlikely to attach much significance to the fact. No, I was wrong there. Everything, absolutely everything was significant. *The patient's toe was sticking through her stocking, a way of telling me that the treatment was unimportant to her, or possibly a cry for help, presenting herself like a child.* But the hole could have appeared during my walk from Highgate to Hampstead.

The first thing I had told her was how glad I was she could see me in the afternoons because I was sure it would make it easier to talk. I was not certain why but whereas some people felt sleepy after their lunch I never had much to eat and it was the time I felt at my best. Whatever that might be, I added, but of course she made no comment so I told her about our house in Highgate and the garden that Muriel had stocked up with herbaceous plants. Then I realised she would think I was incapable of making a garden for myself, not that I would ever know what she thought. It would go down in her notebook but I would be none the wiser.

After that there was a long silence until finally I told her how I found the walk to Inverness Gardens quite enjoyable and it had not given me a headache or made me cough. I described *The Gables* although I was not sure why, probably because it was where Leo was brought up and it was so much grander than where he lived now.

Another long silence so I cleared my throat and tried again. 'Last time I came here I wasn't sure what you wanted me to say. And I'm still not sure. Leo thinks I should tell you whatever comes into my head. He made me read Volume One of Freud's papers and it said treatment requires long periods, six months to three years, but in less severe cases it might be much shorter.'

'You're hoping that's how it will be for you.'

'Getting dressed takes ages and I can't do any of the things I used to do, gardening, mending, cooking. In the beginning Leo used to do everything for me but now I prefer to do it myself unless there are fastenings at the back and I try to avoid them as far as possible.'

'It must be difficult.'

'Yes.' First thing in the morning I had drawn back the curtains allowing pale sunshine to stream through the window. Now it was raining, a heavy squall that pattered on the glass roof of Mrs Moberley's conservatory which was just visible through a small leaded window.

'Can I say anything,' I asked, 'anything at all? Only there is something that's been preying on my mind. Enid, our maid, she comes to the house five and a half days a week although it was less before I was ill. The thing is she's getting married. Not yet, not immediately, she insists she'll wait until I'm better but that's not right, is it? She's bringing her fiancé to meet us this evening. Jim, he's called Jim and he's a painter and decorator. Leo thinks I'm too attached to her. To Enid I mean. So does Archie, my father-in-law although he's too polite to say so.'

'You're worried how you'll manage without her.'

'Yes but I didn't come here to talk about Enid, did I? I've been trying to think of something traumatic that happened when I was a child only so far I haven't come up with anything. Joyce, my sister was ill, she had scarlet fever, and I was sent to stay with a relative. At the time I was only three so I suppose I might have been upset, and frightened of the scarlet fever, and frightened Joyce would die. No I don't think so do you? No I'm sure it couldn't be that.'

More silence. I felt hot and sticky.

'Leo wants things to get back to normal,' I said, deliberately tossing out an ambiguous remark that she would have to clarify.

'Is that what he said?'

'He's losing patience with me.'

'What makes you think that?'

'I suppose he just hates me being ill.' Perhaps I ought to I tell her we had twin beds. No, why should I, it had been Leo's idea and if he was starting to regret it that was hardly something I could be held responsible for. *That way we'll appreciate each other Ursa instead of taking one another for granted.* At the time I had been a little upset but hidden my disappointment. Now I was relieved.

Muriel had given us the beds, Gordon Russell ones of course, and when Leo told her it was twin ones he wanted perhaps he had been aware how much she secretly disliked the idea of another woman in the same bed as her beloved son. Or it could have been Muriel's idea in the first place and Leo had been so embarrassed he had gone along with it.

'Leo's an only child,' I said. 'Sorry, I don't know why I suddenly thought of that.'

'You haven't told me much about him.'

'Haven't I? He's a schoolmaster, he teaches history at a preparatory school. He's tall, like his father but in other ways he looks more like his mother. Oh, you want to know what kind of a person he is, quiet, serious, likes things done properly.'

'What kind of things?'

It was the first time she had interrupted and it put me on my guard. 'I didn't mean it as a criticism, just that he likes things to run smoothly. I do too. Before I was ill he used to get cross if we ran out of something, the fig rolls he likes so much. Now he goes out and buys them himself.'

'You don't feel you can go to the shops.' It was a statement not a question and it stung.

'No. Well I suppose I could, I've come here haven't I, but there's the money, I'd feel silly holding out my purse. Only lately I've been thinking, plenty of people lost limbs in The War and they don't sit around expecting to be waited on hand and foot. Hand and foot! What a stupid thing to say. I expect Freud would read something into that.'

'Losing an arm in The War is not quite the same thing and you have other symptoms, your cough and your headaches.'

'I haven't coughed much here.' I raised my head to see if the cat was in the room but there was no sign of her. 'I've been wondering, do you think I could be allergic to cat hair?'

'How long have you had your Solomon?'

So she remembered his name, although come to think of it she would have recorded it in her notebook along with all the other information about me and the comments about my illness and how genuine it was and how it might have come about.

'Two years. We got him as a kitten a few weeks after we moved into our house. No, you're right, I would have started coughing then. Anyway I've never heard of cats giving people headaches.'

I thought I could hear footsteps upstairs. A daily who had come in through the back door and was busy changing sheets or cleaning the bath? If I were supposed to say precisely what came into my head I ought to ask who it was but I doubted it included questions about Mrs Moberley herself or what went on in her house. Better to return to my childhood, or school. Yes, boarding school was something that would interest her.

'I was sent to boarding school,' I said, then because my voice had come out sounding rather shaky, 'but I wasn't unhappy there, only at first when everything was so strange and unfamiliar.'

'How old were you?'

'Nine.'

'Was your sister Joyce at the same school?'

'Yes but because she's five years older than me we saw very little of each other. My best friend was called Midge – her real name is Marjorie – and we still write to each other. She lives in Paris, she's an interior decorator. She was always artistic – and good at Maths. I expect you need to be good at Maths if you're going to plan other people's rooms. I don't know though, she may just do the decorative part, curtains and covers and so forth. I haven't seen her for over a year.'

I wished I could see the clock so I knew how much time I had left. I could have wriggled my left arm free and looked at my watch but she might have interpreted it as a wish to escape.

'We have fifteen more minutes Ursula.'

So she was a mind reader too. 'Is there anything particular you want to know? Last night when I was lying in bed it occurred to me that if I told you everything that had ever happened to me I would be here for years and years. Should I start as far back as I can remember? Only you're never sure if it's true or you're just going on anecdotes other people have told you.'

'You seem to feel there are rules you have to stick to. Is that something else your Leo put in your head?'

'No. I don't know. But there must be or it wouldn't work, would it? Not rules you could put in a book but unwritten ones so that you're never sure if what you're saying is a waste of time or might be of some use.'

'Why not leave it to me?'

'But how can I? Yes, all right, but you would say if I wasn't telling you what you needed to know?'

No answer but what did I expect. She was wearing the same clothes as before, her "talking cure" outfit. In contrast, I had selected quite different items from my wardrobe, a coffee-coloured crepe frock that must now be all crumpled at the back, and flat shoes with fringed tongues that I had placed side by side on the rug at the end of the couch.

'The first time I came,' I said, sounding more defiant than I intended, 'I worried about what clothes to wear. This time I just put on the first things that came to hand.'

When she made no comment I was determined not to be put off. 'You see, although I've read some of

Freud's papers I know nothing about what's supposed to happen when you see an analyst. Well only what Leo's told me and he couldn't possibly understand, could he, because you can't get things like that from a book and last time I saw you the first thing that came into my head was how the lid of your pen had been left off and the ink would dry up.'

'It did.'

'Did it?' I laughed. 'There you are then, I should have said.'

She made a small sound that could have meant she was smiling and I wanted to see her face. If you are unable to see a person's expression you can never be certain what they think of you. *The eyes are the windows of the soul* was an adage Muriel often used. Funny, since she disliked meeting your eye.

I wished again that I had chosen the chair. On the other hand in an odd kind of way it felt safer on the couch as though I had been given permission to say things I would never normally say because the whole conversation was so unlike talking to a friend.

'Leo's unhappy,' I said.

'What makes you think that?'

'It can't be much fun living with someone like me. And I'm not sure if he likes his job at the school. Archie, my father-in-law, is a doctor, a skin specialist. I used to work for him as a secretary, that's how I met Leo. He has a practice in Cavendish Square. Oh sorry, I think I told you that before.'

'So you've known Archie longer than you've known Leo.'

'Yes.' What was she thinking? Probably that I ought to be talking about myself, not Leo and Archie. 'Muriel,

Leo's mother, thinks I should pull myself together. Not that she says so, not in so many words, but I can tell. As I said, Leo is an only child so naturally she wants the best for him. Well anyone would, wouldn't they?'

I could taste my lunch. Only a small portion of kedgeree but fish had been a bad choice.

'I had kedgeree for lunch,' I said, knowing the food I ate had nothing to do with anything but determined to say the first thing that came into my head. Enid says fish makes you brainy. I think nineteen's a bit young to get married, don't you? Last week, when Archie drove me home from here, he asked why I was so fond of her and I said it was because she was the sort of person I would have liked as a nanny except I never had a nanny.'

My voice cracked and to my horror a tear slid out of the corner of my eye and travelled down to my ear. If I brushed it away she would notice.

'Tell me about Enid.' Her voice was so soft I had to bite my lip to keep from sobbing.

'She's got black hair and she's not exactly fat but she's stocky with large hands and feet but surprisingly slim ankles. Sometimes we have a cup of tea together but we're not real friends because I call her Enid and she calls me Mrs Ingham.'

A clock chimed in another room and I guessed it was a quarter to which meant I only had five minutes left.

'I can't think of anything else,' I said, swinging my legs over the side of the couch, 'and I think it's nearly time to stop isn't it?'

I expected her to stand up but she stayed where she was. 'You seem to be feeling sad.'

'I'm all right. I get weepy sometimes but I think it's just part of my illness.'

'I don't think distress can be described as an illness.'

'No I didn't mean that.' I struggled to find the words but it was no use. Nothing I said came out right.

Mrs Moberley cleared her throat several times. Perhaps she had a sore throat, or a cold coming on. People clear their throats when they feel anxious, I know I do, but there was nothing anxious about Mrs Moberley, in fact I would have said she was the most unanxious person I had ever met, and the most serene. Serene, what an odd word to have chosen. Composed. Tranquil. I opened my mouth to say I had always been a worrier but she came in first.

'Our behaviour is often influenced by ideas of which we are totally unconscious.'

'Is it? Yes I suppose it must be.' I brushed away my tears and this time she did stand up.

'I'll see you again on Wednesday Ursula. Would you like someone to send for a taxi or are you going to walk home?'

'Oh no, I can easily walk.' *Someone* to send for a taxi? Did she mean the person who was walking about upstairs? Perhaps it was her husband, or another analyst. Perhaps they worked in pairs although surely Leo would have known if there were two of them. I wanted to ask but it was too late. My turn was over.

'Thank you,' I whispered, and she inclined her head, leading me down the passage and giving me a fleeting smile before she opened the front door to let me out and closed it firmly behind me.

In half an hour's time Enid was bringing Jim to meet us.

Leo was on edge but I doubted if his mood had much to do with Enid and Jim. When he returned from work he had been unable to contain his curiosity about my first proper session.

'How was it, did you lie on the couch?'

'Yes but I could have sat on a chair. It was left up to me.'

'And?' He waited impatiently for me to continue.

'I can't remember,' I said and he made an irritable clicking sound with his tongue.

'I told her I was at boarding school, the same one Joyce went to.' I paused, trying to recall parts of our conversation. Not a conversation, more a monologue from me with Mrs Moberley making the occasional non-committal comment. 'I said I wondered if my cough could have anything to do with Solomon.'

'Don't be absurd, we've had him for two years, your cough started less than six months ago.'

'I know. Mrs Moberley's got a cat but it wasn't in the room today. It's called Dora.'

'Theodora, a gift from God.'

'No, Dora,' I corrected him crossly.

He stared at me and I knew he thought I was pretending to have forgotten what we talked about. I suppose I was in a way but describing a conversation is never the same as when you were actually there. He had been so adamant that I needed to see a psychoanalyst. Now he resented the fact that I had been somewhere without him.

'Shall we all sit in here,' I said, 'when Enid and Jim arrive?'

'I think Enid would feel more at home in the kitchen.'

'Yes all right.' I hated the way we talked to each

other in such a cold, clipped fashion. For all I knew his day at school had been tiring and frustrating but if that was the case why not say so, why persist in making me feel everything was my fault.

'I found this on the hall table.' I held up a small green book.

'Oh that.' His voice was unconvincingly casual.

'Where did it come from?'

'The school library.'

'I don't believe you.'

He sighed. 'Well there's not much I can do about that. I didn't mean the library the boys use. There's one for the staff.'

'So you think my nerves are the problem.'

'I'm reading it because, having concentrated on the Arts, my scientific knowledge is somewhat sketchy. We had a well-equipped chemistry laboratory at school but I gave up science when I entered the sixth form.'

I almost believed him. It had been his choice to read History at Cambridge but I suspected a part of him felt he should have become a doctor like his father. Knowing Archie he would never have tried to influence him or to let him think he was disappointed in him and to be fair neither would Muriel. All the same it was firmly stuck in Leo's head and would probably remain there all his life.

Taking the book from my hand he turned to a page towards the end. 'Fatty food,' he read, 'is most valuable in building up the nervous system. Fat people are rarely nervous in the sense of having irritable nervous systems.'

'You mean they're fat and jolly. Are you thinking about me Leo? Do you think I'm too thin?'

Ignoring my question he searched for another page.

'Listen to this. "*By a neurotic person the physician means a person whose nerve-centres are too affectable, whose emotions are too easily aroused, whose inhibitions are too weak.*" Does that ring any bells?'

He saw my expression and stood up, laying a hand on my shoulder. 'No wait. Suppose there are twenty people in a room, and the door bangs, three of them may jump up from their seats, while the seventeen others merely turn their heads in the direction of the sound. There's no criticism implied, it's just a question of whether one has a stable or an unstable nervous system.'

'I like the kind of people who jump.'

He glanced at me but decided to ignore my facetious remark. 'According to the author today's young women stand the fatigues of a day's shopping or sight-seeing much less perfectly than their mothers or grandmothers did.'

'What nonsense.' I snatched the book from his hand. 'When was it published? Look, nearly twenty years ago. You could at least have found something more up to date. In any case why do people have different nervous systems as you call them? Is it the way they're born?'

'Unsuitable infant feeding.' He had adopted the authoritative voice he knew enraged me. 'Too little sleep, insufficient ventilation, bad digestion. As the author points out, in many public schools and this certainly applied to mine, the hours devoted to sleep are far too few.'

'But in spite of that your nervous system has suffered no ill effects. I don't know why you read this stuff, I thought history was your subject, and if you think you're helping me you're mistaken.' I turned to the last sentence in the book and started to read aloud. "Though I speak with the tongues of men and of angels, and have not inhibition, it profiteth me, physiologically speaking, nothing." I'd say that was blasphemous wouldn't you?' I broke off, alarmed at my strength of feeling. 'Oh come on Leo, where's your sense of humour.'

He gave a grudging smile and in spite of his annoying book I wanted to reach out and comfort him. He only wanted to be part of my getting better and beneath the iron self-control he had inherited from his mother he was quite sensitive.

'I'm sorry,' I said, and he looked up surprised.

'What for?'

'Oh I don't know. Sit next to me on the sofa and tell me about your day. That reminds me, look what I saw in the Kennel, Farm and Aviary section. *For sale, pedigree male King Charles spaniel, black and tan, four years old, house-trained, over distemper, wonderful companion, excellent temperament.*'

'No.'

'Why not? He sounds perfect and spaniels never chase cats.'

'I've explained before.' He began repeating why he was not prepared to have a dog but before he had reached the third reason we heard Enid tapping on the back door and he took a deep exaggerated breath to indicate that meeting Jim was not something he relished.

'I'll let them in,' he said.

The four of us sat at the kitchen table, drinking tea and eating the fairy buns that Enid had made especially for the occasion. She was wearing a flowered frock that was a little too tight for her sturdy frame although the material was pretty. Jim had put on his best blue serge suit and his shoes were highly polished. He was shorter than Enid, with a crop of sandy hair and small, neat features, apart from the jutting chin that put me in mind of a jockey although I had no idea why since we never went to the races.

'Not a lot I couldn't tell you about painting and decorating.' He handed his cap to Enid and tipped back his chair until I was afraid it might fall over. 'If you need a room painted. Not that I'm here for that purpose. Very nice it is to meet you both, Enid having told me all about you.'

'Not everything,' Enid giggled, 'I wouldn't do that Mrs Ingham.'

I smiled at her, acknowledging with my eyes that she meant she had not told him about my illness. 'Nice to meet you too, Jim.' I had expected him to be a little ill at ease, at least when he first arrived, but so far he had barely paused for breath.

'Sash windows,' he said, 'that's another of my specialities. If you ever have a problem with a window.'

'Thank you,' Leo said firmly, 'we'll bear that in mind. You live near Enid do you?'

It was a rhetorical question but it set Jim off again. 'Tufnell Park. Same house where I was born. Me and Mum and one of my brothers. The other one married and moved up north. My father died a while back.'

'I'm sorry.' Enid had told me about his family but it always seems rude to say you know something like that already.

Leo was sitting next to Jim on one side of the table with Enid and me on the other. Normally Enid smelled of soap, or whatever cleaning material she had been using, but tonight she was wearing scent, something heavy and cloying that I guessed had been a present from Jim.

'Going to teach her to swim,' he announced, 'hardly seen the sea have you?'

'Yes I have,' Enid protested, 'we had a day out at Brighton on my sixteenth birthday.'

'Can't swim though. Think how you'd have been when The Titanic went down.'

Leo gave a snort. 'It was probably rather better if you were unable to swim. In those conditions the cold would have killed you within minutes.'

'Ah but you might have been one of the lucky ones, might have been hauled into a lifeboat, only not immediately so you had to stay in the water a bit.'

'I suppose that's possible.' Leo was starting to enjoy himself and I feared he might be going to tease Jim. Enid would notice. For all her stolid appearance she was far more quick-witted than Leo realised, and almost certainly more quick-witted than Jim.

'Where will you live after you marry?' I asked, not wanting to sound nosey but needing to steer the conversation back to a safer topic.

'With Jim's Mum,' Enid said, and I could tell she was hoping it would not be too long before they had a home of their own.

'Get on ever so well the two of 'em.' Jim grabbed hold of Enid's hand and I envied the open affection between them. 'Since it's all boys she's had she'll be glad of some female company.'

Leo pushed back his chair and crossed one knee over the other. 'Well I hope you'll both be very happy.'

'Thank you Mr Ingham.' For a second time Jim shook him by the hand. 'And don't you worry about

Enid, I'm going to make sure she has everything she could ever want and there'll be no need for her to go out to work, she can stay at home and help Mum. As well as the painting and decorating I have an interest in furniture, buying and selling small pieces, repairing when necessary, getting the scratches out and that, then giving them a bit of elbow grease.'

'A man of many talents,' Leo said.

'Yes, you certainly are, Jim.' I had visions of a house full of old furniture waiting to be done up. 'And very lucky to have found Enid although she knows how sorry we'll be to lose her.'

Enid let out one of her familiar shrieks. 'I told you Mrs Ingham, not until you're yourself again, not until you're fully recovered.' She reddened, covering her mouth with her hand and I remembered how she had told me about an article in *Peg's Paper* that gave advice on how to stop you blushing.

'I told Jim you hadn't been too well,' she continued, 'but none of the details. I had to say because of explaining why we was to wait.'

'Yes of course,' I reassured her, 'but I'm not prepared to ruin your plans Enid. Besides I'm sure I'll be better by August. Would August suit you all right?'

Leo turned his head sharply. 'That's only two months away.'

'I know that Leo.'

Without having it offered Jim had helped himself to another fairy bun and was chewing it slowly, moving it round his slightly open mouth. 'There's people I know if you need any plastering or carpentry. I'm ambidextrous, can use both hands the same. Quite rare that is, one in a million I'd say. Don't forget Mr Ingham, anything what needs doing round the house or garden. Not gardening as such but fences requiring repairs or walls in danger of crumbling.'

Leo nodded. 'As I said I'll certainly bear it in mind.'

During the short silence that followed Solomon walked into the kitchen with his tail in the air.

'Oh he's a beauty.' Jim reached out and ran his hand down the cat's back. 'I like a tabby, that's what we'll have to get Enid, nice little kitten that'll grow into a big 'un and keep the mice down.'

'Come on then.' Enid was finding the visit a strain and wanted to leave but Jim pretended not to hear.

'Something I'd like to ask you about Mr Ingham.' He paused, swallowing the last crumbs of his bun. 'The brother I told you about, the one what's moved up north, he's taken a job at a saw mill, in charge of wooden bungs he is, bungs for beer barrels. Would you say there's much future in that?'

To do him his justice Leo kept a completely straight face. 'Bungs for beer barrels,' he repeated, 'I suppose it would depend if there were any prospects of moving higher up in the firm.'

Jim nodded his agreement. 'That's what I thought. Of course he doesn't actually cut the bungs, he's in more of a supervisory capacity. Always be a need for beer barrels though won't there.'

'I imagine so although it's quite on the cards the wood could be replaced one day by a man-made material.'

'You think so?' Jim looked delighted. 'Better tell him then, hadn't I, better warn him what lies ahead.' He turned to Enid and I was pleased to see the fondness in his eyes. 'Time to make a move. Much as I've enjoyed meeting you both you'll have things to do, won't want to sit here all evening talking about this and that.'

When he stood up and walked towards the door I realised for the first time that he had a limp. An injury incurred during his painting and decorating or was one of his legs slightly shorter than the other? Enid had said nothing about it and neither would I, after all it could hardly be seen as a serious disability and in his own way he was quite a nice looking young man.

Enid slid off her chair, looking first at me then back at Jim. 'Thank you ever so much Mrs Ingham.'

'No, thank *you* Enid. Very nice to meet you Jim and I'm sure we'll see you again quite soon.'

'At the wedding,' he laughed.

Enid gave him a nudge. 'If Mr and Mrs Ingham want to come.'

'Of course we do.' I kissed her lightly on the cheek and she blushed again. 'We'll look forward to it, won't we Leo and it means I'll be able to buy a new outfit and a specially nice hat!'

'Well?' Leo joined me on the sofa. 'What did you think?'

'Hard to tell.'

'Not really.'

'I expect he was nervous.' I tried to think of something positive to say. 'Some people go quiet when they meet people they don't know. Others gabble away nineteen to the dozen. And it must have been quite a trial for him.'

He picked up the newspaper. 'Not the impression I got.'

'As long as he's good to Enid.' I had a sudden picture of her in Jim's mother's kitchen. Would they sit together, exchanging silly stories or was Jim's mother an unsmiling dragon of a woman who would treat Enid like a skivvy? If she was anything like Jim I couldn't imagine she would have much sense of humour.

Poor Enid, but I was doing it again, letting my imagination run away with me when I ought to be concentrating on Leo.

'Leo, you remember our wedding?'

'What about it?'

'And our honeymoon in Falmouth.' There, I had said it.

'You were unwell.' He kept his eyes glued to the newspaper. 'Possibly the start of your present problems.'

'No I wasn't.' I turned away from him to register my disgust. Taking my courage in my hands I had mentioned the unmentionable and all he could do was re-write history and make everything my fault. Except in his terms he had not re-written history, he had simply described what happened in the only way he found bearable.

'Mrs Moberley is a very good listener,' I said, 'and she doesn't seem to mind what I talk about, just makes the occasional comment to show she's heard what I said. I don't know how she'll do it but I'm sure she's going to make me better.'

'In time for Enid's wedding in August?' His voice was high-pitched with disbelief. 'I hope you pay attention to her comments. I imagine they're rather more important than simply an indication that she's listened to what you were telling her.'

There he went again. Every time I said something constructive he used it against me, turned it into a criticism. 'It was your idea I see her and now I've done what you wanted all you can do is criticise. In any case Mrs Moberley says anything I tell her is private and will always be treated in absolute confidence.'

'From me!' His mouth snapped shut and he began clenching and unclenching his jaw.

His angry reaction had frightened me but not so much that I was going to be crushed into submission. 'You can say an awful lot in fifty minutes. Next time I go I'll make some notes on the way home.'

It was no use. I had tried to pacify him and now he thought I was being sarcastic. 'Oh, come on Leo, I only meant it's so easy to forget.'

He glared at me and I stared back, focussing on the tiny mole above his eyebrow. 'Is that what you think Ursula? Easy is it? Except there are some things it's impossible to forget.'

CHAPTER SIX

*'No woman who has merely achieved
success in a business career ever is happy.
The feminine nature craves masculine love
and affection.'*
(Article in Good Housekeeping, 1929)

Joyce and Sidney had invited us to a garden party. Well, perhaps not quite a garden party but a party in their garden. Archie and Muriel were invited too, and Joyce's friend Pamela who helped with the church flowers and Sunday school, and Sidney's new curate who was called Cyril Foster and had a young wife named Beryl who, according to Joyce, needed "taking in hand".

'Are you sure you feel up to it Ursa?' Leo stared at himself in the mirror, not expecting an answer. 'I think I will wear a tie.'

'You look nice with an open-neck shirt and it won't be a formal party, not with all the children scampering about.'

'Who else is going to be there?'

I reeled off the names, including the part about Beryl Foster needing to be taken in hand and he made a face as though to say, how typical of your sister to feel compelled to organise everybody.

'Well I hope it doesn't rain,' he said, 'or we'll all be stuck indoors.'

Having selected a tie and knotted it to his satisfaction he crossed the room without looking at me and I listened to him running down the stairs. Nearly two weeks had passed since my first proper session with Mrs Moberley and as the treatment progressed I felt less and less like talking about it. Perhaps it would have been different had Leo not believed himself to be an expert on psychoanalysis. Mrs Moberley never passed judgement on me although I did sometimes wonder what she was thinking. Neither did she talk about Freud. Leo on the other hand seemed to think it his duty to make sure I understood the theories that lay behind the treatment.

The childhood trauma that was supposed to be responsible for my arm and my other symptoms had been on my mind ever since I began the treatment, but Mrs Moberley had advised me not to search my memory since any event I had forgotten was likely to return of its own accord.

Easier said than done. Had something happened between my parents? And was that the reason I had been sent away to school when I was only nine? Supposing I had done something so dreadful that nobody liked to mention it again because being so young at the time I was not held responsible for my actions. But if that was the case what on earth could it be?

During the party I was going to draw Joyce aside and question her. At first she would deny that any such event had taken place but when I explained that remembering could be the cure for all my ailments surely she would feel obliged to speak out. I thought about Enid and Jim and all the deprivations their respective families must have had to put up with – bad housing, overcrowding, shortage of money – and any problems I might have felt like an indulgence. My stupid arm still hung limply by my side while Enid, who had been brought up in far less privileged conditions, was a strapping girl who had no interest whatever in the contents of her unconscious mind.

The vicarage was much larger than our house, as big as *The Gables* but older and in need of repair both inside and out. The first time I saw it I thought how lucky it was that Joyce cared so little for her surroundings. All this space, she kept telling me, it's so good for the children, and the drawing room so-called will do for parish meetings while we can sit in the old butler's parlour, much cosier.

The previous vicar had been unmarried and had a private income to supplement his salary so he might well have employed, if not a butler at least a housekeeper and a charlady, and someone to look after the garden. Now it grew wild and Helen and Sybil had the run of it, making houses among the rhododendrons and riding their bicycles round the path that circled the house and continued on past dilapidated sheds and an ancient stable block.

Joyce had a maid but she only did mornings, something my sister never failed to point out when Enid's name came up. *You're so lucky with your Enid. Ethel's a good soul and I wish we could afford to have her all day but she's not the brightest star in the firmament.*

If I had been fit enough I would have offered to help prepare for the party, but what use would I have been and doubtless Joyce's close companion Pamela had rallied round. On previous visits Pamela had not put in an appearance and I was curious to know what she was like. Joyce spoke warmly about her, but with a slight air of condescension, and I wondered if she was a real friend or it was simply that they had been thrown together while arranging the church flowers and helping out at parish functions. Naturally Joyce was a leading light in the Mothers' Union but as far as I could tell Pamela had never been married.

My own lack of friends was something that worried me now and again. If Midge had been in England we would have met up often but since leaving school I ought to have made new ones. During the time I worked for Archie I had been too busy, travelling each day between my mother's house in Surrey and Cavendish Square and spending the weekends caring for Mother as best I could.

Not long after she died I had met Leo and somehow there had been no need for friends after that, just the occasional get-together with girls from school, none of whom meant much to me, and the daughter of a neighbour of my mother's with whom I felt duty bound to keep in touch for a time.

Later, when Leo and I moved into the house in Highgate I intended to take an active part in the local community but somehow the plan had never materialised. I knew people in the same street but they were only acquaintances and either they were much older than me or they had families that kept them fully occupied. *Children are great icebreakers.* That was another of Joyce's maxims. *Most of the people I know are the mothers of Helen and Sybil's friends, quite apart from all the parishioners of course.*

So that was the answer, marry a clergyman or have a family. Or if possible do both.

Leo and I had reached the vicarage later than

everyone else. Before we left Highgate he had given the car such a thorough check we could have been setting out for John O'Groats and his unwillingness to get going had almost given me a headache. Still, as it turned out being the last guests to arrive meant it was easy to merge into the throng and take in the unfamiliar faces from a safe distance.

Every so often I caught a glimpse of Helen and Sybil racing round, throwing dandelions at each other and shouting rude names. My two nieces and I knew so little about them, partly because Joyce hardly ever brought them to our house but also because when she did she liked to keep them on a tight rein.

'Slow down!' Joyce yelled, catching Helen by the arm quite roughly, 'you'll bump into someone and send them flying. Go and help Pamela with the food. She's been working jolly hard, needs a break, poor thing.'

A murmur of female voices floated out through the kitchen window. Worthy people from the parish who had come to help while remaining unobtrusive? What had made Joyce decide to throw a party, or had it been Sidney's idea? It was not his birthday – that was on April Fool's Day – and Joyce's was in November. Perhaps it was for the benefit of the new curate or simply one of Joyce's impromptu ideas, Leo had suggested, adding, "I expect she'd been at the cooking sherry".

A harmless enough remark but lately I was so oversensitive I had taken it to mean he thought Joyce was a secret drinker and it had set us off on another of our fruitless arguments. Sometimes I despaired of myself, suspecting I deliberately picked a quarrel in the hope that we would have a tearful reconciliation, but if that was my *unconscious* wish it was doomed to failure.

Shading my eyes – fortunately the warm weather had held out – I made my way towards the trestle tables where a large grey-haired woman, clad in a jade green dress, was busy arranging plates of sandwiches and cakes. If it was Joyce's friend Pamela she was a good deal older than Joyce, at least twenty years by the look of her. That meant the young woman standing by the pear tree must be the curate's wife. What was her name? I had forgotten it already. The curate was called Cyril and his wife was – I struggled to remember. Beryl! So despite Leo's jibes there was nothing wrong with my memory. Cyril and Beryl, it sounded like a music hall act.

Glancing back at Pam but preferring the look of Beryl I strolled across to join her, turning away from the sun and leaning my back against the tree's rough trunk.

'Hello, I'm Ursula, Joyce's sister.'

'Oh.' She blinked several times. 'How do you do? I'm the new curate's wife.'

'I guessed you must be. Beryl, isn't it and you only moved here a few weeks ago.'

'Five. Five weeks to the day.'

I wondered if Joyce had told her about my arm, but why would she? It was not the most fascinating subject in the world. 'Do you think you'll like it in Ealing?'

'We have a nice house, small but convenient. You live in Highgate don't you?'

So Leo and I had been mentioned but only because we would be attending the party. 'I wonder where Christopher is,' I said, immediately answering my own question. 'I expect he's having his afternoon sleep.'

'Yes I expect so. He's sweet isn't he, a lovely little boy.'

I have never been much good at small talk but there

was something about Beryl that made it easy. Perhaps it was because she was so nervous I felt it would make little difference what I said, she would be glad someone was talking to her, taking the lead. Timid people are never a threat.

She was not very tall, only a little over five foot I guessed, and her slip was a fraction too long at the back so that the lacy hem showed below the skirt of her pale pink frock.

'That's my husband over there.' I pointed with my good arm. 'He's a schoolmaster. And the tall man with white hair is his father. He's a skin specialist. I was his secretary before I got married.'

'Really?' She looked as if I had said something astonishing. 'You are lucky. I'd love to have a job.'

'Would you? But surely being a curate's wife is a kind of a job isn't it and when he's made a vicar you'll be as busy as Joyce.'

I noticed her expression and started to laugh. 'Perhaps you could do something else instead,' I suggested, but my laughter stopped as quickly as it had started because we both knew that would be impossible.

She looked so glum it occurred to me she might have had a secret ambition, to be a dancer or an actress perhaps. She was quite pretty and had a nice trim figure and the poor thing was destined to arrange the flowers and teach at Sunday school when all the time she would feel like a chrysalis that was never allowed to turn into a butterfly. Still, if that was how she felt she should never have married a clergyman.

Muriel was walking towards us and I would have to make the introductions. After that I wanted to collar Joyce except every time I looked in her direction she was rushing about as though the party depended on her single-handed supervision. Out of the corner of my eye I watched Helen climb a wall then count to ten and jump down onto the grass.

'You next,' she shouted, and Sybil looked round apprehensively, stepped onto the rickety garden chair Helen had provided and took her turn. She and Helen were almost the same height but Sybil had always been the more fearful of the two. From her vantage point the distance to the grass must have looked frighteningly far and I hurried across to give her a helping hand, only remembering as I reached her that one arm was not going to be much use and I was more likely to make her lose her balance and crash to the ground.

'Come *on*!' Helen yelled, 'cowardy, cowardy custard.'

Sybil jumped and as she did so she must have caught sight of me and swerved to avoid a collision. Landing awkwardly she let out a scream and all conversation stopped as the guests turned to see where it had come from then surged forward to give assistance.

Joyce and Pamela were inside the house collecting more plates of food and that gave Muriel, the first to arrive at the scene, the opportunity to take charge.

'Really Ursula what on earth did you think you were you doing?'

'She wasn't doing anything,' Helen said indignantly.

'Precisely.' Muriel knelt beside Sybil. 'Are you all right dear? No don't try to move, keep quite still and tell me where it hurts. Helen, go and fetch your mother.'

By the time Joyce had joined us it was clear that Sybil had not broken a limb or even turned her ankle.

'Silly muggins.' Joyce gave her good-natured cuff. 'Come and get some lemonade, that'll cheer you up.

You too Ursula, you look as though you could do with a refreshing drink.'

Joyce had made a special effort with her outfit but it was not a success. Her red dress with its sham shirtfront, dolman sleeves, and inverted box pleats had been designed for someone a good deal slimmer. Red had never suited her and the knotted silk scarf with its green and yellow spots made her look like a Christmas decoration.

'I like your dress,' I said, the way you do when you are thinking exactly the opposite. 'Is it new?'

'This old thing.' She grinned at me and I felt awful because that meant it *was* new and I was being unkind even if it was only in my head. One minute I resented the way she tried to jolly me along. The next I was full of remorse.

'It's a lovely party.' I stepped forward to kiss her cheek but she turned her head and I almost got a mouthful of hair. 'I'm sorry about Sybil.'

'Why should you be sorry Auntie Ursula?' Helen protested, but Joyce waved her aside. 'Go and look after your sister.'

'She doesn't like being looked after. She hates me.'

'I met the curate's wife,' I said, hoping to pre-empt an argument.

'Oh yes.' Joyce was looking in the opposite direction. 'What did you think of her?'

'Rather sweet.'

She gave a hollow laugh. 'But not going to be much use in the parish. Too nervy.'

'Perhaps that's why I liked her. We have something in common.'

'Oh, come on.' Joyce screwed up her nose. 'If you

ask me your arm's the result of all that tennis you played at school, and all those gymnastics.'

'But that was years ago.'

'An old injury resurrected by reaching up to a high shelf or carrying heavy shopping.'

'Actually I wanted to ask you something Joyce.'

'Fire away.' She put both hands round her mouth and bellowed an instruction to Pamela about there being more potted meat if she needed it.' Then she turned back to me with a look on her face that resurrected memories of when we were children. 'If you want my opinion it's like a strained back, takes time to heal but gets there in the end. Anyway how are you getting on with the Moberley woman?'

'Did anything happen when I was a child? Something I've forgotten about and nobody likes to mention.'

'Whoever put that idea into your head?'

But before I could say any more Pamela had beckoned to us and Joyce insisted I accompany her to the food table so she could make the introductions.

Over by the back door I could see Leo playing with Helen and Sybil. The game involved a tennis ball and a badminton racquet and I hoped nobody would break a window or hit the ball into the food. Now fully recovered Sybil was jumping up, as Leo held the ball high above her head, and I thought how relaxed he looked and how much happier than when he was stuck at home with me.

Pamela was one of those people you are supposed to admire but secretly dislike. Cheerful, efficient, never pushing herself forward, never saying anything critical, or anything witty since amusing stories, however lighthearted, are usually at someone else's expense.

I listened as she sung Joyce's praises, then Sidney's. Where was Sidney? He was hardly the partying kind. Even so it was not like him to let down Joyce at a social occasion into which she had obviously put her heart and soul.

Joyce read my thoughts. 'Sidney will be along quite soon. He's taking the funeral of an old man in his nineties. Quite a character wasn't he, Pam?'

Pamela beamed. 'Old Mr Wiseacre, he was a lamb.'

'Hail and hearty almost up to the day he died.' Joyce tipped two remaining drop scones onto another plate that still had plenty left. 'Help yourself Ursula, needs building up, doesn't she, Pam.'

Pamela said nothing since that would have meant disagreeing with Joyce or insulting me.

'I hope you're eating properly,' Joyce continued, 'how did Enid get on with that recipe book I lent her?'

'Enid's good at plain cooking but she doesn't like anything fancy.'

Joyce gave a disapproving grunt. 'Well tell her to be more adventurous. I realise actual cooking's out as far as you're concerned but you could always suggest a new dish and oversee her efforts.'

'I suppose so.' I was remembering how Enid had left Joyce's recipe book on the side and accidentally knocked over the jug of stock so that some of the pages had turned shiny with grease. When I returned it to Joyce I would take the blame, not that it mattered now Enid would be leaving. Leo had agreed that for the time being no mention should be made of her marriage to Jim, but when Joyce found out she would make a great to do about finding a replacement. So would Muriel.

'Did you read the section on poultry and game?' Joyce was set on demonstrating my ignorance to Pamela. 'It's so important to know what you're buying isn't it, Pam? Fowls with black legs for roasting and ones with white legs for boiling. Are you listening Ursula?'

'Yes but I need to go and ask Archie something.'

'Right you are.' She looked at me a little wistfully. 'He's like a father to you, isn't he.'

'Don't be silly, only because I used to be his secretary.'

'What's that got to do with it?' She turned away, busying herself rearranging a plateful of corned beef sandwiches. 'Anyway it'll soon be time to bring out the *pièce de resistance.*'

'Layer cake,' she called after me, and I promised to come back when she cut it as I was sure it would be light as a feather.

When I spotted him Archie had been on his own, inspecting a wide border that had more weeds than flowers, but as I strolled across the grass Muriel rushed to join him. She had seen me coming and done it on purpose, and not wanting another lecture on how I should have prevented Sybil from falling off the wall I decided to take a different route and go in search of Leo.

At first he was nowhere to be seen but, wandering down the path that led to the outhouse, I found him standing next to some straggly blue flowers, almost entirely covered in bindweed, and to my surprise he was holding Christopher.

'I thought he was having his afternoon rest.'

'Woke up,' Leo explained, 'doesn't seem to mind me. Placid little chap.'

'He's probably still a bit sleepy.'

'I doubt it. He was yelling his head off.'

'I never heard him.'

'No, well I expect you were round the other side of the house.'

Talk of babies always made me anxious and I was relieved to see Sidney, back from his funeral and hurrying down the path to join us.

'Good to see you both.' Even in his own home he sounded like a vicar greeting his parishioners. 'How are you?'

'Enjoying the party.' Leo offered him the baby but he raised a hand as if to say, no you keep him since he appears so content.

'Fell off my bicycle.' Sidney pointed to his upper lip. 'One of those cobbled streets that bump you up and down no matter how carefully you proceed. How's your new woman treating you Ursula? Does she go in for hypnosis? Jolly brave of you. All sounds a little unnerving to me but I'm sure she knows what she's doing.'

'Yes she does.'

'I'm afraid I'm not well up on such matters.' He had picked up the shortness in my voice and wanted to make amends for his bantering tone. 'What about you Leo, I gather you're something of an expert on the subject. How did you find out about it? There are books are there?'

Leo nodded. 'And journal articles.'

I could see Joyce in the distance, pulling Helen and Sybil apart. Her mouth was opening and closing and from the angle of her shoulders I suspected she was warning them if there was any more squabbling they would be sent indoors.

'My two girls,' Sidney explained, 'recently they've been as quarrelsome as a couple of cats. Just a phase one hopes. I do my best but I'm afraid Joyce bears the brunt of it.'

'I expect it's hard for Helen,' I said, 'having a sister who's only one year younger. I expect she sometimes feels they're lumped together like twins.'

'An interesting idea.' Sidney fingered the scab on his lip. 'No doubt you're becoming quite knowledgeable concerning the whims of human behaviour.'

'I remember wishing Joyce and I were closer in age then wondering if it would be worse.'

'Worse?' Sidney's face lit up with amusement. With his slightly sallow skin, prominent eyes and egg-shaped head he always reminded me of one of the characters in a pack of *Happy Families*. Not the vicar, I don't think they have a vicar, so it must be Mr Teeth the dentist, or possibly Mr Pipe the plumber.

Two years ago he had officiated at our wedding, carrying out his duties with due solemnity and even insisting on giving us a little talk about the commitment we were about to make to one another. Joyce had wanted the reception at her house but Muriel had stood out for *The Gables* and in the end there had been a compromise with Muriel in charge of the catering but Joyce detailed to make the three-tiered cake. Helen and Sybil had been bridesmaids, wearing clothes I found far too fussy and uncomfortable but before I had any say in the matter Joyce had bought the material and pattern and was well away with her sewing machine. Fortunately she had stopped short of making my dress.

Everyone we knew had attended, and a few people that neither Leo nor I had set eyes on before, and since I had no male relative Archie had agreed to give me away. My friend Midge had come to the service but been unable to stay for the reception because her father was unwell and I remember how bereft I felt as she drove away and how I told myself it was wrong to think that way when I ought to be looking forward to a new life with Leo.

Later, exhausted from all the smiling and shaking hands Leo and I had climbed into the Daimler and been driven to the station on our way to a fortnight in St. Mawes. Pushing down the window so I could stick out my head and wave I had watched Archie get smaller and smaller until, afraid I might get a smut in my eye, Leo had pulled me back into the carriage where the two of us had sat side by side, not knowing what to say to each other…

'Do you Ursula?' Leo said and I snapped out of my daydream and asked him to repeat his question.

'I was telling Sidney how you object to discussing your treatment. She's been seeing her analyst for two weeks but none of us is any the wiser.'

'And quite right too, a private affair.' Back in his role as a clergyman Sidney put his two hands together as in prayer. 'You're always in our thoughts Ursula and we have high hopes of a speedy recovery.'

'Thank you Sidney.' He was amiable enough but a little of him went a long way and I was trying to think up an excuse to leave. 'If you'll excuse me I'm just going to walk round the house.'

'Whatever for?' Leo said and I gave a small shrug, speculating as I continued on my way about what he would say to Sidney. *She's somewhat over sensitive these days, finds socialising a little taxing.*

The gravel was full of weeds and the rhododendrons needed cutting back. How much did vicars earn? Someone had once said it depended on the parish and as far as I could tell this was quite an ordinary one, not the most important church in the district. Would Sidney stay in London forever or might he be moved to a church at the other end of the country and if he was would I miss Joyce or be relieved she was too far away to visit often? Now that her children were getting older, more like little people, I ought to make the effort to get to know them, not simply provide presents for birthdays and Christmas.

'Where are you off to?' called Archie and I turned to greet him, unable to conceal my pleasure.

'Nowhere special, I'm not much good at talking to people I don't know.'

'Nor me. Have you had something to eat?'

'A bit, what about you?'

'Tell me about Mrs Moberley. If you want to that is.'

'Oh I do, but you must promise not to tell Leo. I know it's not his fault but he keeps questioning me and then when I try to explain he interrupts and starts talking about Freud, and Mrs Moberley never talks about Freud, only about me.'

He was silent and I regretted my remarks. After all Leo was his son, how could I tell him not to mention something to him?

'Archie?'

'What is it?' His voice was so gentle I was reassured and felt confident to ask him something that had been on my mind for ages.

'Do you ever lie awake worrying about what you should or should not have done? Especially if it's about someone who matters to you a great deal.'

'Are you still thinking about Leo?'

'No, not especially.' But I had answered too quickly.

'We all have our regrets,' he said, taking my hand for a moment then letting it go, 'but I always think it's best to look forward rather than back, after all one can't change the past.'

During the last half hour the sky had become overcast and the air felt muggy. I found a handkerchief and wiped my forehead and prayed the palpitations I sometimes felt in warm weather would not put in an appearance.

'Is she what you expected?' Archie had returned to the subject of Mrs Moberley.

'I'm not sure. No I don't think she is. I suppose in some ways she's quite intimidating, her manner I mean, and the way she talks, but I like her, I'm not quite sure why, and I trust her. I'm sure she's going to make me better.'

He gave me a hug. 'That's what counts.'

'Yes it is, isn't it.' I pulled free in a half-hearted kind of way but not soon enough because he was still holding me tight when Muriel came round the corner.

'Oh there you are,' she said coldly, making it clear she was speaking to Archie, not me. 'Joyce has produced a cake and we're all to have a slice.'

It was such a feeble excuse to justify her search for Archie that I almost laughed. But that would have added insult to injury. 'It's a layer cake,' I said, 'and she made it herself because Ethel's not awfully good at baking.'

'Apparently their range has been behaving badly.' Muriel was standing directly in front of Archie, blocking him from my view. 'Leo was looking for you Ursula. It's fortunate Sybil's none the worse for her fall. She could have broken something.'

'Not terribly likely.' Archie winked at me then made a mock serious face.

'I don't know why you say that,' Muriel persisted, 'I read about a boy with a broken leg who was operated on and died under the anaesthetic.'

'Chance in a million. Must have suffered from some underlying complaint.'

'You look hot.' Muriel turned her attention to me. I suppose it's this humid weather. You'd better find yourself a cold drink. In the circumstances I do think you ought to take better care of yourself.'

'In that case.' Archie took hold of Muriel's arm and steered her round to face the way she had come. 'We'll all go and sample this famous cake.'

Joyce was standing by the remains of the layer cake, fanning herself with a copy of *My Home*.

'Pam's,' she explained, 'tells you what curtains you ought to have and how to cook your brussel sprouts.'

'Where is she?'

'Upstairs dealing with Christopher. Having no children of her own she enjoys changing nappies and wiping posteriors.'

'I wanted to ask you something, Joyce?'

'Ursula!'

'What?' I hated the habit she had of putting a heavy emphasis on the first syllable of my name.

'Go on then, spit it out.'

'I wondered if Helen would like to come over to our house one day.'

'Helen? Whatever for?' Her face conveyed the amazement she clearly felt that I could suggest such a thing. But I refused to be put off.

'I thought it might be good for her to spend some time on her own, away from Sybil.'

'Away from Sybil,' she repeated. 'How would you manage? You may think butter wouldn't melt in her mouth but I can tell you she's at a stage where she plays up at the slightest provocation.'

'Enid would be there. Anyway, don't decide now.' I began to walk away. 'Just an idea and she might not want to. She might find it a bit of a bore.'

When I caught up with Leo it was clear he wanted to leave.

'You've never liked parties have you?' I linked arms with him. 'No, it's all right I'm ready to go home myself.'

'Then why put the blame on me?'

'Don't, Leo.' I dreaded another argument. 'Let's say goodbye to everyone and they'll think we're leaving because I'm tired.'

'Yes all right.' He followed me across the grass to where the curate's wife was standing on her own, pretending to inspect a clump of overgrown catmint. I wanted to grow some for Solomon but Muriel said we had the wrong type of soil. Since there was still no sign of Beryl's husband I murmured something about looking forward to seeing her again and meeting both of them.

'Cyril was so looking forward to coming.' My words, that I had intended to be so bland, had put her into a dither. 'He had to meet someone. It was all so unfortunate, such bad luck.'

'What busy people clergymen are,' Leo

commiserated, but she shook her head.

'No, it was a friend from the college he attended. He was passing through London on his way to Italy. I do hope Joyce understands.'

'I'm certain she does,' I said, thinking how strange it felt being the one to offer reassurance. 'Anyway I'm so glad we've met and I'm sure we'll bump into one another again in the not too distant future.'

Leo was shifting his weight from one foot to the other and I was afraid he might look at his watch. How little men cared for the niceties of life, for keeping things and people ticking over satisfactorily. If it had been left to him he would have jumped into the car without even saying goodbye to Joyce. Were they born that way, feeling no particular guilt if they upset someone, or was it because they were brought up by doting mothers who led them to believe they were so special there was no requirement to behave in such a way that other people would think well of them?

As we drove away there was a rumble of thunder and it looked as though a downpour might descend on us before we reached Highgate.

'Did you enjoy the party?' I asked and unexpectedly Leo turned to grin at me.

'The food was good, if you like potted meat which I do.'

We laughed, and for a brief moment it was like it had been in the beginning when the two of us had driven away from Archie and Muriel's house, relieved to be on our own again. Right from the start Leo had been wary of showing me any affection in front of his mother, probably because he feared it would make her even more possessive. I had found it mildly irritating and it had contributed to my dislike of Muriel. All the same, the enforced self-restraint had made it more fun when we escaped from her clutches.

'I do love you,' I said.

'I know.' For the first time for ages there was warmth in his voice. 'Don't worry, three or four months with Mrs Moberley and you'll be back to your old self.'

'Four months,' I said, feigning mock horror. 'I hope it won't be as long as that.' And even as I spoke I was thinking, what was "my old self", and did I really want to be back with it.

CHAPTER SEVEN

'I have come to the conclusion that it is above all a question of psychological tact whether one should tell the patient some particular thing. But what is "tact"? It is the capacity for empathy.'
(Sandor Ferenczi)

Sometimes it's impossible to recall the content of a dream but the feeling it leaves you with stays with you all the following day. In this case the mood had been dread, not the usual fear of being trapped in a confined place or falling off a cliff or into deep water. In this dream it had been my own fault that I was so afraid. Entirely my own fault and I had cursed myself for being so hot headed.

Except, try as I might I was unable to remember what it was I had feared so much.

Perhaps seeing Mrs Moberley was making me worse and it would be better if I abandoned the treatment. Leo would be pleased, not that he would admit it, but I would know because he was hopeless at hiding his feelings. But I had become accustomed to my Monday, Wednesday and Friday afternoons and in an odd way I would miss them, even though, more often than not, they left me exhausted and confused.

Lying on the couch in the familiar surroundings of the consulting room it was the first time for several weeks I had felt so apprehensive. My bag lay beside me and I felt inside it with my good hand, sifting through the contents in the hope that it would provide the feeling of safety I craved. Powder compact with its own tiny mirror, hairbrush, handkerchief, lipstick, and pills in case one of my headaches decided to put in an appearance.

For what was probably five minutes but felt a good deal longer I had remained silent. Now, as if to announce I was ready to continue, I gave a heavy sigh and began to talk, choosing my words carefully in case they were misinterpreted. 'Leo thinks I'm giving you a distorted picture of myself.'

Silence.

'But he's right isn't he because nobody speaks the truth, not the real truth, at least not if they can help it.'

More silence. I even wondered if she had fallen asleep. It was a sultry day and the atmosphere in the room felt mildly oppressive. Showers had been forecast for later in the day and as Leo kept saying, for want of something more interesting to talk about, the garden would welcome a good drenching.

What I would have welcomed now was a freezing cold bath, or better still a swim in the sea, floating on my back, looking up at the sky, then flipping onto my front, twisting and turning like a dolphin – I was a good swimmer – submerging under the waves until Leo was certain I must have drowned. The first time we swam together he had insisted I splash my forehead with water before entering the sea. What for, I asked and he muttered something about the shock of the cold, and I thought: Muriel, must be, one of her fusses. What a restrictive childhood he must have had. No wonder he often looked so worried.

Since the memory of that swim had come into my head perhaps I should talk about it. But perhaps not. It was the warmth of the room that had set it off, nothing from the past, nothing important.

When I arrived I had been wearing my favourite hat, a straw one trimmed with crêpe de chine. Mrs Moberley had no interest in my appearance and this irritated me a little. I put on my best for coming to see her and for all she cared I could have been dressed in rags. But how did I know this was true? She never remarked on my outfits, why would she, but they may have been noted in her little book if only because they threw light on my character, my vanity.

In spite of my nasty dream I had enjoyed the walk to Inverness Gardens. On the way I had passed a coal cart drawn by two massive shires and it had reminded me about Enid's father and how Enid had described giving sugar to the horses. *Only for a special treat mind. You have to flatten your hand like a plate and keep the thumb well tucked in. Not that they'd harm you deliberate but their mouths are enormous and all them big yellow teeth!*

Good old Enid, she was so straightforward, so lacking in guile. You knew where you were with her which was one of the reasons I valued her company so much. Something else Leo could never understand.

'I had a dream last night,' I told Mrs Moberley, 'I can't remember what happened exactly but it frightened me.'

'Tell me about it.'

'I was alone in a place I had never been to before, a valley I think, with scrubby bushes and rabbit droppings, and all the people who cared about me had gone. No I don't mean they were dead, I mean they weren't there, and it served me right, I had only myself to blame and when I woke I remembered I was coming here and I thought, I won't go and see Mrs Moberley any more, the treatment is making me worse and Leo thinks it's coming between us.'

'Is that what he said?'

'No but sometimes he looks so wretched. He wants me to tell him what we've talked about and on Friday when I said I couldn't remember he started brooding so I pretended I'd told you about when my mother died.'

Another silence.

'And all he said was, "You told her that before didn't you?" and then he started reading out something from *The Times*, all about a pygmy hippo that had arrived at London zoo and how it was six years old and called Diana, and how it was a gift from the Zoological Society of New York. And it wasn't even yesterday's paper, it was an old one that Enid had used when she polished his shoes.'

'A pygmy hippo called Diana,' Mrs Moberley repeated, as though the item had some special significance. Only if it had I could not imagine what it would be.

'Actually I have been thinking about my mother. I thought I knew her inside out but lately I've decided I didn't know her at all. Once she and my father had an argument, a bad one. I don't remember what it was about but later she overheard me talking to him and accused me of taking his side and it wasn't as though we'd been talking about her.'

'You felt you had to choose between your parents. It was impossible to please them both. Just as you feel it's not possible to please both me and Leo.'

'But I'm not here to please you am I?'

I was becoming used to the silences. A model patient, I had learned the ropes and knew what was expected of me. But silence stirs up memories, nearly always painful ones and not everyone thought the talking treatment made you better. In fact plenty of people seemed to believe it had the opposite effect.

'I've been wondering,' I said cautiously, 'has anyone been made worse from seeing an analyst?'

'You're afraid that may happen to you.'

'No. I don't know. Only thinking about yourself so much must make you awfully self-centred.'

'Isn't that why you're here? To try and discover what has made you unhappy.'

'Having a lifeless arm doesn't mean you're unhappy.'

More silence.

'I told you about Joyce's party didn't I? While I was there Sybil, she's the younger of the two girls, fell off a wall and everyone thought it was my fault, I should have caught her, broken the fall. No, that would have been difficult, but Muriel thought I should have stopped her climbing the wall. Anyway, the reason I'm telling you, after they'd finished blaming me they started on her sister Helen. She's a year older but sometimes I feel sorry for her. If she was only one when Sybil was born she hardly had any time to be the baby. I asked Joyce if she could spend the day with us.'

'If Helen could?'

I nodded. I always forgot she was not looking in my direction. 'It would be all right because Enid would be there and coming from such a large family she knows how to look after children.'

'I expect Helen would enjoy that.'

'If Joyce lets her. She may do if someone collects her

and brings her to our house. I suppose Archie might. No, it's not fair to ask him again. Joyce's house is terribly untidy but she doesn't seem to care and I suppose that's quite sensible. Do you think it is? Leo would never stand for it but I expect Sidney's too busy to notice. Sorry, I keep rambling on and none of it has anything to do with my arm.'

'Tell me about your dream. You were in a valley with bushes and rabbit droppings. When you think about the valley does it have any associations?'

'I was given a rabbit once but it had to go back to the shop.'

'Why was that?'

'Joyce had one first. He was called Rupert. Mine was supposed to be a boy rabbit too but it turned out to be female so of course they couldn't live in the same hutch. So Mother took it back.'

'Couldn't she have exchanged it for another male?'

'Yes, she could have done couldn't she. Why didn't she? Is that what the dream was about? Only why was I so afraid?'

This time the silence lasted for several minutes. Archie is paying for this, I thought, two guineas an hour, and I'm wasting his money because I can't think of anything to say.

'My headaches have been better,' I told her, 'and the coughing. If my blessed arm would start working Leo might not be so cross with me. The trouble is, I've been coming to see you for nearly a month and people are losing patience.'

'It's not very long.'

'How many months do you think it will take? No don't answer that, as if you would.' I laughed, hoping she would join in but the only sound I could hear was the faint rustle of paper. More notes no doubt.

Endurance is not one of Ursula's virtues. She hopes for a miracle, or perhaps it is her husband who is anxious for a speedy recovery.

No matter how hard I tried to concentrate my thoughts seemed to jump from one thing to another. First the dream, then the rabbit. No, that was an association so it was all right. Then my symptoms. Now I was going to start on yet another tack. For goodness sake stop worrying so much. You're paying for this, at least Archie is, and you can say what you like or even say nothing at all.

'Freud says little boys love their mothers and see their fathers as rivals so they want to kill them.'

'He called it the Oedipus complex.'

'What about little girls, do they want to kill their mothers?'

'Not literally but they probably feel a degree of jealousy.'

'Anyway it doesn't affect me because my father's dead. And I'm certain when he was alive I didn't want to kill my mother.'

She moved a little in her chair. 'These feelings, if they exist, are normally unconscious.'

'So how does Freud know if they're true?'

'I wouldn't worry too much about Freud, just try to describe your own thoughts and feelings in whatever way seems right for you.'

'Why do men like suspenders?' I asked, instantly overcome with embarrassment and wondering where on earth my question had come from. 'I read it in a book. I must have done. Why do you think it is?'

She cleared her throat and I thought, that's stumped her, but of course I was wrong.

'Perhaps it's because women's undergarments are something of a mystery to them which makes them rather exciting.'

'Really?' I was so pleased she had answered my question I wanted to sit up on the couch and force her to look at me. 'I'm sure if I made more effort I could pull myself together. Do you think I could?'

Silence. But when I twisted my head to look at her, expecting her to be staring into space, she was straightening the shade on her table lamp.

When she let me into the house I noticed she was particularly smartly dressed. A beige crepe dress with a flared skirt and a low neckline. Her shoes were different too. High heels with pointed toes. Perhaps she was going out after she had dispensed with me. *One patient I have to see at two o'clock then I'll be free.* Where was she going? To visit a friend? Or her lover? He might be married so that she could only see him in the afternoon.

'If only I could remember the trauma,' I said, 'the horrendous event that's supposed to have blighted my childhood.'

'It's not always like that Ursula.'

'Isn't it? Then what am I here for? Leo says I'm suffering from repression, conflict between the ego and something or other. He said I was to tell you whatever came into my head but if I describe some of the things we've talked about he accuses me of wasting time with trivialities.'

She cleared her throat and I thought, now you understand what I'm up against, but when she spoke it turned out to be on behalf of Leo.

'Perhaps he feels a little neglected.'

'By me?' I was outraged. 'I'm always home by the time he returns from the school. And there's always a nice supper waiting to be heated up.'

But that was not the kind of neglect she meant.

'I'm sure he's well versed in Freudian theory,' she continued, 'but the theories have as much relation to its practice as a manual on sexual techniques has to the emotion of being in love.'

It took me a moment to take in what she meant. 'Do you mean the talking cure is more concerned with how the patient feels?'

'Put simply that's exactly what it is.'

Outside in the street an errand boy was whistling one of the tunes that Enid liked so much. What would he think if he could see me lying on my back on a couch with my shoes kicked off and my eyes half closed, talking about falling in love? All those strange things going on behind closed doors and we pretend other people's lives are trouble-free and it's only our own that is in such a muddle.

Had I imagined it or was there something different about the couch today? It occurred to me that Dora might have slept on it and the scent of eau-de-cologne was to cover the smell. Or did the scent come from Mrs Moberley, part of the preparation for her visit to her lover? I wanted to giggle but managed to keep it in check. Instead I asked where Dora was, but no response was forthcoming.

'I'm supposed to say whatever comes into my head,' I protested, 'and when I do you don't answer.'

'I expect she's in the kitchen.'

'I wish you'd let her sit in here.'

'She might distract you.'

'She wouldn't. In any case it distracted me wondering where she was. Leo wants us to have a holiday in August, and Enid wants to get married. If I don't get a move on I'll ruin everyone's plans. I asked Joyce if she could remember anything that happened when we were children but she still thinks my arm is because of something the doctors failed to diagnose. Perhaps she's right and I'm wasting my time coming here. Leo thinks I'm secretive. When he talks to me, which isn't often, it's always in an aggrieved voice. He thinks I'm obstinate and I can tell he wishes he had never suggested I came to see you.'

'He's finding it hard.' Her voice was so infuriatingly calm I could have screamed.

'Supposing my arm gets better but Leo decides he's had enough of me.'

'I don't think that's very likely, do you.'

'Yes I do as a matter of fact. What time is it? Is it nearly time to stop?' I looked at my watch. 'Eleven minutes to go and I'm not sure I can stand much more.' And to my horror I started to sob.

A letter had arrived – from Midge. The writing was more flowery than I recalled but there was no mistaking the French stamp. Tearing it open with my teeth, an art I had perfected after watching Solomon rip open a bag containing old fish bones, I withdrew the letter and smoothed it out on the table, then noticed the photograph that had fallen on the carpet.

She was wearing a hat, pulled well down but set at a jaunty angle and the large bow on the front obscured part of her face. But it was Midge all right. The same upturned nose and Cupid's bow mouth, and the mole on her left cheek had become an alluring beauty spot. I stared at it for several minutes, contrasting my sensible string of pearls with her three rows of brightly coloured beads then placing the photograph on the coffee table, I began to read.

Dearest Ursula. Had she always addressed me as "dearest" or was it the result of her new exciting life? *Dearest Ursula, I write with glad tidings to tell. I arrive in London on the tenth of August and will be staying at my uncle and aunt's house in Wimbledon. Do you remember Uncle Bertie and Auntie Mildred, I'm sure you must, or if you didn't actually meet them you must have heard me describe Uncle Bertie's dubious habit of leaving the bathroom door unlocked, by mistake on purpose! Enough of that, I can't wait for us to meet up and exchange all kinds of interesting news, you of your marriage to Leo and me of my life in gay Paree. What have you been up to? Gadding about London buying objets d'art for your smart little house?*

How is the gorgeous Archie, and his not so gorgeous wife? But perhaps the two of you are the best of friends these days. Hope you like the photograph. Do I look older than when you last saw me? I certainly hope not but with my twenty-fifth birthday coming up in a few weeks time I've been making some careful inspections in the mirror, looking for the firsts signs of decline. Oh Ursula I can hear you laughing at the thought of it. Didn't we have fun? I can't think how I'd have survived that awful prison of a place without all the pranks. I wonder if Miss Wesley is still alive. What was it we called her? The weasel! How could I ever forget?

Must close now but keep the second week in August as free as possible. You're not going away on holiday then are you? I'll be in touch.

All my love, Midge.

I was delighted to hear from her, of course I was, but by the sound of it she was living such a thrilling life that she would think mine frightfully dull in comparison. Her clothes would be smarter too, Paris frocks and Paris hats, all the latest fashions and accessories.

I left the letter for Leo to read. He might not approve of the tone of it. On the other hand he would be glad she was coming as it would give me an added incentive to get well. *You won't want her to see you like that.* Not that he would actually say it out loud but we would both know what he was thinking. And he would be right.

Enid had a hacking cough. I heard her in the scullery and went to make sure she was all right.

'It's nothing Mrs Ingham.' She had her back turned, running water into the sink.

'If you're feeling unwell you must go home.'

'No need for that.' She stood back from her sinkful of washing and let the suds drip from her hands on to the stone floor. 'And I can't have caught it from you so don't you worry on that score.'

'You mean because mine's not an infection it's my stupid nerves.'

'Nerves is not stupid Mrs Ingham.'

'No I suppose not.' I was surprised she had taken my remark so seriously.

'Plenty of people suffer with their nerves.' She returned to scrubbing the cuffs of one of Leo's shirts. 'I had a relative, dead now poor soul, suffered from shell shock, that's a kind of nerves isn't it?'

'I'm sorry Enid, was he a close relative?'

'Only a second cousin, something like that. I never met him, just heard about him from my auntie. All I'm saying if you get a bad shock it can set things off. Leastways that's how some people see it.'

'You think I must have had some kind of shock?'

She let the water out of the sink and started squeezing out the clothes. 'I reckon that mangle would be enough to do for your arm. I'm strong, always have been, but don't you try turning it, even when your arm's got itself better.'

So she had abandoned "shock" as the cause of all my troubles and, like Joyce, was wondering if I had damaged my arm and the doctors had failed to diagnose the injury.

'How's Jim?' I asked, sick of the whole subject of nerves, sick of myself.

'Working every hour God gives.'

'Saving up so you can have a home of your own? If there's any way Mr Ingham and I can help. Yes, well once you've fixed a date for the wedding you must decide what you and Jim would like for a present.'

I expected her to protest there was no need for anything like that but she stayed silent, dragging out the mangle then picking up a damp towel and threading a corner through the rollers.

'Cold in the scullery Mrs Ingham.' She raised her voice against the rattle. 'You go back to the drawing room and soon as I've finished I'll bring you a pot of tea and a macaroon. Turned out nicely they did though I say so myself.'

'Yes all right.' She wanted to be left in peace. Since my illness I had taken up far too much of her time and because she was paid to do as I wished she had been obliged to put up with me. Back home she probably complained to her family. *Talk, talk, talk, it's as much as I can do to finish my work when she's all the time interrupting me, wanting one of her chats.*

'No hurry with the tea,' I called cheerily although cheerful was the last thing I felt. When Leo came back I would tell him I had been having cold feet about "the talking cure". No, on second thoughts, that might not be such a good idea. He would be pleased about the cold feet but annoyed that I had changed my mind. *I never know where I am with you Ursula.* Or sometimes he broadened it to include all women. *They're so contrary, seem incapable of thinking something out logically and sticking to it.*

Returning to the drawing room I picked up the *William* book he had borrowed for me from the library, sat down on the sofa and turned to the first page. *William the Outlaw.* At any other time I would have relished the thought of all those new stories – William was a hero after my own heart – but since talking to Enid I was not in the mood. I knew I was too easily hurt but what harm did it do if I kept her company while she put the washing through the mangle? A twinge of irritation was followed by a pang of loneliness. Was it really because she felt obliged to make conversation when she wanted to concentrate on her work? When I mentioned wedding presents perhaps she thought I was going to commiserate about the fact that she and Jim would have to live with Jim's mother.

No! How dense I was being, how thoughtless.

Picking up *The Times* in the hope that it would convince her I was only going to stay a few minutes, I hurried back to the scullery, ready to insist she fix a date for the wedding rather than wait until my symptoms had disappeared.

'There's something I need to say to you Enid.'

'What's that Mrs Ingham?' She dried her hands on her apron.

'You must fix up the wedding for as soon as you like. Mr Ingham's term finishes in the middle of July and apart from the odd day here and there he'll be home all the time until September. Would the end of July suit you?'

She stared at me, with an expression I found impossible to interpret then returned to the mangle. 'Like I said, there's no rush.'

'Yes I know that's what you said.' But I was fighting a losing battle. She was going to dig in her heels and I would be left feeling responsible for ruining her plans and with nothing I could do to make amends.

Perhaps if I tried a different tack. 'I'm going out in the garden in a moment but I must show you this.' I folded the newspaper to an advertisement, with a picture of a woman sitting down and a man leaning over her shoulder. *"Oh Mother!"* I read, putting on a silly voice that I hoped would make her smile. *"Slacking in the morning! You of all people!" "Yes, it's not like me is it? It's since we had our new cook." "Our new cook! Who's she? I haven't seen her." "Oh, she's a treasure! Our new cook is the New World **cooker**. I set the regulo dial which controls the oven heat and when I came back I found every single thing done to a nicety!"* Isn't it the silliest thing you've ever seen?'

Enid let out a gasp.

'Yes, I know.' I hoped the advertisement might amuse her but had not expected such an extreme response. 'Although I suppose it could be quite useful having a dial that controlled the heat.'

'Oh Mrs Ingham.' Her normally ruddy face had turned quite pale.

'What is it?' Had I said something to offend her, something about the *New World* cooker?

As she walked towards me with a beaming smile on her face I remained stock still, trying to work out what it was all about.

'Do you know what you done Mrs Ingham? When the newspaper nearly knocked over the packet of Rinso you saved it with your bad hand. Look at it now, it's resting on the sink.'

While I waited impatiently for Leo to come home I had another go at Freud's Collected Papers, picking a section at random then finding it was full of words I had never come across before.

Apart from the fact that it was Latin I had no idea what *vita sexualis* meant, but in the case of nervous invalids grave disturbances of it took place. The next paragraph was about how patients concealed the truth but Freud became more and more adept at worming it out of them. Different ailments related to different types of sexual noxia, whatever that was. It sounded quite horrid. Frequent pollutions tended to come to light and led to an unsatisfying discharge of the libido aroused. Banished memories returned and the psychoanalysis of hysterics showed that their symptoms were equivalent to compromises in conflict between two mental currents.

It was no use, I could make neither head nor tail of it. Even so, when Leo suddenly entered the room I jumped, dropping the paper on the floor at my feet.

'What are you reading?' he asked.

'Freud, but it doesn't make much sense, and I found another of your library books.' I held it up for him to see. 'Why would the masters at your school need a book about madness?'

'Any number of reasons. A study of nineteenth century novels would provide an assortment of characters suffering from varying degrees of insanity.'

I opened the book where Leo had left a marker and started reading. '*The attribute of the insane patient which is at once the most general, the most obvious, and the most striking, is his apparent irrationality.* You always accuse me of being irrational.'

'Don't be silly Ursa, you know perfectly well I don't think you're insane.'

'What then?'

'I'm not going to argue about it.'

I laughed. I had no interest in the book, I just wanted to build up the suspense. 'I have some news for you.'

'Did you see Mrs Moberley?'

'Yes of course, it's Friday. I was in the scullery talking to Enid, showing her an advertisement in *The Times*.'

'Whatever for?'

'Because it was so ridiculous, making out women get excited about their kitchen equipment.'

'I expect some of them do. I realise how tedious your life has become but – '

'No listen!' I interrupted. 'I was talking to Enid and all of a sudden I noticed she had turned pale and when I asked her what was the matter she said my bad arm had moved, to stop the packet of Rinso from falling over, and now I had it resting on the sink!'

'And was it?'

'Yes, of course! If you don't believe me you can go and ask her. Only don't get too keyed up about it because when I tried to move it deliberately it was no good. But it's a start isn't it.'

He took his diary from his inside pocket and began

flicking through the pages as though he needed to check something important. 'So why won't it work now? Why could you lift it then and now it's gone back to hanging by your side?'

'I don't know. Should we telephone Mrs Moberley do you think?'

He shook his head. 'You can tell her next time you see her.'

'I thought you'd be pleased.'

'Of course I'm pleased and it's quite on the cards it will happen again but you know how disappointed you'll be if several days pass and no more progress has been made.'

'But if I could move it once surely I ought to be able to do it again. The trouble is when I was in the scullery I moved it without thinking and when I try to do it on purpose it doesn't work.'

'Most movements are involuntary.'

'Are they?'

'In the sense that we make no conscious decision.'

'No that can't be right Leo. If you decided to lift your arm.' I demonstrated with my good one. 'You think to yourself, I'm going to lift my arm, then do it. Oh and another lovely thing happened today. I heard from Midge and she's coming to London on the tenth of August, isn't that wonderful?'

He sat on the arm of a chair. 'So if all goes well you'll see her during the second week. Then Enid can get married and after that we'll be free to go on holiday. Where would you like to go? Give it some thought.'

'Yes I will.' I tried to wiggle the fingers of my right hand but to no avail. 'The thing is Leo I still haven't remembered a childhood trauma but I've a feeling Mrs

Moberley thinks the reason for my arm and all the other symptoms might be something quite different. '

His head spun round. 'Why, what did she say?'

'That it might not be so simple.'

'Yes, well she's not infallible. Just try to let nature take its course.'

'Whatever that's supposed to mean.' Why was he always so cautious? Another man might have flung his arms round my neck and covered me with kisses? But I knew the answer to that. He had never been particularly demonstrative and living with me had made him even more guarded. As usual I had only myself to blame and he was right when he said my moods were unpredictable, up one minute, down the next.

He had picked up the photograph Midge had included in her letter. 'I'm not sure I would have recognised her.'

'It's because of her hat.'

'Possibly.' He studied the picture more closely. 'Oh I almost forgot to tell you, one of the boys has won a scholarship to Winchester. Shawcross, the one I gave extra coaching to, the one who's a particularly good spin bowler.'

'That's wonderful Leo and I'm sure his parents must be terribly grateful.'

And there was no trace of bitterness in my voice, even though he sounded far more excited about his favourite pupil than he had been about my arm.

CHAPTER EIGHT

'The womb is an animal which longs to generate children. When it remains barren too long it is sorely disturbed.'

(Plato)

It was her half-term holiday and Helen had come to spend the day with me. When Joyce dropped her off at ten-thirty it was clear she would have liked me to have Sybil as well, and possibly even Christopher.

'I have a meeting of the school governors.' She made it sound like an audience with the King. 'Pam will have the other two. Highly inconvenient for her since she normally does hospital visiting on Tuesdays but she's a good soul, she's rearranged it for tomorrow.'

'What would you have done if Helen hadn't been coming here?'

'How do you mean?' She frowned as if I had said something totally incomprehensible then returned to rummaging in her bag.

I should have been concentrating on Helen but Solomon had gone missing the previous evening and by breakfast time he had still not come back. It had happened before and each time I worried myself sick and vowed never to have another cat. The more people you loved the more you had to lose.

'Calamine lotion for her eczema.' Joyce held out a bottle with its label coming off.

'I didn't know Helen had eczema.'

'Back of her knees. Nothing to worry about but I don't want her scratching at it, and don't give her shellfish or salted meat.'

'You should speak to Archie.'

'Archie?' she said vaguely. 'Oh you mean because he specialises in diseases of the skin. I hardly think it warrants that. What time do you want me back?'

'She can stay as long as she likes.'

Joyce gave a disparaging snort. 'You may regret that Ursula. Ah well, be it on your own head. People think babies are the testing ones but children Helen's age can tax you to the limits. The way she's been behaving lately she's heading for a good spanking.'

I glanced over my shoulder but Helen had vanished and a moment later I heard her greeting Enid warmly.

'I just thought it would be nice for her to have some time on her own.' I said, wondering why I sounded so apologetic. Joyce knew the reason I had invited Helen, not that she necessarily agreed with me. In fact I was fairly certain she thought I was being ridiculously oversensitive on Helen's behalf.

'Yes, well I can see one will be more than enough.' She gave me the irritating smile people reserve for children who have done their best but their best is not up to much. 'So it's all right if she stays all day. What about your session with the Moberley woman?'

'I don't see her on Tuesdays.'

'Nor you do.' She found a handkerchief and blew her nose loudly before calling to Helen. 'Mind you behave yourself for Auntie Ursula. Do as she tells you and don't talk your head off. You can't believe how she can talk! Oh and don't bother Enid when she's trying to get on with her work.'

'Enid likes children,' I said, impatient for her to leave. 'She's been looking forward to seeing Helen as much as I have.'

'I've probably said this before Ursula but I do think it's a mistake to treat servants like friends. Supposing you found something had gone missing.'

'I don't know what you mean.'

'Yes you do. Enid's a good soul but anyone can succumb to temptation, a pendant, a ring. Right, I'll be off.' She glanced at the grandmother clock. 'Good Lord is that the time? Oh, by the way, how's the arm?'

'Starting to improve I think.' Her suggestion that Enid might steal my jewellery was so foolish it was best ignored. 'Some of the feeling's returned to my shoulder. But the rest of the arm still feels very weak.'

'Yes well don't tell me anymore now, I'll ask you again later. '

After she left I joined Helen and Enid at the kitchen table where they were busy chopping up a red cabbage. Of the two girls Sybil was the conventionally pretty one, having her father's small straight nose and her mother's large hazel eyes. Helen's nose was broader and her face rounder but there was something appealing about her. Because of her brown eyes and fair skin Joyce often said she looked like me. Two of a kind, she had once remarked, although whether it was our looks or our characters it was best not to inquire.

Since I saw her last Helen's hair had been cut so it hung straight with a fringe that stopped just above her eyebrows. Previously it had been longer and parted on one side but Joyce had complained how she kept tossing it out of her eyes and was driving everyone mad with the silly habit.

'I gave her the knife that needs sharpening,' Enid said and I nodded my approval and turned to Helen.

'It's lovely to see you, I'm so glad you could come.'

'Mummy's jolly glad to be rid of me.'

Enid let out one of her shrieks of laughter. 'Course she isn't.'

'She is Enid, she thinks I'm a pest. If Sybil and I have a fight I always get the blame because I'm the oldest. It's so unfair, even Daddy agrees, but he's usually out visiting and when he comes back Mummy says we're not to bother him because he's praying or something. Sybil wets the bed.'

'Oh I'm sure she doesn't,' I said, 'well even if she does, it's not her fault.'

Helen wrinkled her nose. 'Anyway she's a baby, she still reads *Peter Rabbit* and *Tom Kitten*.'

'*Samuel Whiskers* is my favourite,' I said.

'Is it?' She gave me a slightly pitying smile.

I began collecting up strands of cabbage and putting them in the bowl Enid had provided. 'You like horses don't you Helen. Have you read *Black Beauty*?'

'No.' She put down her knife. 'There's a copy in the bookcase but it's got a picture in it of a dead horse on a cart. I hate it.'

'That's poor Ginger. What about *The Secret Garden*?'

'Oh yes that's my favourite.'

'Mine too.' I glanced at Enid, afraid she might be feeling left out but she was smiling contentedly, relieved no doubt that Helen's presence would prevent me from going on about the date of her wedding, something that had created an unwelcome degree of friction between us.

Helen might say something. She knew about Jim – I had told her at the party when she made a remark about how much nicer Enid was than their Edith – but I should have warned her not to ask Enid when she was getting married. Now it was too late and I would just have to hope the subject never came up.

'What about you Enid?' Helen popped a piece of cabbage in her mouth and crunched noisily. 'Are there any stories you particularly like?'

'I once read *The Wind in the Willows.*'

'Did you?' Helen sounded impressed. 'Mummy read it to us but it's got quite difficult words.'

Enid nodded her agreement. 'Mum and I are the best readers in our family. My sister Flossie prefers drawing. Makes lovely pictures she does, flowers and trees, got a talent some people say.'

'Do they?' Helen was enjoying the conversation. 'I like drawing, and painting. Sybil spilt her paint water over Daddy's sermon and all hell was let loose.'

I laughed, more because of the expression she had used than because one of Sidney's rather dry sermons had been soaked through, and Helen made a face like her father and spoke in a church voice.

'I can forgive you your clumsiness Sybil but not the fact that you picked up my sermon along with the paper you purloined. Purloined means stole,' she added, 'grown ups like to use words they think you won't understand.'

Solomon was still missing. The three of us had searched the house but without success.

'He'll turn up,' Enid said, 'most likely he'll be hiding in a bush watching the birds.'

'Yes I expect so.' I was worried but I had no wish to spoil Helen's day. 'I tell you what, why don't you and Helen make some peppermint creams.'

'Oh yes please.' Helen jumped up excitedly. 'I'm sure Solomon hasn't gone far Auntie Ursula, cats like to walk alone.'

'Oh you are a one Miss Helen.' Enid began collecting the ingredients for the sweets. 'You'll need to mix together a pound of icing sugar, the white of an egg, a teaspoonful of cold water and a few drops of essence of peppermint.'

'Can I separate the egg? Mummy never lets me and Edith doesn't like us in the kitchen.'

'Course you can.' Enid found a pudding basin and showed her how to crack the shell then keep the yolk in one half of it while the white part ran out. 'Now mix it all up and then you'll have to knead it well and roll it out with a rolling pin.'

'Then what?' Helen was revelling in the attention and Enid was as happy as a lark.

'Then you use a cutter to make little rounds.'

'Have you got a cutter Auntie Ursula?'

'Course we have.' Enid winked at me. 'If Mrs Ingham agrees we could find a box and you could take some home for your sister.'

Helen pulled a face. 'I'd much rather you took it home for your brothers and sisters Enid.'

'Oh Miss Helen you do say some things.'

'No I don't, do I Auntie Ursula? I wish I could live here. No, honestly I do. Mummy wouldn't mind, she's far too busy in the parish and we get under her feet. Did you get under your mother's feet Enid, or does she like children?'

I left them to their peppermint creams and went upstairs to have another look for Solomon. He might have come in when no one was looking. Or he might be stuck up a tree, or shut in a neighbour's outhouse, or stolen by someone who liked tabby cats or wanted to make him into a pair of fur gloves. Why did I torment myself, always expecting the worst? My mother had despaired of me. *The trouble with Ursula she lets her thoughts run away with her.*

But surely it had its good side too. One of my school reports had praised my English essays. *Ursula displays an excellent imagination.* And at least my father had been pleased. Or had I imagined that too?

The day was pleasantly warm so we decided to eat our lunch in the garden.

'You too Enid,' I said, waving aside her token claim that she was not hungry.

'Yes, you too,' Helen chimed in, 'Edith's skinny and mean, not like you Enid. Auntie Ursula's lucky having you.

'Oh I don't think that's quite fair,' I protested, 'Edith's very fond of you all.'

'No she's not. She just pretends to be when there are visitors. Enid said I could play with this box of bits and pieces. You don't mind do you Auntie Ursula?'

'No I don't mind a scrap and if you find anything you like you can keep it. And take something home for Sybil too.'

'Do I have to?' She laughed. 'Actually I don't mind her that much. It's just nice to get away from her sometimes.'

We ate Bovril sandwiches and some currant biscuits Enid had made specially and drank the bottles of pop she had insisted we must buy when she heard a nine-year-old was coming for the day.

The sun had brought out the bees that were buzzing

round the lupins and delphiniums. A thrush was pecking about in a flowerbed and I looked all about in case Solomon was watching it but he was nowhere to be seen. If Sybil had been with us she would have fussed that one of the bees was going to sting her and Helen would have adopted a superior attitude and told her not to be such a baby. Was that how Joyce had treated me when we were children? She had been the one who knew best and I the one who took my lead from my older sister, but Sybil was only a year younger than Helen whereas the gap between Joyce and me had been so great it was surprising we had played together all.

When I was five she would have been ten, and when I was Helen's age she would have been fourteen! Why had our mother decided on such an age difference? Perhaps giving birth to Joyce had been a horrendous experience and it had taken her several years before she felt up to going through it all over again.

While Enid was fetching a bowl of tinned apricots a wasp began buzzing round Helen's head.

'Keep still,' I told her,' and it will soon go away.'

'Yes I know.' She was keeping her eyes tight shut. 'There are heaps of insects about this summer. Mummy puts citronella on our clothes to get rid of the midges and for wasp stings you need vinegar although I'm not sure if it works for bees. They're worse than wasps, they can kill you.'

'I don't think so Helen.'

'And hornets are even deadlier. They're huge with stings as big as…' She indicated with her finger and thumb just how lethal they were. 'And as for snakes!'

Enid, who had returned with apricots, gave a shudder. 'No snakes round here Miss Helen.'

'Are you sure? They could have come from the heath.' She relaxed now the wasp had flown off, changing the subject in the way children often do, jumping from one fascinating topic to the next. 'Mummy makes us have cod liver oil. And Virol, ugh!'

'The malt's to build you up Miss Helen.'

'I don't need building up Enid. Anyway I saw an advertisement for chocolate and it said it was just as good for you. It said most people suffer from milk starvation.'

'Milk starvation,' I said, 'are you sure?'

'Yes, certain. What's this?' She picked up Enid's copy of *Peg's Paper*.

'That's my book,' Enid said, 'full of useful tips it is. This one tells you how to use the juice from a lemon to whiten your skin.'

Oh please don't do that, I thought, hating the idea that she wanted her skin to be lighter, but before I could say anything Helen gave an ear-splitting shriek.

'Look who's scratching up the flower bed.'

'Solomon!' I jumped up, happy out of all proportion. The day was now complete, such a happy day except if I had known then what was to happen a few months later I doubt I would have felt so relaxed.

'Where've you been you beastly cat?' I crouched down to inspect him. 'No don't run away. Have you been fighting?' Helen and Enid were giggling but by the time I turned round both their faces were expressionless. 'Seems right as rain,' I said, and they looked at each other, still with straight faces even though I could see the amusement in their eyes.

'Sorry,' Helen said, 'you were worried weren't you but cats often go missing, that's why I'd prefer a dog, only Daddy says there's enough livestock in the house already. Actually Daddy can be quite annoying.'

Enid looked at me and smiled.

'I'm not joking.' But Helen's expression was so solemn it was difficult not to laugh.

'Sometimes he drives us round the bend,' she continued, flicking back her fringe with a toss of her head. 'Do you like being a maid Enid?'

'Helen!'

'I like working for Mrs Ingham.'

'Some girls are treated like animals. That's what Mummy says.'

I glanced at Enid but she was enjoying Helen's company so much I don't think she would have minded what she said. 'She's right there Miss Helen. I heard of one who had to go without her lunch because the lady of the house caught her doing a dance in the scullery.'

'What kind of dance?' Helen was eager to hear more.

'I expect it was the Charleston.'

'I can't see what's so bad about that. Auntie Ursula?' She paused, drawing back her top lip and making a face like a rabbit. 'I thought when people got married they had a baby.'

'Oh Miss Helen.' Enid blushed. 'What a thing to say.'

'No, it's all right Enid,' I said, 'it's a sensible question. I presume it was a question Helen, you wanted to know why haven't I had a baby?'

'Is it because of your arm?'

'It would be difficult to care for a baby in my present state.'

Enid came in quickly. 'It's getting better isn't it Mrs Ingham but it's still not as strong as it ought to be. But improving every day,' she added.

Helen seemed satisfied. 'Yes, well when it's back to normal I expect you'll have a baby. Only I hope Mummy doesn't have any more. Christopher's such a nuisance and Daddy says he'll be even worse when he learns to crawl.'

I looked at Enid as though to say "that's a relief, now let's talk about something else" but she was concentrating on Helen.

'That's a pretty bracelet, did your Mummy give it to you?'

'No, Pamela, she helps in the parish. She says there's a famine in Belgian Ruanda and children are dying because there's nothing to eat. Where is Belgian Ruanda?'

'It's in Africa,' I told her, 'and I'm sure the government will make sure we send them some food.'

'Pamela collects money for Dr Barnardo's, that's a place for children whose parents have died. Or they didn't have any in the first place. No, that can't be right. How could you have no mother and father? Pamela's looking after Sybil today.' She chuckled with glee. 'Sybil had a tantrum when Mummy said she couldn't come with me. She always wants to do exactly the same as I do. She even wants her hair the same way.'

'Enid has six brothers and sisters.'

'Have you Enid? What are their names? Are you the oldest or the youngest or somewhere in the middle?'

Enid began describing her family and I thought about what it would be like to give birth seven times. Did it become easier or was each time as agonising as the last? Earlier, before Helen and Joyce arrived I had been reading in *The Times* how the prime minister had opened a new maternity unit at a place called Stourport. Someone had described the awful circumstances in which some children were born. One woman had given birth to her baby in a pigsty, and by some miracle they had both survived. Apparently, for every thousand babies born, five mothers were lost. How many did that make in a year? It didn't bear thinking about.

Helen had brought a skipping rope and a yo-yo and was alternating between the two as she listened to Enid recounting stories about her brothers and sisters.

'Your mother must have been expecting all the time.'

'Helen!' I warned, but Enid only smiled.

'You don't mind what I say, do you Enid?' Helen started singing a skipping song, something about sausages on a dish, and Enid joined in, clapping in time with the rope.

They were so easy together, so natural, it made me feel quite priggish.

'Can you skip, Auntie Ursula?' Helen asked and instinctively I put out my hand, only to see Enid and Helen's mouths fall open in amazement.

'That was your bad arm!' Helen squealed. 'Come on have a try. Well if you can't skip you could have a go with the yo-yo. Use your good hand and your other one might forget it didn't work and reach out to steady you. I think the arm's sulking, don't you Enid, I think it's gone on strike.'

Joyce returned at five o'clock when the three of us were back in the kitchen having a game of ludo.

'So sorry Ursula, one thing after another, what a day, how's she been?' She ran her fingers through Helen's hair. 'Haven't overtired poor Auntie Ursula I hope.'

Helen sighed and I thought, she's nine years old

Joyce, still very young but old enough not to be treated like a baby.

When she saw her mother I had expected Helen to tell her about my arm but although I could see from her surreptitious glances at me that the subject was on her mind she must have decided to keep quiet about it. Perhaps she would tell her on the way home but perhaps not. Little girls her age loved secrets.

'A piece of news.' Joyce sat down heavily and kicked off her clumpy old shoes. 'You remember Beryl.'

'The curate's wife?'

'Expecting.'

Helen's head shot up. 'Do you mean she's going to have a baby?'

Joyce nodded. 'Due in January, poor little mite, so we'll have to do something about their heating.'

'Is she pleased?' I asked and Joyce made a tut-tutting noise.

'What a question Ursula, of course she's pleased, she's delighted.'

I glanced at Enid, hoping she would acknowledge with her eyes what an impossible sister I had but she was staring down at the table and her face and neck were scarlet.

'Are you all right Enid?' I was afraid she must have spent too long in the garden although surely people with her colouring never burned in the sun.

She looked up, obliged to reply or she would have drawn even more attention to herself. 'Course I am Mrs Ingham.' Her mouth quivered but she still managed to smile at each of us in turn. But as her eyes met mine my stomach lurched and I jerked the table with my knee, sending the coloured counters flying in all directions.

'Now we won't know who was winning,' Helen said.

'I'm sorry Helen but in any case I think it's time for you to go home. You can come again another day if you'd like to,' I added and she gave a resigned look, as though to say "if I'm allowed to without Sybil" and began putting the game back in its box.

Joyce was well away, oblivious to what had happened to the game of ludo as she related the details of her terribly busy day. 'There's a man on the governing board who claims to know everything there is to know about education and just about everything else too. Old humbug, and the chairman's not a blind bit of use, lets him witter on, wasting our time. He even held forth about the positioning of the new public telephone box.'

'What's that got to do with the school?'

'Precisely.'

As she gabbled on I listened, sufficient to nod occasionally and appear interested but all the time I was wondering how I could have a few words with her in private. Helen's coat was upstairs. I could ask Enid to fetch it and suggest Helen accompany her. No, that would never work and in any case did I really want to confide in Joyce, especially when my fears might be unfounded. Better to talk to Enid first. Or Leo. No Enid, then Leo, although on second thoughts I might need to discuss with Leo how I was going to broach the subject.

'Why are you clutching your stomach?' Joyce pushed her feet back into her shoes and stood up noisily.

'I didn't know I was.'

'If you suffer from dyspepsia you need to drink china tea, gallons of it.'

'I should think that would make you much worse.' I

attempted a carefree smile. 'And in any case indigestion has never been one of my complaints.'

If I told Leo he would say I was imagining it, jumping to conclusions. And short of confronting Enid there was nothing I could do to confirm I was right.

After Joyce and Helen left she had gone to great lengths to avoid being alone with me. *You go and sit down Mrs Ingham. Leave me to get this lot cleared up before Mr Ingham comes home*. Further proof, I thought, because if I was wrong she would have been happy to chat, telling me how much she had enjoyed seeing Helen and what a lovely girl she was turning out to be.

If I were right Enid would have to get married as soon as possible. Why had she failed to tell me? Because she was too embarrassed – or too afraid? Perhaps nobody knew about it, not even Jim. Where were we? The middle of June. It should only take a week or two to arrange the wedding, although when I thought about it calmly there was no need to fix it up in such a rush and in any case it was always possible Enid feared the worst but had made a mistake. Once in a book of Archie's I had read how a specimen of urine had to be injected into mice or rabbits. A positive test was indicated by the formation of blood spots in the ovaries. But how could they tell? By cutting up the poor creatures I suppose.

I turned the pages of *The Times* searching for the section with ladies maids, not that Enid would have been described as a "ladies maid" and not that Leo and I would have been able to afford such a creature. What would I do? How would we manage? Still, with any luck Enid might know of someone who was looking for a job.

On the opposite page there was an advertisement

for *Fellows compound syrup of hypophosphites. If you're "jumpy"*, it said and there was a picture of a man standing next to what was supposed to be a door that had just banged shut making him leap out of his skin. *One teaspoonful three times a day. Just what the doctor ordered.*

Another advertisement was for *Vita-wheat, the British crispbread, for the "slim silhouette" that is part and parcel of the modern emancipated woman.* Oh well, I thought, I might not be emancipated but at least I'm slim.

Enid left, after calling goodbye, but avoiding putting her head round the door as she usually did. I thought of chasing after her then changed my mind and decided to leave it until the following day when I would have given myself time to work out what I was going to say. Perhaps it was not such a disaster. She and Jim would get married and in due course the baby would arrive and amid all the excitement nobody would be much interested in working out how many months had passed.

My eye was caught by an item in the paper about a baby that had been abandoned at Croydon. At first it had been thought the mother had mental problems but the judge had decided she was only borderline, whatever that was supposed to mean. What would they do with her and what would happen to the baby? Enid was terribly young but she would make an excellent mother and everything would work out all right, provided Jim could find somewhere for them to live, and from the little we had seen of him he appeared a very determined young man, and practical too.

Sitting up straight, I attempted to exercise my arm but as usual it refused to co-operate. Perhaps if I counted to five then reached out for the game of solitaire. One, two, three, four. My arm shot out but my hand crashed down on the marbles, scattering them over the rug. With tears of frustration in my eyes I knelt on the floor collecting them one by one with my good hand and replacing them in their wooden holes.

Leo was late. The boys must have a cricket match and he had offered to act as umpire. No, that was next week. Where was he then? He could have telephoned although he probably thought Helen was still with me. Perhaps he had rung when we were out in the garden. No, he would have tried again. I thought about Helen and how good it had been to have someone young and lively in the house and how Enid had enjoyed her company. At least she had up to the fateful moment when Joyce had made her announcement about the curate's wife. Then I remembered the way she had blushed when Helen asked why I had failed to have a baby. At the time I had assumed Enid was embarrassed on my behalf. Now I was not so sure.

The front door was flung open and I pictured Leo laden down with a pile of exercise books he had not found the time to mark. But when he burst into the drawing room his hands were free. He was breathing hard and I thought he must have been talking to the other masters then realised how late it was and left in a hurry.

'Got held up?' I asked but, without even a fleeting look in my direction, he strode across to the window where he stood with his hands behind his back.

'I blame myself entirely.'

'What for?' Something must have happened at the school. A boy had hurt himself. Two boys had got into a fight.

'At the time I convinced myself I had made sufficient checks but obviously they were not thorough enough.'

'I don't know what you're talking about Leo.'

His eyes had been darting round the room. Now he fixed his gaze on a brown and yellow marble I had overlooked.

'I was trying to move my arm,' I explained, 'and it did move a little but then I knocked over the solitaire.'

'For heaven's sake,' he roared, 'do you want to hear what I have to say or not?'

'Yes but I wish you'd calm down.'

His fists were clenched so tightly his knuckles showed white. I waited for him to speak but he kept swallowing and smoothing back his hair.

'Helen spent the day with us,' I said, 'it was rather fun.'

He bent down to retrieve the marble then straightened up again and began rocking back on his heels. When he finally spoke his voice was so loud he could have been addressing a roomful of people. 'Your Mrs Moberley, would you say she sticks to Freud's system of analysis?'

'I've no idea. I expect she does.'

'All right, I'll put it another way, does she believe it's the task of the analyst to reveal as much of the truth as the patient can bear?'

'I don't know Leo.'

'Well perhaps you should ask her. If you want my opinion she's a charlatan. I doubt if she knows what she's doing and she certainly shows little concern for the people she likes to call her patients.'

I opened my mouth to protest but he held up his hand. 'Her husband divorced her. Did you hear what I said? Your precious Mrs Moberley is divorced.'

'How do you know?' My heart beat faster but the rest of my body was rigid.

'I asked someone to check up on her.'

'Why?'

'Why do you think? Because she's not doing you any good. Yes I know you claim your arm moved but I've never seen it.'

'If you weren't so impatient – '

'Impatient! Is that what you think? How many months is it I've endured your cough and your headaches and all the other symptoms you profess to suffer from. You've been seeing the woman for weeks and you're still not back to normal, in fact in many respects I'd say you were rather worse.'

'I don't know what you mean.' I was frightened. But I was angry too. 'I think she's helping me a lot.'

When he spoke again it was through gritted teeth. 'Yes, you do know what I mean Ursula, you know perfectly well. She has children, two of them, although I've yet to discover how old they are or where they are living. With their father I assume.'

'I can't see what's so bad about that.' I thought about the tall young man with fair hair and glasses who had once let me into Mrs Moberley's house. At the time I had assumed he must be her previous patient, although that had seemed unlikely, or possibly that he had come to do some work for her. On the previous visit she had mentioned how she was unable to open the window because the sash cord had broken. Oh, one of ours did that, I said, absurdly pleased that she had told me something about herself, or at least about her house.

Leo was glaring at me as though it was my fault I

had been receiving treatment from a divorcée with two children. 'I had a feeling there was something fishy about her,' he said coldly. 'You knew about it did you? Knew about it but decided to remain silent.'

'No I didn't but even if I had –'

'You haven't heard the worst part yet.'

'You say you asked someone to check up on her, who was it?'

'That doesn't matter.'

'Yes it does. It might not even be true.'

'Oh it's true all right, and what really matters Ursula.' He paused to give emphasis to his next announcement although calling me "Ursula" was enough in itself. 'What matters is that your so-called treatment has come to an end as of now.'

'No I can't do that.'

'It's not up for discussion. She's dangerous, should never have been allowed to practise as an analyst. I assumed they were licensed, or at least someone made sure they were properly trained and of impeccable character.'

'She is properly trained.'

'You don't know that.' He was shouting again. 'Oh don't worry, I blame myself, I took the word of two doctors who specialise in functional disorders but it's obvious now they simply told me what they thought I wanted to hear.'

'Why would they do that? And I'm not going to stop seeing her just because she's divorced.'

His eyes blazed. 'Oh yes you are. If you want further proof of how incompetent and unethical she is, one of her patients committed suicide, threw himself into the Thames.'

'When?' My voice came out as a whisper.

'A year ago, two, what's the odds?'

'So you don't know what actually happened.'

He moved closer and for a split second I thought he was going to hit me and put up my arms to protect myself. Both arms, although Leo was far too agitated to notice.

'What I do know,' he said, 'is that you're not going anywhere near her again. I've talked to the experts and the reason you're so attached to her, it's of no real consequence, just a simple case of transference.'

'Whatever that's supposed to mean.'

'You don't know about it? She hasn't explained? "Psychoanalysis is a process that revives earlier experiences in the form of the current relation to the analyst." If you'd read the material I gave you, you might understand these things.'

'Well I think you're making too much fuss. All I care about is that she's making me better. Her private life has nothing to do with it.'

'Her private life! The death of one of her patients!' But the fight had gone out of him and he sank into the big armchair and sat with his legs sprawled out and his eyes shut. 'I'm sorry Ursa, sorry I lost my temper and took it out on you. It's not your fault, it's mine entirely, but you must see the treatment will have to stop. If it's important for your mental state you can see her once more, to round it off so to speak. In the meantime all I can do is apologise for ever suggesting she was a suitable person to help.'

CHAPTER NINE

'Analyst –baiting is in fact both a popular and relatively safe sport, harming no-one but the unfortunate victims of severe neurosis.'
(Ernest Jones)

Too little sleep leaves you feeling light-headed. Light-headed and unreal. In some ways it reminded me of the first time I visited Mrs Moberley, the day of my assessment, except that had been in Archie's car and now I was on foot.

June the twenty-first, the longest day of the year. Dark clouds scudded across an ominous sky and as I reached what I thought of as the halfway mark between our house and Inverness Gardens I paused a moment to collect my thoughts.

As likely as not – this was my second visit since Leo's revelations – I would fail again in my resolve to tell Mrs Moberley. I hated lying to her and sins of omission were just as bad. And another thing, it affected what I said to her as much as what I avoided saying. So much so that last time I had talked about my mother and wasted most of the ensuing thirty minutes in an agonising silence. Doubtless she had thought I was "resisting", the name Freud gave it when the patient refused to face a painful memory.

A gust of wind whirled round the corner and I was glad Enid had persuaded me to wear my warm jacket. Worry about Mrs Moberley had pushed my concerns about her out of my mind, even made me wonder if I had jumped to conclusions too quickly. Her scarlet face when Joyce announced that the curate's wife was expecting could be explained away by her anxiety that Helen was going to start awkward questions again, not just about me but about where babies came from. Except she would never have done such a thing when her mother was there. Had Joyce told her how women's bodies' worked? Not yet, she was too young, but when she reached ten or eleven what would Joyce say to her? Our own mother had assumed we would be taught such things at boarding school, and we were, but not by the mistresses. It was other girls who enjoyed relating the gory details.

A woman was coming towards me, holding the lead of a West Highland terrier. It was very young, not much more than a puppy and as I passed its body writhed and wriggled and its paws scrabbled at my leg.

'I'm so sorry.' The woman looked vaguely familiar. Perhaps she lived in our road.

'He's sweet,' I said, 'what's his name?'

'Archie.'

'Oh the same as my father-in-law. And he's got white hair too!' It was one of those silly remarks you make when your mind is elsewhere but a chance encounter with a stranger provides a welcome diversion.

'I've seen you before,' the woman said, 'I expect it was on the heath. No I know who you are, you're Mrs Ingham and your husband teaches history at Kingslade.'

'Yes that's right, do you have a boy there?'

'Two and they're both very happy and doing well.'

We exchanged a few more words then went our separate ways. A trivial piece of conversation and on any other day it might have raised my spirits, made me feel I was known in the area, if only for being Leo's wife. Now the thought of it only served to increase my anger. When I left Mrs Moberley's Leo had arranged that Archie would be waiting for me. No it was worse than that, he would be standing on the doorstep with a ready-prepared speech that would inform her that my treatment was at an end. Surely however much I wanted to avoid the subject I would have to forewarn her. How could I bear it if my last visit was taken up with anger and recriminations, but neither could I bear the fact she had no means of knowing I knew. *You remember how I told you Leo resents me coming here. Well, to get back at me he asked someone to check up on you.* Or – *I have to tell you Mrs Moberley, Leo's been checking up on you and he's going to try and stop me coming here again.*

No, that was no good either. She would want to know what Leo had found out. And another thing, if I was honest with myself hearing about the man who had jumped in the river had been a shock. I had been coming for six weeks and not for a single moment had I experienced the slightest wish to kill myself, but six weeks was not very long. What if the treatment became more rigorous and memories began to be dragged out of me, under hypnosis if they had failed to appear spontaneously, and without realising it I slid into a state of such despair I was powerless to control my own actions.

Sometimes I felt she knew the reason for my arm but believed it would never recover its strength unless *I* was the one to discover the underlying cause. *Memories must be brought to light and described in the greatest possible detail.*

As I turned into Inverness Gardens my heart began

to thump. One moment I was determined to stand up to Leo, the next my resolve crumbled. If everyone was against Mrs Moberley, not just Leo but Archie and Muriel too, would I be able to resist them? And another thing, Archie was paying and if he refused to stump up the money there was nothing I could do. Once he had made up his mind there was no changing it. Even Muriel, who saw him as near perfect, admitted he could be pig-headed.

'You seem to be feeling exceptionally anxious.'

'Do I?' After a silence lasting several minutes her words had startled me. 'I didn't sleep very well. I've been wondering what to talk about today. Sometimes I'm still not sure what kind of things you need to know. Now that my arm has moved a bit perhaps could you give me some advice about what I should do.'

'You know I don't give advice Ursula.'

'But why not?'

'Because I'm not here to tell you what you should think or do. In my experience people know the truth about themselves and need only to be assisted to accept this truth.'

'Yes I know that's how it's supposed to work,' I sighed, 'but if it was right I wouldn't need to be here would I? And in any case I don't understand how remembering something makes it go away.'

She shifted her position and her chair gave a small creak. 'If a memory is distressing it takes all our energy to keep it out of our conscious mind. Once it's out in the open there's no longer any need to repress it and our energy can be used productively to come to terms with whatever it was that caused so much conflict and pain.'

'But you said there might not be a single traumatic

event I had forgotten. You said my problem might be something quite different. There is one thing I wanted to ask you.'

'What is that?' Her voice was so gentle I felt a surge of protectiveness towards her. What did it matter if she was divorced? And the patient who jumped in the river might have been in such a bad state there was nothing she or anyone else could have done for him.

'I know it sounds rather silly but do you like me?'

'If I didn't I wouldn't be able to help you.'

Tears filled my eyes but almost immediately I wondered if she truly meant it. It could be how she replied to all her patients if they asked a similar question. After all, she could hardly tell them she disliked them.

'This morning my arm moved again.'

'Tell me about it.'

'I was brushing my hair with my good hand and the bad arm reached out for my hand mirror. It used to belong to my mother. It's silver-backed with a pattern of flowers and leaves and swirly bits.'

When she made no comment I knew she was waiting for me to tell her some more about Mother.

'She wanted everyone to be happy.' I paused, searching for the right words. 'But you can't be happy all the time can you? She wanted us to think she was a good mother and everything she did, even if we didn't like it, was for our benefit in the long run.'

'You and your sister?'

'And my father.'

'He died when you were fifteen.'

'Even then she said it was a blessing he hadn't suffered more than he did. She wanted us to look on the bright side but lots of people are like that, aren't they, and perhaps they're right. It's no use getting morbid.'

'That's how you sometimes feel?'

'In some ways Muriel is a bit like my mother. I suppose the difference is now I'm older I can see through people better. Muriel sounds cheerful enough but you can't help noticing when the lines draw together round her mouth.' I laughed as though I had said something funny, but it was only my nerves. 'Do you mind if I tell you about Enid? But first I'll have to tell you about the curate's wife.'

'You met her at your sister's party.'

'She's called Beryl.'

Sometimes I had mixed feelings about the way she could recall things so easily. Did she study her notebook before I arrived? Presumably she would have to or she would confuse one patient with another. But how many other patients did she have? Perhaps I was the only one. Perhaps all the others had left after the young man threw himself in The Thames.

'She's having a baby,' I said.

'The curate's wife.'

'And it's due in January so she'll have to make sure she keeps it warm. That's what Joyce said. Joyce's daughter came to spend the day with me. I didn't tell you on Wednesday because there were so many other things I wanted to talk about.'

'As I recall you were finding it difficult to talk.'

'Was I? Anyway she's nine and she's called Helen. I expect I told you that before. We had a lovely day together. Enid was there of course and we had lunch in the garden and while we were eating it or it might have been afterwards, I forget, Helen wanted to know why I hadn't had a baby. She thought you got married and…' My voice trailed away.

'What did you tell her?'

'I didn't know what to say.' I picked at a loose thread on the couch. 'But luckily she decided it must be because of my arm and when it was stronger, I mean, *if* it gets stronger I'll probably have one then.' I broke off, realising my words were unclear and she would be wondering if I was talking about what Helen thought or what I intended for myself.

'Anyway, later on when Joyce came to take Helen home, she told us about the curate's wife and I looked at Enid as if to say "here we go again" but she avoided my eyes and I noticed she had gone bright red. She often blushes but this was different. She was scarlet and her hands had shot up to try and cover her face and neck and I thought Oh my Lord, *she's* having a baby too.'

'Have you asked her?'

'Not yet but if it's true obviously she won't be able to put off the wedding.'

I expected her to say, no I don't suppose she will, but she was fiddling with the lamp on the table beside her, and a moment later she switched it on, explaining that the weather outside had made the room rather dark.

People often talk about the weather when they can think of nothing else to say, or when they think someone is going to say something they would prefer not to hear. Did she think my talk of babies was a preamble to bringing up the subject of her children?

'Do you think it's right women have to give up their jobs when they get married? I don't mean people like Enid. No, that's an awful thing to say. But it's true isn't it? If you have her kind of job you're allowed to go on working, you have to because you can't manage without the money. Except I don't see how Enid could come to work with a baby. In *Good Housekeeping* there was an article called "The Best Job for a Girl", written by a man of course. It said women without children were always unhappy and unfulfilled. When my friend Midge comes to see me I'm going to ask her if she's happy. No, I won't actually ask, that wouldn't be fair, but I'll be able to tell, won't I.'

'I expect you will.'

Having said so much I felt emboldened and suddenly had no wish to remain lying down. I wanted to see her expression. I wanted us to be on equal terms. Swinging my legs over the side of the couch I sat leaning forward so that even if the whole of her face was not visible I could tell more or less how she was responding.

'Leo doesn't want me to come here any more.'

'He still feels excluded?'

'He doesn't trust me.'

'In what way?'

'I mean he doesn't trust my judgement. No, I'm sorry that doesn't make much sense. Oh I don't know what I'm saying. It's not that I'm afraid of him, it's just that I can tell how cross he is and it makes everything so difficult. Do you think it will take much longer to cure me? My arm's started working now and again but I can't move it on purpose.'

She was silent, refusing to help me out even though my anxiety was making me feel quite ill. It's not fair, I thought, none of it's fair. When it comes down to it we're alone, each of us, and nobody really cares what happens to us.

'What is it that's making you feel so concerned Ursula?'

But I was unable to tell her. How could I?

Archie was nowhere to be seen. Then I spotted the Daimler down the far end of the road and started to run.

'Hop in.' He pushed open the passenger door.

'But I thought…'

He smiled but said nothing. 'We'll drive to that road that runs along by the heath. There are things I need to tell you.'

He was wearing a jacket he had worn when I was his secretary, navy-blue and double-breasted with wide lapels. His grey flannel trousers looked new though *and* his shirt with its collar attached, and the blue bow tie. Thinking about his consulting rooms made me feel better. Even though I had not been very proficient at running an office I had loved working for him and he had never criticised, only encouraged, always expressing particular gratitude for little jobs I had carried out without being asked. Only two and a half years ago but it felt like another life.

'Leo said you were going to speak to Mrs Moberley.' As the car turned the corner I gripped my seat with my good hand. 'When she let me out of the front door I thought you'd be waiting on the path.'

'Are you up to a walk?'

'Yes of course.'

He started humming under his breath and I thought, I trusted you to be on my side and now you are going to let me down.

We passed the large house covered in creeper that always reminded me of my boarding school and how a girl had tried to climb up a drainpipe then slipped and scraped the skin on the inside of her thighs. Thinking about it made me draw in breath so that Archie felt obliged to ask if I had a headache.

'No I haven't had one for ages. It's just that talking to Mrs Moberley makes me remember all kinds of peculiar things and sometimes I have dreams about the people I've told her about although dreams are strange, not like real life, and Mrs Moberley says we embellish them so they make more sense.'

'I can never remember any of mine.'

'You would if you wanted to.'

He laughed. 'You mean they're too disreputable. Does your Mrs Moberley have a list of symbols? Dreaming you're being pursued by a mad bull means you've been working too hard, or dreaming you've fallen over the side of a ship means you covet your neighbour's wife.'

'No nothing like that. I tell her a dream and she asks what various parts of it remind me of. Leo said – '

'Leo says a lot of things.'

'About Mrs Moberley's divorce and the man who jumped into the river.'

'Wait until we have our walk.'

'Has Leo got it all wrong? Did the private detective he hired muddle up the name and it was someone completely different?'

'I don't think he needed a detective.'

'You mean he did the checking up himself?'

But Archie was being as bad as Mrs Moberley. Silence, the great weapon, it gives the person who refuses to speak so much power. Only whenever I tried using it people got annoyed.

When we reached the heath I could see by the way the trees were blowing that the wind had increased in strength. It was not as dark as it had been during my fifty minutes with Mrs Moberley but at any moment it might cloud over again. What had Archie planned? To explain why he agreed with Leo but to do it gently, not in the brutal way Leo had chosen to impart the news? Knowing Archie he would want to convince me that all things considered it might be best to find a different source of help.

If I refused to fall in line would either he or Leo telephone Mrs Moberley and cancel my next appointment? Or Leo might write her a letter. Yes that was more his style. My fury with Leo was so intense my fists clenched involuntarily, both of them. But when I *tried* to clench the right one again it steadfastly refused to carry out the instruction from my brain.

Archie had pulled up close to Kenwood House where the ground was relatively flat. I am quite up to managing hills, I wanted to protest, but it was my own fault everyone thought me weak and feeble, unable to run my own life. The cough and the headaches had virtually disappeared but at home I still behaved like an invalid, dependent on everyone around me to decide how I spent my time and what I was and was not allowed to do.

I was wearing low shoes which was just as well since the turf was soft and spongy from the previous night's rain. No doubt it would rain again, but what did it matter if I was soaked to the skin. Nothing could make things any worse. All the same I hated having wet feet and if I had been on my own I would have kept to the path.

'I like walking on the grass,' Archie said, 'you never know what you might find.'

'Just seed heads from the trees I should think.' I buttoned up my jacket and thought how wretched England could be and wondered if the weather was beautiful in Paris and Midge was sunning herself by the banks of the Seine.

'You'd be surprised.' Archie replaced his hat at a rakish angle and I listened while he told me how once, when Leo was a little boy, they had found a five-pound note in the long grass by one of the small ponds in Richmond Park.

'And you've been looking for another ever since?'

He laughed and I tried to join in but I was too impatient to hear what he had to say. People who are planning to tell you something unpalatable always put it off, waiting for what they think is a suitable moment. How far would we have to walk before that moment arrived?

'Do you like Bassett hounds?' he asked.

'I like all dogs, you know that, but Leo doesn't.'

'Another of his shortcomings but he's devoted to you Ursula, don't ever forget that.' He smiled to himself. 'There's a dog I meet in Richmond Park. Dottie, she's called and she has the most lugubrious face you've ever seen, not that her face bears any relation to her sunny temperament. Lovely dog, I said and her owner replied, yes if you can stand the smell!'

Once again he expected me to laugh and once again I was too much on edge. 'Well I met a dog called Archie,' I said, 'a West Highland terrier, and I told its owner my father-in-law was called Archie and he too had thick white hair.'

'Is that how you see me, as your father-in-law? I like to think we're friends.'

'Yes of course we're friends.' I began to cough and he turned his head with such a concerned expression that I would have forgiven him anything, even the fact that he was keeping me waiting so long.

'This cold wind's not good for you. You ought to be wearing a scarf.'

'Please Archie, tell me what Leo said to you.'

He rubbed his chin. 'Just the bare bones.'

'And?'

'About the divorce and the poor chap who killed himself.'

I waited for him to continue but he seemed more interested in a woman with two little boys. The taller one was attempting to fly a blue and white kite, running with it until it rose a few feet off the ground then watching dejectedly as it flopped down back to earth.

'Should we give them a hand?' Archie asked.

I sighed. 'But after that you promise you'll tell me why we've come here.'

'Did you say anything to Mrs Moberley?'

I shook my head.

He looked away, rubbing his chin. 'Can't say I blame you.'

'I was going to but I was too afraid.'

Archie picked up the kite and held it above his head. 'Wait for another gust of wind,' he told the boy, 'then when I shout "go!" hang onto the string and run for dear life.'

The second boy was dressed in a sailor suit and looked angelic although a moment later he was on his back on the grass, drumming his heels in fury because he wanted to be the one who flew the kite.

'You can have a turn too.' His mother gave Archie a grateful smile. 'Look, the kind man's helping John to make it fly.'

The kite had risen about twenty feet and was flapping about. 'Unwind the string,' Archie yelled, hurrying across to give the boy some more help. 'But don't let go whatever you do.'

No hang onto it, I thought, or we'll spend the rest of the afternoon trying to retrieve the wretched thing from the branches of a tree. How sour I was being but who could blame me? Just when my life was starting to improve Leo had spoiled everything and if it had not been for Leo I would never have met Mrs Moberley in the first place.

Before we moved on Archie had a few quiet words with the boys' mother and seeing them together it occurred to me they might know each other. Had he met her before, that first time he drove me to Inverness Gardens, or was it simply that he had an ability to strike up conversations with total strangers, an ability that must come in useful when he was talking to his patients. Or possibly that was how he had acquired it in the first place.

'Come along then.' He put his hands on my shoulders. 'Shall we find somewhere to sit down or shall we carry on walking?'

'I do feel rather weary.'

'Over there then.' He pointed to a bench under a tree then strode on ahead and tested the wooden slats to make sure they were not damp from the rain.

As I crossed the grass to join him one speculation followed another. He thought Leo was being unfair. The fact that Mrs Moberley was divorced had no bearing on her work as an analyst. Or, he agreed with Leo but thought it might be best if I saw her for one more week, to round things off. Or he might suggest I saw a different analyst, a man perhaps, or obtained some entirely different form of treatment involving medicine or tablets.

'Rather hard.' He patted the space between us. 'But this won't take long.'

'It's no wonder I suffer from nerves.'

He smiled and I realised that whether what he had to say was something I would want to hear or just the opposite made no difference. Leo had conveyed to him how worried he was and Archie had offered to talk to me because he thought it might come better from him.

'First the suicide victim,' he said. 'Inevitably there was an inquest and various members of the public appeared as witnesses. I spent a good part of yesterday looking up the reports.'

'Were you allowed to?'

'Of course.'

If you know the right people, I thought, but perhaps I was wrong and providing accounts for the public to read was part of the scheme of things.

'Some of the witnesses blamed Mrs Moberley,' he continued, 'but others stated the obvious fact that people who seek the kind of help she provides are likely to be unhappy or even seriously depressed. There was no evidence her treatment had made the poor young chap worse. In fact he appears to have been doing exceptionally well until he returned home one day to find his wife had left, taking their child with her and leaving a note to say she wanted no contact with him ever again.'

'And that was when he jumped in the river?'

'The same evening. Tragic, and I'm sure Mrs Moberley was as distressed as anyone but they would have been hard pressed to hold her responsible. In the event the coroner brought in a verdict of suicide while the balance of the mind was disturbed and no blame whatsoever was attached to Mrs Moberley.'

I picked up a fir cone and threw it at one of the trees with my good arm. 'So Leo's wrong when he thinks seeing her will make me do away with myself.'

'I'm sure he doesn't think that Ursula.'

'Yes he does,' I protested, but Archie held up his hand.

'Now for the divorce. If it hadn't been for the inquest none of this would have come out so it's an ill wind and all that. One of the witnesses, a relative of the dead man, tried to blacken her name and it was left to Mrs Moberley to explain that while it was true that she had left her husband she had every reason for doing so.'

'Did he beat her?'

'She has twin sons.'

'Twins? Identical ones?'

'That I can't tell you.'

'Do you know how old they are?'

'At the time of the inquest they were nineteen so now they must be twenty-one or thereabouts.'

The young man with fair hair, I thought, opening my mouth to explain, but once again Archie held up his hand. 'When they were born there were complications. The first baby was healthy enough but the second was lying at an awkward angle and soon after delivery it was clear all was not well. The child survived but was left suffering severe brain damage, caused by lack of oxygen I imagine.'

'Oh.' I had a sudden picture of a young man with his head lolling and his eyes fixed in a sightless stare. 'Poor Mrs Moberley, how awful.'

In the distance the boy with the kite and his brother had started for home, with the mother carrying the smaller of the two. Archie had stopped talking but I knew there was more to come.

'What happened to the brain-damaged one?' I asked.

'Until he was six or seven he was looked after at home, but as he grew older he became unmanageable and a place had to be found for him in an institution where he could receive specialist care. Mrs Moberley visited him often, still does I assume, but on her own since her husband resolutely refused to acknowledge the boy's existence and appears to have wanted him shut away and never mentioned again.'

'He couldn't do that.'

'As far as I can surmise he laid down an ultimatum. Give up on the boy or leave the house.'

'So she left.'

'Taking the other child with her.'

I felt weak with exhaustion, or was it relief? These days I never knew from one minute to the next whether I was sad or happy, clear headed or confused . 'Does Leo know all this?'

'Not yet. I thought it only fair to tell you first. To forbid you to see Mrs Moberley was unforgivable and as it turns out his fears were unfounded. In fact all in all I'd say it was a quite unwarranted intrusion into her private life. I know considerably less than he does about psychoanalysis but I'm sufficiently well informed to be aware that cutting it short is not just inadvisable but positively dangerous.'

The wind had dropped but the black clouds were so low it was only a matter of minutes before a downpour soaked us to the skin. Enid had urged me to take an umbrella but I had refused and a moment later she had started busying herself in the larder, leaving me wondering what was going through her head.

Archie touched the back of my gloved hand. 'As far as I can gather most female analysts have no children when they do their training and it's exceptional for them to marry before their mid-thirties. Between ourselves I've gained the impression Mrs Moberley is a rather exceptional woman.'

I felt my cheeks burn. 'I should think being married would help you to understand your patients better. Yes I'm sure it would. Leo wanted to find something bad about her. He was the one who thought I needed analysing and now he resents it.'

'Why would he do that Ursula? Particularly since your arm is regaining some of its sensation.'

'He feels left out.'

'I see.' I expected him to accuse Leo of being ridiculous but instead he thought about what I had said then agreed it might be a problem. 'Perhaps he thinks the two of you discuss his shortcomings. He does tend to take life rather seriously. His mother's son wouldn't you say?'

'Actually I hardly talk about him at all. Mostly I tell her about boarding school and when I was a child. That's the whole point isn't it, trying to remember what happened and why it's made me ill.'

'I admit when you first agreed to visit an analyst I did have some misgivings but all in all I'd say it seems to have helped you a good deal. If you trust her as I'm sure you do perhaps you should talk about the present as well as the past.'

'I think she would agree with you there. She never asks questions, well hardly ever, but she listens so carefully, not just to what I say but also to how I feel.'

He gave me a hug. 'Well far be it from me to advise you Ursula, as you know it's not my field, but when Leo suggested you say whatever comes into your head in that instance I think he may have been right. Past, present, whatever you think could be useful.'

A tramp had emerged from behind some trees. He was carrying a dilapidated shopping bag with crumpled newspaper sticking out of the top. Poor old thing, I thought, wanting to give him some money but not sure how Archie would react if I did. 'So you'll tell him it's all right for me to go on seeing Mrs Moberley.'

'If that's what you'd like but it might be better coming from you.'

'But supposing he doesn't believe me.'

Archie stood up and stretched. 'You may find he's more receptive than you imagine and in any case I'm hanged if I'm going to let him bully you, although to do him justice I think he was genuinely concerned when he found out about the suicide case.'

'I feel so terrible I ever doubted her. No I don't, it would be silly wouldn't it to think Mrs Moberley, right or wrong.'

'But isn't that how you do feel Ursula. If I were you I'd trust to your feelings.'

I smiled. 'You're beginning to sound like an analyst yourself. Maybe you'd better give up being a skin specialist and take up a whole new career.'

'Bit late for that, wouldn't you say?' He held out a

hand to check for rain. 'Incidentally, the girl who took over your job has given in her notice. Wouldn't like to come back, would you?'

CHAPTER TEN

"Reflexes connected with the sex organs, reflexes very old in the history of the race, are entirely outside voluntary interference."

(D. Fraser Harris)

Even Leo could understand why Mrs Moberley had left her husband. And he seemed to accept that the patient's suicide had not been her fault. Not necessarily, was how he grudgingly put it, adding, 'in any case I'm no longer sure Freud's theories are correct.'

'How do you mean?'

He cut the top off his egg, the one he had insisted on boiling for himself every morning since my arm had ceased to function. Previously he had eaten two slices of toast and marmalade.

'I've been reading about an American psychologist called John Watson,' he said. 'Watson believes the central theme of psychology should be that only events that can be observed and measured are worth considering.'

He waited for me to comment on what he clearly thought was a momentous announcement but I had no idea what he was talking about, apart from the fact that he had turned against Freud.

'After all,' he continued, 'how can we be certain one person's introspections are the same as another's?'

'I'm sure they're not, but why should they be?'

His expression implied if that was a serious question there was no point in having the conversation. 'Obviously the thought processes in psychoanalysis fall right outside observable events. You've heard of Pavlov's dogs? Pavlov showed that dogs could be conditioned to salivate when they heard a bell. They learned to associate it with food.'

As his spoon plunged into the egg, a blob of yolk jumped out and slid down the shell. 'Yes I know about associations. Mrs Moberley says it's through dreams that the contents of the unconscious can be discovered – by free association.'

'Freud's "royal road to the unconscious". His voice had an unpleasant note of derision. 'Of course the notion of the unconscious is not original to Freud. It was used by German philosophers in the first half of the last century.'

'But they didn't invent analysis.'

'Neither did Freud invent hypnosis.'

'Well, even I know that Leo.' The sight of his egg was turning my stomach. I sipped my coffee and looked away. 'One of Freud's patients, Frau Emmy, had a leg like my arm but she was far worse than me, she had a change of personality and spoke with a stutter.'

'I was wrong when I suggested you might benefit from the talking cure.' He wiped his mouth with his table napkin. 'I wouldn't read any more of Freud's cases if I were you.'

'Anna O was more like me.' I stood up and started clearing the table with my good hand. 'She had headaches and a cough, and terrifying hallucinations, and it was all because she had to nurse her father, and she was extremely intelligent so whatever was wrong with her it wasn't because she was too stupid to make sense of it.'

'Have I ever said you were stupid?'

'No but you treat me as though I'm feather-brained. Hurry up or you'll be late for school.'

What a way to start the day, arguing about the relative merits of Freud and some new person called Watson. And the argument wasn't really about them at all. Was it my fault we kept bickering? Men hate it when their wives are ill, that's what my mother used to say, it makes them anxious and ill-tempered. A wife's duty is quite simple Ursula, to provide a comfortable home for her husband and children.

So it *was* my fault.

For the past few days I had resisted the temptation to question Enid but I could put it off no longer. For her sake as well as my own because think how it must feel having to keep something like that a secret. If I was right, surely by now she would have told Jim but I doubted if her family knew and that included her mother. Of course it was possible she had been afraid she was expecting a baby but it had turned out to be a false alarm.

I found her up in the bathroom, silently polishing the taps.

'Hello Mrs Ingham.' She straightened up, adopting a falsely cheery expression and speaking in the kind of voice that would have fooled nobody. 'I'm having a bit of a spring clean.'

'You had one in March.'

She kept her eyes firmly fixed on the fiddly bits round the plug hole. 'Does no harm to have another.'

'No I suppose not.'

'Mr Ingham likes everything spick and span.'

'And I don't?'

She laughed and I felt a fraud, joining in the laughter when I had come upstairs to tackle her about such a sensitive subject. Should I wait a few moments, talk about this and that, or would it be best to come straight out with it? Knowing Enid she would have picked up on my edginess and knew I had something to say that she would rather not hear, even guessed what it was going to be.

Downstairs I had planned how I would introduce the subject. *I've been wondering Enid, only of course I could be quite wrong. When Helen was here and then my sister came to collect her and she told us how the curate's wife was expecting… Only I noticed you were blushing and…* With any luck at this point she would help me out, but supposing she stared back blankly, not having an idea what I was talking about.

No I was right, I knew I was. The cough she had told me about had not gone away, except now I suspected what I could hear was not a cough at all but her being sick in the scullery sink. Joyce had been very sick when she was expecting Helen and Sybil although she said it had been better all round with Christopher, an easier pregnancy and an easier birth. Not that she had told me any of the details. They would have been reserved for friends of hers who had shared the same experience.

Enid had started on the wall tiles and I was beginning to lose my nerve. Supposing I had imagined the whole thing. The cough was genuine, and when Joyce announced that Beryl was expecting and looked at me, as though to say, "now it's your turn Ursula,"

Enid had simply felt uncomfortable on my behalf. After all, she did blush rather easily.

'Enid?'

'Yes Mrs Ingham.'

'The reason I came up here.'

She paused with the cloth in her hand. 'Was there something you wanted me to do downstairs?'

'No nothing like that. I wondered if your cough was better.'

'Gone Mrs Ingham. Wasn't really a cough, just a touch of hay fever maybe.'

'You don't suffer from hay fever.'

She turned away and I noticed the hand holding the cloth was shaking.

'I may be quite wrong Enid and you'll be cross with me if I am.'

'Why's that, Mrs Ingham?' Her face was scarlet and she was breathing hard.

'We're friends aren't we.'

'Yes, I hope so, Mrs. Ingham.'

'Only I have to ask, are you going to have a baby?'

The cloth dropped into the bath and she covered her face with her dripping hands.

Leo had come home for lunch. It was Thursday, cricket match day but on this occasion his presence was not required.

'It's Hugo's turn to act as umpire, and his wife's responsible for the teas.'

'So when you're the umpire I'm supposed to make tea for the boys.' I was desperate to tell him about Enid but she was still in the house and he might insist on talking to her and that would only make things worse.

He would try to help but choose the wrong words and Enid would be mortified. Admitting the truth to me was one thing, discussing it with Leo would be quite another.

After the showdown in the bathroom I had persuaded her to go downstairs and reluctantly she had allowed me to make a pot of tea.

'But your arm Mrs Ingham, you might scald yourself.'

'The more I use the good arm the more likely it is that the other one will start to work. You sit down and dry your eyes.'

Like a small child she had done as she was told, sitting at the kitchen table with her hands folded in her lap and her eyes fixed on the window behind the sink. The smell of the bones she had been boiling up was enough to make anyone feel queasy so I had moved the pan off the hotplate all prepared for Enid to protest that they needed longer, but she had no interest in the stock.

While we drank our tea I was the one who did all the talking, with Enid responding without opening her mouth. How long have you known? A shrug. Have you told your mother, or your sister? A shake of the head. When I suggested that she and Jim would have to try and find a place of their own she nodded in a hopeless sort of way. When I asked if she would like the rest of the day off she shook her head vigorously. Finally I had decided to leave her on her own for a while but make sure I had another talk with her before she left to go home.

'Don't you have to go back this afternoon?' I asked Leo, afraid he would say he had no more lessons so he had brought the boys' prep books back with him and planned to sit in the garden and do some marking.

'I thought I'd come and see how you were. This morning, at breakfast, I was afraid I might have upset you.'

'You didn't.'

He frowned, not sure if I was still cross with him or meant what I said. 'Any luck with the arm?'

'No but people adapt don't they, like blind people acquire a better sense of smell and touch. I actually made a pot of tea.'

'Was that wise? Where was Enid?'

'I could have lost the arm in an accident. Then I'd have to make do with what I'd got left, and since my cough and my headaches have been better I've made a resolution to stop behaving like an invalid and do some shopping, just small items at first, a loaf of bread or some fruit.'

To my surprise he nodded his agreement. 'If you believe it would help. I've been thinking Ursa, you were right to reproach me. I should have trusted your judgement. I thought I was looking into Mrs Moberley's background for the best of reasons, to protect you, but I think my motives may have been mixed.'

'In what way?' I was astonished at his admission.

'I may have felt a little left out, as though Mrs Moberley had taken over and you no longer needed anything from me.'

'But I never wanted it to be like that Leo. I would have told you more but even though I only see her three times a week so many different things come up, mainly about my childhood, and I get quite tired and don't feel like going over it all again.'

'I understand.'

'From now on I'll try to remember what we talk about. I know, I could write it down when I get home and show it to you in the evening.'

'No need for that but can we make a fresh start?'

'Yes of course. Is that why you came home for lunch? Thank you Leo, that was kind.' I wanted to give him a hug but was not sure how he would react. 'Actually there is something I have to tell you.'

'About Mrs Moberley.' His eyes had a wary expression and in an instant any remaining resentment I felt towards him disappeared. Perhaps people were right when they said arguments sometimes brought you closer and I respected him for being brave enough to admit how he felt. No, not respected, that was a cold, unfeeling word. I admired him.

'Nothing to do with Mrs Moberley,' I said, 'and it can wait. You go back to school and finish your work and we can talk about it this evening.'

I stood up and kissed him on the cheek and he reached out tentatively, being careful to steer clear of my bad arm, except since it had no sensation it was odd how people avoided touching it, almost as if they thought the "illness" might be catching.

When I found Enid again I was hoping she would have perked up a bit. Now that it was out in the open, and there was no need to pretend, she ought to be feeling a degree of relief so I was horrified to see her swollen eyes and realise she must have been crying on and off for the past hour or so.

'What is it Enid? No leave the dishes for now. I'm sorry, I only asked because I wanted to help. You haven't told your mother have you?'

She moved her head from side to side in a weary

gesture that was so unlike her I could have cried too.

'But you've told Jim and I'm sure he agrees you should be married as soon as possible so don't give another thought to my stupid arm, fix up a date and Mr Ingham and I will deal with the rest. Promise?'

When she made no reply I wanted to ask how the deed had taken place. In an alleyway, up against a wall? Perhaps she had thought if you made love standing up you were safe. Or it could have been at the recreation ground, in the long grass. Had she enjoyed it, had it been something she wanted, or had she thought she would lose Jim if she refused to let him have his way? They could have gone out for the day, on the bus or the train, something he had suggested with seduction in mind. Still, how and where was irrelevant now apart from the fact that she might be able to pinpoint the date.

'Do you know when it's due Enid?'

The tears started again and she searched in her apron pocket and found a sodden handkerchief.

'Here, have mine.' I tried to sneak a look at her stomach even though I was certain nothing showed or I would have noticed before. It was true she was quite stout, but she always had been, it probably ran in the family.

Her nose was so blocked with crying she had to breathe through her open mouth. 'Is Mr Ingham still here?' she gasped and when I told her he had returned to work she let out such a wail it sent a shiver down my spine. 'He's gone.'

'Gone? Who's gone?' But I had guessed at once what she meant. 'Jim? When? Where did he go?'

'Up north to see his brother.'

'Oh is that all. The one who makes beer barrels?

Well as soon as he comes back you can tell him what's happened and start making plans.'

'He's not coming back.' She was so distraught she could hardly speak. 'He wrote me a letter, said he loves me but he don't think we ought to be tied down, not when we was both so young.'

'But when you tell him about the baby.'

'I've been in touch with his brother but he don't know where he is, said he was talking of finding work on a farm.'

'I thought he was a painter and decorator.'

'I know but he can turn his hand to most things.'

'Enid, I have to ask you this, does he know about the baby?'

She nodded miserably. 'That's what done it. I shouldn't have told him should I, only meself to blame.'

'No of course you're not to blame. You'd have to have told him sooner or later.' But not until after the wedding, I thought, and the reason the wedding had been put off was because of my arm so it was easy to draw the conclusion the disastrous turn of events was my doing.

'Don't worry Enid.' I leaned towards her, resting my bare elbows on the slightly sticky table. 'It's a rotten show but it will be all right, I promise it will. If you like I could come with you to talk to your mother. No, on second thoughts it would probably be better if you did that on your own, but afterwards Mr Ingham and I will do everything we can to help and you can stay on here as long as you want.'

And then what? Up to that point I had hoped that after she and Jim had settled down together he might agree to her coming back to us, even if it was just for the mornings. Now, any idea of that was out of the question. Still, if I wanted to look on the bright side, although from Enid's point of view there was nothing very bright, the baby was unlikely to be due until February at the earliest and long before then I would be cured. Mrs Moberley would see to that.

The effort of talking to Enid had given me a headache and I decided to lie down for an hour or so before Leo came home. Removing my shoes and dress I stood in front of the mirror and took a long hard look at myself. My mother had sometimes remarked about it being a pity I had inherited my father's square shaped face. Was my face a square? It didn't look that way to me and in any case was one shape really better than another?

I was wearing the pink crepe-de-chine brassiere and knickers I had bought for myself before the wedding. The lace trimming was pretty and I thought what a pity it was that women had to wear suspender belts. Then I remembered the time I had blurted out a silly question to Mrs Moberley, asking her why men liked suspenders and she had said it might be because women's underwear was something of a mystery to them. Only *might* be, because what men found exciting was hardly her line of work, except on second thoughts I was wrong about that. Freud was obsessed with such things and as far as I could tell Mrs Moberley knew everything there was to know about the great professor.

Closing the bedroom door I lay on the bed on my back, with the covers pulled back, wanting to ease my headache but knowing I would be unable to sleep. My body was too restless, and my mind was too, going over everything that had happened, Enid's baby, Leo's investigations into Mrs Moberley's private life, and now his apology which was almost as much of a surprise as the other two bombshells.

Sometimes at night I lay awake for hours, twisting and turning, unable to find a comfortable position, then fell asleep in the small hours but woke at my usual time, knowing I had not had sufficient sleep and would spend the day in a state of irritable fatigue.

On Sunday night I had slept well, a dreamless sleep, except Mrs Moberley said there was no such thing, and woken bursting with energy and looking forward to my visit to Inverness Gardens now there was no need to worry about Leo's investigations. Mondays, Wednesdays and Fridays. In the beginning I had been relieved I would only be going three times a week, instead of Freud's five, but lately I had come to dread the days in between. How had I spent my time before my analysis started? Reading, resting, talking to Enid. It was not enough.

I was desperately sorry for Enid but there was something else. To my shame the thought of Jim making love to her had excited me. It was so wrong, so forbidden. And making love was probably the wrong way to describe it. No words of endearment, just a few token kisses then fingers fumbling with buttons, Enid's dress dragged up, a hand over her mouth if she protested. No Jim, please Jim, but he was too strong for her, or she thought she was supposed to let him do what he wanted and he would call her standoffish if she refused. All over in a minute and not much pleasure for Enid, just the beginnings of a baby inside her.

It was cool in the bedroom but I felt hot and could feel my heart beating faster than normal but not like the old palpitations. Like a bird, I thought, but since I would never have been brave enough to hold one of the thrushes or sparrows, rescued from Solomon, I must have read the phrase in a book. Like a small bird with a fluttering heart. Archie had once said I was his "little dove". Not while I was working for him so it must have been just before Leo and I got married. Yes, now I remembered. Leo had bought me an engagement ring and I had shown it to Muriel in the drawing room then gone to Archie's study to show him too. *You'll be part of the family, my little dove.*

Now, lying alone on my twin bed I longed to be touched, by soft, gentle hands. I thought about the dream, walking on the beach with Archie, and wondered if I should have told Mrs Moberley about it although lately it had seemed less important. I wanted to be touched, but not by Archie, and to be talked to at the same time. Was that what people meant by "sweet nothings"? Soothed with sweet nothings while a finger traced a pattern, first on my cheek, my neck, then…

Had Enid put on weight? I touched my own flat stomach, smoothing it round and round like my mother used to do when I had a pain and wondered how thinking about someone could affect the way your body felt, making it come alive so you became aware of every part of it. Except my right arm of course. Blow my stupid arm, there was nothing wrong with the rest of me and that was what I should be concentrating on, my perfectly normal head and shoulders and breasts and hips and legs.

My fingers touched the skin between my brassiere and knickers, stroking it slowly then more quickly, feeling down to the triangle of soft hair. Everyone had hair in funny places but nobody ever talked about it. I could mention this to Mrs Moberley because nothing shocked her, nothing was unthinkable. She was the most amazing person I had ever met, so clever and so reliable. No that made her sound dull, just about the last way anyone would describe her. *Did* she have a lover and if so what was he like and where did they meet? I pictured them in a bed together, completely naked but not touching, just gazing at each other's bodies. My fingers caressed the warm skin on my inner thigh and without warning an involuntary spasm ran through me making me cry out, half in alarm, half with a totally unexpected sensation of exquisite pleasure.

Leo took the news about Enid better than I had expected.

'Poor old thing, I didn't take to the man but I never thought he'd let her down like that although to tell you the truth I've had a feeling she wasn't quite her usual self.'

'Have you? Why didn't you say?'

'It was only a feeling.' He gave an apologetic smile as if he thought he should have dealt with the situation himself instead of leaving me to broach the question. 'So what can we do to help? Give her money I suppose but would she accept it? I know, we could buy her some of the things she'll need, a cot or a pram. At least she comes from a large family so she won't be on her own. They can't be very well off though and I bet there's not much space in their house.' He frowned. 'I don't suppose she mentioned anything about…'

'What?'

'She does want the baby?'

'Leo!'

'No, I don't mean anything illegal but I believe there

are steps people take, jumping in and out of hot and cold baths, drinking gin.'

'And endangering their health, doing unspeakable things with soapy water, using purgatives and crochet hooks.'

He flinched. 'Who told you that? Anyway it was jolly brave of you to ask her about it and I'm sure it must have been a great relief for her when she admitted the truth.'

'I don't know about that.'

'Oh come on, sooner or later she would have to have told someone.' He stretched his arms above his head and yawned. 'Anyway enough of that, at least for the time being, let's go up to bed.'

'It's not yet ten.'

'Well I'll go up and you can follow.' He paused for a moment by the door. 'I do know how lucky I am.'

'How do you mean?'

'You agreeing to marry me. I'll never make my fortune but with any luck in a year or two I'm hoping to be made head of history. Harold Gregg's nearing retirement age and a few hints have been dropped that they're more than satisfied with my work.'

'I'm sure they are.'

He stayed where he was and I could think of no way of justifying my wish to remain downstairs. 'All right I'll come up with you now. Where's Solomon?'

'Out hunting I expect.'

'Can you call him in?'

'I could try but I doubt if he'll take much notice. Cats love the night.'

'But I need to know he's safe.'

His expression softened. 'Silly old thing,' He took

hold of my hand, something he had not done for as long as I could remember. 'Look he's over there on the window seat. Must have caught something earlier and come back in so he could give it a chance to digest.'

He saw my face and grinned. 'Oh come on Ursa, you know I didn't mean it. He's far too well fed to bother with hunting.'

'Except for the fun of it,' I said.

It was a warm night and I only needed a single blanket over me. Leo was breathing evenly and I assumed he must have been so tired he had fallen asleep almost immediately. I thought about Enid's baby and felt grateful to him for not saying he wished it had been me who was expecting, but with the curate's wife and now Enid I knew it would be what everyone was thinking. After all even nine-year–old Helen had expressed surprise that, after two years of marriage, I was still childless. Then I thought about Mrs Moberley and how much I had come to depend on her and how she managed to be both patient and firm, waiting for me to tell her things in my own time but insisting I think clearly about myself and what had happened to me. When I told Leo I talked mostly about my childhood it was not entirely true. Archie had been his usual perceptive self when he suggested it might be useful if I told her what was going on in my life at the present time. Actually, it was something she had asked me herself. Not much at all, I had replied at first, but needless to say that had not satisfied her. *I'm not just thinking about day-to-day events Ursula, everyone has an inner life too.*

The last time I saw her she had been wearing a two-piece suit I had never seen before. The skirt brushed the back of her knees and I thought how pretty her legs were and wondered where she bought her silk stockings. At Harvey Nichols, price nine shillings and seven pence a pair? I needed some new clothes myself, something more sophisticated than the slightly childish dresses that Muriel had helped me choose and if I could walk to Inverness Gardens surely I could catch the bus to Oxford Street.

Was that where Mrs Moberley did her shopping? Sometimes, lying on the couch, I found myself imagining how she would look in her underwear and was glad she was unable to see my blushes. When Leo told me about her divorce, and about the patient who had committed suicide, I had been angry, but there had other feelings too. I had wanted to rush to her defence, tell him that whatever he found out about her private life I knew she was doing me good and no matter how many terrible things he told me I would still trust her with my life.

Trust was the word I would have used but what I really meant was love. I loved her. It was something that had crept up on me during the two and a half months I had been seeing her and the criticisms of her had only served to make my feelings for her stronger.

Leo's bed creaked and I held my breath, wondering if he was going to say something, offer yet another apology.

'Are you awake Ursa?'

'Mm?' I murmured drowsily, wanting to give the impression I was half asleep.

'I do love you.'

'I love you too Leo.'

'Do you?' To my horror I heard him climb out of bed. 'I'm sorry about Mrs Moberley.'

'Yes I know you are.'

'You do believe me.'

'Yes of course.'

He was leaning over me, breathing hard and I could see perspiration glistening on his forehead. 'I just want to hold you.'

'Not now Leo.'

'Yes, now!' He squeezed in beside me and moved on top of me with his whole weight bearing down.'

'Don't Leo, you're hurting, you'll hurt my arm.'

'How can I?' He tried to kiss me but I turned my head. 'You can't feel it.'

'Yes I can!' And it was true. The sensation had returned, a prickly feeling that ran down to my wrist and on to the tips of my fingers.

A few minutes ago my body had been soft and pliant. Now it was rigid. Leo was pulling at my nightdress but I managed to wriggle my hands free and with both of my arms I pushed him as hard as I could.

'Don't you love me?' His voice was half wheedling, half angry, but he had moved away and was balanced precariously on the edge of the bed.

'I'll be back to my old self soon.' I spoke through chattering teeth. 'In a month or too, maybe much sooner, everything will be all right again, I promise it will.'

'No it won't.'

'Please Leo, get back in your bed and we can talk.'

'What is there to say?' But this time there was defeat in his voice and I knew I was safe, he would never dream of forcing himself on me.

He had said he was sorry for trying to blacken Mrs Moberley's name, agreed that we should buy things for Enid, and in return I had rejected him. But was it really like that? Perhaps it was something he had been planning all day and the apology that had pleased me so much had been simply a way of making me more agreeable to his advances. How could he want me when I was so cold and unresponsive, and worst of all, something so shocking I hardly dare admit it to myself, how would he feel if he knew my innermost thoughts, knew how abnormal I was, what a freak, a married woman who had fallen in love with another woman.

CHAPTER ELEVEN

*'When two personalities meet, an
emotional storm is created.'*
(Sigmund Freud)

When I saw Mrs Moberley the following day I felt naked as though something about me would give away what had happened the previous night. If I had been braver I would have talked about it, told her the bare facts without ascribing any blame and waited to see what she made of it. Instead I repeated Leo's words from earlier in the day.

'Leo says it wasn't Freud who discovered the unconscious mind.'

'That's perfectly true. Freud's contribution was to show the importance which the unconscious assumes in psychoanalysis.'

I thought about this and tried to come up with something intelligent to say but it was no good, I wanted to tell her how I felt about her, how important she had become in my life.

'I was right, Enid is having a baby,' I said, 'and Jim's gone up north and she doesn't think he's coming back.'

'You must be worried about her.'

'She hasn't told anyone else, not even her mother. I think she may be hoping she'll have a miscarriage but things never work like that do they. People who want children don't have any and people who prefer…' I stopped short, aware that without meaning to I had entered a dangerous area and Mrs Moberley would interpret it as a way of introducing a subject that up to now I had avoided.

She made no comment and I thought to myself, this technique is clever. No questions but by remaining silent she forces me to say more. "Babies" hung in the air between us and I was glad I was lying on the couch where she was unable to see my face. But the next time she spoke her words came as a shock.

'Before we go on Ursula I need to tell you that I shall be going on holiday on the twenty-seventh of this month. For two weeks.'

'Oh.' I felt so let down I was speechless. When I needed her most she was going to abandon me. How could she? Surely she knew any progress I had made would be undone by her absence. I was supposed to say whatever came into my head but how could I? Instead I told her I would miss coming but I was glad she was having a holiday and I was sure she must need one.

The silence that followed made me angry.

'That's not true, I said, 'I know you have to go on holiday but I wish it didn't have to be now, just when I've started to understand what I'm supposed to do. And last night the strength came back in my arm although it's not there now.'

'What happened?'

I hesitated, knowing I ought to tell her how Leo had climbed into my bed but reluctant to show myself in such a bad light. 'Something was about to fall on me and I pushed it away with both hands.'

'What was that something?'

'Oh.' My thoughts darted about searching for a

plausible explanation. 'The ironing board.'

She was silent and I thought: she knows it's a lie but lies are grist to her mill.

'Today is only the tenth,' she said at last, 'we shall be meeting seven more times before then.'

'Will we? Yes I suppose that's right. But now I know you're going away I don't want to tell you anything. I'm sorry, you know how selfish I am, how babyish. Sometimes I feel like three separate people. When I'm here I only think about myself but when I'm at home I'm not the same, I want to help Enid, and I enjoyed looking after Helen when she came for the day, and there's a different me that drives Leo mad. I don't know why he puts up with me.'

'Because he loves you?'

Poor Leo, I would have to tell her the truth, but there was something else I needed to say first. 'When I told you about my mother's death you said you thought it must have made me feel guilty because she wouldn't allow me to look after her only I don't think that's right because she was only behaving the way she always did. I was used to it, understood why she didn't want a fuss and I think she was grateful to me for that.' I sighed. 'Now you'll tell me I'm pretending, deceiving myself so I don't have to face up to the truth.

She shifted slightly on her chair. 'It's quite possible for a patient to object to an interpretation on the part of the analyst and for the patient to be correct.'

'Is it?' I was genuinely surprised.

'Anything I say is only a suggestion, not the final word.'

'Yes I suppose it would have to be, wouldn't it, because you only know what I tell you.' I laughed. 'And what I don't tell you. Don't worry I know you can read between the lines.'

'We can all do that.'

'Yes but some people are better at it than others. Men aren't much good. Leo takes everything at face value.'

'Then perhaps you should speak to him in the same way.'

'You mean say things straight out?' I sighed again. 'But it's so hard.'

'What would you like to say to him?'

I hesitated. Now was my chance and if I failed to take it I might never have the courage again. 'After we married.' I coughed but only to hide my confusion. 'After the wedding we went on our honeymoon to Cornwall. It's supposed to be the happiest time of your life and I was happy because I loved him but…' How could I explain? What words could I use?

My face felt hot and sticky. I put up my hand to wipe away the dampness, realised I had used my "bad" arm and hardly cared.

'It was awful,' I said, 'I don't know what I was expecting but I didn't think it would be so bad.'

She must have known what I meant and I thought she would help me out. When she remained silent I sat up, wriggled myself onto the edge of the couch and announced that it was too difficult to describe what had happened when I was lying down.

'Whatever makes it easier.'

'Leo tried to make love to me.' Now my voice was too loud. 'I tried, I really did, but I hated it, it hurt, and he was patient for a bit but then he got angry – because he was upset. He accused me of not loving him, of only marrying him because other people thought it was a good idea. Only it wasn't true except after I'd been seeing you for a few weeks I started to think about things I've pushed out of my mind, like the time when I worked for Archie.'

'Your father-in-law.'

'Yes but he's more like a father. No that's not right either. I was so fond of him, I still am, and I think I may have married Leo because of Archie and they're not the same, how could they be?'

I began to cry, silent tears that ran down my face and dripped onto my blouse. My bag was on the floor and I needed to blow my nose but if I jumped down she would think I was using it as an excuse to escape, not from the consulting room but from thinking about Leo and Archie, only not if I kept on talking.

'It's wrong to compare people.' I snapped open the bag and found a handkerchief. 'And in any case I'm not even sure it's true, about Archie I mean. I feel so confused. Sometimes I think it was better when I pretended everything was all right, only I know what you're thinking, you're thinking it's pretending that's making me ill.'

'No Ursula I was thinking how courageous you've been and how difficult it must have been for you to tell me these things.'

'You mean about our honeymoon? Or do you mean living with Leo for two years when everything is so wrong between us?'

'Have you heard of Dr Marie Stopes?'

'I don't think so. I might have. What kind of a doctor is she? I might have seen her name in *The Times*. It does sound a bit familiar.'

'She wrote a book called *Married Love*. If you want I could lend you a copy. It was written several years ago but some things never change and I think you might find it helpful. Perhaps Leo could read it too.'

'Thank you.' I felt a little disappointed, as though she wanted a book to do the work for her, as if she was afraid of what else I might tell her in case it was too intimate to bear.

Naturally I was wrong.

'Marie Stopes' first marriage was an unhappy one and in the end she obtained a divorce.'

'Oh.' My voice croaked. Because I was afraid she going to tell me that she too was divorced? But she would never do that, not when we were here to talk about me. I longed for her to talk about herself, partly because I was curious, but mostly because it would have meant we were like friends.

She continued talking about Dr Stopes and in spite of the turmoil in my head I listened as carefully as I could.

'After she wrote *Married Love* she had great difficulty finding a publisher. They rejected her book on the grounds that it would frighten women off marriage, and also because she believed that marriage should be an equal relationship between husband and wife. Something some men find hard to accept.'

'But if men earn the money…'

'In the end she found a small company that was willing to publish it and the book was a huge success and had to be reprinted many times although it was banned in America.'

'Why?'

'When you've read it you can tell me what you think.'

'Yes I will. I expect I should have read it before. Before I got married I mean. My mother hated talking about that kind of thing and anyway she was dead by then and I was hardly likely to talk to Muriel. And my friend Midge had gone to live in Paris. Did I tell you she's coming on Saturday?'

'Will she stay at your house?'

'No, with her aunt and uncle but I'm hoping to see quite a lot of her although with all her new friends in France I'm afraid she may find me rather dull.'

She gave a short laugh. 'That I would very much doubt.'

Every time I tried, as tactfully as possible, to find out when Enid's baby was due she gave a shrug and continued with her work at a breakneck pace, rubbing Mansion polish into the furniture, attacking the linoleum with a mop, or making pastry like a mad thing.

Today was no different but this time I refused to be put off.

'Perhaps you're not sure.' It was a clumsy thing to say because it implied that she and Jim had made love on more than one occasion, possibly several times, but I was tired of tiptoeing round the subject, thinking only of her feelings.

She must have known the risk but Jim would have been persuasive, he had the gift of the gab, as Archie called it. *It's because I love you so much. Don't you love me too Enid? No, don't worry, nothing will happen and if it did it wouldn't matter because we're going to get married.*

When they came to the house together had they known then that Enid was expecting? No, I was sure that was not the case or she would never have insisted they put off the wedding until my arm was better. Except poor Enid could have known and, like she always did, put my wishes first.

'I only want to help, Enid.'

'I know you do Mrs Ingham.'

'How have you been feeling? Has the sickness stopped?'

She looked up from the carrots she was scraping and frowned. 'I haven't been sick, not like they say some are. Felt a bit… lost my appetite but nothing to speak of.'

'But you have other symptoms?'

She blushed. 'Just the usual.'

'Yes I see.' What was the usual? I could ask Joyce but then I would have to tell her about Enid and before I could explain she would think I was having a baby and pour out congratulations, followed by a stream of advice about what I should and should not be eating and drinking. More milk, something I hated, less tea and coffee, plenty of greens, and red meat and liver. And how I would need to rest but also make sure I took plenty of exercise.

'Don't you worry Mrs Ingham.' Enid had finished the carrots and drawn up a chair at the kitchen table where she was starting on the silver. 'You just concentrate on getting well. How's the arm been today?'

'I moved it a little when I was with Mrs Moberley and it's definitely starting to feel stronger.'

'And your cough's quite disappeared.'

'And the headaches. I have one occasionally but I think everyone does, don't you?'

She nodded, afraid I was going to return to the subject she so disliked.

'I must ask you Enid, have you told your mother?'
'All in good time.'
'But she'd want to know.'

She held the spoon up to the light. 'If you'd met her Mrs Ingham.'

'I wish I had. I mean I'd like to meet her. And the rest of your family, your father and all those brothers and sisters whose names I can never remember. No, I remember your sister's name. Flossie, short for Florence.'

She gave me a sideways smile. 'So you could tell tales.'

'No, of course not.' It was unlike Enid to make such an accusation and it hurt me. 'All right I won't mention it again, not for at least a month, but only if you promise to tell me if you're not feeling well.'

She relaxed visibly. 'Course I will.'

'That's a promise?'

She nodded again. 'That's a promise Mrs Ingham. How's Miss Helen?'

'You're thinking she might come for another visit? Yes I enjoyed it too. Children come out with such funny remarks, don't they?'

'They do that. You think they're playing and all the time they're listening to what the grown-ups are saying and taking in every word.'

'Enid?'

'Now what is it?'

'You wouldn't do anything silly?'

'How do you mean Mrs Ingham?' She looked puzzled. 'Oh, for a second I thought you meant do away with myself. I know what you're thinking and I wouldn't do nothing like that. Against God's will it'd be. No, I'd never do nothing like that.'

I stood up and gave her a hug, refusing to be put off when she told me to watch out or her apron would leave marks on my dress. Then the doorbell rang.

'Stay where you are Enid, it's probably the delivery boy.'

'Don't you go trying to lift a heavy box.'

'I'll tell him to leave it in the hall.' But when I opened the front door, prepared to give the boy his instructions, I let out a squeal of delight.

It was Midge.

'All right if I smoke?'

'Yes of course.' I found her a glass ashtray. 'Leo does sometimes but not so often lately because of my cough.'

'Oh I'm sorry.' Midge paused with her cigarette holder in one hand and her lighter in the other. 'Never mind, I'll have one later.'

'No, no, I haven't coughed for ages.'

She looked smaller than I remembered, but how could she be? At school I had thought we were about the same height and weight but I could see now I was wrong. She was at least two inches shorter and in spite of her loose-fitting multi-coloured dress I could see that her figure was much curvier than mine. Her face though had hardly changed at all, the green eyes and wavy auburn hair that was parted in the middle and looked frightfully up-to-the-minute, and the large mouth with its bright lipstick.

When she arrived, she had been wearing a grey hat with a petersham band. Now the hat lay on a chair and she had kicked off her black court shoes and was wiggling her toes.

After the initial shock of seeing her a day early, and

all the hugs and kisses, I felt a little awkward, unsure of myself, not knowing what to say or how to be. I had explained in a letter about my arm, and my headaches and cough, but played down the severity of the symptoms, telling her I was on the mend and would be totally cured within a matter of weeks.

'So your arm's almost returned to normal.' She lit her cigarette and inhaled deeply, turning her head so the smoke drifted away from my face. 'What a relief. What was it, some kind of muscle strain? '

I took a deep breath. 'I must tell you Midge or we'll be talking at cross-purposes. I saw dozens of doctor, most of them specialists and there's nothing wrong with me medically speaking. It's all in my mind so I've been seeing someone, a psychoanalyst who lives quite close by near Hampstead Heath. She's called Mrs Moberley.'

'Really? How exciting. Was it Leo's idea, as I recall he was always fascinated by that kind of thing? How often do you have to see her only I was hoping we could have a day out together.'

'We can, of course we can.'

'Is Saturday all right? As I mentioned in my letter I'm staying with my aunt and she's fixed up any number of dreary outings to distant relatives I can barely remember but when it came to Saturday I was adamant. Unless it's a day you like to spend with Leo.'

'Oh no, I'd love to go out. Leo has cricket matches. The boys he teaches. And he was so pleased when he heard you were coming because he knew seeing you would cheer me up. Not that I need cheering up. Your uncle and aunt must be awfully pleased to see you.'

She smiled, as if to say, what is all this Ursula, I wish you could relax and be your normal self. 'Isn't this extraordinary, you married and living in Highgate, and me…' She searched for adequate words to compare our two lives. 'Me still an independent woman with all the antagonism that seems to provoke. So how's the London scene? Living the other side of the Channel I'm quite out of touch although I saw in the paper there's to be a Garden Party at Buckingham Palace at the end of the month.'

'I think they have them quite often.'

'And who gets invited, not the likes of us I imagine.'

'I shouldn't think so.' Did she really want an invitation to meet the King and Queen? It seemed so unlike the old Midge but perhaps she had changed, or perhaps like me she felt a little self-conscious and was simply making conversation.

'Anyway.' She gazed round the room and I wondered what she thought of our serviceable but conservative furniture. 'If you're up to it I have exciting plans for Saturday. There's an exhibition of Art Deco I just have to see and you'll love it too, I know you will. It's in a street off Piccadilly so we can go on the tube and take a look at the new underground station that claims to be the best in the world.'

'That would be lovely.' It was so good to see her but I was tired, from my session with Mrs Moberley and from talking to Enid. Where was Enid? I wanted to speak to her again before she left and reassure her I had no intention of telling her mother, not unless she wanted me to. Now she would leave without saying goodbye.

Midge had started talking about shopping in Paris. *Galleries Lafayette, Bon Marché, Printemps*. 'As soon as you're better you must come and stay. Paris is the heart of good design and many of the designers are women now. As far as London's concerned I hear Bond Street and Mayfair have the most exclusive shops but Oxford Street and Regent Street still attract the crowds. And Selfridges is supposed to be a very glamorous store. World famous lifts, I believe, with an exotic Japanese look and figures representing the signs of the zodiac.'

'They were installed last year.'

'And your best furniture is at Heal's?'

'I'm not sure, you'd have to ask Leo's mother. She's a bit of an expert on furniture. That's what she gave us for a wedding present, Gordon Russell beds, and other pieces too.'

'Workshop in the Cotswolds. So the two of you are good friends now.'

'Me and Muriel? Hardly. I don't think she's ever accepted me properly as Leo's wife.'

'Oh come on, wasn't she one who did the match making?'

'I know.' I wanted to tell her everything, but not now, not yet. 'But she often used to make remarks about Leo's previous girlfriend and once she even called me by her name. As far as Muriel's concerned I'm not a patch on Cicely.'

'Nonsense, you're imagining it. Oh that reminds me.' She opened her envelope-shaped handbag and took out a long parcel wrapped in mauve tissue paper. 'For you! No, on second thoughts perhaps I had better unwrap it. It's breakable and we don't want an accident.' With lightning speed she removed three layers of packaging. 'There, do you like it?'

'Oh it's lovely.' I reached out to touch the porcelain figurine, an elongated woman holding a Scottie dog on a lead. 'Thank you Midge.'

'I remembered how you loved dogs. Actually I thought you'd have one. When I rang the bell I expected to hear loud barking.'

'We've got a cat but Leo's not fond of dogs. Thank you so much, I'll put it on the mantelpiece. No, it's all right, you'd be amazed how well you can manage with one arm once you've got the knack of it. Are you too warm in here? Yesterday was the hottest day of the year but it's cooler today, quite pleasant.'

I knew I was sounding stiff and reserved and it was the last thing I wanted but I was worrying about Saturday. What would Leo say when I announced that Midge and I were going to the West End. Would he try to stop me? Surely if I agreed to go everywhere in cabs and only walk short distances. But he might use the proposed outing as an excuse to lay down the law.

'Now, Saturday.' Midge jumped up as Enid appeared with a tray of tea things.

'Thank you Enid.' I smiled at her but she kept her head down. 'This is my friend Miss Walsh. You remember I told you she lives in Paris.'

'Pleased to meet you.' Enid put down the tray, blushing a little before turning to me. 'If there's nothing else Mrs Ingham I'll be off now.'

'Yes of course.' I glanced at the outline of her figure but there was no discernible difference. 'I'll see you tomorrow and take care.'

After she left I wondered if I should tell Midge about the baby. When I said, "take care" she had given me a look as if to say, that was an odd remark to make to your maid, and I had waited for her to ask if Enid was ill but she must have decided against it.

It would have helped to confide in someone,

someone who was not Leo, but Enid might not like it and if they met again Midge might treat Enid differently so that she suspected I had given away her secret.

She was lighting another cigarette, then she took a quick puff, balanced her holder on the ashtray and offered to pour the tea. 'So you have a maid, lucky old you.'

'It was Leo's idea.' He had hired Enid because he assumed I would soon be fully occupied looking after a child. 'I'm sure I could have managed without.'

'Still, if you haven't been well.'

'And she's been wonderful. More like a friend than a maid.'

Midge gave me another curious look then picked up *The Times*, turning to the entertainments page. 'After we've seen the exhibition we could get a bite to eat then later take in a show. A farewell performance of *The Truth Game*, starring Ivor Novello and Lilian Braithwaite. Certain to be sold out wouldn't you say? What about the Ben Travers at the Aldwych?' She saw my face and misinterpreted my expression. 'No I'm not a great fan of farces myself. Ah but look at this. *La Vie Parisienne* at the Lyric Hammersmith.'

'Perhaps it would be best if we went to the theatre another day, if you can spare the time that is. How long are you staying in England?'

'Not sure yet. Yes, you're right, don't want to overdo things. Now tell me all your news. How's Joyce and her funny vicar husband and those two little girls?'

'Oh didn't I tell you, they have a little boy now too. Christopher, he's still a baby, adorable but I'm sure he'll soon be up to all kinds of mischief.'

'Goodness, poor Joyce, how can she bear it? She has help I suppose.'

'There are always plenty of people from the parish.'

Midge was turning the pages of the paper faster and faster. 'Latest additions to the Zoo,' she read, 'a fishing cat, a jungle cat, and a brush-turkey. What on earth is a brush-turkey do you suppose? Oh, and a letter from Sherlock Holmes, I mean Arthur Conan Doyle.'

'What does it say?' She was so full of life I could hardly keep up with her. Now that she had seen what I was like would she want to spend time with me? She could hardly opt out of Saturday but for all I knew she was regretting the invitation.

'Something about punishing violent criminals.' She folded the paper and dropped it on the floor. 'Well it would be wouldn't it?'

'Yes, I suppose it would.' I smiled but the vivacity had left her face.

'Have you noticed,' she said, 'how you hardly ever hear the word "flapper" these days, or if you do it's because it's become a term of abuse, used against independent women who are seen as flighty and irresponsible.' She gave a bitter laugh. 'People like me.'

'That's ridiculous Midge.' The more she talked the more out of touch with things I felt. 'What's wrong with being independent?'

'It excludes men.'

'Oh I see.' I thought I could hear Leo and wished he had not chosen this precise moment to return home.

'You must have heard the outcry about women taking men's jobs.' She leaned back, squeezing her eyes shut then opening them wide. 'Take no notice, once I get on one of my hobbyhorses there's no stopping me. Now, you've told me about Joyce so what about you and was that the lovely Leo I heard?'

She stood up, giggling. 'I tell you what I'll hide behind the door and give him the shock of his life.' She flattened herself against the wall and put her fingers to her lips.

Leo came in looking much as I expected he would, an expressionless face, except it's impossible to express nothing, "expressionless" means "cross".

'Had a good day?' I asked.

'Same as usual. Have you been smoking? I know your cough's better but I don't think it's a very good idea. In any case I thought you didn't like it.'

'I don't.'

Midge was keeping quiet, waiting her moment, and I was terrified she would make Leo jump and he would dislike it even though he would try to disguise his annoyance. Fortunately she seemed to have had the same thought and made frantic gestures to me that I assumed meant she had decided to play a different game.

'Guess who turned up at the front door,' I said.

'Joyce?' Leo yawned, glancing at the tea things and the extra cup.

'Me!' Midge jumped out, flung her arms round his neck and kissed him making preposterous smacking sounds.

'I thought you were arriving in England tomorrow.' He stepped back to look at her properly. 'You're looking extremely well.'

'Left Paris a couple of days early. Couldn't wait to see Ursula. And you of course.'

'Of course,' Leo laughed, and I thought how much easier it was to get on with your wife's friend than it was with your wife.

'Mind if I smoke?' Midge opened her enamelled case and took out another a cigarette.

'Of course not. Something to drink or is it too early?'

'I'd love one but I'm afraid I'll have to leave in a couple of secs, I'm going out to dinner.'

'But she's coming back on Saturday,' I said, 'and we're going to visit an exhibition off Piccadilly.'

Leo frowned. 'I don't know about that Ursa. It's quite a time since you went out on your own.'

'I won't be on my own, silly, I'll be with Midge. Besides, I walk to Inverness Gardens three times a week and nothing terrible ever happens.'

'I suppose that's true.' He gave me a look as if to say, we'll discuss it after Midge has left. And I knew I was in for a battle but I also knew it was one I was going to win.

CHAPTER TWELVE

*'In my first marriage I paid such a terrible
price for sex-ignorance that I feel that
knowledge gained at such a cost should be
placed at the service of humanity.'*
(Dr Marie Stopes)

Only by learning to hold a bow correctly can one draw music from a violin. I had picked up the book with a mixture of apprehension and excitement, skimming the first chapter and mildly reassured that I was not the only person who had married expecting to be happy then felt a miserable failure. Was that true for Leo as well or did he think me cold and prudish, and what about other married couples, was their life bliss or did some of them at least suffer the agonies Leo and I had endured?

Poor Leo, but as I read on my sympathy for him began to diminish. *The untutored man seeks but one thing, the accomplishment of his desire.* At first, the woman forgives the "crudeness" but quite soon her love revolts although she is likely to keep quiet about this.

Dr Stopes was right, men were beasts, except if Leo and I had been able to talk to one another it might have been different. What would we have said, what words would we have used? There was too much hurt and too much ignorance.

Chapter Three was entitled *Woman's Contrariness* and I thought, this will appeal to Leo, but to my relief the opposite turned out to be true. It described men's exasperation at the way they believed they could do no right in women's eyes because they were so difficult to understand. *Woman's caprice is, or appears to be, a negation of reason. And as reason is man's most precious and hard-won faculty he cannot bear to see it apparently flouted.* But according to Dr Stopes it was normal for women to feel more affectionate on some days than they did on others.

Turning the pages with my "bad" hand I read on, my face becoming stiff with unshed tears. *The young husband may try first one and then the other, and still find his wife unsatisfied, incomprehensible – capricious... Disheartened, he tires, and she sinks into the dull apathy of acquiescence in her "wifely duty".*

Was that what sensible women did? Submitted to wifely duty? Dr Stopes claimed "the horror of the first night of marriage" had been known to drive the woman to suicide or insanity. Surely that was a bit extreme, but perhaps not. She was writing about the women who complied, suffered in silence. My wish for self-preservation had been stronger than that.

Parts of the book were so plain spoken I was shocked but how else could people be saved from their lack of knowledge? Sometimes she used words I had never heard before and some I knew but would never have spoken aloud. *The vaginal canal. The external lips.* And descriptions that made me flinch with embarrassment. *Her husband's lips upon her breasts.* If Leo saw the book he would think Mrs Moberley the devil incarnate.

Alone, apart from Solomon who was purring loudly as he rubbed himself against my leg, I learned how seventy to eighty percent of married woman were deprived of a full orgasm through the excessive speed of the husband's reactions. What was an orgasm? I could ask Midge but would I dare? Midge was not married so was likely to be even more ignorant than I was.

Many medical men now recognise that numerous nervous and other diseases are associated with the lack of physiological relief for natural sex feelings in women. Was that why Mrs Moberley had lent me the book? *A little crest lies between the inner lips.* But unless Leo read it nothing would change. And if he did he would be shocked to the core.

Would I tell him about it? And risk having him try to put an end to my analysis all over again? First I would finish the book, let it sink in. I could ask Archie if he had read it although on second thoughts that was the last thing I ought to do. He would guess why Mrs Moberley had lent it to me and the ensuing conversation would be more than I could bear, quite apart from the fact that he might mention it to Leo. Or to Muriel. To Muriel! The thought of it made me want to laugh out loud.

'Do you like Art Deco?' Midge asked, and before I could answer. 'Silly question, who doesn't? I know the movement started in Paris but it soon spread to London. I imagine it's the rage all over Europe.'

We had found the gallery without difficulty, taking the tube then walking a short distance with Midge talking all the while, about her work in Paris and the amount some people were prepared to pay for an interior decorator.

'I'm afraid I don't know much about art,' I said.

'No? Well that will make the whole experience even more thrilling. With any luck we should see some good pottery and porcelain, even a few pieces designed by Clarice Cliff.'

She meant well but she had a way of making me feel like an ignoramus. Worse than that, she thought me unsophisticated. If Leo and I had lived in Surrey or Sussex I could have presented myself as a country bumpkin but Highgate was within easy reach of all the galleries and theatres so I had no excuse for my unexciting life.

'Clarice Cliff doesn't sound frightfully French,' I said.

Midge laughed. 'I'm not surprised. She comes from Stoke-on-Trent. Her famous "Bizarre" collection was launched a couple of years ago and you've probably seen some of the pieces without realising who designed them.'

'Yes I expect so.'

'The English tend to favour pastels and inconspicuous patterns whereas the French incline toward bolder designs and more garish colours.' She paused to light a cigarette. 'Not that I've exactly made a name for myself but give me time and I'm hopeful I'll be able to branch out on my own and dispense with Jean-Claud.'

'He's the man you work for?'

She nodded. 'He runs the business.'

The day could hardly have been better, a blue sky but none of the stifling heat I often associated with the West End. After breakfast Leo had fussed about what I was going to wear but since he had to leave for work long before Midge arrived there had been plenty of time to decide for myself. I wondered how she would be dressed. In an ultra smart outfit, suitable for visiting an exhibition or in the same kind of clothes she had worn when she had arrived at the house so unexpectedly?

After much trying on and taking off I had settled for a pink herringbone suit with an unfitted jacket and a double collar. It was not new but I had only worn it four or five times and after adding an eau-de-nil silk scarf I was quite pleased with the effect. Midge might think it conservative but it was the best I could manage and trying to compete with someone who lived in Paris and had more money and more opportunity to buy clothes than I would ever have was a forlorn hope. Also I had the excuse that my arm had prevented me from doing any serious shopping during the last few months.

Brown leather shoes with thick low heels completed the outfit and, holding my lacquered straw hat, with a band that matched the colour of the scarf, I had asked Enid what she thought, knowing she would never let me down.

'Oh Mrs Ingham, you look a picture. How's your arm?'

And when I told her it was working rather well. 'There you are then I knew your friend would do you good.'

It was true. Midge was doing me good. Moving round the exhibition hall, from one room to the next, we inspected printed textiles, outrageous wallpaper, and innumerable posters and prints. Then a gallery containing a collection of handmade books where a woman with a cloche hat decorated with replica fruit was holding forth in such a shrill voice that Midge took my arm and guided me away.

'Sounds like a macaw. If you're interested we can always return to those exhibits later.'

Midge was resplendent in an oatmeal linen suit and a black velvet hat with a white artificial rose. We were the same age, give or take a month, but anyone observing the two of us would think she was older than me, and much more stylish.

The next room we entered was swarming with people. A large glass case displayed a hotch-potch of enamelled jewellery, cigarette cases, powder compacts, buckles and brooches, and in another I spotted an exquisitely embroidered evening bag, pink and purple and black.

Midge had made a beeline for a scent bottle in the shape of a bow tie. 'In France there are two different kinds of designers,' she explained, 'those who strive for purity of line and those who cover every available space with stylised fruit and flowers. Some of the customers give me a fairly free hand, others want every inch of their house turned into part of an exotic jungle with each room choc-a-bloc with ornaments and wall hangings.'

'You prefer purity of line?'

'Of course Paris is *the* place for fashion design too. You've heard of Paul Poiret I expect, the man who freed us from the corset and brought in the flat-chested look.'

'Lucky for me,' I joked, 'I've never had much in the way of a bust.'

'You mean you have a delightfully sylph-like figure. Anyway all that's changed now hasn't it. Hair is longer and wavier and waistlines have returned to a natural level, in fact slim curvy silhouettes are all the rage. Do you remember those awful girdles our mothers used to wear?'

'My mother would never have let me see her girdle.'
'All right, what about Muriel?'
'You think I've seen hers!'

'You might have gone for a bathe in the sea together, shared a communal changing room.'

'Highly unlikely.' I considered telling her about an awful shopping trip with Muriel, when she had insisted the sales assistance measure my bust, but my attention was caught by a screen that was rather like the one in Mrs Moberley's consulting room although hers was made of fabric and this one had contrasting shades of inlaid wood. A snake wound round a branch, a tall bird stood on one leg, and a delicate butterfly with tiny dark antennae perched on an exotic looking plant.

A short distance away Midge was going into extravagant raptures over a brightly coloured cocktail shaker with a silver top. 'Colours are so important. Scarlet excites, blue provides peace and quiet and yellow is so clear and luminous, wonderful for children's rooms. Oh and did I tell you about the printed fabrics designed by Raoul Dufy?'

'Leo and I were given a Lalique ashtray for a wedding present,' I said, noticing the name on a card and wanting to sound knowledgeable about at least one of the displays.

'Really? Lucky you.'

I sighed. 'You must think our house awfully old-fashioned.'

'Not at all but if you'd like a few ideas for any of the rooms I'd be happy to oblige.'

'*I* would but I'm not so sure about Leo, he's rather set in his ways, but you will come round again won't you? Have you decided how long you'll be staying in England?'

Her mouth turned down a fraction. 'I'm not quite sure.'

'Don't you have clients waiting for you in Paris? I have an image of you hobnobbing with all the rich artistic people. Do you go to lots of parties, I'm sure you must, and soirées, I've never been certain what they are, but it's a French word isn't it so I expect they have plenty of them in Paris.'

Staring into the distance she gave a little swing of her shoulders. 'Come on I want to show you the amazing wrought-iron furniture I've read about, and some Chinese porcelain vases adapted as lamps, and some cloisonné bowls. Oh look!' She pointed delightedly. 'A Clarice Cliff tea set, isn't it sensational, see the way the crocuses get cut off at the lip of the cups, and the milk jug's the same. And they're not just works of art, they're practical. They do cost an exorbitant amount but anyone would be glad to serve tea out of them.'

Not Leo, I thought, and what would Enid say? *Ooh Mrs Ingham, they're very modern I'm sure but do you really think they're as nice as your willow pattern?*

Midge moved from piece to piece, exclaiming her appreciation, and now and again she saw something she took to so much she could hardly bear to tear herself away. It was infectious and I even began to quite like the gaudy china myself.

'Isn't it all so perfectly lovely.' She took hold of my arm. 'And after we've finished here you'll be famished, we both will. What about a special lunch to buck us up? If you're game I know exactly the place.

I smiled. I was exhausted but whatever she suggested I would go along with it because I so much wanted her to think well of me.

Later I remembered Archie and Muriel saying they had

dined there on their wedding anniversary, the previous year when the place was newly opened. The food, Muriel said, was excellent but certainly not cheap, and Archie had laughed because it was so typical of her, always thinking about value for money.

The entrance was in Swallow Street and stairs led up to the restaurant that had a pictorial view of Regent Street. Although neither of us had been before we were greeted like valued customers and I was a little embarrassed when Midge turned down the first table we were offered, something I would never have dreamed of doing, and asked for a more private one.

'There are things I need to talk to you about Ursula.'

What kind of things? But I knew what they would be. First she would reproach me for forfeiting any chance I might have had of an interesting career and putting all my energy into being a good wife to Leo. And by so doing I would have added to my crime by failing to fight for the rights of women. And then she would admonish me for what she had described as "confining myself to the house".

Best friends at school but how little we knew about each other now. It would be wrong to say we had grown apart but I was painfully aware that all the repeated anecdotes about school were serving to shore up our friendship. The time the French mistress asked a girl called Philippa to describe the rooms in a house then sent her out when she included "le cabinet de toilette". Or the time the doctor came to give each of us a check up and Matron stood by, making personal remarks about our bodily development, or the lack of it.

'She was a sadist,' Midge said, 'no I'm not joking.

Her own dreams were unfulfilled so she took it out on us.'

'What were her dreams?'

'Husband, children, who knows.' Midge lapsed into silence and I thought yet again how, in a few short years our lives had diverged in so many ways and how hers was so much more exciting.

When my arm was fully recovered I would take steps to do something about it, but to do what? Midge was talented, artistic, whereas my only skill was as a shorthand typist. Still, it was a start, and there were possibilities. If Leo let me I might be able to begin at the bottom in the office of a large company and work my way up, just part-time at first so there was time for my duties at home. Only if Enid had gone that would be impossible and, besides, Leo would interpret my wish to have a job as a refusal to have the child he longed for.

The waiter came to take our order and again I left it up to Midge to decide. 'No you choose for me. I know nothing about this sort of food and I expect you're an expert in all kinds of foreign dishes.'

She made a face then laughed and began reeling off names like *Achar Gosht*, *Kerala spices*, and *Peshwari Nan*.

'Sounds delicious,' I gazed round at the other diners. 'Don't stare,' I whispered, 'but you see that man at the table in the corner. Only I think it may be a woman.'

Midge turned her head a little then looked back at me without smiling. 'Have you read *The Well of Loneliness* by Radclyffe Hall?'

'I don't think so. What's it about?'

'Probably never got the chance. It was published last year and your courts declared it obscene.'

Like *Married Love*, I thought, wondering if Midge

had read it and planning to ask her if a suitable moment arrived. 'Does the story take place in Paris?'

'Part of it. There's so much prejudice, mainly from men, but women too. The only acceptable image of a woman these days is "housewife and mother".'

'Oh yes I do agree about that. All those ghastly magazines that tell you how to cook tapioca pudding and turn out children's woollies on your Golden Fleece Knitting Machine.'

'My aunt reads them avidly.' She screwed up her nose with disgust. 'And I have to pretend to look at them too although it goes against the grain.'

'Enid reads *Peg's Paper*.'

But she had stopped listening. 'Your colouring is ideal for one of the new lipsticks.' She studied my face with her head on one side. 'And why not try a marginally lighter shade of powder.'

'Yes all right, I might.' Her advice was becoming a tiny bit tedious but only because I wanted to talk about other more important things. 'Mrs Moberley lent me a copy of a book by Dr Marie Stopes.'

'Oh her,' she said vaguely, and hoping for a surprised reaction I felt let down by her lack of interest but also determined not to be put off from telling her about it.

'She describes "marital rights" as *rape*.'

'Goes without saying.' Midge studied the menu. 'I didn't tell you before but one of the reasons I've considered remaining in England…'

'You're not going back to Paris?'

'Nothing's been decided yet.'

'But you might stay? It would be wonderful if you did and I'm sure you'd find plenty of work in London. Leo's father knows all kinds of influential people. People with money I mean. He could easily spread the word.'

'Ah the famous Archie of whom you were so enamoured.'

'I worked for him.'

'That makes you impervious?' She gave a knowing smile. 'I saw the way he looked at you at the wedding.'

'Don't be silly, he was giving me away.'

'Didn't want to though did he? Would like to have kept you for himself.'

I pulled a face as though to say, how can you be so ridiculous, and returned to the subject of her interior decorating. 'Actually London might be an even better place for you than Paris. You'd have all the most up-to-the-minute ideas and there would be less competition.'

'Not so fast Ursula. My life is a little more complicated than that.'

'Sorry.' I felt snubbed, put in my place. 'Anyway, I thought you loved Paris and you must be fluent in French. You were good at it at school. Now you must be word perfect.'

'That's hardly a good enough reason to stay in a place.'

'No I suppose not.'

For a moment she had sounded like Mrs Moberley. *Hardly a good enough reason.* As far as I could recall she had never used those exact words but she often made me aware how my thoughts rushed ahead, selfish thoughts in the main, and here I was doing it again, wanting Midge to stay in England for my sake when I ought to be asking what *she* wanted and why she had doubts about returning to France.

'I had a close friend.' She took a cigarette from her case and inserted it in a holder that I hoped was made out of bone rather than ivory as I was rather fond of elephants. 'A close friend who turned out to be a morphine addict.'

'Morphine? How awful.'

'Yes it was.'

Did she mean her boyfriend? 'When you say the friend was close…'

'I knew about the morphine but was big-headed enough to think that being with me would provide a cure, even if it took several months.'

'But it didn't work? And here's me, worrying about my silly problems.'

'They're not silly Ursula but you know what it's like when you're fond of someone, things get out of proportion, you need to stand back, take stock.'

'Is that why you came to England? What's his name? Is he French? I suppose he must be. No don't tell me if you don't want to.'

'I'd like to hear about your Mrs Moberley but you may not want to talk about her. I might be asking you to reveal things that are private.' She took several quick sips from her glass of wine. 'Or painful,' she added.

'No I want to tell you Midge. I can talk to her about absolutely anything, whatever comes into my head and at first I kept wondering if that was a good idea, but one things leads to another and it doesn't matter where you start because after a while all the important things come up whether you wanted them to or not. Of course then you have to decide if you're brave enough to talk about them.'

She was listening intently and suddenly I felt shy. Because I had sounded so enthusiastic? Because I had given myself away? But Mrs Moberley had taught me that giving yourself away brings you closer to people. 'In the beginning Leo used to question me and he was angry if I couldn't or wouldn't tell him every detail of what we had discussed.'

'I don't imagine you'd want to do that.'

'No.'

I looked up at her and she was smiling. 'All I meant Ursula, when times are hard we need someone to confide in and that often includes confidences about our nearest and dearest. Or does your Mrs Moberley see all problems as stemming from your upbringing?'

'That's what I thought at first but it's not like that. She's made me see things differently. I mean see myself in a new light. Sometimes it's so confusing but later when I think it over it starts to make sense.' I broke off, blushing. 'Actually I've grown so attached to her I don't know what I'd do without her.'

'I can believe that. It must be an incredibly intense experience. Does she ask you about your dreams? According to Freud almost all adult dreams can be traced to erotic wishes.'

The waiter had brought our first course and as Midge continued to talk I fiddled nervously with the knives and forks.

'It's tough luck about your arm,' she said, 'but maybe in the long run you'll be glad of it. After all if it wasn't for that you'd never have met your Mrs Moberley.'

'Yes that's what I think too. When I first went to see her I thought something must have happened when I was very young, before I was sent away to school, and now for some strange reason it was preying on my mind, but not consciously, and making me ill.'

'But what on earth could have happened that

affected you fifteen years later? Was Joyce any help?'

'No she can't think of anything and in any case she disapproves of Freud. It's true he says if you have a hysterical limb it's because something traumatic happened that you've pushed out of your mind and repressed, but Freud's not God is he?'

She poured herself another glass of wine. 'Anyway you're feeling better.'

'Yes I am.' I picked up my fork and explored my plate of food with some trepidation.

'Go on,' Midge urged, 'you'll love it.'

'Perhaps it's an acquired taste.'

'Then start acquiring it!'

We laughed, but there was something a little frenzied about Midge's laughter and for the first time it occurred to me that she might need me almost as much as I needed her.

'I'm so sorry about your friend,' I said, 'it must be frightfully upsetting.'

She looked down at her plate and I thought she was cross because I had returned to a subject that caused her so much pain.

'If I tell you about it you may not want any more to do with me.'

'How can you say that?' Did she mean she too had used morphine? 'Whatever you've done we'd still be friends. Are you in some kind of trouble? Do tell me Midge. For months I've felt so useless and if there was anything I could do to help… Your friend's still in Paris is he? Is it over between the two of you? Perhaps when you go back things will be better. There must be doctors, clinics. Perhaps he'll miss you so much he'll decide to overcome the addiction.'

'You're wondering if I'm addicted too.'

'No honestly I wasn't.'

'Why not? I could have been but as it happens I've never used the stuff, never would, and no, she won't have booked herself into a clinic. Her name's Solange and I was in love with her, I adored her. But it was killing me and it's over. I won't be going back.'

Leo had found the copy of *Married Love* and was as appalled as I had known he would be. So much so that he had no interest in my day out with Midge, and I certainly had no inclination to tell him about her life in Paris and the lover she had been forced to leave behind.

Naturally the temptation was there. *So you think Marie Stopes is too outspoken do you Leo, well listen to this. Midge was in love with a woman and she's heartbroken. And no, I'm not shocked, well a little I suppose, but not really because all that matters is love.*

Where had that last thought come from? It sounded like the words from one of the songs Enid liked to sing as she stood at the sink, washing the dishes. *Fish gotta swim, birds gotta fly, I gotta love one man till I die.*

Poor Enid, I thought, and then another thought struck me. Imagine a song about a woman loving another woman. Imagine if they played it on the wireless. As if they ever would.

'How many chapters have you read?' I asked.

'Enough.' He had put the book on the floor. 'Return it to her on Monday and we'll say no more about it.'

I was silent, not wanting another argument even though being with Midge had been so refreshing that the gruelling day in the West End had left me full of energy. Nervous energy, Leo would have said. *It will come to no good Ursula, I suggest you go to bed early and have a very quiet day tomorrow getting your strength back. But I haven't felt so strong for ages.* So went the imaginary conversation in my head, accompanied all the while by Leo biting his lower lip, spoiling for a fight.

'My arm's virtually back to normal,' I said, 'I've no idea why, in fact it looks like we'll never know, but these last few days it's grown stronger and stronger.'

'So you'll soon be able to put an end to your analysis.'

'I might have a relapse.'

He glared at me, not sure if I was being serious or flippant. 'That woman has an insidious effect on you. Did you ask her to lend you the book?'

'No of course not, I'd never heard of it.'

Solomon had started sharpening his claws on one of the chairs. Without waiting for an answer to his question Leo picked him up roughly and almost hurled him across the room.

'Don't!' I knelt beside Solomon, afraid he might have injured his leg but he was none the worse and not even particularly affronted. 'If you want to take out your bad temper on someone,' I said angrily, 'take it out on me.'

He gave a snort. 'And watch your arm hang limply by your side again?'

'So you think I was putting it on.'

'Did I say that?'

'As good as.' I was close to tears. 'I had a lovely day out with Midge and now you're trying to spoil it. Anyway she's not going back to Paris, she's staying in London.'

'So you'll be able to see her whenever you like.' His voice had an edge and I thought, you're not just jealous of Mrs Moberley, you resent me spending time with anyone apart from you. Why Leo, why do you have to be so possessive? If it were left to you I would never go anywhere or see anyone. It was so cruel, so unjust, but a small voice in my head still told me I was the one who was being unfair.

CHAPTER THIRTEEN

But isn't "falling in love" a kind of sickness and craziness, an illusion, a blindness to what the loved person is really like, a state arising from infantile origins? The only difference between transference-love and "genuine" love, is the context.

(Sigmund Freud)

It was my last visit to Mrs Moberley before she went away for her holiday and there were so many things I needed to tell her. By now I ought to be used to the calm manner in which she accepted whatever I said. The trouble was I never knew what she was thinking.

Perhaps the fact that she was going away would make me braver, and if I left the important things until just before my fifty minutes was up I would be safe because there would be no time for recriminations. What recriminations? Why did I still expect to be criticised? Because that was how I had been treated all my life although surely that was no truer for me than for anyone else. In "real life" people often express disapproval, especially if something you say or do threatens their cherished beliefs.

I had read the whole of "Married Love", and parts of it I had re-read, all the time listening with half an ear in case Leo came home unexpectedly and caught me in the act. Once when I was studying a particularly shocking bit Enid had tapped on the door and asked if any clothes needed ironing.

'No nothing thank you Enid.' I had jumped at the sound of her and she had noticed my agitation.

'Everything all right Mrs Ingham?'

'Yes thank you.' I wished I could show her the book – it would have been good to discuss it with another woman – but imagine what poor Enid would have thought! Sometimes I wondered how Dr Stopes had been able to write in such a forthright style, and been brave enough to send it to a publisher, but thank goodness she had because now I knew why our honeymoon had been such a disaster. Now, when it was too late.

Before we married Leo had kissed me but nothing more, not very passionate kisses either because he said it was important to him to treat me with respect. At the time I had been grateful. No, that was not quite true, I had known I ought to be appreciative but part of me had felt if he was able to show such restraint it must be because he found me only moderately attractive.

Once I had pushed my hands inside his jacket, feeling the warmth of his body, and the ridges of his ribs. *Don't Ursa.* He had cleared his throat noisily and moved away. Because I had been too forward, I thought, too flirtatious. Now I realised that was not the reason at all. *The untutored man seeks but one thing, the accomplishment of his desire.* And unwittingly I had made this desire harder to restrain.

I wanted to tell Mrs Moberley about it, to tell everything, talk freely about the book and how it had come as such a shock and to say how glad I was that she had lent it to me but that Leo had refused to read it. I wanted to tell her how he had climbed into my bed and how the strength had come back to my arm and I had pushed him away. Nothing had been mentioned about it since, by either of us, but when we talked about the trivialities of the day the unspoken words were louder than the spoken ones.

I could have endured his anger. It was the hurt that was so hard to bear. Why did I always blame myself – Leo was the one who had refused to read *Married Love* – but with a heavy heart I faced the fact that even if he were to read it I had no wish to have him in my bed.

'I've finished the book,' I said, 'but could I keep it a little longer?'

'Of course.'

'Thank you.' Perhaps she had several copies and lent them to all her patients. I could ask her but she was unlikely to tell me and in any case I preferred not to know. The thought that I was merely "one of her patients" was too awful to contemplate. I wanted to be her favourite patient, her only patient. I wanted to be special.

So powerful is the influence of thought upon our bodily structure, that in some people all these physical results may be brought about by the thought of the loved one. It was true. I had tried it. But how could I tell Mrs Moberley that it had been thoughts of her that had stirred me so profoundly? That because of this I had realised she was the one I loved.

Quite unintentionally Midge had allowed me to accept how I felt and shown me it was possible to love another woman. Was Mrs Moberley like that too? It could be one of the reasons her marriage had failed. No that had been because her husband had been cruel and unfeeling.

'I had a dream,' I said, blushing a little because what I was going to say next was a lie. 'It was about you.'

She waited for me to go on.

'You had come round to my house. I'm not sure why but I had been expecting you and Enid had baked a cake.'

Now she would tell me it was wish-fulfilment, dreaming what you wanted to happen.

When she still remained silent I realised I would have to make up some more. 'It wasn't a particularly eventful dream but it made me happy and after I woke up the feeling continued.'

'Dreams are often like that. You may find yourself in a dangerous situation yet feel no fear, or you may be very much afraid of something that in reality is quite harmless.'

But that was not what I had wanted her to say. I wanted her to guess, to make it easy for me. 'You know I told you how I spent last Saturday with Midge?' I hauled myself onto my elbow. 'Well when she was living in Paris she had a friend called Solange and something terrible happened to her.'

'To Solange?'

'She became addicted to morphine.'

Silence.

'The reason I'm telling you, it was dreadful for poor Midge because she loved her.'

More silence.

'No, I mean really loved her. She was in love with her. That's why she's so heartbroken. When she told me I was shocked at first although I pretended not to be, but now I'm not shocked at all, in fact I understand completely why she feels like that because I've had the same feelings myself only until I talked to Midge I was too afraid to admit them.'

'Tell me about them.'

Why was she was making me spell it out when she knew perfectly well what I meant. 'I wish you weren't going on holiday. I know it's selfish of me but it's come at such a bad time.'

'Perhaps a short break will be helpful.'

'How could it be?' I felt hurt and rejected, and angry too. 'Coming here has muddled me. In fact I'm starting to think it's better just to live from day to day, like most people do, never thinking about what's going on in your head, let alone your unconscious mind. Leo doesn't like Freud any more. He's changed.'

'Leo has?'

'No I don't mean in himself. He's found a new set of books and papers about experiments with animals and a baby called Albert who was made to be afraid of a rat.'

'John Watson and the Behaviourists.'

'Oh you know about them. I don't understand what he's talking about. I try but all the time I'm thinking, you were the one who kept on about psychoanalysis and now you've turned against it because you don't like the way I've changed.'

'You feel you've changed too.'

'Yes of course I have, I've just told you!'

'Your feelings for me are quite natural Ursula. We were bound to develop a close relationship.'

'You may think it's natural.' It was the first time I had interrupted her, the first time I had dared to, but she was refusing to take responsibility for what she had done. Only was it her fault if my true self had emerged? Surely that was what psychoanalysis was all about?

She drank from a glass of water by her side then began talking in a quiet but matter-of-fact tone of voice.

'Let me explain a little of what happens during an analysis.'

'I know what you're going to say. You're going to say how I feel is meaningless and it would have been the same whichever analyst I had been to see.'

'It's certainly not meaningless.' She gave a small cough and I wondered if she had caught a cold and in an instant my anger disappeared and I wanted to jump off the couch and tell her how sorry I was I had been so bad-tempered and ungrateful, and how much I loved her, and was it remotely possible that one day she might love me in the same way.

'I think perhaps you're right,' she said, 'and this is not a good time for me to go on holiday. But it's only for two weeks and I have every confidence in you.'

'It's all right.' I lay down again, this time on my front with my hands pressed against my stomach. 'I know you have to have a holiday only there is something I need to tell you because I can't bear it that you don't know. Five weeks ago, when Leo was feeling so upset about me coming here, he made some investigations and found out you were divorced and, worse than that – his words, not mine – that one of your patients had killed himself.'

'Both of those things are true.'

'I didn't dare tell you before but Leo and I had a terrible row and then Archie, my father-in-law, found out about the inquest on the dead man and I'm only telling you now because it was so horrible of Leo and none of it was your fault and he tried to spoil things between us but he was wasting his time wasn't he? You don't mind me saying this do you? Promise you don't mind.'

'I don't mind Ursula but we only have six more minutes left so we must talk about the next two weeks. Will you be seeing your friend again?'

'Midge? Yes I hope so. Since she's not going back to France she'll have to find somewhere to live. At present she's staying with her uncle and aunt but she'll want a place of her own and she'll have to find some work, people who want their houses decorated.'

'Perhaps you can help her.'

'Yes.' She wanted me to calm down before I left. That way she would feel better about abandoning me. Part of me wanted her to feel guilty but another part wanted to reassure her. 'I will be all right,' I told her, and as you say the break might do me good and thank you so much for everything you've done.' I stood up and pushed my feet into my shoes. 'Have a lovely holiday. I won't ask where you're going because it's nothing to do with me.'

She stood up too and walked towards me, smiling. 'I'm going to Cap d'Antibes,' she said, 'with my son, the fair-haired young man who once let you into the house.'

Enid was cutting steak into thin pieces. 'Beef olives Mrs Ingham.'

'Mr Ingham's favourite.'

'Likes his food don't he, and why not?' She held up her greasy hands. 'They had a cure for chapped hands in *Peg's Paper*, you need equal parts of granulated sugar and dripping rubbed well in.'

'Sounds a bit messy and who has chapped hands this time of the year?' But as soon as I had spoken I cursed myself. Chapped hands were not only the result of cold weather, it could be because of time spent with your hands in the washing up water, or on your knees scrubbing the floor. 'Good idea Enid, I'll remember that.'

'And another for wrinkles,' she added, 'but neither of us need worry on that score, not yet awhile. Pearl barley, it said, you have to boil it until something called the gluten comes out, then strain it through muslin and add some drops of something whats name I forget.'

I laughed and she joined in. 'Nice cup of tea Mrs Ingham before it's time for me to go?'

Since she was in such good spirits I had no wish to spoil things by bringing up the dreaded subject. Of course her cheerfulness could be just an act. How many times had I appeared as happy as a sand boy when underneath I was so miserable I could barely bear it?

'I don't mean to pry Enid but have you heard from Jim?'

She kept her head down, spreading the strips of meat with a mixture of breadcrumbs and minced suet. I knew the recipe because Joyce had once given me a lesson. *Add pepper and salt and a little milk then roll up the pieces and brown in hot fat, but not too hot or they'll burn on the outside and the beef won't cook properly.*

'Batter pudding to follow,' Enid said.

'Lovely but I shall put on weight.' Once again I regretted my comment as soon as I had made it, hardly tactful in the circumstances.

Enid allowed herself a small sigh. 'About Jim, Mrs Ingham, he won't be coming back.'

'Are you sure?'

'Flossie bumped into his friend and he said he'd joined a ship. As a carpenter I expect. Do they have carpenters on ships?'

'I'm not sure.'

'Best off without him, that's what Flossie says.'

'So you've told her about – '

'Not yet.'

Having got this far I ought to ask if her mother knew but she had read my thoughts and I could tell from her face that none of her family had been told. 'You can't put it off forever Enid.'

She rammed a skewer through the last of the beef olives. 'Doesn't seem real.'

'But it is real. Isn't it? You are sure. Have you been to the doctor? I could go with you.'

'Don't you worry, it's all being taken care of.'

'How do you mean?'

She noticed my startled expression. 'No, nothing like that, I told you I'd never… And there's no need for doctors, having a baby's not an illness.'

'But there can be problems.'

Her jaw tightened and I could tell she had changed her mind about the cup of tea and was hoping I would go away.

'Please tell your mother Enid, or if not your mother, your sister.'

'Don't you worry.'

'But I do.' I moved towards her but she backed away. 'All right, I won't keep on about it but if there's anything I can do to help, absolutely anything.'

'I know you would Mrs Ingham.' She made it sound like the last word. 'I've left some haricot beans in a pan.' She pointed to the stove. 'They have to soak overnight in cold water with a pinch of soda.'

During the last few weeks she had changed, seemed older than her nineteen years, more self-reliant. Not that she had ever depended on me. I only wished she would. And she was angry too, I recognised the signs, angry with Jim but I suspected there was more to it than that. Was she afraid her family would let her down? From everything she had told me I felt fairly confident they would stand by her. They sounded such a close-knit bunch, something I envied, celebrating Christmas with hordes of friends and relatives, sticking together in times of trouble, or had I got it all wrong, created a romanticised version in my head because that was how I wanted it to be?

Leo had gone out for the afternoon. A walk on the heath, he said, but it was probably just an excuse to get away from me. Now that the school holidays had begun he was free to study his latest passion, shutting himself away for hours on end then appearing with yet another article about the Behaviourists. Freud's papers had been relegated, if not quite to the dustbin, to the bottom drawer of his desk along with the pipe he had once smoked and a jumble of pencils, pens and scraps of blotting paper. Freud had become a dirty word.

'Watson finds Freud's view of human behaviour far too philosophical, almost mystical.'

'Yes well he would.' I had flicked through one of John Watson's papers, believing that forewarned would be forearmed, and was not impressed.

'Why do you say that?' He must have known it would be better to drop the subject. Instead he insisted on drawing me into an argument.

'I don't see what rats running through mazes has got to do with human beings.'

'Ah but that's where you're wrong Ursa.' His eyes shone with enthusiasm. 'Watson is only following on from Pavlov and his work has real scientific rigour.'

'Is that what you'd like to be?'

'How do you mean?'

'A scientist like your father.' It was an unkind thing to say but my head throbbed and he had goaded me.

'Being a doctor is not the same thing at all.'

'Doctors have to study science.'

'Only anatomy and physiology. None of the psychological aspects.'

'Anyway,' I persisted, 'it's impossible to study human beings in the same way you might study animals or insects.'

'Impossible if you start from Freud's standpoint, yes.'

'All right, I'll sit here.' I folded my hands on my lap. 'And you can explain why your behaviourism is more sensible than psychoanalysis.'

But the whole conversation had been doomed from the start. Leo was far too cross to have a reasonable discussion about anything.

Enid had gone home and Leo had still not returned. Out in the garden I began to exercise my arm, moving it backwards and forwards then clenching and unclenching my fist. I had no idea if it did any good. Obviously not in any psychological way but since it looked as though the root cause of it would never be found I had decided the best policy was to concentrate on strengthening the muscles.

Archie had suggested I talk to Mrs Moberley about what was going on in my life at the present time. I had done that all right, taken a huge risk, and then been informed that she was going on holiday. What did *she* think about my arm? Was she still convinced it was the result of a childhood trauma or did she think it had come about because my marriage was such a disaster? And if it was the latter did that mean she thought I had put it on, pretended it had no feeling when, if the truth be told, I could have used it all the time? Only surely Freud believed your unconscious mind could affect your body without you realising it.

I tried to feel cross with her. But it was no good. There was so much I wanted to discuss and I would have to wait two whole unbearable weeks.

The herbaceous border had burst into flower, just as it was supposed to do, although it never failed to surprise me. Unfortunately a day of bucketing rain and raging wind had flattened some of the plants but Muriel, who had spoken to Leo on the phone the previous evening, had assured him they would perk up now the mild weather was back. Hollyhocks and snapdragons and some yellow flowers like small clusters of buttercups whose name I could never remember. When we moved into the house the garden had been neglected but Muriel had soon put that right, arriving with bagfuls of plants and cuttings. *I divided my clumps Ursula. You'll need to do the same in a year's time.*

For the shady part of the border she had provided something called Monkshood but said we would have to enrich the soil. She also said it was poisonous so I was rather relieved when it failed to flourish and had to be dug up and replaced with Lady's Mantle.

Looking round the garden made me think about Midge and her passion for colour. Almost a fortnight had passed since our day in the West End and I was disappointed no other outing had been arranged. I had left it up her to get in touch, assuring her she would be welcome any time but that Tuesdays and Thursdays were best because then I was free all day. Did she think I was too taken up with my analysis to want to spend time with her or was it because she regretted telling me about Solange?

If I failed to hear from her during the next few days I would telephone her aunt and uncle. The trouble was, now that Leo's term had ended it would mean if she came round to the house he would be there and the three of us would chat about this and that and none of the things I wanted to talk about would be possible.

Mrs Moberley had let me down, going away just when I needed her most, and now Midge had done the same. My stomach churned continually and from one moment to the next I had no idea if I was ecstatically happy or filled with guilt and remorse. It was no good Mrs Moberley trying to explain away my feelings for her by saying they were the inevitable result of my treatment. That might be true with other patients she had seen but in my case it was different because I was not just fond of her, I loved her, really loved her, in every possible way.

So what had I done to Leo? I had married him thinking I loved him but that was when I had no understanding of myself. Now I could see it was Archie I had been so attached to, and because Leo was his son I had expected him to be the same as his father when really he was nothing of the sort and any fool could have seen that from the start.

But even that was wrong. I had loved Archie because he was kind to me, and flattered me, and because of his thick white hair and the way he smiled and looked into my eyes a fraction too long, but now that I had met Mrs

Moberley I knew that what I had felt for Archie had been mere infatuation.

Staying at home day after day was so frustrating. Archie had told me an ice rink had opened in Richmond and it cost half a crown to get in and another half a crown to hire a pair of skates. The idea quite appealed to me, if Leo would come too, but I knew what he would say if I suggested it. *Don't try and run before you can walk. To fall on the ice and break a limb would be just about the last straw.* Fuss, fuss, fuss, he was just like his mother, and another thing he had inherited from her: they both had to know best, have the last word.

The telephone started ringing and I prayed it would be Midge. She was psychic and thinking about her had persuaded her pick up the phone, but when I ran back into the house and snatched up the receiver Muriel's familiar voice came on the line.

'Is Leo there?'

'He went for a walk.'

'When will he be back?'

No "Ursula, how are you?" just a demand to speak to her son but there was something about her voice that had made my chest tighten.

'Is anything wrong Muriel?'

'It's Archie. He's been taken ill.'

'Archie?'

'He's in hospital. St Bartholomew's. I'm there now and I need Leo to join me.'

'Yes of course. What happened?'

There was a long pause and I was beginning to think she had rung off when she spoke again, sharply, almost angrily. 'His heart. They think he had an attack.'

A heart attack? Not Archie. 'But he's going to be all right?'

'How long do you think Leo will be? When did he go out?'

'He should be back any minute.' My voice was almost inaudible. I must have forgotten to breathe. 'I'll go and look for him.'

'If you could.' She sounded so calm, so controlled, but that was her way of dealing with a frightening situation. 'It's difficult telephoning from here and I need to be with Archie. He's fully conscious but drowsy from the drugs they've given him.'

Leo was coming through the front door. I called to him and he picked up the anxiety in my voice and hurried towards the phone, smoothing back his hair.

'It's your father,' I whispered, 'I mean it's your mother on the phone. He's been taken ill but I'm sure he's going to be all right.'

Leo returned from the hospital at half past nine. I had not accompanied him because everyone seemed to think it would be better if I stayed at home. *I'll give you a ring as soon as I've seen how he is.* But the phone call had never come and I had spent the entire evening going over all the possible outcomes in my mind. It was not a serious attack. Archie would have to ease up on his work or even retire early but he would be all right if he took care not to overdo things, or it was bad, so bad he was unlikely to survive the next few days. Then what would happen? Muriel would come and live with us and it would be my fault for fantasising about a time when she had gone and Archie had moved to Highgate. Except how could my fantasies have any effect?

I blamed my mother for making me so superstitious.

You've spilled the salt. Toss it over your left shoulder or you'll have a year of bad luck. If little girls whistle they grow beards. Step on a crack, you'll break your mother's back. Poor Archie, I wished I could have gone to the hospital but he was probably too ill to care who was there. Muriel had said he was drowsy. Did that mean he was unconscious or had the doctor decided if he rested when he woke up he would be better? A relative of my mother's had died from a heart attack when he was on the train. No warning, no time to call for an ambulance, he had dropped dead while he was putting his suitcase on the luggage rack. As a child the awful scene had haunted me.

By the time Leo came home I had exhausted myself with useless speculation.

'It's not as bad as they thought.' He sank into his usual chair. 'He should pull through.'

'Oh thank goodness. Are you sure?'

'As sure as anyone can be.'

'But it *was* a heart attack.'

He nodded.

'How's your mother? Perhaps you should have brought her here. No she'd want to be at the hospital. Will she be there overnight or perhaps she could find a bed in a hotel. You should have stayed with her. I can manage perfectly well on my own.'

He rubbed his eyes. 'You know Mother, she wouldn't hear of it.'

'Have you eaten?'

'I'm not hungry.'

'Enid prepared some beef olives.' I sensed he was keeping something from me. 'I could heat them up, I mean cook them. They don't take long.'

'Not for me.'

I balanced on the arm of his chair. 'You are telling me the truth Leo? I'd much rather know all the facts.'

'Do stop talking Ursa I can't hear myself think.'

'Sorry.'

He closed his eyes, drawing in air through his nose then letting it out through his mouth in the heaviest sigh possible.

'Please tell me Leo. Is he dead?'

'No of course he's not dead. Although it might be better if he was.'

'How can you say that?' But perhaps he was paralysed, unable to move or speak. No, that was when you had a stroke. Only they could have made a mistake about his heart. Was a stroke connected to what happened to your heart or was it something to do with your blood?

Leo had started walking round the room and I waited as patiently as I could, knowing any more questions would make my wait even longer.

'It was around two o'clock,' he said at last.

'When it happened?'

'He should have been in his consulting rooms but he'd cancelled all his afternoon appointments.'

'Why?'

'You may well ask.' His stared at me and his voice came out in an angry growl. 'He was with a friend, a woman. He was in her bed.'

CHAPTER FOURTEEN

'Upon my word, I think the truth is the hardest missile one can be pelted with.'
(George Eliot. *Middlemarch*)

Archie had been in hospital for nearly a week but he was on the mend. Having spent several days and nights at his bedside Muriel had returned home and today Leo and I were on our way to *The Gables* and not looking forward to it very much. The circumstances in which the heart attack had taken place had come as an awful shock and Leo was so angry with his father it frightened me.

'How could he be so stupid?'

'At least it wasn't one of his patients.' I had taken the news badly myself but in my case the feeling was more one of hurt.

During the five years since I started working for Archie I had trusted him implicitly. A family man, one hundred percent reliable. I knew how attractive he was to women, myself included, but the fact that he might one day take advantage of this had never entered my head. Well only in my silly fantasies, and fantasies bore no relation to real life, not in the sense that you ever wanted them to actually come true. Or did you? My time with Mrs Moberley had changed my mind about so many things. None of us understood our true feelings, or if we did we pushed them out of our heads as quickly as possible. Mrs Moberley said Freud had written about the conflict between our instincts and the restrictions we had to put on them. For the sake of society, she said, but I think she meant because of the effect our true feelings might have on other people. If we acted on them I mean.

I thought about the day Archie and I had walked on Hampstead Heath and how kind he had been when he explained the reason for Mrs Moberley's divorce and told me how the inquest on the suicide victim had shown that in no way could she be held responsible for the young man's death. At the time I had been so grateful for the trouble he had taken to unearth the true facts, and I was still grateful, of course I was, but Archie in another woman's bed, the thought of it made me weep. Whatever happened I had believed he would never let me down. Let *me* down? What about poor Muriel? How must she be feeling? If I were brutally honest with myself, until a week ago she had been simply Archie's wife and I had been the one who was special to him. How could I have been so selfish, and so naïve?

During the past week Leo had talked to his mother on the phone every day but after each call said nothing about her state of mind, merely relayed the latest facts with regard to his father's recovery. Now we were going to see Muriel I needed to know what to expect.

'How do you think your mother has taken it?'

He gave a small shrug, keeping his eyes on the road ahead. 'Last time I spoke to her she sounded relieved he was better.'

'But it can't be the only thing she feels. Has she said anything about the other woman? Was it serious? How long had it been going on?'

'When he comes home she'll have to nurse him. After what he's done…' His jaw tightened and I realised he assumed Muriel felt the same way he did.

'She may have forgiven him.'

'Oh come on, she's only known about it for a week. Besides she won't want an invalid on her hands. Why should she… The whole business makes me furious.'

'Yes I know.' I was trying to think of something helpful to say, something that would make him plan for the future instead of endlessly going over and over what had happened. 'When he's well enough perhaps they could have a long holiday, go on a cruise.'

'Whatever for?'

'Isn't that what convalescents are supposed to do? I saw an advertisement in the paper. Orient Line Cruises on a new steamer, *"The Orontes"*, visiting Spain, Italy, and North Africa.'

'Well don't mention it to Mother.'

'Any helpful suggestions I'll leave to you.'

'Please Ursa.'

There had been no hint of sarcasm in my voice but I could hardly blame him for being touchy. 'I just meant it would be better – '

'Yes, yes all right. To tell you the truth I haven't an idea what to say to her.'

At this admission I warmed to him a little. 'I should let her do most of the talking. She'll need us to be good listeners.'

'That's what your Mrs Moberley would suggest?'

After that I kept quiet, thinking my own thoughts, but as *The Gables* came into view and a sudden shower lashed the windscreen I recalled our visit in April and tried to remember what my life had been like before I met Mrs

Moberley. At the time I was being pulled in all directions, by Leo who was adamant that only an analyst could cure my symptoms and by Muriel, in collaboration with Joyce, who saw psychoanalysis as the work of the devil. Only Archie had remained neutral, insisting it was a decision I should be allowed to make for myself. Kind, considerate Archie, although the affair could have been going on then and he had been deceiving us all these months.

'Yes you're right,' Leo said, 'leave the talking to me.'

'I always do.'

'I know but since your sessions with Mrs Moberley you've become more outspoken and I don't want Mother upset.'

'Perhaps I should have stayed at home.'

He slowed down to manoeuvre the car between the gates to *The Gables*. 'She wouldn't have liked that.'

'Are you sure? It was your idea I come, I did it for you, but she'll probably resent my presence, want to talk to you on your own. If she does, give me a sign and I'll go for a walk in Richmond Park.'

'Don't be silly.'

'I'm not being silly Leo.' We were heading for another argument. 'I'm trying to think what's best for your mother but whatever I suggest you find fault.'

'Oh you poor thing,' he mocked, 'so we all have to feel sorry for you do we, never mind that Mother's life will never be the same again.'

Pompous idiot, I thought, I've done my best and I'm not going to be made to feel guilty, and neither am I going to let you tell me what I should and shouldn't do.

Muriel was being brave. She greeted Leo warmly, enveloping him in a hug and speaking to me over his shoulder. 'I'm so glad you could come Ursula.'

For once she sounded as though she meant it and in spite of myself I was touched. 'Is there anything I can do Muriel?'

She stared at me as though I had said something incomprehensible. 'Oh you mean make some coffee. Vera will do that.'

'I thought you might want to be alone with Leo.'

'Why would I want that?' Now that she had disentangled herself from him I was shocked to see how much older she looked. The lines round her mouth had deepened and there were dark shadows under her eyes. She had never liked me much and almost from the start our dislike had been mutual. I say almost from the start because the first time she introduced me to Leo I think she must have decided I would be quite a good catch, but that had been before she knew what I was like, and before it dawned on her that "your son is your son till he finds him a wife."

And the irony was she had no need to worry. Leo was just as devoted to her now as he must have been as a small child.

'Have they told you when he'll be able to come home?' he asked.

'Possibly at the weekend.'

'As soon as that? So it could be the day after tomorrow.'

'Or Monday.' Muriel turned away and strode briskly towards the drawing room. 'Yes I think Monday's more likely.'

'What about a convalescent home.' Leo glanced at me briefly to make sure I was following but with no acknowledgement of how difficult the conversation was going to be, no signal of mutual support. 'That would be easier for you Mother.'

Muriel turned to frown at him. 'Do stop it Leo, I'm more than capable of making my own decisions.'

The sofas and chairs, that usually made a wide semi-circle in front of the fireplace, had been pushed closer together and I hesitated, willing Leo to choose the seat that meant he would be between the two of us, but the armchair I had been avoiding was where Muriel wanted me to be.

'Sit down Ursula.' If she was not dressed in widow's weeds her outfit, plain brown skirt, cream blouse, and a jacket that could have belonged to her mother, was the nearest thing to it she could find. 'I'm glad your arm is so much better. I must say I admire you for persevering with your Mrs Moberley.'

'She's going away on holiday.'

Really? One never thinks about that kind of person taking a holiday.'

'For two weeks.'

'Oh is that all. Well as long as it doesn't set you back. If all goes well I imagine you'll be able to finish the treatment by the autumn. As I said, I admire your tenacity.'

She means well, I thought, but why does she have to speak like a nurse whose patient has agreed to swallow some nasty medicine. And surely she realises two weeks feels like an eternity.

The room was stuffy and smelled of turpentine. Some concoction Vera had used to remove a stain on the carpet or loose covers? Thinking about stains produced an unwelcome image in my mind: Archie chair-bound and incontinent, smelling of old people like the time

Mother and I had visited a neighbour who had fallen and broken her hip and been admitted to a nursing home. No, that was ridiculous. Archie was not yet sixty and would soon be back to his old self, although he would have to lead a quieter life.

Normally Muriel was particularly keen on fresh air but today the windows were firmly closed and the whole house had the air of a place where someone had died. That must be how it felt to Muriel, I thought, but as it turned out I was wrong.

We sat in our tight semi-circle for what seemed like several minutes without anyone speaking or moving apart from Leo who kept locking and unlocking his fingers. For myself I felt quite relaxed, relieved perhaps that the focus was no longer on my arm, that my problems had been eclipsed by Archie's illness, and his betrayal. Besides, there was no need to search for the right words because Muriel's expression was making it clear she wanted to be the one to start the conversation.

When she did speak it was to tell us she had needed to collect her thoughts, and her next words were addressed to me.

'All this must have come as a shock to you Ursula. You were fond of Archie.'

'Yes I was. I mean I am.'

'There's something I have to tell you both, something I should have told you before.'

Leo jumped up from his chair. 'His heart's worse than they thought? He's likely to have another attack. What did the doctors say?'

'Sit down Leo. No nothing like that. I realise how upset you must be about the circumstances in which the heart attack occurred but for my part the situation came as less of a shock. It was not the first time he'd strayed.'

Leo sat down heavily. 'How do you mean?' But it was not a real question, simply a way of allowing him time to take in this new kick in the teeth.

'We've been together almost thirty years.' Muriel had the steady tone of someone who prides herself on her self-control. 'And apart from the first four or five I suspect this kind of thing has been going on for most of our married life.'

'You suspect?' Leo's voice was high-pitched with indignation. 'Do you have evidence? Has he admitted it? Why have you never said anything before?'

'I have no wish to go into details Leo.' She picked up a small brass bell. 'I'll ask Vera to bring some coffee or would you both prefer a cold drink?'

'No not yet.' Leo snatched the bell from her hand. 'Why didn't you tell me? How could you let me – '

'Don't Leo.' I tried to stop him but he brushed my words aside.

'Most of your married life? What's that supposed to mean?'

'It means exactly that Leo. Men are not the same as women are they Ursula.'

How could she speak so calmly? Frequently her ability to hide her feelings had made me want to scream but on this occasion I admired her for telling us the truth, admired her and knew she needed to tell us and that having me there was making it a little easier than confessing it to Leo when the two of them were alone.

She noticed my expression and laid a hand on mine. 'It's all right Ursula, Leo has a right to be upset. I didn't tell you Leo because you were only a child.'

'It's been going on as long as that? Are you sure?

Why did you stay with him?'

'These things happen. I'm not the only woman who's had to turn a blind eye to her husband's little flings. I suppose you get used to it and I've never had the slightest doubt we would stay together, mainly because he needs to maintain his reputation for the sake of his work.'

She yawned and I thought about the long hours she must have spent lying awake, thinking over what had happened and what she was going to say to Leo, and how he was going to take it, and how he would behave towards his father now he knew the unpalatable truth.

'Little flings, little flings,' he kept repeating, 'is that what you call them?'

'As far as I could tell none of his associations lasted very long. Now, if you pass me the bell I'll ask Vera to bring us some coffee.'

Leo closed his eyes and took several deep breaths. There was so much he wanted to say but Muriel's tone of voice had made it clear the subject was not up for discussion. She had told us the facts and did not wish them to be referred to again, ever.

I thought about Archie's "associations" and how the word made what he had done sound sordid and grubby. Then I wondered how old the women had been. Younger than Muriel no doubt. As young as me? And how his victims had felt when Archie tired of them and the affairs came to an end. Somehow the fact that none of them had lasted very long made it worse. Archie's playthings, a way of flattering his vanity, or when it came down to it was that what all men would like if they knew they could get away with it? Leo was unlike his father in so many ways but he was still a man, and one who was being denied his marital rights.

Push the thought away. Think about Muriel. And Archie. I knew how his "little flings" would have come about. He was so charming, so attentive, to his patients, and his staff, and to countless others by the sound of it. I had fallen for his charms and believed he was terribly fond of me, and perhaps he was, or perhaps he would have given the same care and attention to whoever had worked for him and later married his son. I thought about his present secretary and how he had joked that since she was retiring quite soon I might like my old job back, and all the time he had been lying to me, if only by omission, and making excuses to Muriel to explain why he was late home, and spending the stolen hours in another woman's bed.

The morning had been arduous but I had no intention of resting on my bed as Leo had advised. I felt light-headed, almost elated, and when Leo decided to call in at the school and collect some books he needed I decided to have another talk with Enid.

'How's poor Dr Ingham?' She had climbed on a chair to reach something off a high shelf that turned out to be a gravy boat.

'Be careful Enid,' I warned. 'He's better, much better. In fact he'll probably be able to go home either at the weekend or early next week.'

'Well that's good news.'

'Yes it is.'

'Liver and bacon pie for your supper. You'll need to put it in the oven for three-quarters of an hour then add a few more slices of potato and let it brown for seven or eight minutes. Mr Ingham likes liver and bacon.'

'Three-quarters of an hour.'

'Then add some more potato.'

'Yes, yes, I heard.'

She stared at me then looked away, collecting plates from the draining board and piling them in the cupboard. 'I got that stain off the bath. Poured a little paraffin on a cloth then washed it away with soapy water.'

'It's you I want to talk about Enid, not the bath, and this time I'm not going to let you put me off.'

At once her expression became sulky. 'You've quite enough on your mind without worrying about me Mrs Ingham.'

'If your mother knew I wouldn't feel quite so concerned. Think how upset she'll be when she discovers you've kept it from her. And annoyed with me too I wouldn't wonder.'

'I won't tell her you found out.'

'I didn't find out Enid, I guessed because of the way you looked when my sister was talking about the curate's wife. And you must have wanted me to know or you would have denied it. No I'm sorry, that wasn't fair.'

'Mum's got enough on her plate.' Her eyes moved from side to side as though she were reading an invisible book. 'Oh yes, I remember. Miss Walsh telephoned earlier, about eleven I think it were, she's coming here at five.'

'Midge? Why didn't you tell me before?'

She gave me a look as if to say, "If you'd given me a chance I would have".

'No don't look like that Enid, I know you think I'm interfering but it's only because I'm so fond of you.'

In an instant the sulkiness left her face and she put up both hands to stem her tears. 'There's things I haven't told you Mrs Ingham.'

'What kind of things? Something to do with Jim? Have you heard from him? Have you had some more news? Please tell me Enid, I do so want to help.'

But it was no good, she was buttoning up her cardigan and for today at least there was no way I was going to get any more out of her.

Midge arrived with a mission. She had been giving it a great deal of thought, she said, and wanted to toss out a few ideas with regard to how the house could be modernised, or "brightened up" as she called it.

'It's a lovely house but it could be even more delightful.' She had brought colour charts that she insisted on showing to Leo. 'Scarlet is stimulating but might be too much in such a small room. What about orange?'

Midge herself was wearing a rather sober outfit, a beige dress with brown pockets and brown piping round the neck. Her hat, which she had tossed onto the sofa, was cream coloured with a brown band and lay in such a position that Solomon might see it as a comfortable nest except he was probably too large to squeeze in.

Leo was smiling to himself. He had no intention of taking Midge up on any of her ideas but it was a welcome change from thinking about his father and he was prepared to humour her. 'I like wallpaper myself,' he said.

'Yes why not?' Midge enthused. 'A recurring motif of birds perching on boughs, or pheasants, yes what about pheasants? English taste in wallpaper is so traditional. The French are much bolder.'

'What about our sofa and chairs,' Leo teased, 'I imagine chintz is old hat.'

'Something more dramatic would do wonders.' She stood back, narrowing her eyes as if to visualise a room transformed. 'Jade curtains would go well with the wallpaper, and to make the lighting more intimate you need wall brackets with those ground glass panels that conceal the bulbs.' She turned to me. 'You loved the oriental stuff we saw didn't you Ursula, especially the lacquered furniture.'

'And who's going to pay for all this.' I glanced at Leo, and seeing how exhausted he looked, knew he would soon start to tire of the game. We should have explained as soon as Midge arrived. Now it was going to embarrass her. 'I have to tell you Midge.' I rested a hand on her arm. 'Leo's father is in hospital.'

'Archie?' She froze.

'He had a heart attack last week, not a bad one and he's much better, he's going to be all right.'

'Oh no!' She snatched a cigarette from her enamelled case. 'You should have said. Here's me boring you to death with my schemes and all the time… I'm so sorry. If I'd known I'd never have come round. Enid should have warned me. Why didn't she? How stupid maids can be, not wanting to cause offence when it would be so much better – '

'No need to apologise.' Leo picked up one of the colour charts. 'Correct me if I'm wrong but I believe I once saw a picture of varnished newspapers used as a substitute for wallpaper. Sounds hideous but it was quite effective in an odd sort of way. You design wallpaper do you, and curtain material?'

'That's what I'd like to do but at present it's simply

my job to select other people's designs. Look, I'd better go.'

'No please don't.' Leo was surprising me with the comfortable way he was talking to her. The news of his father infidelities had appalled him but at the same time there must have been something slightly gratifying about it. The perfect father he had never been able to live up to, the great skin specialist, admired by patients and friends alike, who had turned out to have feet of clay.

Midge had started on the subject of bathrooms. 'Silver paper provides a stunning effect and it's very hard wearing although knowing you Leo you'd like everything in the house to be white. White means "intellectual".

'What about black?'

'Too dark and depressing for a house like this. You want to bring in as much light as possible. There used to be a craze for versions of William Morris wallpapers but that's a bit passé now. I know what you'd like Ursula, a floral design, poppies and marigolds on a black background.'

I gave a faint smile. 'If you say so.'

'No I'm not inventing it. You remember that paper we saw at the exhibition.'

After our day out together I thought we had become close, special to each other, yet here she was talking in an awful superficial voice about things in which I had little interest. Because Leo was there I suppose, or did she regret the confidences we had shared and had come round to make it clear none of it was to be mentioned again.

I wanted to talk to her properly, tell her about Mrs

Moberley, but there would be no opportunity for that. She and Leo would carry on re-designing the house and then she would leave.

'Are you still staying with your aunt and uncle?' I asked.

She hesitated. 'Yes but I'm looking for an apartment, a studio flat in Chelsea if I can find one. If I can afford one! With my kind of work it's absolutely essential I'm in the throng of things.'

'Yes I'm sure.' Archie was in hospital. Mrs Moberley had gone away on holiday and all Midge wanted to talk about was interior decor. When I looked at her it was as though our conversation at the restaurant had never taken place. Was she really speaking in that bright and breezy way because Leo was there or was it because she was desperately unhappy and the only way she could keep going was to rush madly about making plans for her future?

I've fallen in love with Mrs Moberly, I wanted to tell her. Do you hear me Midge, I love her and it's the most terrifying thing that's ever happened to me but also the most wonderful.

Midge was the one person who would understand.

As I watched she held a small swathe of pale blue silk up to the window so that Leo could get the full effect and I thought, you're throwing yourself into your work, trying to escape from the misery of being separated from Solange. You have no wish to listen to my problems.

If I had lost Midge as a confidante how was I going to manage when my treatment came to an end? There would be nobody to talk to, I would be alone. Even Enid had made it clear she preferred not to discuss what was happening to her. But not for long, I thought. Reading between the lines I suspected she had been expecting for at least five months, possibly a little more. That meant the baby would arrive at Christmas.

Today was the first of September. If she had not told her mother by the end of the month I would have to go round to the house and tell her myself. Enid would be annoyed with me, might even give in her notice, but there were more important things to worry about than that, her health and the baby's health too. I had no idea when you were supposed to see the doctor, or how often. Muriel would know but now would be a bad time to ask her, quite apart from the fact that Leo and I had decided to keep Enid's condition to ourselves for the time being.

Midge and Leo had gone upstairs to inspect the bathroom and make plans to cover it in silver paper. It sounded like a cheap option but no doubt it was extremely expensive, far more than we could afford. Perhaps Leo found her alluring, and certainly more fun than I was, although that would not be too difficult.

Solomon was mewing and I wondered if Enid had remembered to give him his supper. 'Come on.' I lifted him up with both hands and held him close. 'You weigh a ton but I can manage you now, only don't turn your head round and bite me or I'll drop you like a hot brick.'

He wriggled to get down and ran towards the kitchen ahead of me. What was it Enid had said I had to do with the liver and bacon pie? Put it in the oven for three quarters of an hour then add more potatoes and let them brown. For how long? I had completely forgotten so I would have to guess then keep an eye on them. Possibly Midge would like some, although on second thoughts that might not be such a good idea.

She and Leo were standing on the landing, talking animatedly. At least she was having a good effect on him but later, after she had gone, he would return to the subject of Archie and I would have to set aside any feelings I might have and devote the rest of the evening to talking him into a more forgiving frame of mind.

Leo was asleep. I listened to his barely audible breathing and in the half-light watched his chest move up and down. I was restless, wanted to feel his warmth but if I invited him into my bed he would jump at it, almost literally, and it would be like before and he would be offended, then incensed all over again. Or else I would do something I had vowed never to do, pretend everything was all right and afterwards hate him for it, and hate myself too.

Since reading Dr Stopes' book I had been forced to accept how incredibly uninformed I had been. *To render a woman ready not only saves her from pain but is of value to the man who gains an immense increase of sensation from the mutuality thus attained.* Leo should have known. But how could he? Muriel would hardly have been likely to talk to him about such matters, and neither, I thought, would Archie, not to his own son. Still, if he knew all about it he could have lent him the book.

According to Mrs Moberley it had been published ten years ago and was an immediate success, selling two thousand copies within the first fortnight and by the end of the year it had been reprinted six times. Why had I never heard of it? Had Joyce read it and if so why had she had never mentioned it but I supposed it was one of those books you read but never talked about.

A girl generally lacks the basic facts and the bridegroom may shock her and then be bewildered by her inarticulate pain. Inarticulate pain. The phrase had stuck in my mind because it described my feelings so well. If only Leo had agreed to read it instead of simply dismissing it as "filth" but what good would it have done? I was terribly fond of him. In my own way I loved him dearly, but not in the right way. How could it be?

CHAPTER FIFTEEN

*'I do not think I am exaggerating when
I assert that the great majority of severe
neuroses in women have their origin in
the marriage bed.'*

(Josef Breuer)

The days had dragged by almost unendurably but at last I was back on the couch, bursting with things to say, but oddly reluctant to begin, like a child who has been separated from its mother and now they are reunited sulks, wanting to punish her for abandoning it. Surely I was not that silly.

The trouble with the "talking treatment" it made you so horribly aware of how you felt. My mother had always accused me of being thin-skinned. Now it was as though the last protective layer had been peeled away, leaving me exposed to every attack, however slight or unintended, Leo's comment about the scones I had baked – *they're better than the last ones* – and Enid's refusal to look me in the eye – *going to give the carpets a good going over today Mrs Ingham.*

When Mrs Moberley let me into the house she had looked different. Perhaps it was her lightly tanned skin, or the pale blue blouse that matched the colour of her eyes, or perhaps it was just that I had been so overjoyed to see her.

I inquired after her holiday and she told me it had been very agreeable and asked how I had been.

'Better,' I told her, 'My arm I mean.'

'Good.' She ought to be able to tell from my expression that in other ways I had not been better at all, but her face gave nothing away, I was one of her patients and she was carrying out the usual pleasantries.

I suppose part of me had expected her to be as happy to see me as I was to see her. After my last visit, when I had admitted my feelings for her, I had hoped we would greet each other like old friends. I was wrong, nothing had changed, and as soon as we entered the consulting room she had made it clear that any discussion of her holiday, anything in the way of an ordinary conversation, was still forbidden.

For several more minutes I was silent. Out of the corner of my eye I saw her cross then uncross her legs. Was I her first patient since her holiday or had there been another one in the morning and had he or she felt the same way I did, with so many things to talk about it was difficult to know where to start.

'Something happened while you were away.' I closed my eyes, blocking out the room, and struggled to come to terms with my disappointment that was quickly followed by resentment and a wish to keep her on tenterhooks. 'Something bad.'

'That's frequently the case.'

'No I don't mean in my head, I mean something real.'

I waited for her to say that what went on in my head was real. Instead she asked if I wanted to tell her about it.

'Archie had a heart attack.'

'I am sorry.'

'No it's all right.' She had actually sounded as if she

meant it.' He didn't die, in fact he should make a full recovery, but there was more to it than that.' I paused, once again trying to raise her expectations although she would see through my game, she always did. 'When he had the attack he was in another woman's bed.'

'Oh dear.'

'Yes it was rather.' I wanted to giggle.

'It must have been upsetting for you Ursula.'

'And for Leo, and especially for his mother. Leo was dreadfully angry with his father and anything I said only seemed to make it worse. We went to visit Muriel while Archie was still in hospital. I thought it might be best if I stayed at home and Leo visited her on his own but he insisted I accompany him. Obviously we'd been to the hospital together but that was different, we were all too worried about Archie's health to think what it would be like if he recovered.'

'How is Muriel?'

'She looks awful but I expect she'll soon be her old self. Sorry, that was a stupid thing to say.' Without realising it I had folded both my arms across my chest. Apart from a slight weakness, that was almost certainly the result of lack of use, my right arm was almost as good as new. Mrs Moberley deserved to know about it but so far I had held back from telling her for fear she said there was no need for me to come and see her again. Or even that her going away seemed to have done me good. No, no more games. Later I would tell her but first I had to finish talking about Archie and Muriel.

'When we reached the house Muriel had arranged the sofa and armchairs so they were closer together than usual and the funny thing was she wanted me to sit in the middle between her and Leo. I've no idea why.'

'Perhaps she wanted you to feel included.'

'Or she may have been afraid of Leo's anger. Anyway after a long pause she announced she had something to tell us, and Leo jumped up, assuming his father must have had another heart attack but Muriel said no, it was nothing to do with his illness. Then she told us it had happened before, the other women. In fact she was fairly certain it had been going on through most of their married life.'

'How did you feel about that?'

'Sorry for her, and for Leo.' I wriggled my back into a more comfortable position and listened for sounds in the street, normal people going about their daily business, but there were none. 'No wonder she's so bitter.'

'What about you?'

'Me?'

'You're very fond of Archie.'

I reached for my handbag. 'I brought your book back. Leo won't read it.'

'Then why not keep it a little longer.'

'There's not much point. He's arranged to attend a series of lectures about John Watson and the Behaviourists. Wednesday evenings at the university. That's the way his mind works now. Humans should be like animals. Animals don't need to read books to tell them how to make love.'

She made no comment and after a moment's hesitation I took the book from my bag and held it against my stomach. How childish I was being, throwing out remarks in a glib, superficial voice and by now I must have wasted nearly half of my fifty minutes.

'My arm is almost back to normal,' I said.

'Do you know why?'

'I thought you'd be pleased.'

'Of course I'm pleased.'

'But it means I'll have to stop seeing you and there are still so many things I haven't talked about. If the book's right why hasn't everyone read it? I suppose most women don't mind as much as I do. I'm too fussy, I expect too much.'

'Is that what you really think Ursula?'

'No. No, it's not.'

In the night I had woken with the covers half off and a cold draught on my neck. Now it felt stiff and aching and I decided to sit up with my back propped against the wall. Since my day out with Midge I had taken more notice of the consulting room and its furnishings and I found myself wondering if she had bought everything herself or had some of it had been chosen by her husband. No, that made no sense since according to Archie she was one who had left and found another house for herself and her son. Suddenly, none of it mattered and all I cared about was the two of us sitting in the room together – and with only twenty minutes until I had to leave.

When I told her about my visit to the exhibition I had mentioned the exotic prints and the inlaid screen that had reminded me of the one that was only inches from where I was sitting. I longed to see the rest of the house, the kitchen, the drawing room, her bedroom. And I wanted to ask her about her two sons, the one who had accompanied her on holiday and his brother whose brain had been permanently damaged at birth.

How bad was he? Did he live nearby? Did she visit him every week? And when he saw her did he know who she was?

Not that I would ever ask because if I did she would say we were there to talk about me, not her. Besides it would be unfair, a way of satisfying my curiosity but causing her pain. Sometimes I indulged myself in a daydream about the pair of us on holiday together. My arm was completely cured so it was all right for us to be friends, and we talked about my analysis and I told her how grateful I was and in return she told me about her own life and how she had decided to train as a psychoanalyst.

Naturally the fantasy would never come true.

'I had a peculiar dream last night,' I said, 'about a train that had come off the tracks and was heading for a forest. When I woke up I tried to write it down but it made no sense and all I could think was that I rather like trains.'

'What is it you like about them particularly?'

'The noise, and the steam, and the fact that you're going on a journey, often to somewhere nice like the seaside, and you don't have to worry because someone else is in charge. You can just sit back and look through the window at the passing countryside.'

'I like trains too.'

'Do you?' Her response emboldened me. 'You never tell me anything about yourself. It's all so one-sided. Yes I know it's meant to be like that but it makes me feel self-centred, and useless. And even if my arm's better I'm not. Actually in some ways it was better when my arm didn't work and…' I broke off, uncertain what I wanted to say. 'Anyway it's not Leo's fault about the book. Even if he read it things wouldn't be any better between us.'

'What things are you referring to?'

'You know perfectly well what I mean.' I wanted her to see my scowling face. I wanted us to sit opposite one another, like the first time when I came for my assessment. 'It was no good on our honeymoon or any of the other times we tried and I can see now it was because neither of us knew what to do. I was upset because… and he was upset when I rejected him. If we'd talked about it… but what would we have said? And now I know more about it, and understand why it all went wrong… I'm very fond of him, I love him, but I don't want him in my bed so it's all too late.'

I was crying and normally when someone cries the other person offers some comfort. Not Mrs Moberley. I expect she thought it was good for me, cathartic. I had no recollection of any of Freud's patients crying but that was probably because they were too afraid of him. Before I came to see her I hardly ever cried, in fact it was difficult to remember a time, not since I was a child. If something upset me I sulked or got angry. Crying was too frightening: once you started you might never stop.

I blew my nose noisily. 'I thought it was no good between me and Leo because I was in love with Archie but long before he was ill and we found out about the other women I realised it wasn't Archie I loved. Is my arm better because I've stopped denying what I am?'

'And what is that Ursula?'

'I know you explained it was only part of the treatment but – '

'I don't think I said quite that but I do want to talk to you about coming to see me.'

'You mean you're going to say I can't come anymore?'

'No.' She stood up and walked towards me. 'Are you in pain?'

'Only my neck. I must have slept in a draught.'

'A cushion might help.' She handed me one, dark blue with gold braid round the edge, then returned to her chair. 'As you know a full analysis can last several years but I think we both agreed that was not what you wanted, or needed.'

'Yes I know I said that but at the time I didn't understand.'

'Tell me what you think of this. I suggest we continue for at least two more months but work towards a time when you feel ready to stop. Having read some of Freud's work you'll be aware that an arm like yours is frequently an indication of an earlier trauma, but in your case I think we've established that's not very likely.'

'You mean it's not because of something in the past, it's because I should never have married and if I'd understood myself better I never would have.'

'Is that what you truly believe?'

'I'm like Midge aren't I, we're two of a kind. When Leo tries to come into my bed all I feel is fear and revulsion. Isn't that terrible? Poor Leo, it's not his fault.'

'Why not stop worrying about these feelings you have and allow yourself a little time to sort out your confusion.'

'But how can I?'

'With my help I think perhaps you'll find you can.'

I tried to breathe more slowly, to calm myself. 'Midge says unmarried women are despised.'

'A little extreme I would have thought although

she's right that there's a long way to go before we have any hope of being treated on an equal footing with men.'

'But how could we be if we're the ones who have the babies. Joyce thinks the answer to everything is having a baby but it's different for her, all those people in the parish to help with the children. Helen's lovely, I wouldn't mind a little girl like that but she might turn out like me and drive everyone mad.'

She stood up and I saw that she was smiling. 'We have plenty of time to talk about these things but not today. No let me pick up your bag and you look after your poor neck.'

Joyce had turned up at the house with all three children. When I looked through the kitchen window I could see her in the garden and felt a twinge of fear in case something else had happened and she had been given the task of breaking the news, but a moment later Enid and Sybil appeared from behind the laburnum tree and everyone burst out laughing.

'Oh there you are,' Joyce called as I came through the back door and started across the lawn. 'We thought you'd got lost.'

'I see Mrs Moberley on Mondays.'

'Yes from two o'clock to three. It's almost a quarter to four.'

'I needed a few things from the shops. You should have said you were coming.' I still felt a little wary about the way she had turned up without warning. 'Is everything all right Joyce?'

She sniffed, searching in her battered handbag for a handkerchief. 'Yes of course, why wouldn't it be?'

Enid had disappeared back into the house and Helen and Sybil were standing together, stroking Solomon, their game spoiled by my appearance.

'I telephoned Muriel,' Joyce said, 'to see how Archie was coming along.'

'He's been home a week.'

'So I discovered. Why didn't you tell me, I was worried? For all I knew – '

'I'd have let you know if he'd taken a turn for the worse.' I turned to Helen and Sybil. 'What were you two playing?'

'Sardines.' Sybil hopped up and down, losing her balance and rolling on the grass. 'One person hides and the others have to look for them. Then if you find the one that's hidden – '

'Ursula knows how to play sardines,' Joyce interrupted, pulling down Sybil's baggy hand-knitted jumper. 'I tell you what, we'll all go inside and perhaps Enid will give you some of the currant bread she was talking about.'

As we trooped indoors Sybil began telling me how two people had drowned in a pond.

I looked at Joyce but she shook her head. 'No, nobody we know. For heaven's sake Sybil, Auntie Ursula doesn't want to hear all your stories. She's been practising her reading and of course she has to seek out the most lurid items in the newspaper.

'A passer-by saw a mackintosh coat on the bank,' Helen explained, 'the drowned man was married to someone else and had four children. I expect that's why they killed themselves.'

'And the keeper at the Eddystone Lighthouse drowned too,' Sybil announced.

'No not the keeper,' Helen corrected, 'only his assistant. He was going up a ladder and he slipped and fell into the sea. You ought to read it more carefully Sybil. It said on your school report you were inclined to make careless mistakes.'

Sybil screwed up her nose. 'Grouse shooting starts today, they had a picture. Why do people like killing birds?'

'It's beyond me,' I told her, 'but I can tell you're very good at reading Sybil.'

'Yes I am. *Eureka weed killer cleans paths and renovates lawns.*'

Even Joyce had to laugh at this and we were still laughing when we reached the kitchen and found Enid buttering slices of bread.

'Would you like your tea in the drawing room Mrs Ingham?'

'No thank you Enid, we'll have it in here.'

Joyce cleared her throat. 'Can I ask you a small favour Enid, only for fifteen minutes?'

'Yes of course Mrs Bryant.' Enid was in her element. She put down the knife and Joyce passed her a scarlet-faced Christopher who was struggling to get down onto the floor. 'Would you mind terribly if they all stayed in here with you? There's something Mrs Ingham and I need to discuss.'

'Course they can Mrs Bryant.'

'Thank you so much.' Joyce was being uncharacteristically polite. 'Christopher has learned how to crawl but so far he can only go backwards.'

'Don't you worry, the floor was mopped this morning and we'll all keep an eye on him. I tell you what, I'll close the door so he can't escape.'

When we reached the other room Joyce sat down heavily, adjusted the navy blue skirt that had ridden up above her knees and gave another loud sniff that could have meant she was going to reprimand me for something, or could equally well have meant she was not sure how to begin.

'Currant bread,' she said with a laugh, 'she's too good to be true, your Enid, like old Mrs Rabbit. Where's Leo?'

'Visiting a friend.'

'I thought during the school holidays the two of you might spend some time together, have a few outings in the car.'

'I expect we will.' Was this why she had come? To lecture me about my marriage, ask if I was doing more of the cooking and shopping? When Leo returned home I was going to claim the beef casserole as my own, only perhaps not. He would be glad I had made the effort but might take it as a sign that my treatment must be nearing its end, and on my way home from Inverness Gardens I had decided I was going to tell him Mrs Moberley was pleased with my progress but adamant that I must continue seeing her for at least another eight weeks, to be on the safe side.

Joyce was staring at her feet. She opened her mouth then closed it again, and it was so unlike her to be lost for words that I felt a pang of fear. A moment later she caught at the hair that had escaped from her bun then gave a sigh that I was sure had nothing to do with Archie. 'The reason I'm here Ursula, there's something I've been meaning to tell you for a long time. I put it off because I wasn't at all sure it was the right thing to do.'

She looked up expecting an impatient interruption

from me but I had learned the value of silence.

'Of course now your arm has more or less recovered I realise...' She broke off, leaving me to guess how she had been going to finish the sentence.

'What do you realise?'

She pulled at a thread in her skirt. 'You've always believed it was the result of a childhood trauma.'

'Only because Leo said so, backed up by Freud.'

'Yes well be that as it may what I have to tell you may come as something of a shock. A long time ago, before you were born, we had a brother.'

'I don't understand.'

'He lived for two days.'

'Two days,' I repeated stupidly, 'why didn't anyone tell me?'

'As I said it was before you were born. I was only four so obviously I can't remember much apart from the fact that Mother was so distraught she took to her bed and a distant relative had to come and look after me. Anyway the reason I decided I ought to tell you, it occurred to me you may unwittingly have picked up a stray crumb of conversation which you afterwards forgot but not before it had been buried deep in your mind.'

Buried in my mind? It was not the kind of expression I expected from Joyce, but then everything about the conversation was unlike her.

'I wish they'd told me,' I said. 'Why didn't they? Did you see him?'

She shook her head. 'He was born too early. Nobody explained what had happened but I imagine his lungs had not had a chance to develop properly, something like that.'

'A boy,' I said, 'a son. What a disappointment I must have been. Mother would have wanted another boy to replace the one she lost and had to make do with a second daughter.'

'Stuff and nonsense, you were the apple of her eye. I would have told you before and now your arm's recovered it seems a little unnecessary but having made the decision I thought I'd better get it off my chest, and Sidney agreed. We discussed it yesterday and he said I should strike while the iron was hot.'

'Did he have a name?'

'John. They called him John. I believe it's required by law that a child be given a name. For the death certificate.'

'After Father. So if I was the apple of her eye why was I sent away to school when I was only nine? Think of it Joyce, the same age as Helen. You'd never send her away would you?'

'I might if we had the cash.'

'No you wouldn't. Was it because Mother was so unhappy?'

'No it was to protect you from Father.'

'How do you mean?' I felt cold and faintly sick. Freud's words jumped into my head. *A little girl looks on her mother as a person who interferes with her affectionate relation to her father and occupies a position which she herself could very well fill.* The words had stuck in my mind because at the time I read them the notion had seemed so improbable.

'He drank,' Joyce said

'Oh is that all?'

'It made him nasty.'

'To me, I mean to us?'

She shook her head. 'Mother got the worst of it.'

'But after he died she wouldn't have a word said against him.'

'No, well people are like that aren't they. They say bereavement is harder to bear if you only have unhappy memories of the dead person.'

'I used to pray I could do something to make her happy.'

'Same here.'

'Did you?' Why had she never talked to me like this before? In the past she had always claimed she remembered very little about our childhood and in any case there was no point in dwelling on the past. 'Joyce, I must ask you, have you read *Married Love* by Dr Marie Stopes.'

'The Stopes book,' she snorted, 'certainly not. I've heard she recommends women use a rubber cap, preferably in combination with a soluble quinine pessary. Sounds impractical and faintly disgusting although I suppose there's some sense in it if you feel your family's complete.'

'There's nothing like that in 'Married Love' but Mrs Moberley says she opened a clinic a few years ago, for birth control.'

Joyce yawned without bothering to put her hand over her mouth. 'She gave you the book did she?'

'Only lent it.'

I expected her to say "whatever for" but even Joyce knew that was likely to open a can of worms.

'Anyway.' She gave another yawn. 'I'm glad I've told you about the baby. It was wrong to keep it from you but you know what Mother was like.' And to my astonishment her voice cracked and a tear slid down her face.

'What is it? Because of our brother?'

'You're not the only one with feelings.'

'No of course not. I'm so sorry Joyce and I'm sure I'd feel exactly the same, if I could remember when he was born I mean.'

She looked me up and down as if to assess my current condition. 'I suppose it's possible Mother's grief over the loss of her son might have affected you. But why now?'

'I don't think it was that Joyce.'

'No?' Her hands were shaking and she clasped them together as she struggled to get control of herself.

'Do tell me why you're crying?'

'I'm not, I've stopped.' She dabbed at her eyes then pushed her hands under her thighs. 'Things would be different if you had a child Ursula. Don't you and Leo want children?'

'Yes of course but…' I broke off, blushing.

'What? Oh that, you just have to grin and bear it, we all do. I remember the name of the book now, 'Wise Parenthood'. It upset the Church of England, and the Roman Catholics even more.'

'What does Sidney think?'

'What about? Oh you mean birth control. He approves of helping poor families who can't afford the expense of more and more children.'

'But surely all women should be allowed to decide how many they have.'

She patted me on the knee. 'Hardly a concern for you Ursula.'

'Please tell me why you were crying.'

'No reason. I'm glad we've had this little chat. I should have told you before but somehow the time never seemed quite right.' And she started to cry all over again.

I stood up and put my arm round her, something I had never done before in the whole of my life. 'Please tell me. If it's not because of our brother it must be something else. Are you ill? Is it one of the children, or Sidney?'

At every suggestion she shook her head.

'What then?'

'Oh what's the use?' Her voice came out in such a wail I feared Enid and the children would hear and come running from the kitchen. 'I criticise you for not having a family but my own life... it's so... listening to the parishioners droning on about their petty little problems, looking after the children and Sidney, plus the church flowers, or a Mother's Union meeting, or Sunday school. I'll be thirty next month and I'm condemned to this for the next thirty years, if I survive that long.'

'But there must be good parts, all those friends of yours, far more than I have.'

'Pamela?'

'Well yes, but not just Pamela.'

'You mean I should count my blessings.'

I sat down again, close to her, so close I could feel the warmth of her body. 'No I don't mean that at all Joyce. I'm so sorry, I had no idea.'

'You remember the curate's wife.'

'Beryl? Yes, how is she?'

'Bovine. People get like that when they're expecting. At first I thought she might turn out to be a bit of free spirit.'

'Yes I liked her.' I remembered our conversation in the garden and how I had thought she might be cherishing a secret ambition. 'And once she's had the baby you'll have plenty in common.'

'And Sidney's so long-suffering,' she groaned, 'I can hardly bear it.'

'Is he?'

'And most evenings are taken up with ironing or knocking up clothes for the children on my wretched sewing machine. Do you darn Leo's socks? No that would have been impossible with one hand. Lucky you, I don't suppose your workbox has seen the light of day for months.'

'But the children are lovely Joyce. Helen's such good company and so intelligent, and Sybil is too, and Christopher's sweet.'

'It's easy for you to say that.' She turned to look at me and her eyes that had been so full of pain showed a flash of anger. 'Since your arm became defunct everyone's rallied round offering help and consolation.'

'Yes I know I've been terribly selfish.'

'I didn't mean that Ursula.'

'Well I did. I'm so sorry Joyce, I had no idea, I thought you were happy.'

'You remember the party.'

'In your garden?' Her hands were red and shiny and I wondered in that silly irrelevant way that sometimes comes to you at such times if they would benefit from Enid's patent remedy.

'And how Sidney turned up late,' she said in the kind of voice that implies the person being addressed is not listening with their full concentration.

'He had to take a funeral.'

'It wasn't just that. The previous night we'd had a terrible argument about the way vicar's wives are supposed to work themselves into the ground, carrying out endless unpaid duties. Sidney said it was a privilege. A privilege! I hit him Ursula, I actually hit him. You must have noticed the mark on his lip.'

'He told us he'd fallen off his bicycle on a cobbled street.'

'Did he?' Her body slumped like a sack of potatoes. 'Well what else could he say, how else could he explain it away? My wife's a husband-beater. If only we could have a proper quarrel, clear the air, but not Sidney, he's far too rational.'

'Leo's the same, at least he used to be. Now he gets so angry it frightens me but I still prefer it that way, only I do know what you mean. You've no idea how many times I've felt like hitting him.'

'But you didn't Ursula, that's the difference between us.'

'No I just felt sorry for myself.'

She managed a feeble smile. 'Is that the choice?'

Sounds were coming from the kitchen, Christopher had started to cry and Enid was singing loudly in an effort to keep him quiet. Any moment now and one of the girl's heads would come round the door demanding that we join them.

'We must meet up more often Joyce. Promise you will.'

She nodded. 'When I have the time.'

'Make time.'

'Yes.'

'I'm so glad you told me.'

'About our brother?'

'And the rest, and I do understand Joyce, I really do.'

Sybil had appeared with sticky crumbs all round her mouth. 'Is it time to go home Mummy?'

'Quite soon Sybil,' I told her.

'No now!'

I expected Joyce to reprimand her for shouting but she was too done in.

'Wait in the kitchen Sybil,' I said firmly, 'and we'll join you in a couple of minutes.

She hesitated, wanting her own way but sensing that it might not be a good idea to make a fuss. 'All right but promise you won't be long.'

'I promise.'

She closed the door behind her and I turned to Joyce who was powdering her face in an effort to make herself look more presentable. Next time we met she would act as though the conversation had never taken place, but both of us would know it had and however much we kept up appearances it would have brought us closer, we would be like proper sisters.

CHAPTER SIXTEEN

"The most striking kind of slips of the tongue are those in which one says the precise opposite of what one intended to say."

(Freud)

I was reading the Births, Marriages and Deaths in *The Times* but as always with a faint sense of foreboding. The births were the worst. You could be merrily counting how many girls, how many boys, when you were brought up with a jolt by a heartbreaking announcement. *A daughter who only survived a few hours.*

Now that Joyce had told me about our brother it added a new piquancy to such tragedies. Had my parents put his death in the newspaper? How could they bear to write the words, but people must do it in order to avoid upsetting inquiries from relatives and friends.

At night, in bed, I speculated endlessly. What would he have looked like if he had lived? What would he be doing now? Would my mother have been happier if one of her children had been a boy? After my father died was her grief compounded by the recollection of a previous loss? John had never had a life, and now Enid was going to bring a new life into the world and Leo and I were the only ones who knew about it, apart from Jim.

In half an hour's time we were leaving for

Richmond. Archie had been home for two days and Muriel had decided he was sufficiently rested to receive visitors. The way she had spoken on the telephone had made it sound as if he were holding court whereas in truth he must be dreading our visit and would probably have preferred to put it off for as long as possible, or to get it over and done with I suppose. It was going to be heavy going.

Still, with any luck Leo would be too afraid of causing a relapse to confront his father with what he thought of him. As for myself I planned to be friendly and sympathetic but refuse to act as though nothing had altered between us. A month ago I would have been devastated by the thought of Archie in bed with another woman. Now I was far too preoccupied with my feelings for Mrs Moberley.

Leo joined me in the bedroom where I was changing my dress for something more suitable for the occasion, at least something that Muriel would find more suitable. Following the first of his Wednesday evening lectures he had immersed himself even more enthusiastically in the writings of the American psychologists, making notes about their theories and experiments in a loose leaf file he had bought especially for the purpose, and asking my opinion of some of the salient points even though he must have known what kind of a response he was likely to receive.

If he wanted some lighter entertainment he sat silently reading *The Times*, something he was doing now although I had no idea why he had brought it up to the bedroom.

'Are you going to wear that jacket?' I asked. 'It's rather shabby.'

'We're not attending a wedding.' He folded the newspaper and dropped it on a chair. 'There's a new Bernard Shaw play on at Malvern. They say it's his worst yet.'

'What's it called?'

'The Apple Cart.'

'Odd title.'

'Not really.' He took two ties from his top drawer and held them up, frowning as though he had an important decision to make. 'You've heard the expression, "don't upset the apple cart", don't ruin carefully laid plans? Imagine what it's going to be like for my father when he returns to work.'

'Perhaps his colleagues know about his affairs of the heart.'

'Is that what you call them?' He moved towards me. 'Need any help with that fastening?'

'No I'll be all right. Watch.' I put both hands behind my neck and secured the hook into its loop. 'Proof wouldn't you say I'm virtually back to normal. Leo?'

'Now what?'

'You know the lectures at the university, can anyone attend them?'

'Don't tell me you want to come too.'

'No of course not, I just wondered.' We stared at each other and I thought, why are you keeping your face so expressionless? Is there something you would prefer me not to know about, something you want to hide? Perhaps he was hoping to give up his job at the school and devote his life to the American psychologists. But how would he make a living?

'I'm glad you've found something that interests you so much,' I said.

'No you're not.'

I turned away, frowning. 'Why do you say that?'

'Sorry.' But there was no warmth in his apology. 'Actually I may have to go out next Thursday.'

'As well as Wednesday.'

'A demonstration.'

'With rats?'

'It's only a possibility. They're going to let us know if they can arrange it. It may not take place.'

It will, I thought, and for no reason I could think of my eyes filled with tears.

Downstairs Enid was washing the dining room carpet with a broom dipped in water to which she had added a handful of salt. *It revives the colours Mrs Ingham, and raises the pile.* During the last few weeks I had tried to persuade her to take more care of herself but my words seemed to have the opposite effect and since her arrival today she had been attacking her cleaning jobs like a mad thing.

'Show me your hand,' Leo said and I held it out like a naughty child.

'What for?'

'Just an article I was reading, someone who claimed you could tell from the lines how eventful a life you were likely to have.'

'Eventful in what way? Good things or bad?'

'Both I imagine.' He traced a finger down my palm. 'Oh yes, very eventful. I wonder if it includes your childhood.'

'Don't Leo.' I had told him about Joyce's visit but his only comment was that it would have been better if she had kept quiet about my dead brother. Now he repeated this, along with an uncharitable comment about Joyce's inability to keep her opinions to herself.

'That's hardly fair Leo, she thought it might be the childhood trauma I experienced. If there was one,' I added, looking him in the eye and meeting his steady, unflinching gaze.

'How could it be,' he said, 'when you weren't even born?'

'Because it might have affected my mother so badly that when she had me, and I turned out to be girl, she was so disappointed she never took to me.'

'From what you've told me that sounds unlikely. In any case, your arm started to get better long before Joyce told you about the baby that died. Why does Mrs Moberley think it's recovered its strength? You must have discussed it. She must have an opinion.'

'It's not like that Leo.'

He tied his tie in a tight knot then pulled it free again. 'So what is it like? She must have a theory about why it happened. *Was* it because of something in the past?'

'Yes I expect so,' I lied.

Leo was telling Archie about the lecture he had attended the previous Wednesday. 'It's impossible to study what goes on in people's heads, makes much better sense to observe their behaviour.'

'But doesn't that rule out much of what it means to be a human being?' Archie looked tired and his face was thinner, his cheeks more sucked in. It's aged you, I thought, and you'll never go back to how you were before. All the same he was making it clear he was quite up to a good discussion.

As I watched the two of them conflicting feelings surged through me, making me want to laugh and cry, the absurdity of Leo talking about everything apart from the one thing that mattered, and the loss I felt that my lovely Archie had been reduced to a gaunt old man. No that was an exaggeration, in the week or two he would be back to his old self. Even so I was painfully aware how in the past I had turned him into something he had never been or, as Mrs Moberley might have described it, I had been influenced by my need for a perfect father which in Freud's terms meant a perfect lover.

'It's a question of being scientific,' Leo persisted, 'if psychology wants to be taken seriously it has to use rigorous methods of inquiry. So far it's been too concerned with introspection and consciousness. If it's to have any validity actual behaviour needs to be observed by dispassionate observers.'

Since we arrived Archie had hardly stirred. Now he pulled himself up in his chair and placed a marker in the P.G Wodehouse he had left open on the table. 'So where did you come across this Watson chap?'

'In the library. As you know I've always been interested in the human mind and Ursula's treatment has provided plenty of food for thought, throwing light on the inconsistencies in Freudian theory. Watson's approach is far more painstaking and meticulous.' He gave a short laugh. 'Can you believe his first paper was turned down on the grounds that he made no mention of what the rats were thinking!'

'Really?' Archie was wearying of the subject. 'Even so psychoanalysis appears to have served Ursula well.'

Leo pursed his lips in grudging agreement. 'Although it's perfectly possible that given enough time her arm would have healed itself without any intervention.'

'What do you think Ursula?' Archie gave me a slightly anxious smile and in an instant I had forgiven him his philandering. Things had changed forever but he was still my Archie, we would still be friends. After all he had never lied to me, not in the sense of making out he was something he was not, and if I had interpreted his fondness for me as something more he could hardly be blamed for that.

'I'm glad Leo's enjoying his lectures. He's out till all hours aren't you Leo?'

'There's sometimes a discussion after the formal lecture ends.'

'Jolly good,' Archie yawned, 'it's a popular topic these days, is it?' He winked at me. 'Are women allowed to attend too?'

'Yes of course.' Leo made no effort to hide his irritation. 'Anyone who's sufficiently interested to read up on the subject.'

Muriel had appeared in the doorway with a vase of pinky-purple daisies. 'Echinacea,' she explained, 'late flowers which with any luck will continue until the end of October.' She placed them on a table by the French windows then turned to smile at the three of us. She was still putting a brave face on it but the strain was showing. 'All right now Leo, that's quite enough for one day, your father has to rest.'

'Oh nonsense.' Archie pushed back a lock of hair. 'What the doctor actually said was that I should do whatever I liked within reason, and talking to Leo and Ursula seems eminently reasonable.'

'In that case.' Muriel put an arm round my shoulder. 'Ursula and I will make some coffee. Come along dear and we'll rinse out the new china or do you think it's too good and I should display it on a shelf?'

'Oh no I'd much prefer you to use it.'

When we arrived I had given her a coffee set decorated with floral motifs in brown, orange and gold. Not as modern as Midge's beloved Clarice Cliff but quite daring in its own way. It had come from a shop in Hampstead and I had been afraid Muriel might not like it but when she cautiously removed the paper and opened the box she was so touched she had shed a few tears and the two of us had embraced.

I had expected her to say "a present for me, whatever for?' but she had known instinctively that I was trying to express something I was incapable of putting into words. *I know what a terrible time you've had and I'm so sorry it never occurred to me that your life might be less than perfect.*

Out in the kitchen I felt nervous all over again. Supposing she made a speech about our new found friendship and I was unable to respond adequately, but she was too astute for that, fragile alliances are best not discussed.

Instead she began issuing orders as to how the coffee pot was to be washed. 'It would be a tragedy if the silly cloth decided to slip out of your hand and the spout got chipped.' And I was happy to fall in line and play the dutiful daughter-in-law whose experience of washing and drying china was so much less than her own.

'Ursula?' Her back was turned but I could tell from her voice that she was about to say something important, a defence of Archie, a request that what she had told us about him was never mentioned again?

'I want to tell you something.' She found a tray and began arranging the cups and saucers. 'It's about Leo.'

'Leo?' Had he complained about me, told her I was failing to fulfil my wifely duties? She would skirt around the subject but we would both know what she meant, and I would be unable to defend myself without being drawn into the kind of conversation no woman would want to have with her mother-in-law.

'When he was born.' She paused as though to allow me time to prepare myself for another revelation. 'There were complications. He was a breech baby. I don't know if you know what that means.'

'No I don't.'

'He was round the wrong way, feet first. They tried to turn him but without success. I won't go into details but there was quite a lot of bleeding and the outcome was that the doctor told me I would be unable to have more children.'

'Oh.' It was so unexpected it threw me for a moment. 'I'm so sorry. Would you have liked to have more?'

It was stupid question and understandably she ignored it. 'The reason I'm telling you this Ursula, I'm aware that you've always found me a rather possessive mother and you're probably right. It's no excuse but as you'll see he was, is, rather special. All the same it can't always have been easy for you.'

What could I say? Make false protestations that I had never thought her possessive? She would know that was not true. I was grateful she had decided to tell me because I knew it meant she wanted the two of us to get on better together, and while she was talking another thought had crossed my mind. Perhaps her love life had been as disastrous as mine. Was that why Archie had strayed? The "other women" had been prepared to lie there and endure it. Or had I got it quite wrong, he was a wonderful lover and Muriel had failed to appreciate him.

So many questions I could never ask.

'Thank you for telling me Muriel and I do understand how you feel.'

'Do you?'

'Yes of course. If you only have one child he's bound to be terribly important, the most important person in the world. After all you are his lover, I mean his mother.'

Would she pretend she had misheard my slip of the tongue? The old Muriel would have done just that, but she was laughing.

'In vino veritas,' she said, 'except in your case there's no need for any alcohol.'

'I'm sorry, it truly was a slip of the tongue. I know what Freud says about them but sometimes he exaggerates to fit in with his theories. At least that's what I think.'

'I'm sure you're right Ursula and isn't it just typical of Leo to force you into a Freudian analysis then change his mind about the treatment and turn his attention to something quite the opposite and from what I can tell even more outlandish.'

'Muriel?'

'Now what is it?'

'Not long ago Joyce told me something rather sad.'

Her head jerked up and I realised I had introduced the subject badly. 'No not about her or the children, or Sidney. She said we had a brother but he died when he was only a few days old. It was before I was born and nobody said anything about it when I was child. He was called John.'

She left her coffee making and embraced me for a

second time. 'How terribly upsetting for you Ursula. I suppose they thought they were doing the right thing not telling you but it does seem a little unnatural.'

'I think it was because Mother was afraid I would feel unwanted, a second girl when she would have liked a boy to replace the one that died.'

'Oh I'm sure she never thought that.'

But I could tell from her voice that she found it a plausible explanation.

On the way home Leo was full of joie de vivre. No mention had been made of lunch and we had been happy to leave soon after midday, with promises to return in a day or two and good wishes all round. Muriel had kissed me and I had responded warmly. I was still a little wary of her but I respected the fact that she had made such an effort to improve things between us.

After her humiliation at the hands of Archie she could so easily have become colder and more distant. Instead I felt we were united in our suffering at the hands of men. Not that Muriel would have seen it that way, but Archie was no longer the charismatic figure who put her in the shade and I expect she felt some justifiable pride in the fact that she had kept going through what must have been some very trying times.

As we drove through central London I closed my eyes and listened to the rumble of trams and the occasional shouts of market traders. Our visit to *The Gables* had been less of an ordeal than I expected. Archie was recovering and however Muriel felt about the circumstances of his heart attack she was prepared if not to forget, to try and forgive, and perhaps she was comforted by the fact that he was unlikely to risk the same thing happening again.

'I told your mother about my brother,' I said.

'Oh yes.' Leo glanced at me then back at the road. 'Joyce hadn't said anything to her then.'

'Of course not.'

'You say "of course not," but they discussed your symptoms behind your back. At the time they were as thick as thieves.'

'Only because they were both worried about me.' Why did he always have to make people appear so unpleasant?

Pulling myself into a more upright position I turned my attention to the hat shop we were passing with its absurd concoctions in the window, although they might well have appealed to Midge. Then I thought about Archie and Muriel, eating their lunch together while discussing our visit and glad to have something new to talk about no doubt. Muriel would tell him about my brother and they would both express surprise that Joyce had waited until my arm was better before breaking the news.

After what Joyce had said about her and Sidney, and her life as the wife of a vicar, I could understand why she had started thinking about herself and wanted to include me in her childhood memories. Also, having a baby brother who died soon after he was born could be seen as the reason for my arm and all the other symptoms, an unlikely reason perhaps but so much more acceptable than the real one.

'Your lectures sound interesting,' I said.

'They wouldn't interest you.'

'I didn't say they would,' I felt angry out of all proportion. 'I was thinking about you.'

'I'm sorry.'

'But you're not really.' I was so agitated I was unable to stop myself. 'You treat me like an idiot as though I hadn't a brain in my head.'

He tightened his grip on the steering wheel. 'That's not true Ursula.'

'Well that's how it feels.'

'Perhaps it does but feelings are not a very reliable guide to the facts.'

'Oh Leo,' I sighed.

'What?'

'Never mind, let's talk about something else. Your mother told me about when you were born. You were a breech baby. I think that's what it's called.'

'She told you when you were out in the kitchen?'

'We were just chatting about this and that.'

'This and that? Oh about Enid I suppose.'

'You know what women are like.' My laugh sounded horribly false. 'No I haven't told her about Enid. We decided not to, remember?'

So he was blissfully unaware that his mother had been in danger of bleeding to death. One day I might mention it and he would say, "yes, my father told me, but made me promise not to say anything in case it upset her." Or else he would be surprised, and possibly hurt that I had been told something he felt he deserved to know, and I would explain it by saying that Muriel must have decided there was no reason for him to know but that when something awful happened – like Archie's heart attack – people seemed to feel the need to exchange stories about other upsetting events.

Sometimes it was as if everyone inhabited a secret place that they must disclose to the world on pain of death. But when the pretence of a jolly life broke down it freed them to express their true feelings. Now I was becoming morbid but during my time with Mrs Moberley I had come to understand why most conversations were so superficial. Nobody wanted to hear about your unhappiness because it might stir up their own thoughts and feelings, ones they preferred to deny.

Midge was not like that. It was true last time she called round she had only talked about the house but that was because Leo was there, and when I visited her in her new flat it would different.

'What are we having for lunch?' Leo asked and I returned to the present with a jolt.

'Left overs I expect but there's a beef casserole for supper.'

He licked his lips and I laughed, telling him he was like one of Pavlov's dogs.

'Did you make it Ursa or is it one of Enid's efforts?'

'Enid's but she's going to teach me how. She'll have to won't she or what will we do when she leaves to have the baby?'

'When did you say it was due?'

'I'm not sure and I don't think she is. Sometime round Christmas, plenty of time yet but I've said if she doesn't tell her mother by the end of the month I'm going to go round and tell her myself.'

'Enid won't like that.'

'No she won't but it's not fair leaving us as the only people who know, and if Jim really has done a bunk that means the baby will be another mouth to feed and Mrs Drummond will have to make plans.'

'Mrs Drummond? Oh yes, I'd forgotten she had a surname.'

'Honestly Leo.' I gave him a playful push. 'Goodness knows where they'll find room for everyone. According to Enid her two youngest brothers already share a bed and she and her sister sleep in a tiny room.'

'They'll manage,' he said and I nodded my agreement although my thoughts had returned to Mrs Moberley and how much I needed to talk to Midge about her and Solange. Or would she find that too painful? And were my feelings for Mrs Moberley really the same as Midge's for Solange or was I in such a state of confusion I had mistaken one kind of love for another?

I have often wondered what would have happened if we had stayed at *The Gables* for lunch. Muriel had not offered food, either because she feared the four of us sitting round the table might lead to an argument or because Archie was tired. Or perhaps she thought, correctly, that we wanted to go home.

I remember the exact time we arrived back in Highgate because Leo looked at his watch as the car came to a stop and announced that it was ten past one and he was starving.

At the front door I paused to remove my hat – Leo was inspecting a mark on the car's paintwork – then froze. Had the sound come from the garden or was it in the house? It could be Solomon. But it had not sounded like a cat, it was too human. Wrenching open the door I thought for a moment I must have imagined it. The high-pitched shriek could have come from a child. As far as I knew there were no children living close by but one might be visiting or there could be several of them, playing a wild game of pirates in a nearby garden.

'Leo,' I called and as he joined me in the hall a low

moaning sound came from the direction of the kitchen.

'Enid?' I started running along the passage but Leo overtook me and held me back.

'Let me go in first. She may have cut herself or spilled boiling water.'

'Shall I call Dr Sawyer?'

'Not yet.'

For a few brief moments I stood outside the kitchen as instructed, but it was no good, the uncertainty was too much to bear, and however bad it was I had to see for myself.

At first sight the room looked empty then I realised Enid was on the floor behind the table with Leo bending over her. The moaning had stopped but she was on all fours, like an animal, gasping for breath and when I reached her I could see that her face was contorted in pain.

'What is it?' I slipped, almost losing my balance on the wet linoleum. 'Did you fall? Have you hurt yourself?'

Her breathing became easier but a second later she let out an ear-splitting scream and began writhing in agony and at the same moment Leo caught my eye and simultaneously it dawned on us both what must be happening.

'She's having a miscarriage,' I said. 'Call Dr Sawyer. Quick!'

Leo raced from room and I was left, helplessly wondering what I was supposed to do. 'It's all right, Enid, it's all right. Try not to worry, try to stay calm. The doctor will be here very soon.'

Her forehead was pressed against the cold floor. 'Stay where you are,' I ordered her although what else could the poor thing do. 'I'm going to fetch a blanket.'

Leaping up the stairs two at a time I dragged the eiderdown off the nearest bed and ran down again almost bumping into Leo who put out a hand to steady me. 'Dr Sawyer's on his way.'

Enid was crying out in pain again, loud bellows that sent a shudder through my body. Could you die from a miscarriage? If you lost enough blood it might be possible. Muriel had lost blood when Leo was born. I knew nothing about such matters but if something that had been growing inside you forced itself out before it was supposed to... Folding the eiderdown in half I attempted to ease Enid onto it but without any success. She tried to speak but no words came out, just a jumble of sounds that ended in another deafening scream.

'Don't say anything,' I knelt beside her. 'Does it hurt terribly? I'm so sorry. The doctor will be here any minute now.' My eyes had been drawn to a pool of blood, at least I thought it was blood but on closer inspection it turned out to be the smashed remains of a jar of bottled plums that Enid must have dropped. The red juice had spread out in the shape of an island, the Isle of Wight. What a stupid thing to be thinking. Should I clear it up in case someone cut themselves or... I turned back to Enid and found Leo bending over her, breathing hard.

'I can't help it Ursa, one of us has to look and see what's going on.'

'Oh no, poor Enid, we can't.' I picked up what I thought was a wet cloth that turned out to be her underwear. 'All right, I'll look.'

But Leo had abandoned his inhibitions and adopted the role of a doctor. 'Try to keep calm Enid. You'll be all right. I'll do whatever needs to be done.'

'Don't miscarriages just happen on their own?' I whispered.

'I don't know.' He had his hand on the back of her neck and I thought, what good is that going to do but what else was there, apart from trying to reassure her.

Kneeling beside her again I repeated what I hoped were soothing words but they were soon drowned by another series of screams, another bout of excruciating pain.

'Come here Ursa.' Leo's voice was quieter, almost awe struck.

'What is it?' I joined him, forcing myself to look between her bloodstained legs and saw to my horror that something dark and wet had appeared, a pink dome-like shape covered in slimy streaks. 'What is it? Oh no! Wait Enid, please try to wait!'

'No don't.' Leo disappeared, returning with a cushion. 'Breathe in and out Enid, faster, pant like a dog.' He smoothed back her wiry black hair and I thought, you're as fond of her as I am, you can't bear to see her suffer. 'When you feel the next bad pain coming push hard. Yes now!'

The noise was so loud I wanted to cover my ears. It lasted for several minutes and all the time I could see the terrible pain in Enid's eyes.

'That's it,' Leo urged, 'come on, it'll soon be over, just keep breathing in and out.'

And to my amazement she did as she was told, until the next pain overcame her and she let out a fearful shriek, then another, and another, and the baby's head emerged.

Leo cradled it in his hands. 'Well done Enid, well done, you're doing really well, not long now.'

I dabbed at her damp forehead with my handkerchief. 'It's all right, it's all right.' And she arched her back, leaning forward with her chin on the floor, and producing scream after scream.

'The shoulders,' Leo announced, 'look Ursa it's amazing.'

'Is it all right?' I peered between her legs at the stretched skin surrounded by sticky slime and clots of blood. 'It's too soon, it will be too small.' And with a slithering rush the baby slid out and flopped onto the eiderdown with Leo still hanging onto its head.

'Is it breathing? Is it alive?'

'Keep still Enid.' He picked up the baby and gave it a hard thump on the back.

'It's all right Enid,' I reassured her, 'It's over now and you've been terribly brave.' Then the doorbell rang twice and leaping to my feet I tore through the house, sliding on the polished tiles and catching hold of the stair rail to steady myself, and as I regained my balance and let Dr Sawyer into the house the baby began to yell.

CHAPTER SEVENTEEN

*'Men's statements about the sexual impulses
of women often tell us less about women
than about the person who makes them.'*
(Havelock Ellis)

Enid's baby had arrived early – but not that early. The two of them had been admitted to hospital where it had been estimated that the baby was three or four weeks premature but all things considered surprisingly strong and healthy. Enid had been allowed home the following day and Dr Sawyer told us it was likely the baby would be able to join her by the end of the week.

How could we have failed to notice her advanced stage? But she had always been well built and, as her sister Flossie pointed out, even their mother had put down the increase in weight to Enid's sweet tooth.

I blamed myself. Leo and I had been the only ones who knew she was expecting and we had been too preoccupied with our own problems, although Leo insisted I was being unfair on myself. After all I had tried to talk to Enid on innumerable occasions and each time she had refused to discuss when the baby was due. Had she known all along and resolutely refused to face facts or was she so ignorant of such matters that the birth had been as much a shock to her as it had to us? Having brought the child into the world Leo took a proprietary interest and was touched when we learned that she was to be called Erica. Leo's second name was

Eric. As for me I was full of admiration for the way he had taken over when he realised Enid was about to give birth. How had known what to do? But when I asked him he had played down his contribution.

'Babies bring themselves into the world.'

'Yes but sometimes things go wrong.' I thought about how Muriel had almost bled to death. 'There are complications.'

'To tell you the truth Ursa I was as unnerved as you were. Fortunately it was a relatively easy birth and not much was required from us.'

'No, that's not true Leo, you knew all about the panting like a dog, and pushing. You were wonderful.'

'I must have read it somewhere.' But he was pleased I was so impressed.

Flossie had offered to come three mornings a week, to do the cleaning and washing, and I had taken over the shopping and cooking. Unlike her sister Flossie was tall and thin, and so different in appearance from Enid in every other way that it was hard to believe they came from the same family. She did exactly as I asked and was perfectly polite and obliging but she lacked Enid's warmth.

'Enid's that impatient for you and Mr Ingham to see the baby.' She threaded the tie of her apron and pulled it tight. 'When will you be visiting?'

'If that's all right we'd love to.'

'She doesn't like the feeding.' Flossie gave a slight shudder. 'Says it hurts.'

'But it's so much better than a bottle.' I was repeating Joyce's words. For myself I knew nothing about babies and the thought of breast-feeding made me shudder except if it were your own child I supposed you might feel differently.

Flossie tipped Rinso into a bowl and I thought about the day Enid had turned pale when she saw my "bad" arm resting on the sink. Only four months ago but it was difficult to remember how the useless limb had hung by my side and I had been so certain it was unable to move, or rather that I was incapable of moving it. According to Freud I had transformed "psychical excitation" into "chronic somatic symptoms", or to put it more bluntly I had expressed my misery through my body. Once I had insisted Mrs Moberley tell me the absolute, honest truth. Did she think I was pretending, that I had made a deliberate decision to acquire a "hysterical limb" so that Leo would feel it would be unfair to try and make love to me. *No I don't think that Ursula, mainly because it would be impossible, your arm would have moved involuntarily.* But in the end it did, I said. *Yes but only when you were beginning to become aware of the underlying reasons for your unhappiness.*

Flossie was watching me out of the corner of her eye. 'Will you be calling round then Mrs Ingham? Enid's been fretting.'

'Has she? Surely she doesn't think we're cross with her, that's the last thing Mr Ingham and I feel, and of course we'd love to see the baby, and Enid, and the rest of your family. Would Saturday afternoon be all right?'

'Whenever it suits Mrs Ingham. I'll tell Mum, it'll give 'er time to prepare.'

'Yes but please ask her not to go to any trouble.'

Flossie gave me a look as though to say "of course she'll go to trouble if you and Mr Ingham are visiting", and began sorting the washing into neat piles, the clothes that needed ironing and the ones that could be aired and put away.

'Visit Enid?' Leo spoke the words as though I had suggested a visit to a house of ill repute. 'I couldn't possibly.'

'Why ever not?'

'In the first place she wouldn't like it.'

'Yes she would. Flossie says she's desperate to show us the baby.'

'Desperate? Hardly the word she would have chosen. I do wish you wouldn't put words into other people's mouths Ursa. Where does she live? Kentish Town isn't it. If you think I'm driving over there.'

'It's not very far.'

'That's hardly the point.'

My face had flushed scarlet with anger and disappointment. 'But you were there when the baby was born Leo and Enid was so grateful she named her after you. Surely you want to see her. She'll have put on weight but still be a little scrap.'

'You go if you feel you must.' He took out his pocket diary although why he needed it heaven only knew. Perhaps it had become one of Freud's "need-fulfilling objects" like a soft toy or a well-sucked blanket.

'I tell you what,' he said, and I realised my anger had alarmed him a little, 'when Enid returns to work you can suggest she brings the baby with her one day. She wouldn't get much work done but the two of you could discuss child care, it might come in useful one day.'

'I doubt if she will be coming back.'

He frowned. 'I thought her mother had offered to look after the baby.'

'Flossie says she doesn't think Enid wants to leave it.'

'Oh well, Flossie seems hard-working enough, more so than Enid if anything and better organised by the sound of it.'

But I miss Enid, I thought, I miss our conversations, and her kindness, and above all her sense of humour. And why has Leo refused to accompany me? Is it really snobbishness – he doesn't relish a visit to the house in Kentish Town – or was I mistaken when I thought the birth of Enid's baby had brought us closer? We were still not close enough for Leo's liking and I had a feeling there was something on his mind, something he was avoiding telling me about. At this point my own mind closed, just as it had always done in the past when something came into it that was too awful to contemplate.

When I told her I would be visiting Kentish Town on my own Flossie had suggested I accompany her on the bus after she finished her work.

'That way you wouldn't get lost.'

'If that's all right with you Flossie.' I had been planning a taxi but the bus would be better. Mrs Drummond might not like a taxi arriving outside her house and in any case it would make me feel like a grand lady visiting the poor and after Leo's snobbish outburst that was last thing I wanted.

'We live in Countess Road,' Flossie explained as we walked together to the bus stop, 'not far from the station, then a bit of walk but it doesn't look like rain.'

'No it doesn't.' I had brought my umbrella just in case but regretted it almost at once as I also had my handbag and a small parcel for Enid. Still, it was one of my larger bags and I could probably squeeze the parcel inside.

As we turned into Archway Road I asked Flossie if Erica was a good baby. 'I know nothing about small babies but my sister says there are contented ones and fractious ones and they seem to be born that way.'

'Babies is babies Mrs Ingham, just needs feeding and changing.'

'But she looked so small.' I regretted my words at once, afraid I had embarrassed Flossie by reminding her I had been present at the birth, but she looked quite unperturbed.

'Mum says it's a bit thick Enid never told us.' Flossie raised her voice against the rattle of a passing lorry. 'Too scared, I said, and that made her even crosser. Still, what's done's done and don't you worry Mrs Ingham you'll be ever so welcome.'

Don't you worry Mrs Ingham? Did she mean her mother blamed me for what had happened? Not Enid having a baby, I could hardly be held responsible for that, but the fact that it had arrived without warning.

'Quite warm for the time of year,' I said, not wanting to discuss Enid behind her back, and Flossie gave me a sly smile as though to say "you're mentioning the weather because you don't want to think what it will be like when you meet Mum."

If Leo had agreed to come it would have been different. How could he be so horrible, especially when he knew how much it meant to me, but it was no use relying on other people, you had to learn to fend for yourself.

When the bus pulled up a few minutes later I took a step forward and almost spilled the whole contents of my bag.

'Down the front,' Flossie shouted and I climbed on,

struggling to keep my balance as I hurried to join her.

We sat close together but not actually touching because both of us were quite slim, whereas the seat in front was occupied by one of the largest women I had ever seen and it would have been impossible for another passenger to sit next to her. Her hat was pulled well down and a thick shawl covered her immense shoulders and every so often she gave a hacking cough and Flossie glanced at me as if to say, "not used to travelling on the bus are you Mrs Ingham, taxi cabs is more your style."

She had her return ticket so I had to ask her which stop we were going to.

She held out her hand for some loose change, counted out the right money and returned three coins. 'You'll want a return or will you be going home in a taxi?'

'Oh no on the bus. Yes, a return ticket please.'

During the journey I attempted one or two topics of conversation but Flossie responded in monosyllables so I gave up and looked through the window at the passing traffic and the mothers hurrying their children in and out of shops and the men, some of them quite smartly dressed, others in shabby suits and flat caps.

Archway Road met up with Highgate Hill and across the other side of the junction, although it was not on our route, was Holloway Road where Dr Stopes had opened her first family planning clinic. One day I would try to find the place, might even nerve myself to go inside. They would assume I needed advice about limiting my family and when I explained I was childless they would think me quite unsuitable to help. Only perhaps not. Mrs Moberley had encouraged me to take risks. *People can only say "no" Ursula and that's not the end of the world is it?* Not if you feel sure of yourself, I thought, except that must be the way people gained confidence. They took risks and it made them feel better about themselves.

Enid had told me plenty of amusing anecdotes about her family but said little about the house where they all lived. Two up, two down I had always imagined, wondering occasionally how the nine of them fitted in although recently two of her brothers had married and moved out. As I recalled she and Flossie, and the twins, and their parents of course, lived in the four small rooms. No, the family consisted of five boys and two girls so that meant I had left out another brother. What were all their names? I could have asked Flossie but I was afraid of her sharp tongue and hoped her mother would be more like Enid, large and homely and good-natured.

When we alighted from the bus I tried to memorise a few landmarks that would help me on my return journey. A laundry, a greengrocer's and a rather grim looking building that turned out to belong to an obscure religion with a name that was new to me.

'We cross here.' Flossie looked up and down the road then darted between the traffic, expecting me to follow. I hesitated, not sure I wanted to take the risk, and was then obliged to stand on the pavement while a beer dray pulled by two huge grey horses passed slowly by.

When I joined Flossie I apologised for keeping her waiting but all she said was that the area was not much like where I lived, was it, no grass or trees or fancy front gardens.

'No but the shops are handy,' I said, regretting my

words at once in case she thought them condescending.

'Down here then second on the right and first on the left.' She spoke so fast it was difficult to memorise. 'Don't you worry I'll walk you back to where you catch your bus home.'

'Thank you Flossie, if you're sure you don't mind.'

She gave a slightly unpleasant laugh. 'Don't want you going round and round in circles till the dark creeps up on you.'

The streets were narrow with small terraced houses on either side, back-to-backs people called them but surely not literally since they must have yards that separated them from one another. A group of boys, and a single girl who was taller than the boys and dressed in a faded cotton frock, stopped their game of hopscotch to follow us with their eyes and I felt conspicuous and overdressed in my dark blue two-piece suit and matching hat.

It would be strange seeing Enid in her own home and even stranger seeing her nursing Erica. Would she think back to the birth and feel mortified that Leo and I had been present at such an intimate occasion or had the whole painful episode been wiped from her memory, forgotten in the excitement of having a new baby.

Joyce said that was what happened. *You forget Ursula, you have to, or you'd never be prepared to go through it again.* Well that was something to look forward to if it ever happened to me.

'Number fifty-two,' Flossie announced. 'Down the end there past the lamp.'

Children were playing in this street too, younger ones than before, and I thought about the time when Enid's baby would be the same age as Helen but with few of her advantages, no garden with a swing and a sandpit, no music lessons or dancing classes. Life was so unfair in so many different ways but perhaps the mistake was in imagining things were ever meant to be fair.

When we reached the house Flossie pulled open the front door and stood back for me to pass and I stepped inside and waited in the dark slightly forbidding passage that led to narrow wooden stairs. All of a sudden a tall gangly boy ran down them, flattening himself against the wall as he squeezed past then sprinting off down the street.

'Our Mick,' Flossie explained, 'he's shy of strangers, doesn't know what to do with himself. His twin's just the opposite but he's out, found himself a job.'

I was watching Mick's receding figure when a voice made me jump and I turned to face a woman who, in almost every respect, was an older version of Flossie.

'Mrs Drummond?'

'Come along in then.'

'Thank you so much.' She ushered me through the first door on the left into what turned out to be an unwelcoming room with a beige carpet, with a pattern of swirling green leaves and pink flowers, and hardly any furniture, just a sofa and a high-backed wooden chair. The mantelpiece was covered in large china ornaments, most of them horses, and the room had an unlived in feel but that might have been because of the faint scent of camphor.

Dressed in a dark skirt and a floral blouse, with a large shiny brooch covering the top button, Mrs Drummond looked quite a bit younger than I had anticipated and was still a good-looking woman with her light brown hair scraped back into a neat bun, not like Joyce's roll that was always escaping into wispy strands. Enid must take after her father, I thought, I expect he's shorter than his wife and more heavily built and with darker colouring.

'I like your wallpaper,' I said, wishing Enid was there to break the ice, 'it's pretty. Is it new?'

She ran her hand down the embossed wall. 'Cost half a crown a yard. Given to us by a man where my Tommy works. Doug hung it only last month.'

'Enid's father.'

'That's the one.'

'How is Enid?'

'She's told you about her brothers and sisters? Billy and Tommy are married and Len's staying with his uncle in Peckham so we're not such a crowd as we used to be.'

'That makes things easier I expect. How's the baby?'

Once again she ignored my question. 'Sit yourself down.'

'Thank you. Mr Ingham was very sorry he couldn't come but it's the start of the new school year so he's rather busy but I hope Enid will come and visit us when she's feeling up to it.'

Mrs Drummond remained silent, silent and intimidating.

'Is Enid in the kitchen?' I asked, determined not to be daunted. 'Perhaps we should go in there, or she could come and join us.'

'Just as you like.'

Flossie had disappeared and I thought I could hear her upstairs although it could have been another member of the family. As I followed Mrs Drummond down the passage I began to wonder if Leo was right and Enid was not looking forward to a visit. Supposing it had been Flossie's idea. I could imagine she might be someone who liked causing trouble and she could have told Enid it would be rude not to invite me and poor Enid would have shrugged and said, "all right then, you'd better ask her."

If that was the truth I felt bad about it but when we entered the kitchen the whole atmosphere of the house changed and I was sure I was wrong. A picture of the old queen looked down on a row of nappies drying on a line in front of the range and there were other pictures on the wall too, prints of the countryside and one of what could have been the sea front at Brighton. Next to it was a pipe rack, but with no pipes in it, and beyond that a small shelf with a glass paperweight and a Toby jug with a three-cornered hat. The smell of baking gave the room a homely feel and I was relieved when I spotted Enid, sitting close to the wall, squeezed in between a coal shuttle and a wooden crib on rockers, and almost hidden by a table with a white cloth.

'Oh there you are Enid.' I moved towards her and she gave a faint smile and looked away. 'How are you? It's lovely to see you.'

She said nothing and for a few moments the three of us endured an awkward silence that was broken by Mrs Drummond placing her hand on the crib.

'Lent us by Mrs Davis who lives next door but one.'

'Can I have a look?

'That's what you came for Mrs Ingham.'

'Yes of course.' I leaned over the crib but all I could see was part of a tiny red cheek. The rest of the baby, including most of her head, was wrapped tightly in a white blanket and the shape it made was so small she could have been a doll.

On the bus I had prepared what I was going to say to Mrs Drummond. *Flossie says Enid may want to come back to us later but not just yet and if she did it would mean you had to look after the baby and I'm sure you've more than enough on your hands. Just do whatever you think best, don't worry about me and Mr Ingham, and don't worry if there are any doctor's bills.*

Now none of it seemed appropriate. What had I expected to find? A careworn middle-aged woman, old before her years? Enid's mother had the air of someone who was well able to deal with whatever life served up. I had no idea what they had in the way of amenities, an outside privy and no running water but a communal tap at the end of the street? And where did they all sleep? The twins in the front room on the sofa, Mr and Mrs Drummond in one of the bedrooms, and Enid and Flossie in the other? And now there was the baby too.

'Don't take up much room do they.' Mrs Drummond was pouring boiling water into a brown teapot. 'Leastways not until they learn to crawl and you can't turn your back on 'em an instant. I've had seven, all born healthy excepting one of the twins and he's turned out the biggest of the lot. Sit down then Mrs Ingham. What are you doing Enid, perched on that chair like you're glued to it?'

I chose a rocking chair then wished I had chosen somewhere else since every time I moved a muscle it squeaked. All the same, I was starting to relax. 'My sister has a ten-month-old baby,' I said, 'no he must be eleven months now isn't he Enid? Yes, his birthday's in less than two weeks time, I mustn't forget.'

So far Enid had not spoken a word and it occurred to me how odd it must be for her having her mother and me in the same room. I suppose I had thought the baby would make things easier but clearly Enid was finding the situation uncomfortable and I knew how she felt. People behave differently according to who they are with and faced with two people, both of whom knew her so well, she was at a loss how to be or what to say.

'Must have given you quite a turn.' Mrs Drummond's face was expressionless apart from a slight twitch of her mouth. 'She'd told you hadn't she, you knew she was expecting.'

I had been prepared for this, Flossie had forewarned me, besides her mother would have questioned Enid who would have been unable to deny the truth.

'I kept urging her to tell you,' I said. 'That's right, isn't it Enid. And naturally I had no idea the baby was due so soon. January I thought.'

If I had hoped for a reassuring smile from Mrs Drummond I was out of luck. Still watching me intently she waited for me to continue.

'You see, what happened,' I began, 'my sister's nine year old daughter had come to spend the day with us and later when my sister came to collect her she mentioned someone I knew, the wife of her husband's new curate who was having a baby in the New Year. Up till then it had never occurred to me… We were all in the kitchen and – '

'And you saw our Enid's face and put two and two together.'

'I still wasn't at all certain.'

'But when you questioned her she broke down.'

I hesitated, trying to work out how best to defend myself without making things worse for Enid. 'I know Enid was going to tell you but – '

'No I wasn't,' Enid said hotly and her mother and I swung round to face her. 'I knew what you'd say and Mrs Ingham was ever so kind.'

'I spoke to you about it several times didn't I Enid.'

'But she never let on when it was due, just like it was with her mother.' Mrs Drummond saw my face and gave a satisfied smile. 'That's something Enid's not told you then. My sister Liza, only seventeen she was, took up with a fellow what traded in horses, old enough to be her father and vanished into thin air same as Enid's Jim has.'

'I had no idea.' I glanced at Enid but she was looking down at the baby.

'Got through the birth all right,' Mrs Drummond continued, 'or so we thought, then got a blood clot and was dead within the hour. We took Enid in when she was three days old and our Len was still a baby.'

So that accounted for Enid looking so different from Flossie, and from her mother. Why had Enid failed to tell me she was adopted? Perhaps it had never occurred to her to say, or perhaps she felt bad about it, one of the family but not quite, although I was sure Mrs Drummond would have treated her the same as the rest.

The baby was making snuffling noises. I opened my bag to take out the present I had brought but Mrs Drummond misinterpreted my action and thought I was going to give her money.

'No need for that Mrs Ingham.'

'It's only a little matinée coat.'

She nodded, taking the parcel and handing it to Enid. 'I just thank the dear Lord you and Mr Ingham came back to the house when you did. All on her own poor girl, doesn't bear thinking about.'

'She was terribly brave. It must have been so frightening for her.' I broke off, aware I had started to talk about Enid as though she was not in the room. 'You were wonderful Enid, we were proud of you.'

Mrs Drummond ran her tongue round the inside of her cheek. 'Always said that Jim was up to no good. What did you think of him Mrs Ingham? Shifty look round the eyes. And talk! I never heard a lad go on the way he did.' She gave a contemptuous laugh. 'All a pack of lies, making out how clever he were and how he could turn his hand to just about anything.'

'I only met him once,' I said.

'Only takes the once though don't it.'

She knew she had put me in a difficult position but she was still angry with Enid, and with me too I expect. Wanting to put an end to the talk of Jim, Enid had lifted the sleepy baby out of the crib and carried her over to where I was sitting.

'Let me see her properly.' I watched as the blanket was unwound. 'Oh she's lovely Enid and she's put on quite a lot of weight hasn't she.'

'They lose a bit at first.' Mrs Drummond spoke like the expert she clearly was, 'but this one's a fighter, feeds for two.'

'Does she? I'm so glad.' I was remembering the bloodstained little body that had flopped onto our kitchen floor. What a transformation! She was still tiny but had lost her blotchy newly born look and if Leo could see her surely he would forget his inhibitions. In a few weeks time I would invite Enid to bring her round to the house – if necessary Flossie could accompany her – and we would all indulge in some baby worship, free from Mrs Drummond's censorial gaze.

'Erica,' I said, touching the baby's forehead with the tip of my finger. 'Mr Ingham says it's Latin for heather. It's a lovely name.' I thought about Exmoor's heather covered moorland and the little valleys with streams running through them, an area we had visited often as children, and once again before my mother gave up holidays and became an invalid. How far away it all seemed from Countess Road and how many things had happened in the intervening years, and how much I had changed.

'Give her to Mrs Ingham,' Mrs Drummond commanded and Enid placed the baby in my arms where she lay staring up at me with slightly squinty eyes. One day she might have Enid's dark wiry hair but just now she was bald, apart from a faint covering of down. She had none of the cuddly chubbiness I associated with Joyce's babies but that would have been when they were older, possibly three or four months, and none of them had been premature.

'She's a little beauty,' I said, wondering where the expression had come from and supposing I must have read it in a book. 'I'm so glad she's doing so well.'

Enid looked at me and there were tears in her eyes. 'Thank you Mrs Ingham. No I mean for what you and Mr Ingham done and I'm ever so sorry – '

'No please don't be,' I interrupted, 'Mr Ingham's proud of how he brought her into the world. When you're ready you must bring her round to show him. He'd have come today but his new term's started so he's back at school.'

I thought about Mrs Moberley and how I would describe my trip to Countess Road. *I visited Enid in Kentish Town and met her mother and saw the baby, and Mrs Drummond wasn't at all what I was expecting, rather alarming but a good soul underneath, and it was so strange seeing Enid with a baby of her own.* That was the trouble these days, wherever I went, whatever I did I found myself preparing a description of it in my head for Mrs Moberley's benefit. What was I going to do when there were no more visits to Inverness Gardens? Leo rarely listened with his full attention and if he did he only wanted to know the bare facts, not how a particular event had made me feel. Still, there was always Midge.

I picked up my hat, ready to leave, but Mrs Drummond took it from me and placed it on a hook on the back of the door. 'Haven't had your tea yet Mrs Ingham or one of my Eccles cakes.'

'If you're sure, that would be lovely.' I turned back to Enid. 'Enid's cakes are a legend in our house, aren't they Enid, and poor Mr Ingham's having to make do with mine at present although he tries not to complain.'

When I returned to Highgate I found Midge waiting outside the front door, looking alarmingly up-to-the minute in loose fitting trousers and a slouch hat.

'Where've you been?' She made it sound as though I had no right to leave the house. 'I've been waiting nearly an hour.'

'You should have phoned. Come inside and I'll tell all.'

'What is it?' She had picked up the excitement in my voice. 'A secret assignation?'

'Don't be silly. You remember Enid?'

'Your maid?'

'She's had a baby.'

I enjoyed the look on Midge's face. 'A baby? How could she have done?'

'I knew she was expecting,' I explained, 'but we thought it wasn't due until after Christmas. It's a little girl and she's going to be called Erica, after Leo because his middle name is Eric.'

Her face dropped and I began to laugh. 'Only because he was the one who delivered her! We came home and found poor Enid in absolute agony and I thought she was having a miscarriage, we both did, and then we saw the baby's head. It was incredible Midge, I've never known anything like it.'

'I shouldn't think you have. Rather off-putting I should imagine.'

'Yes I suppose so.' I disliked the way she was pouring cold water on my enthusiasm. 'But if there was someone there to help it would be quite different. Poor Enid was all alone.'

'So next time I see you…' She extracted a cigarette from her enamelled case and lit it at lightning speed.

'Leo just took over,' I told her, 'I'd never have believed it. All I did was run upstairs and fetch an eiderdown for Enid to lie on although she was in too much pain for it to be any use. On all fours she was, arching her back. Leo held the baby's head and waited for the rest of it to emerge. We'd called the doctor but he arrived too late.'

'How ghastly.' Midge inhaled deeply. 'Rather you than me.'

Why did she sound so down? Was she having difficulty finding somewhere to live? Had she run out of money? If so I would offer to help although I was not sure how Leo would feel about it.

'That's where I've just come back from,' I told her, 'Kentish Town where Enid's family live. And she was adopted and I never knew, taken in when her mother died of a blood clot. Her real mother was Mrs Drummond's sister but they look after their own don't they.'

Midge blew out a ring of smoke. 'How on earth did Leo know what to do?'

'Fortunately the baby was the right way round. I think the worst part must have been before we arrived on the scene except Leo said afterwards he was afraid it might have had the umbilical cord round its neck.'

'He is knowledgeable. Because of having a doctor for a father I suppose.'

'The only trouble is when I asked him to go with me to visit Enid he wouldn't.'

'Perhaps he thinks he did his bit when the baby was born.' She paused and I realised she had come to tell me something and so far I had given her no chance to speak. 'I'm sorry Midge, here I am babbling away not letting you get a word in, it's just it was all so amazing and now Enid's sister Flossie comes three mornings a week to help with the cleaning and she's very efficient but I feel quite bereft without Enid. Would you like some tea? Yes of course you would. I made a cake. Yes me! And it turned out better than you could ever imagine although I haven't actually tasted it yet so you'll have to take pot luck.'

We sat on the sofa with Solomon curled up between us.

'Leo will be sorry he missed you,' I told her, 'he thinks you've done me a world of good.'

'You've done me good too Ursula.'

'I can't see how.'

'You listened, hardly anyone does that but I expect it's something your Mrs Moberley taught you. Are you still seeing her?'

'For one more month.'

'And then? Oh that reminds me, I've discovered a perfectly splendid centre for arts and crafts in Kensington Church Street, pottery and jewellery, and some hand-blocked textiles that would send you into ecstasies.'

'Perhaps we could go there together. Could we, do you think?' Midge was making an effort but she looked tired and strained and, feeling on edge, I reached out to stroke Solomon. 'Now you're going to stay in England,' I began, but before I could finish she cleared her throat and my heart sank because I guessed what was coming next.

'The reason I came round without warning you first I've decided to return to Paris tomorrow.'

'Tomorrow?'

'No don't look like that and I know what you're thinking but Solange needs me, I can't just abandon her.'

'And you miss her desperately.'

'Oh I do love you Ursula, you're the only person I know who would have said that.'

'I love you too,' I said, 'and you're right, I do understand.'

She looked away, it was all too much for her, and for me although I had become quite good at silences and the kind of moments most people seem to find so excruciating.

'I must tell you,' she said and I prepared myself for another confidence, but she only wanted to describe an evening gown she had seen in Peter Robinson, georgette with an embroidered bodice and yoke, and how it would have suited me beautifully because I was exactly the right shape.'

'We'll keep in touch won't we,' I said, 'and write often.'

'And you can come and visit. Leo too if you think he'd like it. How's he enjoying the lectures?'

'Oh he told you about them did he?'

She nodded, putting up both hands and rubbing her eyes. 'Who else goes to them? Are they open to anyone?'

'I've no idea. I suppose so. He comes back very late and one week he went out on Thursday evening as well as the usual Wednesday.'

'Present for you. Open it carefully, it's rather fragile.'

'I have two good arms now,' I protested, removing the wrapping and unfolding the white tissue paper to reveal a miniature garden with lakes made of mirror-glass, and bridges and temples.

'Like the one you admired at the exhibition,' Midge said and I noticed how her voice shook a little.

'It's absolutely lovely.' I placed it on a small table close to the window and returned to the sofa and gave her a hug. 'Thank you so much, I shall miss you such a lot.'

'Me too Ursula, you'll never know how much. And don't worry about Leo, I'm sure there's an innocent explanation.'

'How do you mean?'

'Your worry about his evenings out.'

Fear flooded through me. Like father, like son, that's

what she was thinking. Leo had found a woman who provided what I had been denying him. He loved her. They loved each other. He was going to leave me, biding his time until he was sure my arm was fully recovered and the scandal of his father's infidelity had started to fade.

'Don't look like that Ursula.' Midge gave my hand a squeeze.

'You think he's found someone else.'

'No of course I don't, not Leo, he adores you. I was just afraid that might be… might be what you were thinking.'

CHAPTER EIGHTEEN

*"The polar bear and the tiger
cannot fight".*

Sigmund Freud

October and the leaves were falling and *Marshall and Snelgrove* was advertising tweed coats with lamb fur collars, priced at seven and a half guineas, and I was on my way to Inverness Gardens for the last time.

Another page in *The Times* had a picture of a three-quarter coat, available in rifle green tweed. What did it mean, *rifle* green? Did women as well as men stalk deer on the Scottish hills? How could people enjoy it and why did my thoughts keep jumping all over the place? I had rehearsed in my mind all the things I wanted to say to Mrs Moberley but it was no use, she would know it was a prepared speech and would still expect me to be spontaneous and tell her whatever came into my head.

Sometimes I wondered if Freud encouraged his patients to tell him stories that confirmed his theories. Mrs Moberley never did that and if anyone mentioned Freud it was likely to be me. Because of Leo I suppose although now he had no interest in the Great Doctor and spent his spare time poring over articles describing how rats could be taught to find their way round mazes or press a lever that delivered a pellet of food.

As I passed the house that I often thought looked like a smaller version of *The Gables* I wondered how Muriel and Archie were spending all that enforced time together. Leo was convinced it must be a nightmare but perhaps Archie's illness had brought them closer, or was Muriel finding it impossible to forgive him, not for his "little flings" of which she had become accustomed over the years, but for the way in which his infidelity had been made so public? But she *would* forgive him, I thought, because to do otherwise would make her life impossible and when it came down to it people were realists and did what was in their best interest regardless of the rights and wrongs of the situation.

Once, in the paper, a report of court proceedings had described how a woman had attempted to murder her husband with a razor. The husband, who had survived the attack, wanted to forgive her and admitted to having wasted money on gambling, and given her cause for jealousy, and the case had been dismissed. Would the pair of them live happily ever after? It was hard to imagine how they could.

I pictured Muriel attacking Archie physically, but it only made me smile. Muriel would never risk untidying her hair and Archie, the old Archie, would have been able to restrain her with one hand tied behind his back. In her frustration Joyce had hit Sidney but in the main adults fought with words that could deliver far more savage blows. Poor Muriel, it was strange feeling sorry for her and even stranger that I had started to think about her with some affection. Lately she had permitted herself small moments of weakness which had endeared her to me so much more than when she insisted on appearing immune to all pain and suffering. Of course being Muriel she could have been shrewd enough to realise this.

My fear that Leo was finding solace with another

woman had disappeared. Since Midge returned to Paris he had been kind and affectionate, telling me I needed to get my strength back and murmuring how there was plenty of time, something I took to mean he would put no pressure on me to allow him his marital rights. To show my gratitude I had cooked some special meals. Roast leg of pork with onions and sage, followed by a date and apple pudding, was my biggest success and Leo had been gratifyingly surprised. *You'll soon be as good a cook as Mother and you're definitely better than that sister of yours.*

Now that my treatment was coming to an end I would spend as much time as possible with him and encourage him to talk. No mention must be made of *Married Love* but I hoped as we became closer we would find a way to lose our embarrassment about such matters.

Inverness Gardens was deserted apart from a black and white mongrel relieving itself against the pillar-box. Before I left home I had made a batter pudding and put it in a greased tin. I expect you are supposed to cook them straight away but in this instance it would have to wait. It took thirty minutes so I could put it in the oven when Leo returned from his lecture. Batter pudding was something Enid hardly ever made – she knew it was not one of my favourites – but Leo liked it, served with stewed fruit.

Mrs Moberley's house came into view and I checked my watch to make sure I was going to arrive on time, not too early, not too late. So far I had never bumped into one of her other patients – I expect she left a decent interval between us – and today it was the last thing I wanted to risk. Once, the thought that I was ending my treatment when someone else was carrying on with theirs would have been too much to bear, but with the help of Mrs Moberley I had been preparing myself for several weeks and knew I had made the correct decision. When the time seems right, she had said, leaving it up to me to decide, and when we reached the fifteenth of September I had told her, a little reluctantly that two more weeks felt about right and she had nodded her agreement.

My arm was functioning normally, in fact as far as my body was concerned I was fighting fit, and as far as my feelings for Mrs Moberley were concerned I could accept my love for her without guilt or blame because I no longer wanted her in my bed, it was a deeper, stronger love. Perhaps Freud was right about the way patients *transferred* their childhood feelings onto their psychoanalyst but for my part I know it was much more than that. Mrs Moberley had listened and understood and my gratitude towards her had coincided with a sexual awakening brought about by Dr Stopes' book. Or was I quite wrong and it was simply a response to being allowed to feel so close to another human being. Whatever the reason that was unimportant now, all that mattered was that Mrs Moberley had cured my arm and in the process changed my life. Now it was up to me to make the most of it.

When she let me into the house she gave no indication of what a momentous day it was and I followed her into the consulting room, undecided as to whether to lie on the couch or sit on a chair. If I chose a chair she might still sit with her back half turned, when what I wanted was for it to be like the first time when I came for my assessment and we sat opposite one another in front of the hearth.

The room felt pleasantly warm and I experienced an instant of pure joy when I saw Dora curled up on the rug. Because it was my last time Mrs Moberley had allowed her to remain in the room with us.

'Would it be all right if I sat on a chair today?' I asked.

'Of course.' She turned her own chair to face mine.

'Thank you for letting Dora stay.' I held my breath, afraid it had not been deliberate and she would say there was no need to thank her, Dora must have padded in without her noticing.

'I know how fond you are of cats.'

'Yes I am.' Tears threatened but I blinked them away. 'Only now I don't know what to say.'

A familiar silence followed but silences no longer alarmed me and one question was uppermost in my mind.

'If my arm or any other part of me stopped working again would I be able to come back?'

'I don't think a weak limb would be a prerequisite do you?'

Until then I had kept my eyes firmly fixed on my shoes. Now I looked up and saw she was smiling. 'How is everything?' she asked, 'have you heard from your friend in Paris?'

'A letter arrived yesterday. She and Solange are back together and Midge is trying to find someone who can help her but the trouble is she thinks she can give up the drugs without attending a clinic. Solange does I mean. '

'And Archie and Muriel?'

'I'm not sure. They seem all right but you can never tell can you, about other people's marriages.'

I flinched. Other people's marriages? What about

my own? 'Enid's baby is doing well,' I said hastily, 'she's eight weeks old now and Enid's sister says she can smile.'

'Flossie is still helping you?'

'Yes.' I had never known her to ask so many questions. 'She's very thorough but it's not the same without Enid.'

Dora stood up and stretched then sank to floor again and curled up in a ball. 'I wish we could be friends,' I said, 'proper friends.'

'I know Ursula but I explained how that won't be possible. An analyst and her patient build up a very special relationship. Meeting as friends would destroy it.'

'But you've helped me so much. It seems all wrong just to walk away.' My voice started to falter. 'And never come back.'

'You have a life away from here.'

'Yes and I know what you're going to say. I must concentrate on being a good wife to Leo.'

She laughed and I did too.

'I do love him.' I paused. 'Do you think I ought to have a baby?'

'I can't answer that for you Ursula.'

'I don't think I'd like being at home all day and if you have one baby people expect you to have another, so it won't be lonely I suppose, and now I'm better there are so many things I want to do.'

'What kind of things?'

'Well.' I felt myself blush. 'You know Dr Stopes' clinic in Holloway Road? Is it still open?'

'And there are several others now. Certainly one in Walworth. And she's no longer alone in her campaign.

She founded the Society for Constructive Birth Control with financial help from her second husband.'

'Then that's what I'd like to do. Help women who are as ignorant as I was. And ones who want to limit the size of their family. Enid's mother had seven and I've heard of people with twelve or even more.'

'You'd find there are plenty of women who'd be glad of your help. Have you discussed your plans with Leo?'

I shook my head. 'I think I hoped Enid's baby would be a turning point for us but how could it be? We talk about the house and Midge's plans to make it look more fashionable, and about Muriel and Archie, and John Watson of course and his rats.'

She stood up and took at book from a shelf. 'It's not as much at odds with psychoanalysis as you might think. I've read some of Watson's work and the gap between the two theories is not as wide as it at first appears. We're all affected by what happens to us. If something hurts us we try to avoid a recurrence of the pain. If something makes us happy we try to repeat the experience. In the same way rats memorise events, either unpleasant or rewarding.'

'Yes I can see that. It's an awful thing to say but since he found out about his father Leo has become much more…' I searched for the right word. 'Self-assured. I'm glad for him, I suppose I am, but he still insists my arm was the result of a childhood trauma I'd repressed.'

'Perhaps if you explained that it was a response to an immediate situation you were unable to deal with in any other way. Not just the sexual difficulties but other feelings surrounding your parents and your sister.'

'Yes I'm sure you're right. Joyce and I get on so much better now. I don't think my arm had anything to do with the brother I never knew but her telling me about it was important.' I reached down to stroke Dora. 'And the fact she was brave enough to talk about herself. We're all so frightened aren't we, frightened of being hurt, and sometimes if you reveal your weaknesses people take advantage of them.'

We sat in companiable silence for several minutes. I could hear the ticking of the clock but I no longer felt my time was ebbing away.

'I'm so grateful to you,' I said at last, 'and I'll never forget you as long as I live.'

'And neither will I forget you Ursula. Whatever you decide to do I wish you all the luck in the world.'

On my way home a voice called my name and the woman I had met once before, the one who had two boys at Leo's school, quickened her pace to catch up with me. She was carrying a large bag of shopping in one hand and hanging onto her hat with the other to stop it blowing away.

'I think I live in the next road to you Mrs Ingham. You must come to tea. My name's Gwen. Gwen Mason.'

'Thank you, I'd like that. I'm Ursula.'

She shifted the bag from one hand to the other. 'We're going on holiday next week but may I get in touch with you when we return?'

'Yes please do. We live in the house with the wrought iron railings.'

The first time we met I had thought her rather plain. Now I could see she had beautiful eyes with thick dark lashes, and underneath her hat her hair was probably thick and dark too.

'Hugh and I haven't been away on our own for

years,' she said, 'and the children will be perfectly happy with my mother.'

'How many children do you have?'

'Three. Tom and Robin are at school but Susan's only four.'

I smiled, pleased she was being so friendly.

'Fortunately my mother lives just round the corner,' she continued, 'I don't know what I'd do without her. Do you have a family?'

'Not yet.'

She laughed, the way people do when they have no means of knowing if a stray remark is of great significance or unimportant.

'Enjoy your holiday,' I said.

'And we'll meet up when I get back,' she called, 'better dash, I think it's going to pour.'

As I walked home I tried to picture myself in Gwen Mason's shoes. Two boys at Kingslade and a little girl of four, a comfortable home, a holiday with her husband while her mother looked after the children, it sounded pleasant enough. I wondered what her husband was like. Easy-going and jolly, I thought, the kind of father you see in advertising posters in the train, on all fours on the carpet with children climbing on his back. Then I thought about Joyce's party and how Leo had held Christopher, and how happy he had looked, playing with Helen and Sybil, and how much he wanted a child.

Inspired by Midge's enthusiasm for clothes I had bought a new frock. It was made of green jersey wool, cut on the bias, with a scooped out neckline, and it was much more figure hugging than anything I had worn before. I wondered what Leo would think of it and as I studied my outline in the long mirror I realised that wearing it this evening, for the first time, was a kind of test. If he paid me a compliment I would give him a hug. If he failed to notice, or worse still made a derogatory remark I would… What would I do?

The frock had long sleeves that made my arms look rather thin. On the other hand, since it was not the kind of garment that allowed for any bulges, it was fortunate I was so slim or, as Midge more tactfully put it, delightfully sylph-like.

I thought about my "bad" arm and how difficult it had been to get dressed and how easy it was now in comparison, something I would never have appreciated without the months of struggling. Pleasure was relief from pain or frustration – that was what Midge believed – a perfectly ordinary meal when you were starving hungry, a glass of water when you were practically dying from thirst, or lovemaking when your lover returned after weeks away from home.

I remembered how I had once felt about Archie, and the dream, Archie and me on the beach! Pure fantasy and it had been the same when I imagined Mrs Moberley in my bed, although thinking about it now made me blush.

Leo's lecture began at six-thirty and lasted an hour so, even allowing for a hold up on the underground, he should have been back by now. If I took the meat rissoles out of the oven he would complain they were cold. If I left them in it much longer they would become inedible. His pocket diary lay on top of the revolving bookcase, along with his silver propelling pencil and a Latin primer one of the boys had dropped in the school drive. The Latin primer was smeared with mud and I wondered if the boy would get into trouble although accidentally dropping your book was hardly a hanging crime.

Picking up the diary I flicked through the months until I came to the date of the first lecture. Leo was meticulous about engagements so I was not surprised to see that eight Wednesdays had a neatly pencilled-in entry. Lecture: six-thirty pm. Eight consecutive Wednesday evenings but no entry for this evening, which was not surprising since this was week nine. My heart thumped in my chest and I felt a flutter in my throat as though a large moth had lodged there and was trying to escape.

Months ago, when I told Mrs Moberley I feared he would lose patience she had said she thought it unlikely. Why? Why had she said that? And how could I have been so trusting, taking everything she said as the gospel truth? But it was no use blaming her because, as she had never failed to point out, it was not her job to tell her patients what to do. Desperate for reassurance I hung onto the affection Leo had shown me during the previous weeks. But it could have meant nothing, no, worse than that it could have been a way of concealing what was going on in the rest of his life.

Moving from room to room I searched for Solomon, calling his name even though I knew it was pointless since he never took any notice unless it was feeding time. Dragging open the back door I peered into the darkness, searching for two round yellow eyes. Something moved in the bushes but it was only the wind stirring the leaves. *Solomon, where are you? Please come back, please.* I stood still, listening, straining for the slightest sound, then my head swam and I realised I had been holding my breath and quickly drew in great gulps of cold night air.

The evening was supposed to be special, Leo's favourite food and afterwards we would talk and I would ask him about his lecture and tell him how Mrs Moberley had said John Watson's theories were not that far removed from Freud's. Where was he and who was he with? He had said nothing about an extra lecture or a demonstration of rats in a maze.

Upstairs the door to the airing cupboard was ajar and I found Solomon on a pile of pillowcases and ignoring his protests carried him to the bedroom where I sat on the edge of my bed, stroking his back, harder and harder until he lost patience and jumped down. Self-pity overwhelmed me. I had brought it on myself, taking Leo for granted and refusing to allow him into my bed. How could your mind tell you your arm was unable to function? What *was* your unconscious mind? Mrs Moberley had never explained. It was Freud's fault I had been sent to Mrs Moberley and fallen in love with her and treated Leo so badly he had fallen in love with another woman. Freud would have described it as my unconscious wish fulfilment but he would be wrong. He was often wrong.

A gust of wind rattled the sash windows. Leo would come home, find me sitting there in tears and feel so sorry for me... or more likely be so irritated... or fail to notice what a state I was in.

Solomon was washing his foot but when I started down the stairs he ran after me and if I had let him he would have accompanied me out of the house and down the path to the gate. Lit by the street lamp a figure appeared in the distance and at first I was sure it was

Leo but as it drew closer it turned out to be an elderly man in a long tweed coat. He nodded in my direction, murmuring something about the wind and rain, and I hurried back into the house and stood leaning against the hall table, not even bothering to switch on the light.

The grandmother clock struck the half hour and Leo burst through the front door, taking off his coat as he walked, and asked why I was skulking in the dark.

'Oh I'm sorry,' he added, 'your last visit to Mrs Moberley, it must have been a wrench.'

I followed him down the passage and into the warmth of the kitchen. 'How was your lecture?'

'All right. Same as usual.'

'Was it about rats in mazes?'

'The point of it is to understand how people learn.'

'Rats aren't people.' I opened the oven door and lifted out the dish with its six dried up rissoles and the two baked potatoes that were supposed to accompany them.

'The reason I'm late.' He rubbed the bridge of his nose. 'I had to call in at the library and return a book.'

The kitchen smelled of the turpentine I had used earlier in the ... attempt to remove a stain from a ... placed Leo's food in front of him and he looked up inquiringly because there was only one plate then picked up his knife and fork. 'You've eaten have you? As I said I had – '

'Yes I know. To return a book.'

The batter pudding mixture had separated into a pale unappetising concoction with a watery brown layer on top. Tipping it down the sink I ran both taps, not caring when water bounced off a spoon and spattered the front of my new frock. A strip of darkness – Joyce called them owl holes – was visible between the kitchen curtains which were slightly too narrow for the window and as I tugged at them I thought about a play Muriel and Archie had taken us to see. It was set in a cottage on the moor and the off stage sound effects were amazingly realistic, wind roaring, rain pattering, and just like Leo the leading actor had made his entrance with damp slicked-back hair and a rain-soaked coat.

That was what I felt like now, an actor in a play. He was having an affair with a woman he had met at the lectures, someone who understood about stimulus and response whatever that was supposed to be, and rats who pressed levers. How long had it been going on? Presumably they met each week although this was the first time he had been so late. Where did she live? Somewhere close to the university? And what did they talk about? Or was there no time for talking? A mad dash into each other's arms and a desperate scramble to remove their clothes…

'What are you doing over there?' Leo had his elbows on the table and his chin in his cupped hands.

'There *was* no lecture,' I said, watching as one of his elbows slipped and his head almost hit the table. 'You left your diary on the bookcase. The last one was a week ago.'

I expected him to bluster, invent an extra one, a discussion or demonstration, but he was silent.

'You left your diary out on purpose,' I continued. 'That's what Freud would have said. You've met someone haven't you? No don't pretend, I'd prefer to know the truth.'

Pushing aside his untouched food, he cleared his

throat, playing for time. 'I've met a lot of new people.'

'What's her name?' My voice was steady and I felt unnaturally calm. Outside an owl hooted. I thought it was an owl. He would want a divorce. I would have to divorce him for infidelity. We would sell the house or perhaps he would keep it but I would move out. Then what? I could visit Midge – I had an open invitation – and if I liked Paris I might settle there and find myself a job. It would be a fresh start, quite exciting and certainly not the end of the world. 'Her name Leo.'

'Dora.'

Dora, the name of Mrs Moberley's cat. The anger I had kept in check welled up. I hated him. He had forced me to see a psychoanalyst then resented my attachment to her and tried to blacken her name, then when that failed...

'There's a library in Holborn,' he said, 'with a good psychology section. She told me about it when – '

'How long have you known her?'

He made an absurd calculation in his head. 'We didn't strike up a conversation until the third lecture. I think it was the third.'

'What does she look like?' The tap was dripping, needed a new washer. I gave it a hard twist, in the process knocking my hip against the hard edge of the sink and relishing the pain.

Leo stood up and gripped the back of his chair. 'After Enid's baby and the business with my father I hoped things would be different between us.'

'You refused to go and see the baby.'

'What's that got to do with anything?'

'You knew how much it meant to me.'

He frowned, looking up at the ceiling then down at

the floor. 'If you want the truth I couldn't face seeing Enid, not after I'd been there at the birth.'

That threw me a little. I could understand his embarrassment. Not that I going to admit it. 'Well, why didn't you say?'

His eyebrows twitched. He had noticed my new frock. 'Is that one of Midge's?'

'My frock? How could it be? I'm at least three inches taller.'

'Really?'

'Yes, really.'

Folding his arms – Mrs Moberley said it was a way of protecting yourself – he let out a long self-pitying sigh. 'You only married me because you were in love with my father. No don't interrupt. You couldn't have him so you decided you'd make do with his son. You remember Freud's "Miss Lucy"? When she admitted she loved her employer Freud asked why she hadn't told him before and she said something along the lines of, "I didn't know. I didn't want to know. I wanted to drive it out of my head and not think of it again." And because she repressed it she lost her sense of smell, apart from an imagined smell of burnt pudding. Burnt pudding, lifeless arm, all makes sense doesn't it?'

I picked up his plate of uneaten food. 'I didn't love Archie like that.'

'I thought you wanted us to speak the truth.'

'Until a few weeks ago I thought I loved Mrs Moberley.'

'It's called transference.'

'That doesn't mean I didn't love her. I thought I was like Midge. Midge and Solange. You kept criticising and everything I said made you cross. Mrs Moberley listened, tried to understand. And you wouldn't even read Dr Stopes' book – '

'As a matter of fact I did.' He had his back turned, pretending to be looking at the picture on the wall, a drawing of a hare that had belonged to my father.

'I don't believe you,' I said.

He shrugged. 'Not much I can do about that. *The woman forgives the crudeness but sooner or later her love revolts and she has nothing but scorn and loathing…*'

Heat rose up my neck and suffused my face. 'Why didn't you say? I suppose by then you'd met the woman at the lectures.'

'The woman at the lectures as you call her is in her late forties with two teenage children and an insurance broker husband.'

I should have kept quiet, let him talk, but I was too upset, and too afraid. 'That doesn't mean… Some men like older women.'

'She shared my interest in John Watson, and like me she has a job she dislikes and like your Mrs Moberley she was a good listener.'

'I didn't know you disliked your job.' My face ached and my words came out mechanically. 'You never said. You never tell me anything. Why didn't you say? What would you like to do, experiments with rats?'

'I'd have to retrain if I wanted to do that.'

'I'm sure Archie would give you the money. Guilt money for all his little flings.'

He stared at me and I tried to work out what he was thinking. That once I had been a nice, charitable person and now I was bitter and sarcastic? That all the things he liked about me had disappeared. It was so unfair. Anyone would think I had pretended my arm wouldn't work, and that couldn't be right because Mrs Moberley said it would have been impossible.

When he spoke again there was no emotion in his voice, only weariness. 'After you started seeing Mrs Moberley you changed. Yes I realise it was inevitable, my own stupid fault believing your arm could be cured but the rest of you would remain – '

'So I'm right, you preferred me as I was before.'

'Did I say that?'

'You didn't have to.'

He turned to face me and I had never seen so much anguish in his eyes. 'I love you Ursa, I always have.'

I should have said "I love you too" but the words refused to come. 'What did you think of the book?'

'The Marie Stopes? It made me realise what a stupid, clumsy – '

'No don't say that.' I hung onto the table to steady myself. 'I was just as ignorant. Did you tell your friend Dora what a bad wife I was? When you didn't come back this evening I thought you were going to leave me. Are you going to – '

'Is that what you want?'

'Oh Leo, I just want us to be happy.'

He moved towards me and I hung back then held out my arms and we clung together until Solomon appeared, letting out high pitched mews, asking to be fed.

'We can talk about it,' I said, 'not just the book. If we tell each other how – '

'Oh Ursa.' He buried his face in my hair. 'I know you're right but you'll have to bear with me. Unfortunately I inherited my mother's reticence rather than my father's easy charm.'

'People can change. And as for your father…'

He gave a short Leo-like laugh and bent to stroke Solomon's head. 'It's all right for you, cat.'

'He went missing too,' I said. 'I thought he'd been run over then I found him in the airing cupboard.'

'His favourite place.'

'Leo?'

'Mm.'

'We will be all right, won't we? You can change your job and I'll…' But now was not the time to tell him how I hoped to work at one of Marie Stopes' family planning clinics. He would be disappointed, he wanted a baby and perhaps I did too. 'Leo?'

'Now what?'

'You know I'd do anything – '

'Anything?'

'Well…'

He gave a wry smile that turned into a grin. 'Soup? A sandwich? No, eggs, scrambled eggs on toast, that's what I'd like, and a pot of very strong tea.'

AUTHOR NOTES

Before becoming a writer Penny Kline taught in a London school, then re-trained (she has a PhD in Psychology) and combined part-time lecturing with work as a psychotherapist. She is the author of six crime novels about Bristol psychologist, Anna McColl. She has also had plays broadcast on Radio 4.